IMMORTAL

GENE DOUCETTE

Immortal
By Gene Doucette

GeneDoucette.me

Cover by Kim Killion, Hot Damn Designs

For Gene Doucette Sr., who loved this book.

"Gilgamesh, where do you roam? You will not find the eternal life you seek. When the gods created mankind, they appointed death for mankind ..."

— —THE ALEWIFE, FROM THE EPIC OF GILGAMESH

PROLOGUE

The dream is always the same.

It starts on the hunt—running hard through the tall grasses in the heat of a blazing, midday sun. My tool is a stick with a sharpened stone tied to the end of it. It's the second crudest weapon imaginable, barely one technological step up from a heavy rock. I would say it resembles a spear, but that's misleading because throwing one of these would be a stupid thing to do. Rather, one is advised to hang onto it until close enough to stab something. Even then you'd better hit the thing you're stabbing in just the right place or the point will bounce off bone and you'll have succeeded only in pissing off something much bigger than you.

There are four of us in this chase, and we're tired. We've been after the beast for two solid days without food or water. We want to stop, all of us, but we won't because this is our job.

The youngest one keeps lagging behind. It's his first time on the hunt, and he's only just discovered it's not a lot of fun. We call him the Kaa, which is what we call all the young ones. He won't get his name until he's made his first kill. Which will be soon, provided he doesn't quit on us.

The thing we are hunting—our name for it is a somewhat un-

spellable guttural noise—is wounded. We hurt it the first time we tried to bring it down. As the leader I remain many paces ahead of the others, stopping periodically to check for tracks, and for blood. I'm a very good tracker.

The dream leaps ahead to the moment we finally come upon our prey. It is, in the modern parlance, a giant cat of some kind—a lion, or a cheetah. Only it's not exactly, as this dream is taking place tens of thousands of years ago. It is perhaps an evolutionary offshoot of a lion or a cheetah. There were few of them then and none of them now.

We find it lying in the grasses, no longer able to run, its breathing halting and uneven. I summon the Kaa as this is his moment, the moment when he becomes a man.

With great pride he steps forward and raises his spear, meaning to strike the creature's soft underbelly, which lies exposed. But I've made a mistake. The cat-thing isn't quite ready to die yet, and just moments before the killing blow is struck it lashes out with its sharp claws and catches the Kaa in the stomach.

In shock and pain, the Kaa lurches backward and unfortunately drops his spear.

Never drop your spear.

The cat is upon him before the three of us can do much of anything about it.

I jump onto the animal's back and wrap my arm around its neck, rolling him on top of me and then throwing him away from the Kaa. (The Kaa is mortally wounded already and will die without reaching his manhood. This I know without looking at him.) Then the three of us surround the cat as it decides which of us is the greatest threat. It settles on me. With a mighty lunge, it pounces.

The creature bites into my shoulder with its sharp, jagged teeth—not a mortal wound, but painful—but I get the better of him, sliding my sharpened stone spear between his ribs. We land on the ground together. I feel its jaw slacken and the teeth slide loose from my flesh as it dies.

Pushing the dead thing off me, I rise. I am bleeding from my own wounds and also covered in the creature's viscera. And I am happy. I howl in triumph.

It's at that moment she appears. She walks out from the tall grasses, a pale white woman with long red hair, devastating blue eyes, and a regal carriage that speaks to me of royalty not yet even imagined in this time and place.

Her clothing varies from dream to dream: a Victorian dress; a sari, simple peasant rags; or a smart business suit. And sometimes she's wearing nothing at all. She looks down at the dead thing, and then at me. She speaks. Her voice is an ice-cold splash of water and seems impossibly loud.

"Urrr," she says, tears streaming down her face, "how could you?"

And that's when I wake up.

PART I

ECHOES OF A BYGONE TIME

CHAPTER 1

I have no idea how long I've been here.

The problem is they took my watch before making me change out of my clothes. One of the reasons I'd gotten that particular watch was because of the calendar feature on the bottom of the face. Most people can keep decent track of what day and month—and year—it is without checking, whereas I've been known to lose entire decades. Which, I guess, is normal for someone like me.

Can't complain too much about the cell. Not that I am all that familiar with cells in general. Let's say it looks better than the ones on television. It has a comfortable cot and a real pillow, a clean toilet, and a functional sink. No mirror. Probably figured I'd break it and use the pieces as a weapon. Or use the pieces to hurt myself. Which I wouldn't do, but I can understand why they wouldn't appreciate it, at least before they're done with me.

Without the mirror I have no idea what I look like any more. My face, which I'd kept clean-shaven for the better part of the past century, is now sprouting the first stages of a beard, and the hair on my head is starting to grow back. I bet with a good enough look at my reflection I could use that to determine the length of my captivity.

How had I ended up in this state? There's the real question. I'd have to go back to the day I woke up behind the futon.

~

My first thought, upon waking up, was that sometime the previous evening I'd become paralyzed in a tragic accident of some kind. I was almost entirely unable to move, largely because all four of my major limbs had fallen asleep and were not nearly as interested in awakening as the rest of me.

It took a little work and a lot of wriggling to ascertain that I wasn't paralyzed. I was simply pinned behind a futon. The smell of stale beer, tipped ashtrays, and vomit triggered vague memories of a party of some kind, one that I may even have been invited to. There was also the outside chance that the futon belonged to someone I actually knew, but that was, statistically speaking, a long shot.

I'm actually something of an aficionado in the "waking up stuck in strange places" department. I've woken up in hay lofts, under a butter churn, on roofs, in a choir loft (twice), under tables, on tables, in trees, in ditches, and half-pinned under a sleeping ox. One time in Bombay, I woke up to find myself lashed to a yak. This was my fourth futon. You'd think I'd have been used to it by now.

I could hear an American-style football game playing on the television, meaning first, someone else was in the room watching the game, and second, I was still in the United States. If I was exceptionally lucky, I was still in Boston, the last place I could recall being in.

My guess was whoever was in the room was also sitting on the futon, because the futon was rather heavy, and past experience suggested most unoccupied futons are easy to dislodge with minimal effort.

"Hello?" I said.

There was a lengthy delay, long enough for me to think I hadn't been heard. Then, "D'you hear that?" someone said. Man's voice, unaccented English. Okay, still in the United States, possibly not in Massachusetts any more.

"Yeah," his friend said. They were both on the futon.

One of them peeled back the top and looked at me through the back support. "Hey, dude," he greeted.

College student. Had to be.

He and his buddy stood up and pulled the futon away from the wall, affording me the opportunity to crawl to the center of the room. They pushed the futon back, sat down again, and continued to take in the game while I lay there and waited for the tingling sensation in my arms and legs to subside. That accomplished, I made a half-hearted attempt to get to my feet, but discovered that was far too difficult, due to a screaming hangover, which almost never goes well with bipedal movement.

"How's it goin'?" one of my new friends asked, without taking his eyes off the game. "You need any help?"

"I'm fine right here, thanks," I said.

"'Kay."

If you're thinking they were acting terribly nonchalant about discovering a stranger behind the living room couch, you've never been to a collegiate keg party.

"Beer?" he offered. "We're still draining the keg."

~

After two cups of beer from my prone position on the floor I managed to gain my feet, struggle into the only other non-floor-position seating in the place, and watch a goodly portion of the football game.

I don't understand American football. If you're going to line a bunch of behemoths up in front of a bunch of other behemoths and ask them to hit each other as hard as they can, why tell them they can only hit one another a certain way? Too many rules, that's the problem.

The Romans did it right. Plus, back then the combatants were slaves and didn't command massive signing bonuses. So, that's two points in favor of the Romans.

My bleary-eyed cohabitants shuttled between active interest and practical catatonia. Once in a while one of them would muster up a "good play" or "run, dude," but that was pretty much it. We did work out basic introductions. The one on the left—blond, gap-toothed, wearing nothing but shorts and sneakers with no socks—was named Gary. On the right—jeans and T-shirt, barefoot, black hair, black skin—was Nate. A more detailed review of their character and standing would have to wait.

By the time the game ended I was on my fourth beer and had probably overstayed my welcome, but I've never been one to much care about that sort of thing, so I sat where I was.

"So, you live around here?" Nate asked.

"I guess," I said. "Is this still Boston?"

He looked at Gary. Gary looked like the kind of person who enjoyed holding people's heads under water.

"Yeah, still Boston," Gary said. "You know, you don't look much like a student, Adam."

I'd given them my current American name, chosen more or less at random. Lately, I've taken to picking appellations alphabetically, the same way the weather bureau picks hurricane names. Zigmund was my last name but I dropped that after only a couple of months. Hard to travel around the U.S. with a name like Zigmund, I have to say. I've gone by hundreds of different names, including, of course, the one I was born with, which was really more of a grunt.

"Grad student?" Nate inquired. They were both sobering up enough to feel a little uncomfortable about me. And I was a bit too tipsy to lie.

"Nope. I just saw there was a party and dropped in."

This might not have been true. I might have come with somebody. I couldn't remember.

"But you do have a place of your own, right?"

"Not so much, no."

"You're a homeless guy?" Gary asked, mustering up some incredulity.

"Well, in the sense that I don't currently have a place to live, yes. But I have had a lot of homes."

"Geez," he said profoundly.

"C'mon," Nate said, "you can't be more than, what, thirty?" The reasoning being, aren't homeless people all a lot older?

I took a sip of my beer and decided, what the hell. "I don't really know how old I am."

"What, you were adopted or something?" Gary offered.

"No," I said, "I just lost count. I'm immortal."

You have to be a little careful about dropping that bit of information in the wrong place. I've been called a witch, a blasphemer, a devil, and a few other unpleasant things depending on the where and the when. But college students—and bar drunks for some reason—tend to be okay with it. Which may explain why I spend so much time with college students and bar drunks.

"Cool," Gary said after an adequate pause. "You wanna crash here for a while?"

~

A couple of things about being immortal:

First of all, I'm not a vampire. I get that a lot, even during the day when I should be in a coffin or a crypt or something. (Very few vampires bother to sleep in a coffin, if you must know. Lugging one around everywhere you go is inconvenient, and it almost always attracts the wrong kind of attention. I did know a vampire who had one, but it was mostly a kinky sex thing for her.)

I'm not invincible. Also, no super-strength, X-ray vision, power of flight or any of that. I eat, drink, sleep, and shit just like everyone else. I just stopped getting any older at around age thirty-two.

Why thirty-two? No idea.

I have all my hair in all the proper places, and a relatively slight build that doesn't seem to get any larger whether I lift weights or binge. To put it in a way a twenty-first century person might understand, it's like someone hit pause on my existence.

I'm pretty sure I can be killed. I can certainly be hurt, and have on several occasions been very close to death due to one near-mortal wound or another. If I wanted to—I think—I could take my own life, although obviously this hasn't been tested. Now maybe you're not the type who ever considered suicide, but—and you'll just have to trust me on this—when you live this long, it comes up. I was suicidal for two solid centuries once. That was during the early part of what they now call the Dark Ages, in medieval Europe. Suicidal tendencies were *de rigueur* at the time, and I'm nothing if not trendy.

I don't know how old I am. My earliest memory is something along the lines of "fire good, ice bad," so I think I predate written history, but I don't know by how much. I like to brag that I've been there "from the beginning" and while this may very well be true, I generally just say it to pick up girls. But it has been a very long time, and considering I'm not invincible or super-strong, that's nothing short of miraculous.

Oh, I do have one other thing going for me. I can't get sick. Universal immunity. That's a fairly big plus. Not as much of a big deal now as it was back when the average life span was in the low thirties and we measured the seasons by what plague was in vogue at the time but still, it's the gift that keeps on giving.

I'm currently white-skinned, but I wasn't always. I pretty

much blend with whatever culture I'm hanging out in, which is a very useful trait when you think about it. Of course I never fit in anywhere for the long haul, not after people around me all start getting old while I don't. So I move around a lot. You know, before locals start getting out the pitchforks and torches and what-have-you.

I try to keep up with the rapid advancement of modern culture, something I liken to sprinting in wet sand. I owe a lot of what I understand about the world today to television and movies, which are a true godsend to a guy in my situation. Likewise, I keep up with language pretty well, that being a survival skill I took to heart just around the time language was first invented.

I've been rich a couple of times. I still am, I think. I just don't live the life. That whole material wealth thing got old fast. I mean, creature comforts are nice, but immortality does funny things to the whole making-something-of-yourself imperative that people who expect to die someday go through. I hang onto enough money to get by because it's the easiest way to acquire alcohol, which I'm much in favor of.

Speaking of which, if you want to know what I've learned in my extended time on Earth it is this: beer is good.

I've never been much of a deep thinker.

~

We finished tapping out the keg that evening, and I immediately earned my stay by providing funds for more alcohol. After that we got along fine.

Turned out Nate was a history major. You'd think with me being immortal I'd be able to help him with that.

"No, no, this isn't right," I said, skimming Nate's copy of *The French Revolution: a cartoon history*. We were sitting at the table—a cheap folding card table—in their dining room. Books and papers were strewn across the surface, leaving precious little room for one to put one's beer.

"C'mon, I got a test on it tomorrow," Nate said, staring unappreciatively at me. "What's wrong with it?"

I tossed the offending tome onto the floor.

"The French Revolution was a street brawl that got a little out of hand. Everything that came after that was a massive rationalization."

"Pretty sure I can't say that tomorrow."

"I can tell your professor myself. You want me to? I was there. He'd probably appreciate my input."

"Cut that out, man," he said, picking up the textbook.

"Sorry. Maybe you should drink some more. I find it helps."

"No, I gotta study. Seriously."

Nate wasn't much fun sober.

Gary was the more laid-back of the two. He didn't know what his major was, but he'd shown a great talent for keg-tapping with a minor in drooling. From the kitchen he said, "That's so cool," as regards my immortality. He said this every twenty minutes or so, usually unprompted. In the kitchen, he was fighting a losing battle with a team of roaches that reportedly held a box of *Cocoa Crispies* hostage this morning and were unwilling to end the siege twelve hours later.

"It's not cool if it gets me an F on this," Nate barked.

"So, you'd rather just regurgitate what these books tell you than know what really happened?"

"Exactly."

"No quest for truth? Where's your spirit of exploration?"

"You never went to college, did you?"

He had me there. So, I let him be and joined Gary, which was just as well. When you're immortal you find there are only so many faces in the world, and to me Nate looked exactly like a Bantu tribal prince I used to hang out with. I kept having to remind myself not to speak to him in Xhosa.

In the kitchen, Gary was standing on the counter with a can of insecticide and firing indiscriminately into the cupboard, undoubtedly rendering everything in there inedible, including the compromised *Cocoa Krispies*.

"Any luck?" I asked.

"It's only a matter of time, my friend. They can't hide behind the macaroni forever."

My money was on the roaches, and I was about to say words to that effect when something under the kitchen sink made a loud bump.

"The hell was that?" Gary asked.

"Really big roach?"

Granting the bugs a temporary reprieve, Gary hopped off the counter and pulled open the door leading to the underside of the sink.

"Aahhh!" he shouted. He scampered back like he'd just seen a human head.

"That's who you remind me of!" I exclaimed.

He looked at me like I was insane. (Not an unreasonable assumption. I was insane for about eighty years in Macedonia. Long story.)

"What??"

"Roman soldier named Cassius. He was afraid of anything with hair."

Gary pointed to the sink cabinet mutely, bringing me back to the present.

Nate popped his head in. "What's going on?" he asked.

"Tell me you see that too," Gary said.

I leaned down and pushed the door open. He was hiding behind the garbage disposal.

"Oh, hey, Jerry," I said. "What are you doing down there?"

CHAPTER 2

Had a particularly unpleasant day today. Kopalev called it a "general physical." I think it was just an excuse to shove his hand up my ass. But I've never had a physical before, so how would I know? Maybe that's standard procedure. If so, no wonder men avoid doctors whenever they can. Felt like he was looking for car keys in there or something.

He's a pretty cheery guy, Doc Kopalev, or Viktor, as he keeps telling me to call him. Sometimes it seems as if he's unaware I'm not precisely a volunteer. And I get the impression he hates his boss—or partner, depending on whom you ask—about as much as I do, which makes me wonder why he's doing this. Pretty sure he's here of his own free will.

I'm eager to probe him for details but that might have to wait, just because the whole hand-up-ass thing is going to take some time to get past. Haven't had anything like that done to me since Athens. Didn't enjoy it then either.

~

I first met Jerry about two years ago, in Pittsburgh. Nice guy, but one of those types you can only stand in short bursts. First time we met we were inseparable for about three months, during which time he managed to nearly get me arrested five times. Which may very well be why I left Pittsburgh for Cleveland—I can't remember. Jerry never got arrested either, of course, and if he had they wouldn't have been able to hold him for long, given he's only about ten inches tall.

Gary was decidedly freaked. He held up the can of bug spray defensively as Jerry rose to his feet and crawled out from under the sink.

"You wanna tell frat fucker to ease up over there?" Jerry asked.

When he spoke Nate leapt five feet straight backward, knocking over the trash can behind him.

"Christ," Jerry said, spotting Nate, "another one. Boo!"

They both screamed.

Jerry is an iffrit. Iffrits are crude little beasties with poor impulse control and vast appetites for all sorts of debauchery—basically Freud's id personified. It makes them a tremendous amount of fun, but only when one is in the right mood.

"It's a ... little person ..." Gary said.

"HEY!" Jerry blasted. It's hard to believe a voice that loud can come out of something that small. "I'll fuck you up, frat boy."

"Guys, guys. He's a friend of mine. Calm down." Neither of them looked interested in calming down. "Look, he's harmless."

"Fuck you, Adam," Jerry said. He liked to think of himself as a bad ass. Hard to pull off when the only thing you can justifiably intimidate is a Ken doll.

"Jerry ..."

Nate took a cautious step closer. "He's ... naked."

"Yeah, what's up with that?" Gary agreed.

Like every other iffrit I've ever met, Jerry preferred to go without clothing. And, he had a hard-on. Again, pretty much like every other iffrit I ever met.

"Suck on it, asshole," Jerry said, grabbing himself demonstratively.

"I'm gonna be sick," Nate muttered.

It was all starting to come back to me: Jerry showing up unexpectedly in Boston, us following a crowd to the party ...

"Must'a passed out ..." Jerry said. Then he noticed the empty keg we had yet to return, and looked at me, aghast. "Are they OUT OF BEER? What the FUCK are we still DOING HERE?"

"There's some in the fridge," Gary pointed out helpfully.

"Aces," Jerry said. He ran to the refrigerator, yanked it open, climbed in, and shut the door behind him.

Gary and Nate stared blankly at the door, then at me, then at the door again.

"Wow," Nate said.

"Totally," Gary agreed. "Dude, we gotta throw another party."

~

There are a lot of human-*like* species out there, on the fringes. An average person might encounter one such species in an entire lifetime, if lucky. (Or unlucky. Many can be quite nasty.) I, of course, have met all of them.

You've probably come across an iffrit once or twice without even realizing it. You just mistook it for something else. For instance, Jerry told me he once lived for nearly a year in the Metropolitan Museum in New York pretending to be a very excited Greek statuette. When the place closed down at night he'd sneak into the executive cafeteria and polish off the liquor supply. They fumigated the place four times and fired three sets of guards before someone figured out that the ugly Hellenic Adonis knockoff in the corner changed poses every day.

~

Nate and Gary threw another party on Thursday, which is evidently the start of the weekend when you're in college. I certainly wasn't about to complain, and Jerry didn't mind at all. As crude and brazen as iffrits generally are, they all adhere to the basic survival imperative and avoid being seen—as themselves—as much as possible, so he appreciated a roomful of people he could come out and party with. And Jerry could party.

"He's so *cute*," exclaimed one buxom blonde gleefully as Jerry performed one stunt after another.

"I'll show you *cute*, sweetie!" he exclaimed, grabbing himself again.

This generated a raucous round of laughter.

"Hey," I said to the blonde, "I'm immortal, you know."

"Uh-huh. Oh look!" Jerry was giving himself a blow job. Again. How does a guy compete with that?

Frustrated at having been thoroughly upstaged by a talking kewpie doll, I grabbed Jerry off the mantle. "Okay, gang. Let him rest, he'll be here all week."

"C'mon, Adam!" Jerry complained loudly. I wended my way through the crowd and carried him into the bathroom, shutting the door.

"What are you doing?" he asked. "I was doin' great!"

"You need a time-out," I said. "Before one of those girls makes the mistake of assuming you're harmless."

"Jealous?"

"Very. Asshole." Sometimes swearing at him is the only way to communicate. Iffrits are much like New Yorkers in that way.

"Fuck you. I think the blonde likes me."

"Fine, but you're cramping my style."

"Chasing younger women again, Adam? You dog."

"Only because I don't know anyone my age. Now calm the hell down or I'll flush you."

"You wouldn't dare!"

"Watch me."

He plunked himself down on the bar of soap and sulked. I made a mental note not to use that soap in the morning.

"What are you doing in Boston, anyway?" I asked. "Thought you were having too much fun in Cleveland."

Jerry had followed me from Pittsburgh to Cleveland which, I presume, was one of the reasons I left Cleveland for Boston.

"I didn't tell you?" he asked, perking up.

"You might have. I don't remember."

If this hasn't been made clear already, I can be something of a blackout drunk. Immortally speaking, it's sort of convenient sometimes.

"If I tell you, will you promise not to flush me?"

I considered it.

"Okay. But no funny stuff tonight. I plan to crash here for a while, and I don't want you wrecking things."

By funny stuff I meant Jerry's peculiar brand of seduction—get a girl drunk, wait for her to pass out, and then spend the rest of the night in her pants. I mean that literally. That blonde wasn't going to think he was so cute after she found him curled up in a post-coital slumber in her panties.

"I saw her," he said.

"Saw who?"

"Her. I saw *her*. Fuck, Adam, the one you keep talking about. I saw her."

I stared at him.

"You're lying."

"Bright red hair and pale skin, just like you said."

"She's dead. I told you that."

"Didn't look dead from where I was sitting. Creeped the fuck outta me, too. Swear to Baal, my scrotum got sucked right into my asshole when I looked at them blue eyes."

I could have sworn I never told him what color her eyes were. My heart skipped several beats and threatened to stop altogether. Had he actually seen her?

"Where was this?"

"I was polishing off the JD supply at Sully's, right? You remember, that little dive on the East side? Yeah, so I was up on the bar and showing myself a good time when I saw her face. In the window, I mean. Peeking in on me. Think she was looking for you."

I grabbed him by the little shoulders. "Did she say anything? Did you talk to her?"

"Oww! Shit no. I just ... you know, stared back. I told you, that chick freaked the fuck outta me. Anyway, I blinked, and she was gone."

I let go of him.

"All right."

I thought she was dead. It didn't seem possible. But why would he lie?

"Listen," I said, "thanks for telling me. You didn't have to come all the way here for that."

"Hey, no prob. This place is a better bar town anyway. So you wanna open the door now?"

I opened the door and let him scamper out to continue his Iffrit Unnatural Acts performance. He stopped in the doorway.

"Hey, what the hell is she, anyway?" he asked.

"I don't know."

"I don't think she's human, bud. Seriously. Not that I give a shit about your ass, but I'd do everything I could to stay the fuck away from her."

"Yeah," I said. "Thanks."

Not the first time I'd gotten that warning. Probably wouldn't be the last. He couldn't understand. Every other face I've known eventually aged, sagged, and died. Jerry's would, too. But the first time I gazed at the red-haired woman with the haunting blue eyes was over ten thousand years ago. Human or not, she was the only other immortal I'd ever seen.

CHAPTER 3

The thing in the cell next to mine is definitely not human. It's much too strong.

I've been hearing this pounding noise every night since I got here. Kind of like the sound of distant artillery. Never knew what it was until this morning, when Ringo took me on my daily walk to the lab. We strayed a bit closer than usual to the second building, and whatever's in there attacked the door. I swear, the door nearly buckled. Which is pretty amazing since just a cursory glance would tell you the whole structure is reinforced with steel.

More tellingly, Ringo flinched. It takes some kind of big ugly to make a thing as nasty as Ringo flinch.

They don't let it out. At all. Or feed it. I think they're just waiting for it to die of starvation.

I just might know what it is.

~

I was in America the last time I saw the red-haired woman.

It was 1922, and I'd ended up in Chicago at the height of

Prohibition. (Why anyone in their right minds would want to ban alcohol is beyond me. What I was doing in a country that banned it ... well, that's a story for another time.) I was dating a girl named Irma, who fancied herself a flapper. Irma was a college girl, technically, but hardly spent any time in classes, which came as a bit of a shock to her moderately well-off, stoic Protestant parents when they got around to looking at her grades. She'd discovered illegal booze, short skirts, and heavy petting sometime around her freshman year and said, *bring it on*. Which was what I liked about her.

I do date, in case you were wondering. I am also—and this I consider a welcome byproduct of my immortality—completely sterile. Imagine if I wasn't. Between my direct descendants and their offspring, we could people an entire continent. I think about these things.

But yes, I do see women. Men too, at one time. I spent about a century and a half as a homosexual. It ended up being far too much work, so I didn't keep it up. (You never really appreciate women until you've tried pleasing another man. Just trust me.)

My relationships don't last long, mainly because it's hard to grow old with someone when you don't grow old. Consequently, I'm often the Courtier, Secret Lover, or more recently, the Transitional Boyfriend. Most of the women tend to be fairly young from a societal standpoint (*young* meaning something different depending on which century we're discussing) and in the exploratory phase of their sexual lives.

Okay, and I like younger girls. Sue me.

It was a Saturday night, and we were in a speakeasy called *Looie's*. You wouldn't know it was a club by looking at it because *Looie's* was in the basement of a former fish market in a rundown neighborhood on the edge of Lake Michigan. It was an ugly, dark place that always smelled of cod and human sweat. The cement floor was covered in sawdust and on Saturdays, there was a live jazz band that was nearly impossible to hear because so many people came to dance that the sound of scuffling shoes over the sawdust and cement made a rasping noise that drowned out almost everything else, and also because the amplifier hadn't been invented yet. The bar—an extra-long wooden table hastily erected by Looie himself—only served bathtub gin and sacramental wine, neither of which tasted particularly good.

I loved the place.

I began that memorable evening standing at the end of the bar, watching the Saturday night masses bump each other on the dance floor, and watching Irma. She was standing in front of me bouncing up and down with the kind of effortless grace I always admired and never had. (Immortal and utterly without rhythm, that's me.)

"Come on, Rocky, I wanna dance!" she pleaded.

I was calling myself Rocky at the time.

"You *are* dancing."

"With *you*, stupid!" She undulated her way over to me and rubbed up against my side, which made me think of doing something with her other than dance.

I looked into her eyes and smiled. She really was beautiful. Maybe today she'd be something less than special, what with almost no chest to speak of and a figure that could be described as boyish. But her legs were long, her eyes were a fascinating green, and she had a nose that was nearly as perfect as Cleopatra's. (Or so I've heard. Never met Cleopatra.) Her brown hair was cut in what might be called, fifty years later, a Dorothy Hamill style. I gave her a decent kiss, which she deserved.

"You go dance," I said. "I just want to watch you."

She put on a pouty face, pecked me on the cheek and sashayed away, all beads and feathers and silk.

I really miss her.

"Hit me, Looie," I requested of the bartender/owner, in his own language.

Looie was a first generation Italian. He spoke with a heavy Northern accent and, despite having lived most of his life on the south side of Chicago, was far more comfortable in his family's native tongue.

I'm fluent in about a hundred different languages, most of which are no longer of any use to anybody. Aramaic, for instance, isn't doing me any good anymore. Someone once suggested I had the "gift of tongues" but that's not true. I've just been around long enough to gain fluency everywhere I've been.

Since language changes far more quickly than I do, I try to practice as much as possible, to pick up on any modern nuances that might have come about since I last visited a particular region.

"More the same, Rocky?" he asked, in Italian.

"Do I have a choice?"

He winked at me. *"Just a moment."*

He ducked under the counter and resurfaced a few seconds later with a new glass for me. I took a sip.

"Scotch!" Twelve-year-old scotch, at least. Made the bathtub gin taste like piss water by comparison.

"Not for most," he said. *"Just for friends."*

"I thank you," I said sincerely.

"It is no problem."

This is another good reason to be fluent. I'd known Looie for only about six months, but the minute I greeted him in Italian I was his favorite customer.

Plus, I did do him a favor once. Looie's sacramental wine came via the usual channels (i.e., a faux Rabbi with an imaginary constituency. The Rabbi's name was Frank and he was about as Jewish as I am) but the bathtub gin was a homemade affair. When Looie first opened his little nightspot, a nephew named Santino was his mad scientist, and Santino mixed a pretty fine concoction. So fine, he was stolen by a local family for their own string of illicit bars, and Looie was forced to shut down temporarily because he knew nothing about making his own alcohol.

So, I gave him a few tips. Actually, I built a still for him, a slightly modern version of what an alchemist named Aloysius showed me back before the Enlightenment. Except where Aloysius used sheep intestines, I used rubber tubing.

"Where did you get the scotch?" I asked him.

"I made some new friends," he said mischievously, giving me a sly wink.

That could have meant anything. In Chicago, in the Twenties, it almost never meant anything good.

On the dance floor, all race and class distinctions had broken down completely. I saw that Irma was swinging with two very limber black men and a white woman wearing a fur stole that looked, to my somewhat trained eye, to be genuine sable. Nobody cared anymore who they were dancing with, which undoubtedly would have had the idiot Puritans who authored the alcohol ban in the first place pitching fits, had any of them been there.

"What kind of friends?" I pressed Looie. *"You're not selling out, are you?"*

Looie had been under pressure to join one of the Chicago families, and I was one of the few people who knew about it.

"I may be, my friend," he said. *"I am tired. This business is for the young."*

"Business is great and this is the best place in town. Everybody knows it. Why mess that up?"

He smiled.

"It will be no less good with another man behind the bar."

"It's not the man at the bar, it's the man at the door, and you hire the man at the door."

I was speaking metaphorically. The doorman was another one of Looie's nephews. He was somewhat slow— not apparently fluent in either Italian or English—but he did comprehend each night's password. My point was, Looie's nephew let everybody who knew the password through. Under new ownership, that could change. Most of the other speakeasies in town were stratified according to race, class, and musical preference. Franchised, in today's lingo.

"We will see," he said simply. Then, hailed at the other end of the bar, he toddled off.

I checked on Irma again, but with the surging crowd it was difficult to spot much more than her raised hands. Fairly soon I was going to have to join her, but I wasn't nearly drunk enough yet to try dancing. I downed my scotch. Still not drunk enough.

That was when I saw her.

The surprising red hair is always the first thing I notice. Even in the poor lighting of *Looie's* it stood out quite clearly, almost glowing. I squinted. She turned. I met those magnificent eyes. It was definitely her.

"Hey!" I called out uselessly. Nobody could hear me, and if they did, *hey* was pretty non-descriptive anyway.

I ran to the dance floor and started to push my way through, positioning myself between the red-haired woman (she was at the far end of the floor, near the band) and the exit. In the past, every single time I spotted her, she was either too far away to reach or somehow managed to slip off before I could get to her. I wasn't going to let that happen again.

Then fate intervened, as it always seemed to. Just as I started forcing my way through the dance floor crowd, the front door—which was made of solid iron—blew open with a loud BANG that startled everybody and knocked Looie's corpulent nephew backward several feet. The band came to a discordant stop, and as one, we turned to see what had just happened.

From where I stood, I could see right up the short flight of wooden stairs and outside. A car blocked the entrance. It was fitted with a wooden beam—a rudimentary battering ram. Someone crashed their car specifically to take out the door.

Keep in mind this was pre-fire code and an illegal establishment to boot. And the front door was the only public exit.

I had a very bad feeling about this.

The room remained silent, all except for Looie's nephew, who was groaning unpleasantly. I think we all knew what was coming next.

The first Molotov cocktail spun into the room, shattered on the wooden railing, and started spreading fire down the stairs. The second made it all the way to the edge of the cement floor and caught on the sawdust. The third reached the wall near the bar about two feet from where I'd been standing a minute earlier. It caught as well, as it should have. Except for the cement floor, the entire building was made of wood.

I had landed in the middle of a Chicago-style hostile takeover and asset liquidation.

As you can imagine, I've been in quite a few tight situations in my long life. One of the first things I learned was if there's going to be a mob panic, don't be standing between that mob and wherever it is they all want to go. The second thing I learned was, don't try to run through fire.

Other than me quickly stepping in the direction of the bar—to where I was less likely to be trampled—the first person to make a move was one of the black guys Irma had been dancing with. He ran up the flaming steps, and it was like a spell being broken because a second later everyone else was behind him. I wanted to scream out that this was an incredibly stupid thing to do, but the decision had been made and nobody was interested in listening to what I had to say. *Get out,* they all agreed, *before the steps are gone and the fire has reached the rest of the room. Get out because we don't know about any other exits. Just get out.*

I saw Irma fly past and managed to grab her by the elbow, yanking her in the other direction despite multiple hysterical protestations.

"We have to get out!" she shrieked.

"Not that way!"

"There's no other way!"

"Of course there is," I said confidently.

But was there? We were below street level and all the windows were half-sized, covered on the outside by iron bars, and nine feet from the floor. Great security if you don't want people breaking in and stealing your supplies. Bad idea if you desperately need to escape, the door is barred, and the stairs leading to that door are on fire.

The sound of gunshots filled the air, and I ducked instinctively. Whoever started the fire had decided to discourage any attempts to get the hell out of the place by shooting a tommy gun through the space between the top of the doorway and the hood of the car. Interestingly, this only managed to affect the people who were actually hit by bullets. Everyone behind them kept trying to plow through.

"You see?" I said to Irma, who I was still holding back. "We can't go that way!"

I scanned the back of the room. There had to be another door, and there was. It was on the far side of the bar. I'd never even noticed it before. Better, it was open.

I threw my fur coat (it was the style) over Irma and dragged her through the door. It led to a small back room that smelled even fishier, and a narrow wooden staircase which led upstairs. At the top, sitting in front of the door and crying, was Looie.

"It's locked!" he cried, in Italian.

"Unlock it!" I commanded.

"No, no, no. It's barred. It's ..." And then he continued his weeping.

I stormed to the top of the stairs, pushed Looie aside, and threw my weight into the door.

It wouldn't budge. He was right. Whoever took care of the front door also knew there was another exit and had taken care of it. Great.

In another minute we would all be unconscious from smoke fumes, and another minute after that we'd all be dead.

"Looie," I barked. He couldn't even acknowledge me, so I slapped him hard across the face. *"You know this place better than anyone. There HAS to be another way out!"*

"No, no, no other way ..." He was inconsolable. At the bottom of the stairs, Irma was curled up and crying all over my coat. I could hear the rising panic in the other room.

People were burning. This was getting to be as bad as Rome, albeit on a much smaller scale.

I started ticking off what I knew about the building.

It was on Lake Michigan. Everyone knew that.

They used to sell fish upstairs and gut and store them on ice downstairs, which was why the place smelled of fish all the time. That was also why the basement floor was cement, because melted ice can just wreck a wood floor.

Fish.

I knew a lot about fish. I worked on a fishing trawler once, in Galilee. We never used a place like this, though. No, we had to clean the fish on the boat, salt it, and get it to market right away, because nobody had invented the ice machine yet. It was messy work. We'd slice the fish up the middle, pull out the bones, and toss the bones and the guts overboard.

It was stupid when I gave it a little thought. Who cleans fish in a basement? What do you do with the guts?

What *did* they do with the guts?

I grabbed Looie and pulled him to his feet, dragged him to the bottom of the stairs, and sat him next to Irma.

"Watch her!"

I took two steps back into the main room and immediately discovered there was almost no breathable air left. The smoke had gotten thicker and the ceiling was nearly engulfed, and the heat from the flames was palpable. At the front of the room, the wooden staircase had collapsed, and I could see several bodies already piled up nearby, either victims of the fire or victims of the sons of bitches on the other side of the doorway. Those that were still alive were in pretty much the same state of paralysis as Irma and Looie.

Me? I had an idea.

Back when I first saw this old fish market, what came to mind right away was that the building was surely about to tumble into the lake, because it jutted over the water a good five feet. Now I was thinking you don't build a building hanging over the side of a lake unless you've got a good reason.

There was one part of the floor that wasn't just cement plus sawdust, and that was where the band played. An area rug defined the space. Coughing madly, I managed to push the equipment out of the way—thoroughly destroying a snare drum in the process—and pulled up the rug.

Under the rug, at the edge of the wall, was a trap door.

It was where they threw the bones after cleaning the fish, and where the runoff from the melted ice traveled. And since it had been years since anyone used it—based on the rust buildup—there was a good chance the guys outside didn't know it was there. Looie didn't even know it was there.

I grabbed the metal ring and yanked. It opened with an unpleasant creak and there was the lake. Best of all, nobody was standing there with a tommy gun.

Stifling the impulse to just jump down and get away, I instead ran back to Irma and Looie, grabbed them both, and got them to the trap door. Irma—by then resigned to the idea that her life was over—refused to recognize the significance of the opening, so rather than wait for her to get her head together, I just pushed her out. Hopefully the cold water of Lake Michigan would snap her out of it in time to understand she was supposed to swim.

"Looie," I said. *"I need you to look out for her. I'll be right out."*

He nodded and patted my hand, then dropped out of sight, hopefully not on top of Irma.

I crawled and crouched my way to the front of the room, looking for anyone who wasn't dead yet so I could show them the way out. This was no easy task, as the smoke was getting heavier and there was a good chance the ceiling would be collapsing at any moment.

I managed to find about twenty people and point the way—including Looie's nephew, who was miraculously still breathing when I unburied him—before things got dicey.

I was dragging a somewhat portly and thoroughly inconsolable woman across the floor when a fire-engulfed support beam landed between me and the trap door. I had no doubt that in another second the rest of the ceiling was going to join it, but the woman wouldn't budge. I tried to scream at her to get her fat ass up and start moving them legs, but I'd been breathing smoke for about five minutes. My lungs felt like they were on fire and there was a good possibility I'd permanently damaged my vocal cords. (A future as an immortal mime flashed before my eyes. I didn't like the idea at all.)

Not knowing any other way to get the fat lady to pick herself up—and not entirely willing to leave her behind (although she was sure pushing her luck)—I leaned over and pulled her skirt up past her hips.

If you ever need to get someone's undivided attention, the very best way to do it is to expose their undergarments. People are weird.

"Hey!" she screamed.

It worked. She rolled to her feet.

Still unable to speak, I grabbed her by the back of the neck and pushed her around the fiery beam and to the trap door. She barely fit through, but she did fit, thank goodness.

I took one last look back, but there was no way I'd make it for another trip, not without a good long dose of fresh air first.

I dropped through the door. Seconds later, that second ceiling beam came crashing down, and then the building began its inevitable collapse.

The water was wonderfully cool and only about four feet deep, so I didn't even have to concern myself with drowning. Even more pleasant was the air. I promised myself not to ever take air for granted again.

"Rocky," someone called out to my right. I followed the voice, and ended up emerging from underneath the lip of the old fish market to find myself eye level with a short dock.

"Over here, my friend," Looie said in Italian from atop the dock. He offered me a hand. Beside him, two of the men I'd just helped save were pulling the fat woman out of the water.

I accepted Looie's hand gratefully and mutely, as I still couldn't speak.

It would be days before I could utter anything, so I never got a chance to ask Looie if he'd seen a woman with bright red hair emerge from the club. Because I sure never did.

CHAPTER 4

At least I'm eating well. There is a decently-stocked kitchen on the base somewhere and possibly a gourmet chef, because today's dinner was the finest example of beef bourguignon I've had since before the French Revolution. Granted the plastic fork and the egregious lack of wine to accompany the meal ruined the effect, but I'm still impressed.

I would kill for a glass of wine, or a beer, or a shot of anything up to and including rubbing alcohol. I'd been dry for over five days before getting here and haven't had a drink since, meaning I'm in the middle of possibly the longest stretch of sobriety I've lived through for a century. This just makes me grouchier, if that's possible.

~

Shortly after the fire that destroyed *Looie's*, Irma found God, pretty much signaling the end of our relationship. Especially when she insisted God saved her from the fire, which I took a bit personally, as I was there saving her and a bunch of other people at the time, and I never once saw God. Too bad. I could have used the help.

It turned out Looie's mistake was in selling out to the wrong mafia family—although the question of whether there is such a thing as a *right* mafia family is debatable—and ending up an important piece in a turf war he knew nothing about. Not willing to risk making the same mistake again, he got out of the speakeasy business altogether. He ended up using his savings to open a small shoe store.

I stuck around Chicago for a while longer, even though I was pretty well convinced my red-haired foil was dead, which meant I had little reason to stay. It just didn't seem possible for her to have gotten out of that fire intact, not if she was anything like me —although maybe she wasn't.

I ran through the possibilities again. Vampire was one that was most likely, as they are hypothetically just as immortal as me. Except I'd seen her in the daytime more than once. And, every vampire I ever met had black eyes. Possibly she was a vampire that didn't need to hide from sunlight and had blue eyes, but that's a bit like saying something is a cat except it walks on hind legs and has no fur or whiskers.

I don't know any other sentient humanoids that have a get-out-of-death clause. Other than me. And I don't have porcelain skin and haunting eyes. So, she might be like me, but was she the same thing as me?

What was she?

Mind you, I'd run through all this before, thousands of times. I've taken suggestions, too. A succubus I used to hang out with insisted my red-haired mystery girl was death incarnate, meaning my endless search for her was actually a complex working-out of my immortality issues.

(A note: succubi are notorious amateur psychologists and have been since well before Freud. In fact, I have it on good authority that Freud stole his whole gig from a particularly talkative succubus he used to know. And if you don't believe Freud knew a succubus, you haven't read Freud.)

I didn't find the argument convincing. If I am to believe in some sort of anthropomorphic representation of mortality, I should first develop a belief in some higher power, or at least in life-after-death.

I'm a pretty sad example of what one should do with eternal life. I've never reached any higher level of consciousness, I don't have access to any great truths, and I've never borne witness to the divine or transcendent. Some of this is just bad luck. Like working in the fishing industry in Galilee and never once running into Jesus. But in my defense, there were an awful lot of people back then claiming to be the son of God. I probably wouldn't have been able to pick him out of the crowd. And since I don't believe there is a God, I doubt we would have gotten along all that well.

I probably wasn't always quite so atheistic. I don't recall much of my early hunter-gatherer days, but I'm sure that back then I believed in lots of gods. And also that the stars were pinholes in an enclosed firmament. There might even have been a giant turtle involved. I distinctly recall a crude religious ceremony involving a mammoth skin and lots of face paint, too, and that was probably a religious thing of some sort. But after centuries on the mortal coil I've come to realize that religion is for people who expect to die someday and want to go to a better place when that happens. It doesn't apply to me.

Anyway, I sat around for days and mused over these and other subjects, mainly pertaining to my mysterious red-haired bugaboo. Gary and Nate were decidedly nonplussed about it, especially since I almost never moved from the futon except to get more beer—which I was still paying for, by the way.

"Man, can you at least shower or something?" Gary asked one evening.

"Later," I muttered.

"How 'bout now? I wanna watch the game."

It did me no good to ask which game. There was always a

game, sometime, somewhere, that absolutely had to be watched. ESPN may eventually be the end of Western civilization as we know it. And I should know, having witnessed the end of Western civilization at least four times.

We stared at each other for a while, and then I reluctantly ceded the futon.

"You should get out or something," he recommended as I got to my feet and stretched out the muscle kinks.

Nate, from the kitchen, agreed. "Clear the cobwebs, dude. Get some night air."

They'd obviously decided that having an immortal as a house guest wasn't nearly as fun as it sounded.

I should have seen this coming when they kicked Jerry out. (Literally. Nate drop-kicked him). But Jerry had left about two dozen stains on the walls, copped a feel on three girls who will probably never speak to Nate or Gary again, and clogged the toilet twice. He was asking for it. Me, I just bought more alcohol and stunk up the futon. Was that so bad?

"What's it like outside?" I asked, taking the hint and running with it.

"It's nice," Nate said quickly.

"Very refreshing," Gary added.

"Sleep on a bench refreshing or head for the bus station refreshing?"

"It's ... brisk," Gary amended.

"Kinda chilly," Nate agreed.

"I got an old coat if you need one," Gary offered.

~

It was indeed brisk, and the old coat Gary gave me smelled vaguely of vomit. To help cut the chill, I took a half-empty bottle of vodka that I might have also paid for. Then I started walking in the general direction of Chinatown, on the other side of which was South Station.

I decided being poor in Boston in November really sucks. And the damnable thing was I couldn't even remember how I'd ended up in Boston in the first place. Last time I'd spent any time there was in 1912, and there was nothing that compelled me to stick around then. Possibly I just hopped aboard a train at some point, not much caring where it went so long as it had a bar car, and rode until it came to a stop. Wouldn't be the first time I'd done that.

I was thinking it was time to consider accessing a larger quantity of funds. As I said, I do have some. I'm just not exactly sure how much. I kept walk-around money in my bag, which was in a locker in South Station, which I hoped was always open because that was also where I planned to sleep. The rest of my money was in a Swiss bank account, so to get at it I was going to have to make a few calls. I don't think the Swiss issue ATM cards, but I never really checked.

Sobriety was also something to consider, although it should be noted I was considering it while gulping vodka. The idea that the red-haired woman was still alive was something worth sobering up for. Maybe it was time to start looking again. It would end in frustration, as it always did, but it was still something to do.

About two blocks from my destination, I saw something curious: a hooker.

At least I assumed she was a hooker, because if she wasn't, her fashion sense was abhorrent. She was dressed in knee-high leather boots, a denim miniskirt (which she'd manually torn along the side to expose half of her left buttock,) and a faded black sleeveless half-shirt that read "Appetite for Destruction" on the front. Her hair was black and very large—length and height—and she'd gone overboard completely in the make-up department. Her skin was a pale white.

What made the view so curious was that it was about ten degrees with the wind chill, and she didn't look cold at all.

"Lookin' for fun, baby?" she asked as I approached.

I sized her up once again, up close. No trembling in the wind at all, and she didn't appear to be strung out on anything. Her nipples weren't even erect. And it was just as cold next to her as it was everywhere else.

"Do I look like I have any money?" I took another swig of the vodka, now almost gone.

"Who said anything about money?" she asked coyly. "I'm just looking for a good time."

I smiled. "Sure you are. What's your name?"

"Brenda." She grinned with her lips tight over her teeth.

"Brenda. You're a vampire, aren't you?"

"Excuse me?"

"It's okay. I'm not on a crusade or anything." I held up my open palms. "No wooden stakes. See?"

(It should be noted that wooden stakes don't work, so don't try it. You'll just piss off the vampire.)

"Go away," she ordered, spinning on a spiked heel and pretending I wasn't there.

"You must be a young one."

"You're crazy," she shouted over her shoulder. "I should call a cop."

"Go ahead. That'll be fun."

A car slowed for her. She gave the driver a little show, leaning over and shaking her fairly impressive pale breasts. He decided after some consideration to shop elsewhere.

"When was it, twenty years ago?" I asked. "Couldn't have been much more than that."

She turned and looked at me long and hard. Not threatening, just curious.

"Twenty-seven," she admitted.

"Thought so."

"You're not one, are you?"

"Nope."

She circled me. I think she was trying to be intimidating, and if I found vampires frightening, she might have succeeded. But the truth is the percentage of vampires that are also evil killers is about the same as the percentage of normal people who are also evil killers. Brenda didn't look like a killer; she looked like a mall rat.

"You smell like vomit," she said, her nose crinkling.

"It's the coat. It's a loaner."

"How did you know I was a vamp?"

"Maybe you noticed how everyone else is dressed in layers? The *Guns 'N Roses* concert shirt doesn't help either."

"I like it," she insisted.

"It's very fetching. But the band broke up a long time ago. You haven't learned how to keep up with the times is my point. But you're young. That always takes a while."

Brenda stopped circling and met me face-to-face. "And how would you know?"

"I know a lot of vampires. And I'm older than I look."

I extended my hand.

"I'm Apollo," I said, giving her the name she was most likely to have heard.

"No *way*!" she exclaimed. "The one-who-walks-by-day?" She grabbed my hand and squeezed, *just* a bit too hard.

"Oww," I said.

"Sorry. My strength, it's ..."

"I know. It's something to get used to, isn't it?"

I'm something of a legend in the vampire community, if you hadn't already guessed. I'm most often described as another vampire but without a sun weakness. I gave up trying to correct the misapprehension about three centuries ago. The name Apollo

—Greek god of the sun—was given to me by a vampire named Magnus in the eleventh century. It certainly wasn't because of my stellar physique.

"Wow, I can*not* believe I'm talking to Apollo!" she gushed. "The one who made me told me *all* about you! You're like, a legend!"

"This is a treat for me too, really," I said. "Look, I have to pick up something from the train station, but I was wondering if I could ask a favor."

"Anything!"

"Great. Because I need a place to crash."

"O-okay. It's not much ..."

She was already reassessing her opinion of me. That was fast. One of the drawbacks of being a legendary figure is that inevitably the legend outstrips reality. She probably thought I had magical powers and could leap tall buildings in a single bound.

"Brenda, I guarantee I've seen worse. I only need a place to stay for a night or two, and then I'll be out of your hair."

"Sure, but ... it's just that I haven't eaten yet ..."

"Right. Tell you what, if you can't snag a quick bite while I'm gone, you can nibble on me. We'll call it my rent for the night."

She brightened, provided that's possible for the undead. "You'd let me do that?"

"Sure. Just don't go nuts or anything."

"It's a deal!"

"Great. I'll be right back."

I left her to her street corner and made my way to South Station, where I hoped my bag was where I left it.

As I found out later, around the same time Brenda and I were negotiating the rent for my stay, something unpleasant showed up at Gary and Nate's. Something that was looking for me.

~

Brenda lived in Chinatown, a short three blocks from the corner she was working. It was a second floor apartment above a restaurant that specialized in something called "hot pot," which I later discovered means "come boil your own dinner."

The word "apartment" needed translating, too. It was one room plus a toilet that had evidently been installed in a closet, with a bucket and a sponge instead of a tub. I wasn't getting that shower.

I might have credited Brenda with being far enough along to realize she didn't actually need to sleep in a coffin except that the place was so small it nearly qualified as one.

It did have a bed, though. Clean sheets, too. This made some bit of sense, especially if Brenda brought any clients to the place. Vampires have an acute sense of everything, but their sense of smell is particularly exceptional. I imagined she washed her sheets after every appointment, probably at the all-night laundromat around the corner.

She shut the hallway door, cutting us off from the dangling bare bulb out there and plunging the room into total and complete darkness. (The windows were heavily shuttered, for obvious reasons.)

"I told you it wasn't much," she apologized, moving freely in the dark.

"Brenda, I can't see anything."

"Oh, sorry. I figured you could see like me." A flame sputtered to life in her hands, which she marched over to a candle resting on the windowsill.

"I don't pay for electricity," she explained. "No phone either."

"That's okay."

"Boy, you're really a lot like them, aren't you?" she observed.

"Like who?"

"Humans. You've ... ass ... what's the word I want?"

"Assimilated?"

"Maybe, yeah." She sat down on the bed. "No strength, no eyes ... and hey, your heart is still beating." Good hearing being one of the aforementioned heightened senses.

I sat next to her. "I'm not a vampire. The truth is, nobody knows what I am, exactly. I sure don't."

"Wild," she said, with about as much sincerity as one can say that particular word. "So, you don't drink blood or anything?"

"Nope. I eat rare steak from time to time." I polished off the last of the vodka and started to roll up my sleeve. "I assume you're still hungry."

Her eyes lit up. "Yeah. But, you know, only if you want to."

A point about vampires. They can and do have sex. I've tried it. It's not bad. A little cold, a little dry ... it's kind of like screwing a very lively statue. Usually the vampire is doing you a favor because they're not particularly turned on by intercourse, although that's not always true with the younger ones. Drinking blood, however, is an orgasmic experience nearly every time, hence her enthusiasm. Yeah, she had to eat, but there was more involved. In a lot of ways it's more fun watching them eat than having sex with them.

"A deal is a deal," I said, extending my arm. "I assume you know how to stop yourself."

"Oh sure. Haven't lost a John yet."

"How's that work?" I asked. "Do you wait until after they're done, or during?"

"During, usually. That way we're both having our fun."

"And they don't mind?"

"Nobody's complained yet. And when I do it well, they don't even notice." I found it hard to imagine not noticing one was being bitten, but that's me.

She held my wrist lovingly. "Cheers," I said.

With a grin, she bared her fangs and dug in. It only stung for a second. Then the two of us leaned back slowly onto the bed, Brenda in a blind frenzy of rapture and me watching her. Lying there, it occurred to me how very much she looked like Eloise.

CHAPTER 5

Viktor is getting more talkative each day. He really isn't a bad guy, despite all the poking and prodding. I assumed I'd be dealing with your basic mad scientist type—if there is such a thing—purely based on what he's trying to accomplish. But he's hardly mad at all, just a little loopy. Everybody on his team is friendly, actually, and come in varying shades of loopiness. Best of all, they let me hang out in the lab even when my part is done. Which is great, because these guys are all very talkative.

Today Viktor spoke at length about my telomeres and how they don't get any smaller. He feels this is very important, but unfortunately I can't figure out why; the phrase in layman's terms *apparently doesn't mean anything to him. I just nod and let him talk, hoping something of use will come out of it.*

He's obviously hoping I pick up on some of his excitement. I think that would make this easier for all of them, knowing I was happy to donate my freedom to the cause. And because every time I smile about something they start talking more, I've learned to accommodate them. If I'm lucky, soon they'll start talking about the others.

~

I met Eloise in the winter of 1356 in France, while I was working in the castle of Enguerrand de Coucy in Picardy, the northern region near the border of the Holy Roman Empire. Picardy was almost perpetually snowbound, and the castle was 200 years old already at that time, so the damn place was as drafty as hell, but it did have a few things going for it. Foremost, it wasn't Paris.

I have developed likes and dislikes regarding major cities over time, and one thing I've learned is you have to pick your spots. For example, Caesar's Rome was a fine place to be, as was Aristotle's Athens. But Paris and London up until the World Wars were almost completely intolerable, as was early New York and early Berlin. Basically, Paris in 1346 was one gigantic smelly sewer, which made some sense, as neither the flush toilet nor deodorant had been invented yet. And the plague only compounded the problem. Nobody knew quite what to do with plague victims, so they usually stayed where they dropped and just added to the overall bouquet.

Altogether, I was pretty happy in my drafty old castle on a hill overlooking nothing in particular. It was quiet, not nearly as smelly, and the plague rarely made it to us. (Not that I personally had to worry about it, but stinky dead people are stinky dead people and I'd just as soon rather not have to deal with them.)

Strictly speaking, I was a servant. I don't like to put it that way because Lord Coucy was a generous man who treated most people he met with a reasonable degree of respect, so I never felt much like one. And my singular talent, the one that got me the room in the castle instead of the hay loft in the stable, was that I was literate. Coucy could read and write as well as the next man but nobody else in the place could, which made me, simple peasant that I was, extremely valuable, especially when he was away.

And he was away all the time. This period was later known as the Hundred Years' War on account of France and England kept fighting each other over French sovereignty. (Or something. They just didn't like each other. Still don't.) While he was off fighting various noble battles—which France invariably lost—I kept up correspondences and maintained the books, looked after Mme. Coucy, and basically hit on the staff whenever I could.

The castle was built on the peak of a hill, with thirty-foot walls that made three-quarters of the keep virtually impregnable to everything except the march of time. The fourth side was open to a small village, itself surrounded by a low wall, with gates at the far end that were lightly guarded on most occasions and not at all in times of war. One might think the opposite made more sense, except that nobody bothered to attack us during war. Most of the battles took place in Southern France, in places like Poitiers and Crecy.

There were no guards at wartime because all able noblemen went to battle. I was an able man but I was not noble. I wasn't even French. I claimed to be a Jew from Venice. (I did not look particularly Jewish, per se, but nobody in Picardy had ever seen one so I got away with it. Intolerance reared its head on occasion, but I had the protection of the lord of the castle, so I stayed pretty well out of trouble.) What noblemen remained were advanced in age and had already seen too many battles in their lifetimes, so busied themselves with maintaining order in the Coucy-le-Chateau in the lord's absence.

One such man was an old codger named Lord Francois Etienne de Harsigny, who for some reason liked to be called Lance. Lance was fifty-two and should not have been alive. He only had one foot and one eye, suffered from gout, and always smelled of gangrene and poppies. The foot he lost in the Battle of Crecy. I don't know when he lost the eye, but I suspect its absence was indirectly what caused the loss of his foot. To compensate—for the foot at least—he would strap the boot from his armor onto the stump. It didn't do him a damn bit of good when he walked but it helped when he rode. Harsigny served as castle regent in 1356 while Lord Coucy was yet again away to battle.

On one disturbingly cold winter's morn, Lord Harsigny bade my presence in the main hall for a matter of grave importance. The hall was where the lord of the castle served as *de facto* judge and jury for local disputes among the peasantry. When I arrived, I found a local smithy weeping over the body of his wife.

"Lord Venice," Harsigny called when I entered. He called me Lord Venice in public out of respect, for I had no actual title. Serge was my common name at the time. "Attend."

I went straight to the smithy, a pleasant man named Albert with whom I'd had many dealings in the past. Albert was a tanner. He made an excellent leather waistcoat, one of which I was wearing.

"Albert," I asked, "what has happened?"

He looked up at me, mute with grief, and lifted the cloak from his wife's body.

Something had torn her throat out.

"What say you, Lord Venice?" Harsigny asked.

It has been said that the Dark Ages were the worst time to be an intellectual, and while the argument has some merit, I'm living proof that there will always be room for the learned, provided one shops one's talents long enough. Harsigny called for me because I was the only man in town who was well versed in logic, and because I knew my history better than most, for obvious reasons. Not that Lance was a fool by any stretch.

"Where did you find her?" I asked Albert.

"Outside the walls," Albert whispered. "She'd gone to the well near dusk at my behest. When she did not return ..."

"Albert, the well lies within the walls. And you found her outside?"

"Yes, Lord Venice."

"When was this?"

"We found her this morning after looking within the keep for much of the night."

I examined the wound more closely. Her head lay at an unnatural angle, and there were teeth marks on her neck and shoulder. Some kind of animal had done this. But there were no other marks on the body, which made no sense. Animals don't kill for sport; they kill to eat. Why hadn't she been eaten?

"What would have made her leave the walls at dusk?" I asked Albert.

"She would not have!"

"No. I suppose not."

It would have been easier on all of us if she had, but he was right. Only the foolish or the extremely well armed drift beyond the keep walls at night, especially in winter when the wolves are hungry and desperate enough to consider going after a person. But no wolf had ever dared stray so far inside as to reach the well, and no wolf was strong enough to drag an adult woman such a distance—by the throat—alone. Nor, I suspected, would any wolf have the inclination to do so.

"We need to see where she was found. Can you show us?"

~

We rode to the gates, in part because Harsigny rode everywhere (he'd stable his horse in his quarters if he could) but also because of the air of importance men on horseback tended to carry. It was a serious inquiry and the villagers—all of whom were by then well aware of the murder—needed to understand that we were taking it seriously. Otherwise I'd have gone alone and walked, which is what poor Albert had to do. His wife's body was left in the care of the castle staff, where a priest had been called and the preparations for her funeral pyre were being made. (It was too cold to bury the dead in the winter in Picardy.)

Before we reached the gates, I stopped at the well.

I dismounted and left Albert to hold my horse. Harsigny remained on his steed and walked along beside me.

We were fortunate that it hadn't snowed during the night, or there would have been no point.

"Wolf?" Harsigny asked quietly.

"I can't imagine how." A crowd had followed us through the town, forcing us to speak in hushed tones.

"I agree. Perhaps were it a child ..."

I crouched down near the well. A lone bucket rested on its side, next to an area of kicked up snow.

"There," Harsigny said, pointing. "The imprint of a head."

I saw no such imprint.

"You are too close to the ground to see it, Serge."

I went to the area he described and brushed back the kicked-up snow to find a fresh bloodstain, frozen and glistening.

I looked in the direction of the gates. There was no trail, or rather, not the right kind of trail.

"She wasn't dragged, Lance," I said quietly. "She was carried."

"Impossible. You saw the wound. No man did that."

"I agree. But no animal walks on hind legs and carries a twelve-stone body in his arms either."

"Few men could do so," he pointed out.

"True. Come, let's see where they found her."

~

The spot was barely thirty steps beyond the gates. The snow still held the shape of the woman's body. It appeared she'd been summarily dropped and then abandoned. Unfortunately, any tracks that might have been useful within the area had been trampled over from when the villagers first found her. Still, I walked a wide circle looking for something to help resolve the scene.

I stopped when I reached a particularly deep set of prints. They were driven into the permafrost, nearly deeper even than Harsigny's armored horse, and at an angle that pointed toward the wall. It was, I reflected, the same angle one might expect if one stood atop the wall and fired an arrow directly into the ground.

It was quite obviously impossible, but it looked as if someone had leapt from the wall.

Harsigny rode up to me.

"I'm of a mind to declare this the act of a wild animal," he said. "We could arrange a hunting party, catch a wolf or two and be done with it."

"Aye," I agreed. "That would settle things down. Until it kills again."

He looked at me appraisingly with his one good eye. "Yes, that would complicate matters. What are you thinking?"

"I am thinking that in order to determine what really happened to our leather smith's wife, we need to ask the person who witnessed it."

"You think there was a witness?"

"The body was left here, no? It wasn't eaten, or buried, or burned, or taken to the woods. It was just dropped. Whoever killed her and moved her to here was interrupted."

"We must find this person!"

I nodded. "Let me conduct my own inquiry. Quietly, when not followed by half the village. It would be for the best."

~

Lord Harsigny was preeminently a man of his age. He did not deal well with deception, intrigue, or skullduggery in general. Any such deceit was, above all, a sin, and it was the duty of nobility to set an example for the peasantry by not engaging in it. (His church, meanwhile, had built a hierarchical structure that—at that time—depended a great deal on deception, intrigue and skullduggery, but I was never one to identify hypocrisy when doing so might get me killed.) Thus, I knew he would want nothing to do with my investigation, which required that I go about the town disguised.

I had two reasons for this. One, it's hard to get anything done properly with a small crowd following you around, as always seemed to happen when I, or anyone else who resided in the castle, ventured out. Two, no crowd would fully appreciate the manner of person I expected to find.

Not to say that I was putting on a putty nose or any such thing, but I did trade in my furs for less expensive clothes: old boots, a grimy pair of pants, a torn shirt, and a hooded cloak on loan from a stable hand. Fully attired, and with the cloak secured, I looked more or less like everyone else in the town.

I waited until late in the day before leaving the castle proper, slipping out through the stables. Not surprisingly, there were few people about. The idea that there was a wolf out there that dared venture past the gates and was strong enough to drag an adult woman from the well more or less guaranteed I'd be walking the alleys alone. Also, it was terribly cold, much colder than in the morning, although my lack of proper clothing may have contributed to that particular opinion. I had to keep the hood closed up tight to protect my face from frostbite, and since the cloak stank of turnips, this was not entirely pleasant.

I reached the wall near sunset. My area of concern was on the town side of the wall. The snow there was almost perfectly virginal, which helped a great deal.

At just about the same point on the wall where the heavy impression outside the gates had been made, I found a matching set. These were not nearly as deep and the angle was fairly straight but the evidence was clear, provided one's world view allowed for such a thing. Somebody had stood in that spot and jumped to the top of the wall.

I knew of a few beings that could have made that jump—and the complementary one on the other side—and most of them preferred to come out only at night.

Working from the embedded prints, I was able to locate the trail that led up to them. They were made by someone who was running. Someone with small feet. Small, unshod feet.

I followed the path backward. It snaked through the untrammeled part of town behind the huts and beyond the main thoroughfares, making it easier to locate, but a frustratingly drawn-out process nonetheless. And with the sun failing and snow on the horizon, I was worried I'd soon lose the trail.

Abruptly, it came to a stop. I'd walked more than halfway back to the castle—albeit a roundabout way—and found the tracks ended at a heavy imprint similar to the one outside the wall. She—or he, although I was convinced I was dealing with a she just based on foot size—had jumped to that point from somewhere.

The best guess was a small enclosed barn thirty paces away. It was a bit taller than most of the buildings around it, so it probably had a loft of some sort, and possibly even a trap that led from the loft to the roof. Theoretically, my prey could have simply used the barn rooftop as a launching point after jumping from another rooftop, but these were not the finest of structures. Traveling roof-to-roof would more often result in one crashing through thatch and into someone's living room.

I walked around the barn once and found no footprints leading to or away from it outside of my own, so it hadn't been in use since at least the last snowfall about a week ago. Horses need to be tended to daily, thus, no horses. Then whose barn was it, and what did they use it for?

I creaked open the door, and with a whiff of the inside air, I had my question answered. It was a tannery. Albert's tannery, presumably, as he was the only tanner in town. I slipped in and shut the door behind me.

It was perfectly dark inside. And I'd stupidly neglected to bring a lantern with me.

Nobody born in or around the twentieth century can fully appreciate how absolutely paralyzing nighttime was before the invention of the light switch. If we wanted to see after sunset we risked death by fire or asphyxiation. If we didn't want to see, we risked banging our shins on something made of stone or getting eaten, neither of which was good. Hence, we mainly just got a lot of sleep. I was somewhat worried about the getting-eaten problem, especially if I was right about what was sharing the barn with me.

I slipped a tinderbox from my pocket and felt around for a lantern. Luckily—perhaps in anticipation of the light switch—Albert had one hanging by the door.

I put down the lantern and knelt beside it, trying to spark a flame.

"What are you doing?" whispered someone from above. "Are you mad? Can't you smell what's in here?"

I stood up unsteadily, for fear that I was about to get pounced upon.

"I know it *smells* awful ..."

"It smells awful and it can burn."

The voice was coming from the loft. It was a woman's voice, soft and melodic with the accent of a peasant, which certainly fit the surroundings.

"Then why is the lantern here?"

A fair question, I thought.

"Albert and Louisa are not stumbling fools. They light it outside in the moonlight and then close it before entering."

"And you?"

"I do not need it. I can see fine."

"I imagine you can."

She fell silent, which was bad because it meant I couldn't tell where she was any more.

"Are you here to kill me?"

This time her voice came from the ground to my left. She'd moved closer and I hadn't heard a thing. Somewhere in the back of my mind was a voice reminding me how incredibly foolish it was to corner a vampire.

"You already know I'm not."

"No," she agreed. Now she was behind me. I wanted to turn around, but I also really didn't.

"Turnips," she said.

"It's borrowed. I'm usually a much better dresser."

I felt her step closer and tried very hard to remain calm and keep my heart rate down, especially after she pulled back my hood and began smelling my neck.

"You know something about what I am?" she purred.

"I know a great deal about what you are."

"And you are afraid. I hear it in your heart."

Damn that heart. "I've been better," I admitted.

Yes, I know I said vampires don't frighten me. So, sometimes they do.

"You tracked me from the wall."

"Yes."

She licked my neck. I didn't know whether to be mortally terrified or incredibly turned on. I opted for both.

"Why?" she whispered.

"A woman was killed."

Her finger traced my earlobe. Wow.

"And you think I may have been responsible, yes?"

"No. I think you saw what was responsible. You were on the rooftop when she was attacked at the well, I imagine. I think you ran from here to the wall and ... interfered with it."

She stepped away from me, and I exhaled.

"This is true. Her name was Louisa. You should use her name, Master Turnip. She was kind to me."

Haltingly, I turned around and pushed open the door, admitting some moonlight. She remained in the shadows just beyond the doorway.

"Did you kill the thing that took her?" I asked.

"I fought it. But it soon realized I was no easy prey, and fled. I would have followed but ... it was barely sunset. It ran west. You see?"

I understood. In the winter the sun tended to dip below a rise at the edge of our little hill at sundown. She didn't dare risk following it over that rise.

"The people in this village call me Lord Venice," I said, extending my hand. "Or Serge."

She extended hers. I bowed formally and kissed her hand. Even vampires appreciate a little class.

"I am Eloise, milord Venice," she said, with a light curtsey. "The villagers have no name for me."

She stepped into the light.

Eloise was dressed in rags, her pale flesh exposed in many places, although not in any really fun places. Her feet were bare, but clean. Her unkempt black hair cascaded down her back, extending as far as her waist. And her large black eyes were mystifying. She was one of the most beautiful things I had ever seen, which is saying something.

"Tell me, Eloise," I rasped, my throat suddenly quite dry, "what was it? What was the thing you saw?"

"I don't know. It walked like a man, but ... I have never seen anything like it before."

"Perhaps I have."

"You know much of the world, don't you, Master Serge?"

"More than you can imagine."

"I can imagine a great deal."

I smiled. "I'm sure you can. Now, I'm going to need a favor from you, Mademoiselle Eloise."

"Are you?" She smiled back, all mischief and melody.

"Yes. I am afraid that thing will come back again. I need you to help me hunt it down and kill it before that happens."

~

The following day brought snow to our little Picardy hilltop, forcing most of the locals inside to huddle beside the fire and do whatever it was we all did before network television. (I myself tended to do a great deal of reading, but the illiterate majority? No idea.) I was busy for much of the day in the armory, preparing for the hunt.

"I should go with you," Lance said for the umpteenth time as he watched me run through the process of loading a crossbow with one hand. This was not easy, just in case you're curious. Twice I nearly ended up with a bolt through my lower thigh.

"I'll be fine," I insisted.

He grabbed the weapon from me. "Rest the butt against your hip, damn you. Like this." He illustrated his point. "You see?"

"How about if I just load it with two hands?"

"On horseback? You plan to rein your horse with your teeth?"

"I'll figure something out."

"I should go."

I sighed. "Do you trust me, milord?"

"Absolutely."

"Then believe me when I say that I need to hunt this thing without you. It's not that I question your valor or your skill. But I *am* protecting you. There are some things in this world that man is not meant to see."

What I didn't say was that I was far more concerned with what was joining me on the hunt than what it was we were hunting. Historically, people don't much care for vampires.

He pointed the bow at me, not as a threat but because it happened to still be in his hand while he gestured. Having a one-legged man with no depth perception pointing a loaded crossbow at one's chest was mildly unnerving.

"And you?" he asked. "Are you not a man?"

"I am." I pulled one of the many broadswords I had to choose from out of its scabbard and attempted to wield it. It was weighted poorly. "Beyond that fact, how much are you prepared to know of me?"

I should mention that as greatly as I enjoyed the Coucy-le-Chateau, it was getting time to move on. I'd been there for nearly twenty years, and even a half-blind old warrior like Lance had taken note of the fact that I hadn't aged a day. As I counted Lord Harsigny a dear friend, I felt I could trust him not to overreact. But it was only a matter of time before someone accused me of being a devil. The whisperings among the staff had already begun.

Lance squinted at me, uncertain how far he was willing to push this conversation, his curiosity waging a battle with an innate interest in keeping his understanding of the world unmolested. He put down the crossbow.

"I trust your wisdom, Serge. You know that I do. And I know that you drink from a font of knowledge most of us have never tasted." (God, I miss the poetry of classical French.) "But I worry that in your zeal to ... protect me, you are committing a fatal error. And that sword is much too heavy for you."

"Is it?"

"Take the half sword."

"What, that little thing?"

"It is sharp, and you will be able to swing it with speed and force. Speed is what matters in close combat."

"I know that," I said.

"I assume you will be facing an opponent who is not armored?"

"Not necessarily."

He rubbed his face in exasperation. "It is a man?"

"An animal. But with a ... tough hide, let's say."

"God save you, Serge. You should be bringing the dogs. You cannot face this thing alone."

I wouldn't be alone, but it struck me that this would be a bad thing to say.

~

We went through another hour of combat instructions with no more complaints from Lance that he should be going. I was pretty sure he still planned to follow me, but I didn't bring it up.

I am actually extremely well-versed in a variety of combat techniques. If, for instance, Lance handed me a blow dart I could probably hit a fly in midair with it. The problem is that weapons change over time and from region to region, and sometimes I just don't have the energy to keep up my studies. If I thought I could take my prey with a quarter staff, I'd probably be all set. But this was going to require steel, and the last time I had used a sword they were much lighter, and considerably flimsier.

At dusk I made my preparations. I was offered a suit of armor, but I turned it down. Those things are deathtraps, if you ask me. Sure if I'm jousting or attacking archers in a fixed position, armor might be good. But I needed flexibility, so I wore a light chain mail vest and the thickest leather waistcoat I could find.

My horse, Archimedes, was fitted with armor and a heavy saddle, neither of which he was accustomed to. He complained about it bitterly.

"God speed, Lord Venice," Lance said as I climbed upon Archimedes. He handed up the sword and helped fix the crossbow to the side of the saddle.

"And you, Lord Harsigny," I replied. "I expect I'll see you in the morning, but if I don't, take good care of the castle for me or I shall be forced to haunt you."

A signal to the stable hand and the stable door was pushed open.

"And don't follow me, my friend," I added. "Some things are best left unseen."

"I can barely see as it is," he smiled.

I shook his outstretched hand. One way or another, I didn't expect to be returning to Coucy-le-Chateau. I think we both knew it.

I rode hard through the small town and reached the gates in a matter of minutes. A casual onlooker might have assumed I was a messenger on a grave mission of some sort, which was fine.

Once past the gates I trotted alongside the wall for a ways before coming to a stop. I listened. The night was dead silent. Perhaps Lance had decided to take me at my word that it was best he not follow. More likely he'd wait an hour, rally his bloodhounds, and track me. But there wasn't anything I could do about that.

Momentarily, I was joined by Eloise. She dropped from the wall and landed before Archimedes, who nearly unhorsed me in surprise.

"Thank you for coming," I said, trying to calm down my mount.

"It's a worthy battle." She put a hand on Archimedes' head. Most animals don't react well to vampires at all, but Eloise seemed to offer him a soothing influence. "And I owe this beast for what he did to Louisa."

"Would you like to ride up here with me?"

"I can keep up." She looked at me appraisingly. "You know my motives. But why do you do this? You are no warrior."

"It killed a woman," I said simply.

"No, there is more. Something personal?"

"Can't I do something noble out of an innate sense of duty?"

Honestly, I didn't know why I was doing it either.

"Perhaps." She didn't look like she considered this a sufficient answer.

"Are you trying to talk me out of going?"

"I am trying to figure out who you really are."

"Same man I was last night."

"Last night you smelled like turnips. Tonight you smell of leather and mystery."

I smiled at what I took to be a compliment. "We're wasting time. Can you still track him through the fresh snow?"

"Of course," she said, bounding off. We followed.

There is something beautiful about vampires on the hunt. If they want to, they can outstrip a horse in full gallop, all the while appearing to move effortlessly.

Like most vampires, Eloise didn't run as a human might. She employed her arms as well as her legs, looking a bit like a large bloodsucking rabbit.

Every few minutes she would come to a full stop, listening and smelling the cold air for traces of an odor I had no hope of picking up myself. These moments were followed by a slight change in direction. We soon found ourselves at the edge of the woods.

I miss woods. It wasn't at all long ago that much of the world was covered by forest. Now I have to hop on a plane to get to a decent one. This particular set of woods wasn't terribly large but it was lush, and in the summer months utterly dark at all times. Visibility improved in the winter only ever-so-slightly. Our saving grace was that it was the second night of the full moon.

"It lives here, in these woods," Eloise said, sniffing. "Precious little else does."

"No wolves?"

"None I can detect. This thing could have frightened them off. It is large enough."

The implication that there was such a beast that could have chased a pack of wolves from its natural feeding ground would no doubt have terrified a lesser man. Okay, it scared the crap out of me too, I won't lie.

She pushed on at a slower pace out of respect for Archimedes, who found it difficult to maneuver between the trees. Eventually we penetrated deep enough into the forest that I questioned precisely where it was I had initially entered. At least Eloise seemed to know where we were going, although at times it appeared she had us traveling in circles. She stopped when we reached a small clearing.

"We are being followed."

I looked behind us but saw nothing. "It may be Lord Harsigny. He's probably got his hounds on my trail."

"No, milord, not a man. The thing we hunt is hunting us."

"For how long?"

"The past hour."

I examined the clearing. It was the largest we'd come across since entering the woods. Visibility would never be better.

"We make our stand here," I said.

She agreed. "You should turn; it comes from behind."

I trotted Archimedes to the farthest point in the clearing and turned around. Eloise stood in front of us in the center of the clearing and fell to a crouch.

"Can you smell it?" she asked.

"No."

"It reeks of brimstone. What manner of thing is this?"

That was what I was afraid of.

I lifted the crossbow and loaded a bolt. I could hear it now. It must have known we'd stopped and concluded stealth was no longer necessary. I could see trees quivering as it closed the distance.

And then it burst into the opening.

It was huge. I was eye-to-eye with it from atop Archimedes. It was covered head to food in leathery scales that I knew from prior experience to be greenish in the daylight but which appeared to be a shade of brown by the light of the moon. Its face was triangular, ending in a large jaw with a slightly rounded snout, its nostrils emitting a gust of steam and its body a quiver of muscles. It was humanoid only in the most superficial sense, although it did stand upright. Its fingers—four of them, and no opposable thumb—ended in talons that looked like impressive weapons.

"Now you have seen it," Eloise yelled over her shoulder as the creature fell forward onto its front paws and prepared to charge. "You tell me what it is!"

I raised my crossbow. "That," I said, "is a dragon."

~

Like so many other legendary creatures, humankind never quite got dragons right. Number one, they didn't fly. Number two, I never saw one breathe fire, although their breath was awful and they did smell like sulfur for reasons I have never been clear on, so people probably embellished that just a little bit. Number three, they averaged out at between eight and ten feet tall, which is a far cry from the enormous dinosaur-like monstrosities of myth.

Dragons weren't traditionally very smart, which may have been a contributing factor in their eventual extinction. You'd think something this brutally predatory should have figured out a way to stick it out otherwise, like the demons have. But most dragons would just as soon eat each other as anything else, which is not the brightest survival approach I've ever heard. They were not, however, so massively stupid that they made a habit of eating humans. Even on some basic level, most of them understood that killing a human will attract more humans, and more humans is invariably bad. This one must have been pretty desperately hungry, then, when it went after Albert's Louisa. And since it never got to eat her, we must have looked like filet mignon to him.

It was a male of the species—male dragons tended to be bigger—and he was considerably larger than average. Large enough to make me wish I'd brought a few dozen more people with me, plus maybe an extra vampire or two.

~

The dragon identified the immediate threat, which would be Eloise crouching in the center of the clearing.

They took turns growling at each other. It was clear the dragon recognized her from their previous encounter, and also that he wasn't the least bit afraid. He even appeared eager for the rematch, as was Eloise.

With unexpected speed, the dragon pounced.

Eloise met him in midair, getting close enough to avoid his lunging claws and scoring a brutal hit on what would have been his unprotected manhood were he more man than lizard. He squealed, but I had to think it wasn't too terribly painful given he was covered in heavy scales, even down there.

Eloise rolled to her feet and spun around to watch him land cleanly, and like that they were at each other again.

They shortly achieved a sort of *détente*, as she clearly had him outclassed in terms of quickness, but he was stronger and much better protected. So, while none of his fierce attacks connected, none of her furious counterattacks had any effect either.

"Are you going to fight?" she shouted at me, ducking a vicious swing and wondering where the hell her backup was.

"You're doing fine," I said.

Were I to insert myself into the battle, the best I could do was offer him something else to swing and miss at—or not miss, which would be infinitely worse—and my sword would fare little better than her nails, teeth and fists. I stood my ground.

I had a game plan. I really did. But there was no point in explaining it to Eloise since she was a critical element in that plan.

As they continued their furious skirmish, I took note that the dragon's fighting style was almost all offense. It worked out well for him. Eloise was getting more and more frustrated as her every blow, cut, and slash glanced harmlessly off his hide.

"I thought you faced one of these before!" she yelled.

"Me? No. I've seen them. Never fought one."

"This would be a good time to start!"

I was completely in awe of what I was witnessing. In my lifetime I had seen some extraordinary life-or-death struggles between countless manner of beasts, some quite fearsome. This battle between vampire and dragon topped them all.

In a telling sequence, I watched Eloise bring her palm up into the dragon's long chin, a powerful blow that unbalanced him temporarily and sent him tumbling backward. Seizing the opportunity, she drove forward hard.

Then I saw what I was looking for.

The dragon brought his right forearm up in front of his chin to ward off her attack and swung down with his left arm. It was his first defensive maneuver.

Everyone has a weakness. The trick is figuring out what it is in enough time to take advantage.

But before I could do anything about my newfound knowledge, Eloise made a mistake. Ducking under his left arm, she sprang forward, leaving herself open for a shot with his right arm. He swatted at her head, connecting with a devastating impact that sent her tumbling backward and exposing her belly. He followed it up quickly with a *coup de grâce*, a deep slash across her stomach that would have been mortal had she been human. Bleeding badly, she fell to her knees. The dragon stood over her, looking eager to finally eat something and probably feeling pretty good about having won the battle, too. But before he got around to doing anything more permanent to her, I fired my crossbow bolt. It struck him in the shoulder, penetrating just far enough to get his attention. Then I drew my sword and slid off Archimedes' back. The dragon looked up at me, confused, apparently having forgotten I was even there.

"Now you face me!" I shouted, not so much to be heard as to inspire a little belligerence on his part. I wanted him to forget about Eloise and focus on me. It worked.

The dragon roared. Terrible sound, that. Made my testicles shrink. I pointed my sword at him defiantly.

"You killed a human, lumpy. That's against the rules. Now I have to kill you."

And then the most curious thing happened. The dragon spoke.

"Kill ... me ... ?" he grunted.

Dragons don't really have the right equipment— brains, vocal chords—to hold a conversation, so it was a guttural rasp at best. But I understood it all right.

"Yes, kill you," I said defiantly. "Come on, let's get it over with."

I took several paces away from Archimedes—he was just about ready to panic—and staked a spot of nice open space, standing tall, in profile, sword in my right hand, behind me and partly obscured.

"KILL ... ME ... ?" he repeated. Maybe it was the only thing he knew how to say.

With a bloodcurdling bellow he charged, arms outstretched, leading with his claws. I was expecting just that kind of attack, as it was the one he'd opened with when he first closed the distance between himself and Eloise.

Then it was all a matter of timing.

I stood my ground until an instant before his claws struck,

ducked straight down, then bounced up again. I brought my free hand up under his chin, popped his head back, and exposed the one place on his entire body he saw fit to protect: his neck. Next came my sword, which I lined up point-first with the soft spot in front of his throat. His momentum did the rest.

The dragon's charge carried us both across the snow. The sword was jerked from my grasp, and as I flew through the air, I was forced to alter my priorities slightly to make sure I didn't end up crushed under him or the victim of a broken neck after an awkward landing. He ended up on his side a few dragon-sized strides away, unmoving.

I got up slowly. A sharp pain in my left side—the creature's knee had slammed into me there when we tumbled—suggested I had a few broken ribs. But I got off easy by comparison.

My sword was buried nearly to the hilt in the center of the dragon's neck.

I knelt down beside him and found he was still alive, but only just. His eyes, so bloodthirsty a moment earlier, looked sad now. Pleading.

"I warned you," I said.

Putting the heel of my foot on his shoulder—which still had a crossbow bolt stuck in it—I managed to yank the sword free. The dragon's head lolled backward, his body no longer obeying any commands. Then I swung the sword down at the still-exposed neck and cleaved his head from his shoulders. I could have let him suffer and die on his own, but I was feeling merciful. Also, I didn't know enough about dragon physiology to be entirely positive I'd administered a mortal wound. Removing his head seemed pretty final, as is generally the case with most beings.

I watched the blood pour out of his body for a few seconds, then tossed aside the sword and went to check on Eloise.

There are actually a fairly large number of ways to kill a vampire. (Or, re-kill, I suppose, since they are supposedly already dead. I never entirely bought into that whole "walking undead" thing, though. I suppose that's an argument for another time.) Chop a vampire up into enough pieces—or simply decapitate them—and they'll stay dead. Fire works, too. And there's the whole sunlight thing, which is extremely effective. But wooden stakes, as I've said, don't work at all. Nor will gutting a vampire, although the latter will hurt a whole heck of a lot and take a very long time to heal.

Eloise was curled up in a fetal position and clutching her stomach. She'd managed to keep her intestines inside by holding them there manually. Not a pleasant sight. I could have finished off what the dragon had started, were I so inclined. This was probably what she was thinking when she looked up at me wearing an expression of pleading similar to the dragon's.

I sat down in the snow and pulled her head into my lap.

"You did well."

"Did I?" she whispered, sounding very afraid. The pain must have been extraordinary.

"Yes." I pulled back my sleeve and thrust my bare wrist under her nose. "Let me help. Drink."

Blood kicks everything in a vampire's system into high gear, and that includes healing. Think of it as a battlefield transfusion.

A bloody tear streamed down her cheek. "Thank you," she said, baring her fangs.

It took her a few minutes to get her fill. She finished around the same time Lord Harsigny reached the clearing.

CHAPTER 6

Another day, another meal with mushrooms in it. I think they scored a deal with a mushroom merchant or something because lately that's all I'm getting, and it's a little tiresome.

Might just be I'm going crazy with nothing to do. Even prisons have libraries, you know? It's like they want *me to sit around and plot ways to escape. And I am seriously considering escaping.*

Granted, even if I get out of my cell, I still have to contend with the guards I can't possibly overpower, the fence, and the desert. Not the best odds in the world.

~

Brenda the vampire hooker reached her limit at around the same time spots started to appear in my vision, which worked out pretty well for both of us. (This is another thing most people don't understand about vampires. Their limit is about four quarts. Only malevolence or severe starvation would lead them to consider overfeeding.) I reached across the bed and slowly pried my wrist from her mouth. She was half asleep, so I helped her the rest of the way onto the bed and then, very lightheaded, I lay down next to her.

It had been centuries since I'd thought of the late Francois Etienne de Harsigny. Like so many thousands that came before and since, he was someone I called friend. That's the truly awful thing about being immortal, in case you were wondering. Everybody dies eventually. Even the vampires. Some of them end up slain by stupid mortals who think they're acting in the name of whichever god is fashionable at the time, but most end up as suicides somewhere around the three hundred year mark.

The way it works is you spend the first century doing all the things you always wanted to do, the second century doing things you never thought you'd want to do, and the third century doing whatever's left. Then one night you look around and realize that not only have you done everything there is to do, you're no longer interested in doing any of it ever again. Suddenly death seems like an interesting option, if only because it represents the one experience left on your checklist. Compounding the problem, vampires young and old routinely suffer from depression. Never being allowed to see the sun ever again has that effect.

And as I've said, when it comes to depression and suicidal thoughts, I've been there a few times myself.

Another unfortunate fact about immortality could best be explained by Harsigny's reaction to the scene in the clearing. There I was, his trusted friend, nursing a vampire in the snow next to a slain dragon. After all this time, I can still see the stunned expression on his scarred face.

Historically, mortal humans haven't dealt well with the unknown. Their usual reaction is to kill what they don't understand. Harsigny, willing up until that point to ignore the obvious fact that I never aged, was forced all at once to come to the only conclusion his ideology would allow: his trusted friend was some sort of demon. And for a God-fearing fellow like him, my apparent demonhood was something he wasn't willing to overlook. (Considering what real demons are like, this was a bit of an insult, but I let it go on the basis of the fact that Harsigny had clearly never seen one.) Thus, my days in Coucy-le-Chateau came to an abrupt end, all thanks to my charitable decision to rid Picardy of a human-eating dragon. Sometimes that's just the way it goes.

Harsigny was gracious enough not to run us through right then and there—which was good, as I didn't particularly want to have to kill him, too—and he did let me keep Archimedes. He even gave us some gold in exchange for the guarantee that we'd leave immediately and never return.

History wasn't particularly kind to him, so while I'm quite certain he's passed on, I don't know when or how because there's no historical record of his existence. Enguerrand de Coucy I do know about. He lived many more years after my hasty departure before dying in the Battle of Nicopolis. I regretted not speaking to him one final time before I left, if only to apologize for leaving.

Eloise and I traveled from Picardy through the Holy Roman Empire and into Italy, where we witnessed the church schism firsthand. Boredom eventually led us to Egypt, where I regaled her with tales of pyramids and sphinxes and long-dead kings. Eventually we drifted apart, although I can't for the life of me remember why.

As I trailed off to sleep beside my new friend Brenda, it occurred to me—not for the first time—that death was the only constant in my life. If it weren't so depressing, I'd laugh at the irony.

~

Brenda nudged me awake with a glass of orange juice in her hand. "You okay?"

I sat up slowly and took the glass. "What time is it?"

"Daytime," she said. It was impossible to tell with the windows masked.

"Yeah, but what time is it?"

"Dunno. I don't own a watch. What do I need one for?"

True enough.

The juice was cool and tasted supermarket fresh. "Where'd this come from?"

"I have a cooler under the bed," she explained. "I like to keep juice on ice, just in case. I figure the Red Cross gives OJ to its donors, I should do the same thing, you know?"

"Do you charge extra for it?"

"No, silly, it's free," she smiled. "You know ... you taste, um, you taste really good. Has anyone ever told you that?"

"I bet you say that to all the boys."

"I'm serious! It's really weird, your blood it's, like ..."

"Old," I offered. "I have heard it before. I'm a very old vintage."

Brenda smiled again. She had quite a nice smile. Had she reached her mid-twenties, she would have been a brilliantly attractive young woman. I wondered what made her decide to arrest her development younger than that. Eighteen, I guessed. Possibly it wasn't her decision, but that was very unusual. When you meet a vampire nowadays you're generally meeting one who chose the life.

"How do you feel?"

"A little lightheaded," I said, "but that's the worst of it. Can you hand me my bag?"

The bag was one of those nondescript army duffel bags. I bought it off an RAF paratrooper in 1952. It contained seven of my lives.

About two hundred years ago, I realized if I was going to continue to travel freely about the planet, I was going to have to officially establish myself. Back in the day a guy could wander from place to place, and his word was pretty much the only identification he needed. Now I need a passport, name, and nationality to get from country to country and sometimes from state to state or town to town. Fortunately, every lawful society has an unlawful element, so it's usually not that tough to pick up a new ID whenever I need one.

I dumped the contents out on the bed. It wasn't much: a change of clothes, the seven passports (they were each good for another two years), a shaving kit, about twenty grand in cash, and the passbook for my Swiss bank account.

"Wow!" Brenda exclaimed, specifically regarding the cash.

"It's just walking-around money."

"Forget walking, why don't you buy a car!"

"It'd use up most of the cash. Plus I haven't driven one since 1965, and that was a disaster. And if you think I'm going to drive in *this* city ..."

"What's this?" she asked, her eyes drifting across other items.

"That's a bank book."

"Cool."

She flipped it open and frowned at the handwritten notes inside. "What language is this?"

"It's a code I invented a long time ago," I said, "so nobody else could read it."

By the way, thank God for the Swiss. I gave up on everyone else's banking system long ago, but they're still going strong. Plus, nobody there seems to have a problem with the fact that I should have died over fifty years ago.

"How much do you have?" she asked.

"A lot."

"Yeah?"

"Yeah, but I don't know how much. I haven't asked for a balance in a while."

"So, you could be, like, a billionaire or something."

"Could be, but I doubt it."

She actually had a point. My last directive was made in 1957 and that was to allocate a portion of my money toward the purchase of U.S. tech stock. This was after I'd gotten drunk with an English mathematician who spent the evening prattling on about the Manhattan Project. About ninety percent of what he told me was top secret, but he was really, really drunk. I think I even told the Swiss to pick up some IBM stock. I don't remember. (I was mad drunk myself when I made the call.) It wasn't the first time I made a snap decision like that, and while this one may have worked out okay— provided I actually made that phone call and wasn't imagining the whole thing—most of them didn't. For example, I once put a load of money down on commercial zeppelin travel. And don't even get me started about perpetual motion machines.

"I wish I were rich," Brenda said wistfully.

"You will be," I said.

"Yeah? Can you see the future?"

"No. But if you want to be rich, you can. It's just a matter of patience and discipline and finding a bank that's open at night. You'll figure it out." I picked up the cash. "I don't think I need a car. But I definitely need to do some shopping, and maybe a shower and a shave. You don't happen to know where the nearest Y is, do you?"

~

Brenda did me one better. It turned out there was a community bathroom, with a real shower, down the hall from her almost-apartment. It was perhaps the filthiest place I'd spent time in since nineteenth century London, but it had hot water and a mirror.

An hour later I emerged into Chinatown, clean-shaven and less odorous, although my clothes were still as crappy as ever, hence the need to shop. My plan was to hit the nearest big bank, set up an account in the States, transfer some money into it and live the high life for a little while, or at least until winter was over. But to do that I had to show up dressed somewhat better than a guy who just woke up in a gutter.

I headed for the nearest subway station, my bag over my shoulder and my coat tightly wrapped. (It wasn't a whole lot warmer than it had been the night before. Why couldn't I winter in the tropics?)

My path to the train took me past a news vendor who looked nearly as cold as I was. Ordinarily I pass newsstands without pausing to examine headlines, because only rarely do any of them make sense to me. The last time I sat down to read a paper was in 1992.

But on this particular day something made me look up. Don't know what it was. Fate, I suppose. And this time the first headline I saw did mean something to me.

STUDENTS BRUTALLY SLAIN, it read.

It was about Gary and Nate.

I skimmed the first two paragraphs, just enough to discover that I was a prime suspect.

CHAPTER 7

The longer I sit here running through everything, the more aggravated I get.

I was so stupid. I should have cut and run the minute I read that headline. It's what I'd have done a hundred years ago, and exactly what I did *do in response to the Whitechapel murders. I fled to the States before someone decided to point a finger at me. I knew the victims then, too. Did I stick around to catch their killer? No, I did not.*

But then nobody ever did catch their killer. Maybe that was my motivation this time around: delayed Jack the Ripper guilt.

Anyway, that was my shot. That was when I should have left town. Or the country. Instead I waited until New York, and by then it was too late.

~

According to the full story—I went and bought the paper —Nate and Gary were assaulted with a blunt object. This told me hardly anything, as there are a whole mess of blunt objects one could use to kill a person, starting with an automobile and working down. (I didn't think they were run over in their living room but you get my point.) The place was also ransacked, and the police were speculating that robbery might have been a motive. Then there was this sentence: "Police are looking for a local drifter who may have spent some time in the victims' apartment."

That wasn't much, but I knew tomorrow it would be "a drifter named Adam" and the day after that, one of Gary and Nate's party friends would cough up a description and I'd be looking at a composite sketch of my face on the front page. They'd say it was just *for questioning,* but I didn't have one of the most well developed alibis on the planet. If you start digging deep enough into any of the names on my passports, you'll quickly find that none are genuine. And Adam isn't even one of those names. Worse, the only person who could possibly prove I wasn't in the apartment when they were killed, was a teenage vampire hooker.

In my favor, I was probably the only "drifter" in town with twenty grand on hand, so I could get out of Boston pretty fast and be done with it whenever I wanted. It was a much better option than jail. (Astonishingly, I'd managed to avoid long-term imprisonment for most of my life. Good thing. Can you imagine me under a life sentence?)

But there was a nagging little voice in the back of my head that needed to know who killed Gary and Nate. I hate that little voice. It always gets me in trouble.

So, I stuck with my original plan, which was to get to Newbury Street and shop for a decent set of clothes, plus a few other goodies, like a watch. For good measure, I stopped in a hair salon. When I returned to Brenda's hole in the wall a few hours later she almost didn't recognize me.

~

"You're bald!"

"What do you think? Do you like it?"

"It's ... I don't know ..." she circled around me, examining the damage. I'd also gotten my ear pierced. With the Armani suit thrown in, I looked like a pimp.

"Hang on." I slipped on a pair of Ray-Bans. "Now?"

"Yeaaah, that's better. Jesus, you look completely different."

"That's what I was shooting for."

"What, are you on the lam now?"

I thrust the newspaper into her hands.

"Apparently, yes."

She read the article while I explained who the mysterious drifter was.

"You didn't do this, though, right?" I guess this is a polite question when you're a vampire.

"Of course not."

"Had to ask."

"Well, I didn't," I repeated.

"Okay," she said. "I wouldn't have minded, you know. I think if you were, like, this big killer or something ... that'd be sorta sexy, actually."

I snatched the paper from her. "Boy, did you make the right career choice."

"Hooking?"

"Bloodsucking." I dropped my new leather satchel onto the bed (the duffel didn't work with the suit) and zipped it open.

"What is that smell?" Brenda of the hypersensitive nose asked.

I pulled out the bag of goods. "Oh, sorry about that. It's diced garlic." Garlic doesn't fend off vampires, by the way. They just really hate the smell. "Also mushrooms, fennel seed, balsamic vinegar, and this ..."

"Molasses?"

"It's the critical ingredient."

"You know, there's a McDonald's right down the street."

"It isn't for me. You don't by any chance have a hot plate, do you?"

~

She didn't, but the old Asian lady down the hall did. She wasn't initially all that interested in helping us, up until I sweet-talked her in Mandarin. (I'm not really fluent, but I know enough to get by.) She even loaned us a saucepan.

An hour later I had a deeply foul-smelling dish that no human would ever consider eating, even on a dare.

"Ugh, God, I'm gonna be sick," Brenda declared.

"Maybe I shouldn't have done this in the apartment," I said.

"I may have to move."

"Sorry. Are you ready to go?"

"Go where?"

"The alley down the street. Come on, the sun's down already."

"Is this some sort of immortal trick or something?"

"Yeah. Hurry up."

~

I set the saucepan on the ground at one end of the alley and then joined Brenda behind the dumpster at the other end.

"Now what?" she asked.

"Shh. Now you watch for me. Your eyes are better from here."

"What am I looking for?"

"Focus on the top of the pan," I said. "You'll know it when you see it."

"Is this magic? Did you cast a spell or something?"

"Of course not," I said. "There's no such thing as magic."

She looked at me with the kind of disbelieving expression

only a vampire can give to an immortal man who doesn't believe in magic.

"Honest," I added.

"Whatever." She refocused on the pan. And we waited.

About an hour passed, and I was still crouched uncomfortably behind the dumpster watching the back of Brenda's head while she stared down the alley. She stood dead still the entire time, and I swear she didn't blink once. Police would do themselves a service by hiring vampires specifically for stakeouts.

Finally ... "What the hell?"

"What do you see?" I asked.

"I don't *know*."

"Something flew into the pot, right?"

"Yes, but ..."

"Did it fly out?"

"No. What the hell was that?"

"That is what we're here to catch."

I led her back to the saucepan, and crouched down to say hello to my new friend. Stuck in the molasses about knee deep was a tiny naked woman with mosquito wings.

"Hello," I said to her.

"Iza stuck," she said back.

"Yes, you are," I said, picking up the saucepan.

Brenda stared at our prize with naked astonishment. "What *is* it?"

"This," I said proudly, "is a pixie."

~

Back in the room, I placed the ensnared pixie on the bed while Brenda lit a few candles. The pixie just pouted, which is something they're very good at. They are, unfortunately for this particular pixie, very *bad* at resisting the smell of mushrooms, garlic, and fennel. (The part they eat is the mushrooms. It is possible to tame a wild pixie with just raw mushrooms, but difficult to catch one that way, and we were on the clock.)

The average pixie is somewhere between three and four inches tall, with gossamer wings and, scale-wise, simply fantastic bodies. Most every one I've ever met was a blonde, and I mean that both literally and in the intellectual sense, although calling them stupid isn't really fair. They're simply innocent. If Jerry the iffrit is the devil on your shoulder, a pixie is the angel on your other shoulder. Not that either species is particularly good at advice, but you get my point.

You may have encountered a pixie once or twice in your life and not known it. And since they move faster than anything else I've ever seen with wings, if you did see one it was for the merest of seconds, just enough time for you to convince yourself your eyes were playing tricks.

"Hello," I said to my new friend.

"H'lo," she said back, then repeated, "Iza stuck."

She wasn't afraid, just annoyed at being stuck. It's not that I'm naturally non-threatening; it's that it would never occur to her to *be* afraid. Think Adam and Eve before The Fall, if that helps.

"It's a little tiny girl!" Brenda said. She was still dealing with this.

"Yes, as far as I know, they're all girls."

"Then how do they ... you know."

"I never figured out how to ask one. They don't seem to understand the concept."

"Iza stuck!" the pixie repeated.

"Right, sorry," I said. "What's your name?"

She looked at me blankly.

"Iza. Iza stuck."

"Oh." Silly me.

"Iza?" I said, "would you like me to help you get unstuck?"

"Uh-huh."

"Okay, I'll do that, but I need you to do me a favor."

She looked unsure. "Big favor?"

"No, a small favor."

"Iza small."

"Yes. That's why I'm asking you. Can you read, Iza?"

Iza brightened. "Iza read!"

I held up the newspaper and pointed to a word. "Can you read that line for me?"

She squinted at it for a few seconds. "'Nay-than-eel,'" she read.

"Good! And that one?"

"'Gah-ree.'"

"Very good!" Ooh boy, this was going to take a while.

"Favor done?" she asked.

"No, that wasn't the favor, Iza."

She pouted again. "Feet are mushy."

"I'm sorry about that. Iza, do you know what a police station is?"

CHAPTER 8

More mushrooms in today's meal and I only just realized I'm an idiot. They aren't for me and never were.

Evidently a certain somebody has been making herself useful in the kitchen. The only problem is, I'm pretty sure I can't trust her. Not after all that's happened. I guess it's possible she's also a captive of some kind but if she is, I'd wager she's got much better digs than I do.

After lunch today, I took the fresh mushroom garnish and spread it around the vents. You know how in movies there always seems to be human-sized air vents just begging to be used by an escapee? No such luck here. These vents are along the wall on the floor and the ceiling, about a half inch wide and not fashioned for a decent escape attempt. Doesn't mean something can't get in through them, just that I can't get out.

We'll see if it works. Then maybe I can figure out what she's really up to.

Besides, I have nothing better to do.

It took the entire evening to explain to Iza exactly what I needed from her, a maddening procedure not unlike trying to deliver shoe-tying instructions to a mentally challenged child who's never seen a shoelace. Twice, Brenda threatened to eat Iza, just for the heck of it. Finally, when I was sure Iza had it down, I freed her with some hot water in the sink down the hall. (And permanently clogged the sink with molasses. Oh well.) Iza could have flown off after that, but this is where the artless nature of pixies is a good thing. It was beyond her grasp to consider not doing something she'd promised to do.

So, the next morning I stood across the street from the downtown police station, with a pixie on my shoulder and a fresh bottle of peppermint schnapps to keep me warm.

"Do you have the camera?" I asked under my breath.

"Uh-huh. Heavy."

She had the smallest commercially available camera I could find strapped to her bosom. It was barely an inch long and a centimeter thick. Took digital images. Cost a bundle. When I'd bought it, I flashed back briefly on a Renaissance painter I knew who had to hire three men and a sturdy donkey to carry his painting gear around, and who took six months to complete a single portrait. Bet he would have hated the twenty-first century.

"Sorry," I said.

"Iza okay."

The camera was a necessity. I couldn't rely on her to comprehend what she was being sent to examine, much less convey it to me. Ideally I would have asked Jerry to do it—he's smarter, and would do it much more quickly in exchange for the bottle in my pocket—but it would have taken too long to find him. There were just too many bars to choose from. This way was imperfect, but ultimately faster.

"There's an open window on the second floor. Do you see it?" I asked.

"Iza see."

"Okay. Good luck."

She buzzed off. One might think that even if the three-and-a-half inch pixie was difficult to see, the slate gray micro-camera flitting across the street would be obvious, but as I said, pixies are very fast. Not even owls bother with them. I lost sight of her myself and I knew to look. I still stood there for a few minutes, looking for some definite indication she'd made it to the window, but getting none, I moved on.

~

A pixie saved my life once, back in the first century AD. Of course, we didn't call it that back then. We didn't call it anything back then, because the Roman calendar was still in vogue. (Every time I come across a new calendar, I have this bizarre need to go back and figure out when everything happened in my life according to that calendar. It's a bit anal, but I have a whole lot of free time. And between the Greek, Roman, Hebrew, Egyptian, early Christian, Islamic, Julian, and Gregorian calendars—among others—I had to do this often. My personal favorite calendar was one used by a small equatorial African tribe, which held that every day was Tuesday. Inaccurate, but very convenient.)

I was living in a small harbor town called Herculaneum, on the Bay of Naples. The whole area was a vacation spot for wealthy Romans, sort of an ancient equivalent of the Hamptons.

I liked it there. It was warm and breezy and pleasant, and I didn't have to do any fishing, something I'd grown tired of. I worked as a gardener, of sorts. Farmer, really, which I'm pretty good at. (Most jobs I've had have been variations on hunter-gatherer and farmer. I was one of the first to say "Hey, if we grow our own food, we won't have to hunt it down all the time." Mostly, I was just tired of moving around constantly, but you have to admit it was a pretty good idea.) I was working for a fat old Roman named Adolphus. He was a retired prelate and acted like one, but he gave me room and board, appreciated the yield from the modest garden I tended, and otherwise left me alone, which was about all one could ask for.

I had been having a problem with my olive tree. I'd spent a couple of years nursing the thing to health after the last caretaker nearly killed it by not watering it enough (olive trees need a *ton* of water) and this particular summer was supposed to bear the fruits of my success. But while it did produce healthier olives than before, the yield was still low. It was incredibly frustrating. I was beginning to think maybe the tree was suffering from some sort of root disease, but that sort of thing usually manifests itself in the bark somewhere and I saw no evidence of that. I was baffled.

It took half the summer before I considered perhaps the problem wasn't with the tree at all. Perhaps I had a vermin problem. Despite the difficulty of imagining a rat climbing the tree and dangling off a branch to prey on my olives, it was the only thing left to consider.

Intent on solving the puzzle, at the next full moon I camped out at the edge of the garden—motionless, hidden beneath a sackcloth—and I waited. Shortly after the moon reached its zenith, I caught some movement in the tree. Mind you, I didn't see anything there, but the leaves on one of the branches twitched and an olive fell. A few seconds later, another branch jerked and another olive fell. Still, I didn't see anyone or anything. I'd have thought a ghost was responsible, except there's no such thing.

Unwilling to sit around and watch the whole tree being denuded, I sprang to my feet wielding a broom I'd brought for just this occasion, and went at the tree swinging.

It is a known fact that most creatures will run in the face of a well-swung broom. Even some larger creatures, like tigers.

Honest. But instead of frightening whatever-it-was away, I just annoyed it.

"Hey!"

I stopped swinging, as evidently the tree had gained the power of speech.

"Almost hit!" The pixie hovered in front of my face and pointed at me accusingly.

"Oh. Uh, sorry," I said.

This was the first time I'd seen a pixie, but I had heard of them before, so I wasn't completely stunned at the sight of one.

"Okay," she said, then flitted to the ground and picked up one of the olives, which she proceeded to eat. This is what I mean by naive. Any other creature, when facing a human swinging a broom might think, *The human is trying to hit me with the broom. Perhaps I should flee*. A pixie thinks, *He was trying to brush the dust out of the air and didn't see me.*

"Hey, stop that," I protested.

"You want?" She offered me the olive. "Is good."

"No, I mean stop eating the olives from this tree."

"Is good," she repeated, taking another bite.

"Yes, I know it's good. It's my tree. That's why I want you to stop taking all the olives from it."

"Silly." She continued eating.

"No, not silly. Please don't." I repeated, "It's my tree."

"Not your tree. Ground's tree. Tree's tree. Tree's fruit." Munch, munch, munch. It was exasperating.

"I grew tree," I tried to explain. You ever notice how your syntax changes when you're talking to an idiot? "Tree is for me."

She frowned. "Tree is for you?"

"Yes, tree is for me."

"Silly."

"No, not silly." I was ready to take another shot at her with the broom.

"Silly. Moon for you?"

"No, the moon is for everyone," I said.

"Tree is for everyone."

Pixies, the first communists. I decided to change tactics. "Do you like the fruit?"

"Good fruit."

"Is there anything else you like to eat?"

She thought about it.

"Mushrooms."

"You like mushrooms?"

"I like."

"Better than olives?"

"Okay." That might have been a yes. Hard to tell.

"If I got you some mushrooms," I asked, "would you stop eating the olives?"

She ran through her options carefully. "You have mushrooms?"

"I can get mushrooms."

"Okay."

"We have a deal?" I asked.

"Deal."

"What is your name?"

"Win."

"My name is Antony."

And that's how I made friends with a wild pixie. Every night I'd leave out a plate of mushrooms I'd either bought in the market or picked myself, and she left the olive tree alone. Every now and then I'd hang out in the garden and strike up a conversation with her. Once I got used to the interesting syntax and the Edenesque world view, it became a fairly easy matter, and by the end of the summer I even felt like I'd made a friend.

You can never have too many friends. They especially come in handy in bad times, like on days you discover that you're living at the base of an active volcano.

~

I've seen my share of volcanoes, mostly from a distance, which is how you want to see one, if you're wondering.

The closest I'd ever gotten—up until that day in Herculaneum—was during the Minoan empire. I was working on the island of Crete as a fish merchant when a massive volcano on a nearby island—it's called Santorini now; we called it Thera back in the day—basically wrecked the whole region. I mean wrecked. Earthquakes, showers of ash, and this nasty junk called pumice. It killed thousands of fish—which put me out of a job—and took down the Minoans almost completely. Plato even wrote about it, although he called the island Atlantis. (Between you and me, Plato was a hack. All that crap about higher forms and caves? He was drunk when he wrote it. I know. I was there. And Aristotle? Seriously obsessive-compulsive.) After that experience, I swore I'd never set up shop anywhere near an active volcano ever again. Nonetheless, sixteen hundred years later there I was at the base of Mount Vesuvius, which nobody even knew was a volcano. My own fault, I guess, for trusting mortals to check that sort of thing.

The morning began as most did on the Bay of Naples: sunny, breezy, and generally pleasant. If anything, it was too calm. I did notice as I tended to the garden that there were no birds. Unusual, but not terribly so.

It was just past noon when Win showed up.

"Ant! Ant!" She called me Ant because Antony was too difficult. Pixies prefer one-syllable words.

"What are you doing here?" She always slept during the day. Pixies are not strictly nocturnal, but do prefer coming out at night.

"Must go!" she insisted, landing on my shoulder and shouting in my ear.

"But you just got here."

"Ant must go!"

"Where?"

"Away! Away now!" She was almost hysterical.

"Win, calm down. What is this about?"

"Bad sky come."

"What, a storm? A hurricane?" I've lived through a few hurricanes, too.

"No, hot!" she exclaimed. "Hot fire sky!" Like that helped.

"Honey, you need to take a breath and add some words to your sentences, or this is going to take a while."

"Just go!"

"Where do you want me to go?"

She looked around anxiously. "Boat?"

"I don't own a boat. And you know I can't fly. Now seriously, what's this about?"

Just then, the ground rumbled. It felt like Naples had indigestion. I knew that sound.

"Oh," I said. "Hot fire sky. A volcano."

"Mountain goes up," Win confirmed. See, now if she'd said that right away I would have gotten it.

I looked at the peak and saw a faint curl of smoke work its way out of the center.

"How long do you think I have?" I asked her.

"Ears hurt."

She felt the same thing that had sent the birds away. Not the best forecasting method around but not bad either.

Just then the mountain ejected a larger mass of smoke and running seemed like a very good idea.

"Okay," I said. "Let's run, shall we?" The proper thing to do would have been to warn Adolphus and his wife first, but they were in Rome on business at the time, so I was obligation-free. I ran.

I headed down the hill, taking the most direct path I knew of to the shore. Any boat close to the mountain would be rendered useless by a big enough pumice rock or flaming ember—wood boats and all—and I was betting that any boat owner with half a brain would know this and act accordingly. Getting on one of those boats before they left would be a good thing.

And then, as I was halfway to the dock, Mount Vesuvius erupted. It began with an earthquake tremor, which knocked me off my feet, prone and looking up at the top of the mountain, and in a position to see something amazing. The entire top cone of the mountain rocketed skyward in a million pieces propelled by an enormous column of ejecta that spread outward in all directions. It looked a bit like those mushrooms I'd been picking for Win, only writ large and much deadlier. As horrifying as it was, I don't know that I've ever seen anything quite so magnificent.

My immediate and very human reaction was to sit there and watch, as one rarely gets a chance to see something this extraordinary. (I'd been sleeping when the volcano off Crete blew.) Fortunately I had Win to watch my back.

"Move now!" she urged, tugging at my earlobe.

Snapped from my reverie, I got to my feet and stumbled down the hill as the ashes began to rain down from the initial blast. I'd gotten about twenty paces, still turning from time to time to admire the view, when a massive chunk of pumice landed right where I'd been admiring the volcano. That sealed it. It was time to get the hell out of Herculaneum, and fast.

As I sprinted through town, I came across dozens of neighbors who didn't seem at all inclined to motivate themselves toward the shore. They just stood there and watched. Either they simply didn't comprehend the peril they were in or they knew there was no place to run and figured they might as well catch the show. I wasn't quite at that point. I'd swim to Capri if I had to.

When I reached the shore I found ... no boats.

"Oh, crap," I said.

"Where boat?" Win asked from her perch on my shoulder.

"It's the middle of the day. Everyone's fishing in the bay right now."

"No boat?" she clarified.

"No boat."

Another massive blast from the mountain shook the Earth and sent me to my knees. Ashes were starting to rain down in force and the sky had darkened considerably. Clouds were forming over the mountain. If prior experience served, lightning would be next.

I shuffled through my options quickly. There weren't many. "Win, do you know where Torre del Greco is?"

"Tory ... ?"

"... del Greco. It's down the beach from here. I need you to fly ahead and see if there are any boats there. I know you can fly very fast."

"Very fast."

"Yes. See if there are boats there."

"You stay here?"

"I'm going to run as fast as I can along the shore. I'd just like to know if there'll be a boat waiting for me. Okay?"

"Okay."

"And Win? If the air gets too bad and you don't think you can make it back to me, don't. Just fly off to somewhere safe. I'll be all right."

"I come back."

"Only if it's safe."

"I come back." She zipped off.

I knelt down and removed my sandals.

Nobody should ever be forced to run in sandals for any length of time. I wore them because everyone else did, but considering I went something like fifty millennia without footwear, for me they were more of a contrivance than a convenience. Plus, you ever tried running in the sand in wood sandals?

I looked up and saw what looked like a giant rain cloud

rapidly losing altitude. It was a volley of heavier ashes, and they looked hot. Time to run again.

As I said, my muscles don't seem to grow over time with exercise. I'm about as strong and fast as I was in the beginning. But that's all right because I was always a good runner. At one time I had to be. It was how we hunted. There were animals that were faster, sure, but we could run for days without getting winded.

I took off down the beach. The sand made the going a little rough, but nothing unmanageable. I would have made excellent time if I didn't have to breathe. Unfortunately I did, and that became a difficult thing to do when the ash fall really got going.

About halfway to Torre Del Greco I had to stop just to find some air. It was a bit like trying to run while breathing through fifty lit cigarettes. I fell to my knees and cupped my ash-covered hands over my mouth, but when that didn't make a difference I tried removing my toga and breathing through that instead. This helped. It left me stark naked, but people back then weren't nearly as uptight about that sort of thing as they are today.

Behind me, I could see that the town was on fire. The second floor of most of the buildings in Herculaneum were made of wood rather than the stone used on the bottom level, and a lot of that wood had surrendered to the hot ash and pumice. I wondered if the people now understood that this was not something to patiently wait out. Probably they would do the same as I did and flee to the water line. Maybe they would be safer there. I was thinking it might be a better idea to find indoor shelter and wait it out, but that was because I was trying jog in an ashtray.

My eyes were burning, so I splashed some water into my face to rinse them. Then I started running again.

When I reached Torre del Greco I found an abandoned shoreline. No boats. No pixie. She'd apparently chosen discretion over valor. And it looked like I was screwed.

Collapsing in a heap at the edge of the water I panted hard and tried to kick loose the ash that had nested in my lungs. The water was cool, so I lay down in it and let the tide splash loose some of the mottled grime coating my naked body and soothe what had to be at least a couple of second degree burns on my back. I imagine I looked something like a mud sculpture prior to the finishing touches.

I could still see the western side of Vesuvius from my vantage point, and it appeared things were not going to end well for my about-to-be-former residence. A gush of lava had lipped out of the top of the mountain and was arcing its way right for the city. It moved extremely slowly, but it was most surely moving, and there was nothing that could possibly stop it except the water.

I began to regret my decision to simply up and run. In practical terms, there were horses available. No doubt one or two of the wealthy landowners had thought of this and were now someplace with less airborne ash. In humanitarian terms, I could have convinced at least one or two people to go with me along the shore ... so they could die in Torre del Greco, like I was evidently about to. Okay, so following me wasn't always the best idea. Win certainly must have come to that conclusion.

"Hey! Get up!"

My tinny-voiced pixie had returned. She was hovering above my face and looking quite sternly at me.

"Why?" I asked. "No boats. And, it's a nice view."

"Stupid."

"I'm stupid? You should get the hell out of here while you can, Win."

"Win found boats."

I looked up and down the shore again. "Where?"

"Not here. No boats here. Found boats down there."

I thought about it. "Stabiae?"

"Don't know."

"But there are boats there?"

"Yes. Hurry!"

I got back up again and half-ran, half-walked to Stabiae. I wanted to quit a dozen times, but Win wouldn't let me. (She would have made an excellent personal trainer.) It helped that the closer I got, the milder the conditions got, with the shower of pumice and heavy ash replaced by a light ash shower that wasn't half as scalding. Still, it was nearly the next morning when I reached Stabiae. Win had been right. There were boats.

~

We ended up stuck in Stabiae for two more days. Nowadays when you think of a boat you think sailboat or motorboat or rowboat. We had flat, ugly beasts with square rigged sails that were entirely dependent on favorable winds. I made myself fairly useful on board a ship owned by an excitable fellow named Pompanianus, and I got to meet the recently deceased body of Pliny the Elder, but other than that, it was a dull, unpleasant couple of days marred by the intense feeling of impending doom.

When the winds finally smiled upon us, we set out for the open waters of the bay with as many living persons as we could fit on six ships (two owned by Pompanianus, four consisting of Pliny's fleet). Herculaneum and the landward town of Pompeii were both gone by then. We all hoped that more had escaped death and simply chosen a route deeper inland to flee the mountain.

The ships quickly spread out to take advantage of the winds. As I stood on the deck of Pompanianus's largest vessel, I looked across at one of Pliny's smaller ships as it receded from us. On the bow, facing me, was a tall pale woman with striking red hair.

~

We landed on Capri, where I remained for another two years. (It was six months before I stopped coughing up ash.) Win stayed with me up until her death, which came about a year after the Vesuvius eruption. An unfortunate fact about pixies is that their life span is only about twenty years, so it was not a big surprise for either of us. I buried her in an olive grove.

Many hundreds of years later, I got a chance to see a museum exhibit showing some of the artifacts uncovered in Pompeii and Herculaneum. It was, to put it mildly, a strange experience, especially since I recognized several of the preserved dead. I also saw my broom on display. I considered reclaiming it but decided it would take more effort than it was worth.

Historians had long speculated that Herculaneum got off easy by being wiped out by a large mud flow, and for a while I thought maybe I'd been wrong about the lava. But I was vindicated by the recent discovery of skeletal remains and half-preserved bodies when the beach houses on the shore were excavated. It looked like half the village opted to wait it out rather than flee, and died when lava engulfed their refuge.

I still feel kind of bad about this.

CHAPTER 9

So far, the mushrooms don't seem to be doing anything, except adding to the overall bouquet of the room. Maybe I was wrong. Maybe I'm losing my mind.

I'm wondering now who's in the third cell. I know the one next to me is occupied, and I know who's in the fourth cell—I think—but the third one is a mystery. I initially assumed it was unused, but lately I've been hearing noises that have me thinking otherwise. Viktor and the others have been mum about it—as they have been about everything except the tests they're running on me personally—but that just makes me more curious. I might have to ask one of them point blank.

Whoever it is in there, he's in a lot of pain. I can hear the moaning. Is he a volunteer, or a prisoner like the rest of us?

~

Waiting for Iza to return, I sat in a coffee shop two blocks from the police station reading the morning paper and enjoying—if one could call it that—a bitter latte sweetened by a splash of schnapps.

My relationship with alcohol is complicated. Give or take a

few days here and there, I haven't been dry since the speakeasy fire in 1922. By all normal human standards that would make me a raging alcoholic, except that by those same human standards I would also be dead by now, if not from old age then from cirrhosis of the liver. But eighty years for me is like a glass of wine with dinner for anybody else.

Many times over my long history, I have allowed myself to become entirely dependent upon alcohol, to the point where I now make advance plans anticipating that I'll be drunk for a decade or two. The unspoken understanding is that I will eventually either grow tired of drunkenness, or something interesting will happen that demands my undivided attention.

You might think this is terribly naive, and perhaps I should just admit that I'm being stupid, as I am clearly already an alcoholic, but I don't think it's altogether fair to apply that term to me. More to the point, I think if you gave any drunkard immortality he would eventually pull himself together with a century or two to work on it. And trust me, alcohol is just about the only way to get through the duller periods of history. For instance, I spent most of the tenth century in Spain when there was simply nothing to do except drink wine. Everybody else did anyway.

Not that I'm lumping twenty-first century America in with tenth century Spain. On the contrary, the last hundred years had been very interesting, and despite being sauced most of the time, I've kept up-to-date on the big stuff. But I've also been in mourning pretty much since that 1922 fire, which upset me perhaps more than I realized.

One thing that hadn't improved with time was the coffee. I'm not sure when bitter coffee became cool, but I don't like the trend. Still, I drank away, because that's what one does when one wants to fit in with the upscale crowd these days.

~

The update on the murders in the morning paper (reading the paper two days in a row had to be some kind of record for me) wasn't any more enlightening than the initial story had been. It was mostly a lot of puff about Gary and Nate and how everybody loved them and so on. Attaching presumptive sainthood to murder victims is a time-honored tradition, so I can't say I was surprised by any of it. Can't say I knew them well enough to contradict anything either, and they were nice enough for me to want to go through the trouble of finding out who killed them, but still ... You'd think there was someone, somewhere—other than Jerry—who didn't like them.

On the hard news front, the papers were a day earlier than predicted with the artistic rendition of my face. It was a pretty good likeness.

It was a bit unsettling seeing my own face in the newspaper. Historically, I've gone to great lengths to keep myself in the background, just in the interest of survival. I've lived through one Inquisition already, you know?

I moved on.

Paging through to the crossword puzzle, a full-page ad caught my eye, mainly because it was addressed to me. Also, it was in classical Latin.

The Latin was pretty rough, penned no doubt by a modern scholar who didn't appreciate the subtleties of the spoken language. And since nobody spoke Latin outside of the Vatican, I guess this was understandable. But I understood it all right.

Translated, the message read:

For the Eternal Man

We are trying to find you. You do not have any reason to fear us. You do not have to run. We want to help you and we believe you can help us. We have the answers to many questions. Stay where you are and we will find you. Do not make this any harder than it has to be.

The message was unattributed and the paper did not note who purchased the ad.

I didn't know what to make of it. On the one hand, it sounded like a friendly attempt to establish a dialogue. On the other, it made it clear "they" were after me in some capacity, possibly the same capacity that resulted in two dead college students. It was an offer of knowledge and a threat all wrapped up into one cryptic passage—don't run, don't be afraid, don't move and don't make this any harder than it has to be. Very convincing. If there's one thing I know, it's that the minute someone feels obligated to tell you not to be afraid of them, that's the time to start being afraid of them. I wondered how long these little letters had been getting printed. Maybe I should have started reading the newspapers sooner.

~

As I sat there at my little, two-persons-max table, contemplating the passage and deciding whether I should wait until I'd heard from Iza before hopping aboard a transatlantic flight to someplace remote, someone sat down opposite me.

If you've ever hung out long enough in a Starbucks you know this isn't a terribly uncommon experience, especially when all the other tables are taken. Usually people bother to ask first if the chair is being saved, but ... Anyway, I tried to act nonchalant and flipped ahead to the crossword puzzle to look busy.

"Hello," my table-mate said. I looked up briefly. He was dressed in a sports coat and a white shirt, no tie. He had a couple of gold chains around his neck with symbols hanging from them that he probably couldn't identify the meaning of at gunpoint. He was white-skinned, stocky in build, and looked to have some Norwegian ancestry in him. I was singularly disinterested in having a conversation, so I pretended to be a foreigner. Which I sort of am.

"I don't speak any English," I said in German. Middle-high German, which nobody speaks any more. I didn't feel like running the risk that he was fluent in the modern form.

Most of the time when someone hears a foreign language they don't probe. And they almost never ask what language it is, just so long as it sounds like an actual language. This doesn't always work. I once spent a half hour trying to get rid of an inquisitive elderly wino in a bar in Ontario while speaking Sanskrit. Sometimes people just can't take a hint.

This appeared to be one of those times. He smiled as if I had responded in the King's English and said, "I'm fine, thanks."

I nodded and tried to go back to my paper. Five letter word for draining aid. Sieve?

"How about this weather?" he added.

"You are ugly and smell like pig dung," I suggested helpfully.

"Yeah, it looks like snow to me, too."

This would have been amusing, if it weren't so very annoying.

"Look," he whispered, leaning forward conspiratorially, "I know you speak English. You're reading the fucking paper. Okay?"

"Your mother eats raw salmon," I offered. Was this guy slow?

He snatched the paper from my hand. Now we were past the *invasion of personal space* phase and fast approaching the *punch you in the nose* phase.

He slapped the paper down on the table and pointed to the artistic rendition of my face, circa two days ago.

"I know who you are. Now let's talk in the same language for a bit."

For the first time, I noticed that the coffee shop was half empty. There were four empty tables he could have chosen from. I should have been paying better attention.

I snatched the paper off the table.

"I am the god of cabbage," I declared angrily. With any luck somebody would step up and ask him why he was bothering the foreign guy.

"All right, all right," he said. "Do me a favor. Look under the table. I have a gun pointed at your balls right now."

Well now, that was obviously a trick, right? If I peek under the table, I clearly understand English. And for all I know he's got his penis out or something. The correct response was to ignore him. Except I knew as soon as he said it that he wasn't kidding. So, I peeked. He wasn't kidding. I sat up again.

"What is that, a .22?" I asked.

"It's a .38. Makes a little 'pop' when you pull the trigger, sounds like a wine bottle uncorking."

"That's nice. What do you want?"

"I want you," he said, smiling.

"I'm charmed. Are you a policeman?"

He laughed. "Hardly."

"Well then. If you're not a member of law enforcement, why should I go anywhere with you?"

"Because I've still got a gun pointed at your balls?"

"It would look terribly silly if I got up and we walked out together with you holding a gun to my groin, don't you think? One almost never sees that sort of thing."

"You could give me your word that you'll leave quietly," he suggested.

"Supposing my word isn't worth anything?"

"I think it is."

"That's mighty trusting of you."

He leaned forward and grinned. "Here's what I know. I know you're old enough to remember a time when there were no words."

He was wrong, I think. I don't remember any fully preliterate societies. But close enough. Who the hell was this guy? Did he work for the people who sent me the message in the paper? Was he the guy who sent it?

"Do I have your attention now?" he asked.

"Sure. What do you want?"

"I want you to sit right there for a second."

He pulled a black case out of his jacket and slid it across the table.

"Open it," he said.

I popped it open and found a syringe.

"We just met and we're already doing heroin?" I said. "Seems sudden."

He leaned forward and whispered, "Keep your goddamn voice down. Now I want you to take that and inject yourself with it."

"Um, no?"

"You want to spend the rest of your very long life without your balls?" he asked.

I was amazed that our dialogue had gone unnoticed. You'd think this was far enough off the conversational beaten path to send up a signal or two to somebody. But everyone was stubbornly minding their own business.

I picked up the syringe and examined it.

"What's in it?" I asked. Not that I had anything to fear regardless. Nobody had invented anything yet that could poison me.

"It's the only way I have to verify your identity. It's concentrated *botulinum* toxin. It'll kill a man in about fifteen seconds. If you are who you're supposed to be, it won't do anything to you."

"I never claimed to be anyone special," I pointed out. "That's all you. And you seem convinced already."

"I am convinced. But if I don't test you I don't get paid."

I laid the syringe on the table and examined it.

"How's it work?" I asked.

"What do you mean?"

"I've never used one."

He sighed and rolled his eyes. I wasn't kidding. I really had never used a syringe before.

"Find a vein," he said. "Your wrist is fine."

I laid my hand flat and palm-up on the table and looked at it. "Like that one?" I asked, pointing to the largest vein I could see.

"Yes, fine." He was getting impatient. All except for the gun under the table, I was sort of enjoying this.

"Okay," he said. "Insert the pointy end into the vein at an angle, and then push the plunger down. And don't do anything stupid like sticking me with it. You kill me, I kill you."

And so, at gunpoint, I gave myself my very first intravenous injection. It was a little painful. I don't think I have a future ahead of me as a junkie.

When I was finished and the fifteen seconds wherein I continued to be alive passed uneventfully, he said, "Good, now put it back in the case and slide it over to me."

I did as I was told. He returned the case to his inside pocket.

"Now what?" I asked.

"Get up. I'm parked about two blocks down the street."

"Where are we going?"

"We'll get to that later. Do you know how to drive?"

"No." He tapped the gun barrel against the bottom of the table. "Yes."

"Good. Let's go."

He stood. I stood. He was much taller than he looked when sitting in the chair. A full head-and-shoulders taller than me. I remember when I used to be the tallest guy on an entire continent. At this rate, in another century or two, I'll be the shortest.

I led the way out the door, leaving behind the bitter, spiked coffee and the paper while he trailed, keeping close enough so I knew he was there but far enough so it didn't look like I was being coerced.

"To the right," he said. "Down the alley, then left."

"I just met you, you've got a gun pointed at my back, and you want me to go with you down an alley?"

"Yep."

"Just checking."

It was a fairly unremarkable alley. Not too narrow, with a couple of trash cans, a dumpster, and a fire escape ladder just out of reach. Pretty typical. But it was long and it was out of view to the public at large, and there was nobody else in it.

At a convenient moment, I spun around and hit just the right spot on his wrist to compel him to drop his gun, which I caught with my free hand. With one sweep of my leg I buckled his knees, and just like that I was standing over my erstwhile captor holding his gun with him kneeling before me.

Here's a little bit of advice if you ever meet an immortal and feel like challenging him to a fight. It is simply impossible to live this long and not pick up a few hand-to-hand combat techniques here and there. I was a black belt before there was such a thing.

Not that I'm bragging.

"Well," my new friend said, "that was impressive. Did you break my wrist?"

"No, but you may have to give it a couple of minutes before you try and use it again. What do I call you?"

"Stan."

"What's this about, Stan?"

"Can I get up?"

"No."

"It's just that my knees kinda hurt."

I pressed the gun against his forehead.

"All right. I'm a bounty hunter."

I pulled back. "That's a new one. Who put a bounty on me?"

"No idea. It's a private contract. Very under the table."

"Sounds illegal."

"That's sort of splitting hairs, isn't it?"

True enough. It had to be illegal, as the police had only been looking for me for two days. This was about something else.

Stay where you are and we will find you.

"Dead or alive?" I asked.

"Alive."

"That's heartening."

"With allowances for wounding."

"You're over-sharing. What were you supposed to do with me once you found me?"

"Call a number."

"What number?"

"The job came with a scrambled phone. It automatically calls the correct number, so I have no idea."

"That's convenient," I said. "Did the syringe come with the package, too?"

"Yes."

"Where's the phone?"

"In my car," he said, adding, "look, my knees are starting to hurt here."

"Oh, stop whining. Keys?"

"In my pocket."

"What kind of car?"

"Caddy Escalade. Black."

"Nice ride," I commented. I didn't know what an Escalade looked like, but I knew what a Cadillac was.

"I make a decent living," he said. "Look, I really wasn't going to hurt you. You seem like a nice enough guy and all."

"Thanks, Stan. I need to know something else. A couple of nights ago two friends of mine were beaten to death in their apartment. You know anything about that?"

"No," he said.

I cuffed him in the ear with the butt of the gun. "Oww!" he cried.

"Try again," I suggested.

"It wasn't me, all right? There are other bounty hunters out there. You're worth a lot of money to somebody."

"How much?"

He hesitated. "Five million."

"Wow." I know inflation has changed the relevance of the word "million" but that still sounded like a lot.

"Yeah, wow," he agreed. "So, now everybody is in on it."

"How'd you find me?"

"Lucky," he said. "I saw your picture in the paper. I was heading to the police station to ask for details on the case. Figured they had a lead on you. But then I saw you outside."

Guess my big makeover wasn't as thorough as I thought. "Cops just hand out information like that?"

"I'm FBI."

"No shit?"

"No shit."

"Show me."

I let him pull out his wallet. He handed it over. It looked real enough to me, but then what do I know? I pocketed it.

"Thought you said you weren't law enforcement," I said.

"I said I wasn't police. And I'm not acting in an official capacity at this particular moment in time."

"The ID says you're based in San Antonio. They let you drive off whenever you feel like it?"

"Technically I'm on suspension."

I smiled. "You're a bit dirty, aren't you Stan?"

He didn't respond.

"Okay, you can stand up," I said.

Stan pulled himself to his feet with help from the wall, while I checked both ends of the alley. Didn't look like anybody had noticed us.

"Thanks," he said. "Now what?"

"Now we have a problem," I admitted.

"Yeah?"

"Look at it from my perspective, Stan. You're a killer. You know how I know that? Because you were willing to accept the consequences of your little injection without blinking. Now I can't let you go because you'll just try and find me again, and next time you probably won't give me a chance to disarm you. And I'm not at all fond of the whole being-turned-in-on-a-bounty thing in general. I'm more of a free spirit in that way."

"I could just walk away," he said, his voice rising somewhat. "Forget we ever met."

"I don't think you'd do that. Plus, you know what I look like. You could put that information to pretty good use. Maybe make a little money out of it."

"I wouldn't," he insisted.

"Stan, Stan, Stan. I'm not stupid. I didn't get to live this long by being stupid. I'm sorry, but when you think about it none of this was my idea."

"But ..."

I pressed the gun up to his chest and fired, once. It made a little pop like a cork. Just like he said.

CHAPTER 10

Today I saw him watching as I walked to the lab. He's got a nice big office on the other side of the compound, with a nice big picture window to look down on his subjects. I'm sure all he sees when he looks at me is dollar signs, but that doesn't mean he's not enjoying the fact that he beat me. Although I suppose I could just be projecting, because it sure as hell bugs the crap out of me that I let someone like that put me in this position.

The encounter—if you call staring at a hundred paces an encounter — brought home the idea that my escape plan is going to have to involve killing him.

But an escape plan would be good first. I definitely need to start with one of those.

~

"You did what?" Brenda asked. This was much later.

After taking poor, foolish Stan off the list of things I have to worry about, I strip-searched his car for items of interest—which I found—and then took the most circuitous route imaginable to return to Brenda's, on the off-chance there were any others like him following me.

"I didn't have much of a choice, did I?"

"You could'a hit him over the head or, or turned him in to the cops, or ..."

I was busy checking out the contents of Stan's car, which I'd dumped out on the bed.

"You're not thinking straight," I said. "You're a vampire, you should know about this. Think in terms of predator/prey."

"What?" Brenda was freaking out, which resulted in her voice getting louder. Almost too loud. Among the many things that are amplified by the vampiric transformation are the vocal chords. I remember Eloise used to hunt rabbits by shrieking at them, which either stunned or killed them outright.

"I've never killed anybody!" she nearly shouted, and I swear the walls quivered. Apparently she'd rethought her whole "being a killer is sorta sexy" thing.

"For Baal's sake, keep it down," I said, clapping my hands over my ears.

"I haven't," she repeated, much quieter.

"I know," I said, lingering near the things on the bed that I very much wanted to delve into. But I was going to have to calm down my hyperventilating vampire friend first. (Ironic, as vampires don't need to breathe.) I stood up and stepped toward her.

"Don't touch me!" she exclaimed, and I bet they heard that downstairs.

"I won't," I said. "Look, just ... calm down a minute, okay? Yes, I could have clubbed him over the head and run off, but what would that have gotten me? He'd already found me once, and he wasn't going to be as careless about it the second time. If I just wounded him, I couldn't guarantee he'd never tell somebody else where I was and what I currently look like. I couldn't go to the police, because who do you think they would believe? The word of the FBI agent, or the word of the guy with no legitimate identification who's already a suspect in another murder?"

She glared at me. "You didn't have to kill him," she insisted.

"If he had to, he would have done the same to me."

Blood tears started to well up in her eyes. I'd clearly overestimated the prowess of the modern vampire. The ones I'd known over the centuries were fundamentally aware that they were killing machines and were largely okay with that.

"I didn't think of you as someone who could really do something like that," she added quietly.

"Neither did Stan," I pointed out. "But I didn't live this long by being polite."

~

I committed my first murder when I was twelve.

I wasn't even aware of my immortality at the time. I was just trying to get by. It happened when our little band of nomads happened upon the hunting grounds of someone else's little band of nomads, and one thing led to another. This was almost literally at the dawn of man, so "us good, them bad" was just about the only thing that figured prominently in our philosophical outlook.

Using a heavy stone—very much in vogue at the time—I crushed the skull of an enemy warrior who couldn't have been much more than ten years old, feeling no particular remorse about it, because again, they were "them." We won the fight and rewarded ourselves by raping several of their women. Because that was *also* very much in vogue at the time.

Violence continued to be the norm for the vast majority of my life, peaceful existence the exception. It may have seemed like things quieted down a bit once we all figured out how to farm, because farming begets society and society develops laws, and laws enforce peace in the interest of the greater good. But society is just another kind of tribe and it eventually bumps into a larger one, and there's more violence, only then it's called war.

In those early days, I must have been directly responsible for hundreds of deaths and indirectly responsible for possibly thousands. Sometimes it's just what you have to do.

The advent of civilization—an overly optimistic word—didn't change things as much as one might think, because no matter how large a city or empire became there was always another "them" to go out and kill. And when organized religion really got going ... well, there's a fantastic excuse to murder people in bunches.

My point is that despite the patina of civility coating most of modern society, underneath it is a thick layer of savagery. Many people go their entire lives without even realizing it's there. I've never had that luxury.

~

I returned to my immediate concern, which was the stuff I'd been able to carry from Stan's Escalade. I would have just driven the car someplace where I could search it thoroughly, but that struck me as a dangerous thing to try. There was too much I didn't know, such as whether his car could be tracked or whether he would be found and connected to the car soon enough for the police to consider looking for it. (Also, I'm a terrible driver.) Instead I took what I could, tossed his keys into the sewer, and left the scene.

I found only two things worth keeping—a large square suitcase and an oversized manila folder.

I slid the contents of the folder onto the bed and examined them by candlelight. There wasn't much, just the phone Stan talked about and a two-page info sheet.

Page one had a bad black-and-white photograph of me. It was recent. Within the last six months recent. I couldn't fathom how anyone managed such a photo, as I take great precautions in that regard.

The rest of the page was notable for its lack of information.

.

Name: Various

Age: looks early thirties

Sex: Male

Race: Various

Height: 5' 11"

Weight: 180 (Approx.)

Hair: Various

Eyes: Brown

Scars, other identifying marks: None

Clearly, whoever sent Stan knew enough to list race as various, which is not the sort of thing one customarily sees in a tally of vital statistics. I flipped to page two.

Target is an immortal man, but in all appearances and mannerisms a normal human being. He is immune to all diseases but can be physically harmed with ordinary weaponry. He typically travels alone but has been known to befriend humans, and also various underspecies. He prefers to use cash when he travels. (Source of cash is unknown.) He will rarely stay in one place for an extended period. He was last spotted in Cleveland.

Target is not usually armed. However, he is extremely cunning and is not to be taken lightly. His greatest weakness is his penchant for alcohol, which makes him sloppy and overly reliant on strangers.

Goal: Target is to be taken ALIVE. Use of lethal force—or damage caused leading to his subsequent demise—will result in nonpayment or forfeiture of payment. Once you have safely secured and positively tested target, contact is to be made via the enclosed phone. NO OTHER FORM OF CONTACT IS ACCEPTABLE. Transfer of target and the necessary payment arrangements will be negotiated at that time.

"What does it say?" Brenda asked quietly, not yet willing to approach the bed, or me.

"It says somebody out there knows more about me than they should," I said. "Strengths, weaknesses... everything except who wants me and why."

"Oh. Has this ever happened before?"

"No. This is new."

I popped open the black case.

"Oh my," I said.

Brenda came around to the bed to take a look herself.

"Is that real?" she asked, looking at what appeared to be a disassembled sniper's rifle.

I pulled out the barrel. "Looks to be. Can't say I'm surprised."

The gun only took up the top half of the suitcase, so I pulled on the little flap in the front and checked underneath. Cash. Lots of it.

"Can't say I'm surprised at that either," I added.

"How much is that?"

"About fifty grand. Bounty hunting wasn't the only thing Stan was into."

"What do you mean?"

"I think he did a little contract killing in his spare time. Looks like the FBI had a good reason to suspend him."

Brenda cocked her head, much in the way a dog does when he hears a distant whistle. "Your pixie's back."

"Good timing." I started pulling cash out of the suitcase and stuffing it into my own bag. "I've got to get going."

"Go? Why?" she asked. "Where are you going?"

"What would you do if you just killed an FBI agent in broad daylight?" I asked. "I'm getting the hell out of town."

PART II

THE NOOSE

CHAPTER 11

Viktor spent half the day today talking to me about how "exciting" my immune system is. Says he's never seen anything like it before and that he would give anything to be able to present me to a few geneticist friends. He ran through a list of the things he'd exposed me to—his lab is evidently a bioterrorist's wet dream—and could not stop raving about how well my body had handled it. All I could do was shrug. It's not as if any of this is a huge surprise.

I think I'm starting to annoy him, having yet to come around to his way of thinking. On the other hand, he hasn't come around to my way of thinking either, and I've got the weight of history on my side, because you don't just introduce something like this to the world. It should be done much more gradually, and there are a few important steps along the way that will end up being skipped.

Viktor agrees that there will be issues but is so very convinced of the general goodness of mankind that he's sure they will be overcome. He's obviously never witnessed a genocide up close before.

~

Ah, New York. Like Boston on steroids. Every other city in the world, with the possible exception of Tokyo, looks like a suburb compared to New York City. The sights, the smells, the unbelievable noise of a few million representatives of impolite humanity jammed together in all its glory. I kind of hate the place.

Right off the train I had to defend myself against two guys who wanted to carry my bag for me, neither of whom were official representatives of the train station (as specifically outlined by the announcements made every ten seconds over the loudspeakers), and at least one of whom would probably take off with the bag the instant he reached the street. Once I fought past them I had to turn down a guy offering to sell me a half-price copy of the New York Times he'd stolen five hours earlier from a newsstand, two homeless people who just wanted my money and didn't even bother with a preamble, and a man who desperately wanted Jesus to save me.

And this was just on the train platform.

New York is the one place in the world that actively encourages rudeness, because that's the only way to get past the fake bag carriers, homeless people, newspaper thieves, Jesus freaks, and everyone else who wants something and isn't afraid to ask for it, repeatedly, at close range. Try to ignore them and they'll step in front of you. Tell them you're not interested and you might as well be speaking Farsi. But tell them to fuck off and they get that just fine. It's like a secret handshake.

I may be the only person on Earth who can state unequivocally that there has never been a city quite like New York before. Hopefully there never will be again.

A short trip on the marvelous subway system and I reached Forty-Fifth Street and a lovely little boutique—I'm being polite—called Ivan's. Or that's what everyone calls it. On the street sign it just says PAWN SHOP. And in case one needs services beyond pawning one's ill-gotten goods, there are additional hand-lettered signs taped up all over the windows: check cashing, money transfer, loans, phone cards for sale, fortunes told. I didn't need any of those things.

I pushed my way in, immediately greeted by the odor of illegally bought tax-free Russian cigarettes. A young fellow I'd never met before sat behind the counter (said counter being glass; a display case showing an extensive array of watches, some still engraved with the previous owner's initials) chewing on a lollipop and reading the latest issue of something called *Maxim*.

"Hello," I greeted.

"Hey," he said, not looking up. Must have been an engaging article.

"I need to see Tchekhy."

He looked away from the magazine, sized me up, looked back down. "Nobody here by that name."

"I see. Do you smoke?"

"Hmm? No."

"Then you can imagine my confusion, because I happen to know Tchekhy does smoke. I know what brand he smokes, and I can smell that brand right now. I can even see some smoke coming from behind that black curtain to your left."

That got him to close the magazine. He slid off the stool, calmly put the magazine down, and pulled up the front of his shirt to reveal a snub-nosed revolver tucked into his pants. "There is nobody here named Tchekhy," he repeated slowly, as I evidently had a learning deficiency.

"That is a stupid place to put a gun," I said, in Russian. *"You'll shoot your dick off."*

Now he was confused.

"Who are you?"

"Tell him Efgeniy is here. And be quick about it."

"Fuck you," he muttered, walking through the curtain. Kids these days.

A few seconds later Tchekhy poked his head out.

"Efgeniy! Come!" he waved.

He led me through the curtain and down the unlit staircase. We passed the surly counter help on the way, and Tchekhy cuffed him on the side of the head, almost as an afterthought. I resisted the urge to do the same.

The basement of the pawnshop is geek paradise, and Tchekhy Ivanovich Gruschenko is its undisputed master. There are a half-dozen computers, printers, scanners, and things I have no name for, whose purpose I don't understand. (What little I do know about computers I know thanks to Tchekhy, but there are a few things he won't explain to me because doing so would make me "legally liable." Which is just as well. I don't think I would understand it anyway.) Cables run along almost every single portion of the floor to power all of the equipment.

A corner of the basement is devoted to portraiture, which comes in handy when manufacturing bogus IDs. Another corner holds a couch, which is about the only thing in the whole basement I know how to use. Keeping the place from overheating are two floor fans and a severely overworked air conditioner shoved in the only window. His power bill would be insane if he ever actually paid it, but I don't think he does. I think he steals electricity directly from the city. When he turns everything on at once, the streetlights dim.

Tchekhy doesn't fit the profile. He's a tubby little second-generation ex-pat Russian with too much hair in too many of the wrong places. Back when the United States and the Soviet Union were playing nukes at twenty paces, he was a major dealer in espionage, but nowadays he gets most of his work from the Russian mafia and poor immortal bastards like me.

Tchekhy stepped into the nest of equipment in the center of the room to access a Styrofoam cooler nestled between two box computer thingies, extracting a Coke. I tiptoed my way after him —I'm always afraid I'm going to step on a live wire—and sat in a squeaky old office chair.

"So, my old friend," he began, popping open his Coke and nestling into his own chair, "you need new passports already?" Behind him a large flat screen monitor was displaying what looked like live satellite images of South America. He hacks into government surveillance just for kicks sometimes.

"Not just yet," I said. "I need a different sort of favor today. Two, actually."

He perked up. "Really? Anything illegal?"

"Only marginally."

He looked disappointed, as any good anarchist would. I reached into my bag and pulled out the miniature camera Iza had used.

"There are photos of a police file in this. I need to read them." I tossed him the device.

"Digital," he said, examining it. "USB port. Very light. Very expensive?"

"Moderately."

"Very sleek. Can I keep it?"

"When you're done, sure."

"You are too kind."

"I know. It's a failing."

"And the second thing?" he asked.

"That's a bit more complicated."

I explained the matter of the bounty while he fiddled with the camera, plugging it into one of his stations and pulling up the digital photos. By the time I was finished, the printer was already running.

"And this man who had the papers?" he asked.

"He ran into a bullet. It was very sad."

"*Da,*" he said simply. No wailing and gnashing of teeth from him on the subject of murder, nor did I expect any.

He pulled the sheets of paper from the printer and handed them over without examination. "So, there is a wealthy person out there who knows a few more things than he or she ought to about your unusual nature. He or she is placing anonymous advertisements in newspapers and hiring armed men to hunt you down. And you wish for me to find out who."

Needless to say, Tchekhy is aware of my immortality. If anybody were to notice I don't age it would be the guy taking my photograph every seven years. (You have to take a new photo every time because of wear and tear on the old photo, but more importantly because clothing styles change.) You might be thinking his knowledge would make him a prime suspect, because after all, somebody had to cough up information, and for this particular someone, secrets are currency. But I've known Tchekhy since he was ten years old, which was when his father Ivan—who also did my passports—introduced us. And I was there fifteen years later when Ivan was dying prematurely of lung cancer, when Tchekhy took an oath in front of him to keep my nature secret. Then we all got outrageously drunk. That's the kind of loyalty you can't buy.

"Let me see the contract."

I handed him the manila folder. He pulled the phone out first.

"This is very interesting," he said.

"How interesting?"

"You say this is a scrambled phone?"

"That's what I was told."

"Satellite, no doubt. I wonder what manner of encryption it uses."

"That's your department. I'm no good at that stuff," I said.

"Have you used it?"

"No. I think it's only good for one phone call. I figured I'd wait until you'd seen it."

"Very smart."

"So I've been told."

He put it on one of the nearly clean counters and waved a peculiar device—it looked like an old TV antenna, complete with tin foil—over it. "That's lucky," he said.

"What is?"

You carry the electronic device of a man you killed. Did you consider that it might have a tracking mechanism in it?"

"Uh, no."

"It does not. But it could have."

So much for me being smart.

Tchekhy reached into the cooler and pulled out a bottle of authentic Russian (meaning cheap and crappy, much like their cigarettes) vodka. He took a long swig of it, then capped the bottle and tossed it to me.

"This will take some time," he said. "I will order pizza."

I took a swig of my own. It made my hair follicles tickle. Russian vodka does that.

"Don't let me get in the way," I said, finding my way to the couch.

~

Two hours later, the vodka was gone and I wasn't anywhere closer to any answers. I was half-drunk however, so at least I had that going for me.

Tchekhy was doing his mad hacker thing with at least four different computers, pausing occasionally to light another of his foul brand of cigarettes. I considered breaking into his reverie to see if he'd actually found anything yet, but I held off. Something I learned a long time ago was to never interrupt a genius when he's in the middle of something. Did that to Newton once. God that man had a temper.

The police report and I were getting along okay, but I was seriously contemplating calling lead detective Caldwell and asking him where he learned such abysmal penmanship. I mean just awful. Before the printing press people gave a damn about their handwriting, you know? Thank goodness there were lots of pictures of the crime scene to work with.

The door to Gary and Nate's apartment had been kicked in rather efficiently, the impact removing a portion of the door jamb. Detective Caldwell called this "signs of forced entry." (Or, *songs of foreign entree,* depending on one's interpretation.) Gary and Nate were both found in the living room on the floor. Contrasting the way the room looked in the pictures with what I remembered, they'd put up a pretty decent fight. The futon was upside down and the coffee table had been broken in two by something large. A fist had gone through the TV screen. Above the wall near the upset futon was a bloody splatter. Detective Caldwell thought one of the victims (or *vicms*) had been thrown there, which was scary because the mark was more than halfway up the wall. It's not easy to throw a guy that far with that much force, no matter what you may have learned from pro wrestling.

The autopsy photos left me seriously reconsidering my vodka-and-pizza dinner. Neither of the guys was recognizable. Frankly, if Nate hadn't been black I would have been unable to distinguish between them. It was, as the good detective pointed out, a classic case of overkill. As in, the guy—or guys—who killed them kept hitting them after they were clearly no longer alive.

Caldwell ran through possible blunt objects (*blond opreds*) that could have served as a murder weapon, leaning toward an aluminum baseball bat. He also figured on at least two bad guys, just because no one person could have done so much damage to two healthy young men like Nate and Gary.

The good news was this almost entirely ruled me out.

He was wrong about there being two guys. I thought again about calling to tell him this, but that was just the vodka talking. He would never believe me.

Two things caught my eye. One was the coffee table. It had been splintered by a strong horizontal blow across the middle. A baseball bat could maybe do this, but it would take a while, and I was pretty sure that Gary and Nate wouldn't have waited around to watch. No, the blow to the table had to be collateral damage during the struggle. The weapon had been a very strong forearm.

The second thing was Gary's face. It had been caved in by a powerful blow administered while he was either pressed up against the wall or on the floor. It was the kill shot and it hadn't been done by any bat. I could clearly see the indent of three knuckles, the middle one raised slightly to a tapered point.

It was obvious what had done this. I didn't blame the police for not recognizing it. They'd probably never seen a demon's handiwork before.

CHAPTER 12

Demons are not—as has been so often assumed—supernatural minions of some higher (or lower) evil deity. They're not supernatural at all, any more than pixies, iffrits, or vampires. Or me. They're just another race—or underspecies, as my unnamed nemesis called them.

This is not to say demons are in any way capable of being nice. Not at all. Demons are the worst combination of big, strong, and nasty on the planet. Worse even than dragons, because dragons were just animals and animals don't have enough self-awareness to be evil. Demons do. They understand money and they understand violence and they don't care about much else. Also, unlike dragons, they managed to avoid extinction, possibly because something deep in the cavernous recesses of most demon brains is the understanding that survival and secretiveness go hand in hand.

But keeping a low profile is only one reason demons still walk the Earth. Another is usefulness. They're the ultimate mercenaries and really come in handy during wartime. Alexander the Great had ten demons on retainer when he conquered most of the known world. Hammurabi had twenty-five. Genghis Khan had thirty, and rumor had it he was one himself. (I don't believe the rumor—a demon would make a lousy general—but I never met Genghis Khan, so I could be wrong.) The biblical Goliath was also a demon, which should tell you plenty about the accuracy of that little story, because it'd take a hell of a lot more than a stupid slingshot to take out a demon. (David actually lured Goliath under a cliff face and had some friends drop a big rock on him.) I wouldn't be a bit surprised if a few of today's governments had one or two demons on the payroll, although with modern weaponry their talents are more useful to drug cartels and the like.

It is notoriously difficult to kill a demon. Their skin is much thicker than human skin (but not as hard as dragon hide), they don't burn easily, and if they have a heart, nobody has been able to figure out exactly where it is. At the Battle of Troy, I saw a demon run through with a pike three times in three different places and keep on coming. It took twenty men to hold him down and two working with heavy battle axes to cleave his head from his shoulders.

You've probably seen one. I don't know how they move about in today's world because I haven't laid eyes on one for over a century, but I know they usually favor baggy clothes and hats to obscure their obviously non-human features. You might be thinking professional American football would be a good place to find a few, but I don't think it's violent enough for them.

The extraordinary thing about demons is that they don't rule the world. They reproduce normally—I've never seen a female demon, but I know they exist—and they were around back when it really wasn't all that hard to take over the world. (Pretty much everyone took over the world at least once back in the day. I even thought about it a couple of times.) For some reason, it just never seemed like there was enough of them to truly dominate.

Why there are so few demons was one of the questions I

posed to the only demon I ever had a face-to-face conversation with. Unfortunately, he was not all that forthcoming.

I was living in Carthage at the time, in one of my occasional incarnations as a wealthy man. By modern reckoning this was around the third century BC, and I was making a fine living as a merchant, shipping goods—mainly ivory, but also a little gold and silver—mined or hunted in the more savage sections of middle Africa. I had customers from Tyre to Corsica, three boats to move product, a couple hundred employees, a few dozen slaves, and one of the largest houses in Carthage. (Don't get on me about the slaves. It was expected. Besides, I've been a slave myself, on four different occasions.)

Business was pretty cutthroat back then, as things always are when money is involved.

As a side note: I thought money was a bad idea way back when it was first invented. I remember the moment very clearly. This guy owed me a sheep, but instead of giving me an actual sheep he gave me five coins he said were worth the same as a sheep. "But I can't eat round pieces of metal, asshole," were my exact words. It took me a while to get on board with the concept is all I'm saying.

I always had somebody trying to edge in on my business, much as I had done to others when I first built my little empire. My trump card was always time, especially in an era when the life expectancy was somewhere in the mid-forties. Most of the town thought I'd made some sort of pact with a deity—a few thought I *was* a deity—but nobody ever organized a lynch mob over it. Carthage was nice like that.

What was not nice was the two harbor problem. Carthage had two harbors, but only one of them was within the city walls. That was where they put all the war vessels. Important when you're one of the first empires in the Western world and therefore spend a good amount of time defending said empire (and the first of the Punic Wars was only thirty years away), but annoying when you want to do business. I had to operate my ships out of the second harbor.

Every time cargo was loaded or unloaded—and I always oversaw these things personally, because nobody trusts a Carthaginian—I ended up spending the day beyond the protection of the city walls. This was my biggest business advantage because I wasn't robbed blind by my captains—others were—but also my biggest disadvantage. Cities in those days were built to keep the rabble out, you see. Not at all like today's cities, which are clearly designed to keep the rabble in. Every night I spent beyond the walls of Carthage was a night I took my life into my hands.

Not to say I didn't have protection. I employed private guards who followed me around everywhere and did a very effective job of scaring away the standard blackguards. And because I wasn't about to sleep on the dock, I kept a modest home a short walk from the pier.

On this one particular evening, after a long day helping unload a shipment of silver from southern Spain, I retired to my modest home and immediately sought refuge in my personal bath.

A lot of people are under the impression that it was the Romans who invented the concept of the bath. Those people don't know what they're talking about, because I was using baths before there were Romans. Trust me, it's one thing to deal with a lifetime of dirt and grime when that lifetime is thirty years. It's quite another when that lifetime is counted out in millennia.

Anyway, so I took a bath. And after a very relaxing hour or so I emerged into the atrium to find a demon sitting on my couch.

"Hello," I greeted amicably. One must always be amicable when faced with a demon. Not that it helps any.

"Hello," he grunted back.

The demon was as ugly as the rest—protruding jawbone with

a double row of jagged teeth, a pug nose, and a small set of horns, all covered in a dark brown skin.

"Are you Amilcar?" he asked.

"I am. I see you've gone and slain my guards."

He had. My very expensive bodyguards were lying in a heap in the corner. I imagined he'd frightened off my slaves. Nice of them to warn me.

"They were not interested in letting me in," he said, matter-of-factly, referring to the bodyguard stew. "I'm afraid I broke them."

"They at least tried to earn their money, didn't they?"

"Oh, I don't know. Didn't put up much of a fight. And that one there started crying when I tore his leg off. Very unprofessional. Why don't you sit down?"

I did. No use arguing, even when one is in the midst of a blind panic. I was nearly naked and completely defenseless, having left my sword outside near the tub.

This would never have happened in the city, where demons are stopped at the gate. Somebody knew enough about me to know when I was vulnerable.

"You're very eloquent," I said. "I didn't know your kind could speak in sentences."

"Don't like to. It's easier to kill a guy than it is to talk to him, you know?"

"Actually, I'm really fond of talking."

"I can tell."

Already this much conversation had exceeded the demon's comfort level. He kept fidgeting, and his eyes darted around the room as if maybe hoping another guard would pop up so he'd have someone to kill. Why he wasn't killing me was the question of the day.

"So, what do I call you?" I asked.

"Whomp."

"Whomp? Your given name?"

"It's the sound people make when I hit them in the chest."

How charming.

"What can I do for you, Whomp?"

"My employer is interested in your shipping routes."

"Oh? Which ones?"

"All of 'em, I guess. He wasn't real specific. Lemme see if I can remember this ... he said he wants, um ... maps, names of buyers, names of sellers ... oh yeah, and whoever gets your ivory for you? He wants his name, too."

"I could just give you my ledgers," I suggested.

"You know, I asked him that. 'Why don't you just steal the guy's scrolls,' I said. He said that won't work. Says they're unreadable."

Which meant whoever hired the demon had already seen my ledgers, which were written in a pre-Phoenician language using alphanumeric symbols I'd invented myself. (It's the same code I use in my Swiss bank book.) The code was nothing a good linguist couldn't have deciphered eventually, but we didn't have linguists back then. We barely had languages.

"So, you want me to translate all of them?" I asked.

"You could just tell me."

"Last count I had a hundred and seventeen buyers, Whomp."

"Okay, then translate."

"That'd take days. Plus none of the scrolls are here. I could head back to Carthage in the morning, get started right away and let you know when I'm all finished. How's that?"

"I'm thinking maybe my employer didn't think this through real well."

"I have to agree."

"Enh. It was worth a try."

He stood up. He was more than two heads taller than me.

"So, that's it?"

"Yeah. Now I gotta go to the other plan."

"Um, is that good?"

"Good for me, sure. Maybe not so good for you, just cuz I gotta kill you now."

"Is that really the backup plan?" I asked.

"He said if you don't cooperate I'm supposed to kill you."

"But I am cooperating."

"Yeah, but he doesn't know that and I get paid either way."

"How about if I give you something now? Like the name of the ivory dealer?"

Useless information, because anybody who approached my contact other than me would be killed in about a second and a half. I like to go directly to tribal leaders for my ivory.

"I don't think that'll make a difference," he said.

"I should start running, then."

"If it'll make you feel any better."

So, I ran. Whomp unfortunately was standing closer to the entrance than I was and, not knowing how quick he might be—despite their size, demons have very good reflexes—I didn't want to risk going that way. Instead I headed back toward the bath, which was outdoors. The demon was right behind me, proving that he was indeed very quick for his size.

When I reached the edge of the stone bath, I vaulted it, landing safely on the other side next to my clothes and more importantly my sword.

Yes, I carried a sword. As a wealthy man, I never had much need for it, but my reasoning was better to be too well armed than not armed at all. I knew how to use it, too. I was even foolish enough to think my skill might be sufficient to defeat a demon, even without a couple of friends, a big boulder, and a cliff face. I've gotten wiser with age.

Whomp came barreling out of the house just as I reached my sword. Focusing all his attention on me and not expecting a spa to be in his way, he fell in.

"What the hell is this?" he asked, splashing around. He was about waist deep.

"I call it a bath. Do you like it?"

"Don't usually like water," he admitted. "But this is nice. Heated?"

"There's an oven underneath."

"No kidding."

"Really," I said.

"After you're dead, you think I could have it?"

"I don't see why not."

He climbed out, and I foolishly stood my ground on the cool grass beyond the bath. We were on the crest of a small treeless hill, with Mount Byrsa in the distance on one side and the shore on the other. And with no other houses anywhere close by—I was easily the wealthiest landowner in this little area—we were utterly and completely alone.

"Nice sword," he said. "Thought you was gonna run."

"I decided to give this a try first."

He shrugged. "Okay."

Whomp swung his right fist at my head, a hypothetically lethal blow that caused the air itself to whistle in protest and surely would have proven disastrous for me had I not ducked. My response was a comparatively feeble counter-swing with the short sword aimed at his exposed right side. The blade dug into his skin, but barely penetrated more than a thumb's-width and drew no blood. If he were a man he would be wondering where the bottom half of him had gone off to.

His response was to swat at me with his left arm, much the way one might attack a harassing bug. The shot hit me in the shoulder. I tumbled over and away from him, finding my feet quickly and luckily hanging onto my sword.

"You're pretty quick for your age."

"I keep in shape," I said, rotating my shoulder to see if there was any permanent damage. "Why, how old do I look?"

"Somebody told me you were the oldest man in Carthage. Must've been thinking of someone else."

"No, that's me."

"Huh."

In two quick steps he was on top of me, both arms out and seeking to grab and possibly hug. This would be the preferred attack, I guess, if one wanted to stop getting stuck with a sword. The charge left both of his sides exposed, but since I'd already taken an unsuccessful swing at his torso I wasn't about to try it a second time.

Instead, I jumped aside and swiped at his leg. Nearly got the sword broken in two, but it did trip him up and he even yelped in pain just moments before landing flat on his face. I seized the opportunity and lunged at his neck, but he'd already begun to roll over. He caught the blade with the palm of his bare hand and swatted it aside. If he were a man, he'd be down one hand.

Still on the ground, he kicked me in the stomach. I staggered backward, desperately seeking air, which was not immediately forthcoming. This left him plenty of time to get back up to his feet.

"This is fun," he said. "You're a lot better than those guards of yours. They just stood around and hacked at me."

My reply was to gasp for breath.

"We about done here?" He was leaning over me the way one might if one were examining a dead bird. Overconfident, he left his neck unguarded.

I pushed his raised arm aside and brought the sword around, this time catching him in the neck with the strongest force I could muster.

It was about as effective as the shot to the torso.

"Aahhh," he uttered, less in pain than in aggravation. He shoved me away. "Just give it up, will you?"

"Can't," I said.

I'd pretty much run out of ideas. A part of me knew this battle was going to end up more or less the way that it had, but as I'd never attempted to kill a demon before I figured I owed myself the chance to try it at least once. Stupid me.

Whomp sighed dramatically and then charged again. Having tried the duck-and-counter and the step-aside-and-sweep already, I went for the only idea I had left. Charge back.

What followed was somewhat like a joust, with my sword pitted against his fist. We both connected. He hit me with a glancing blow that exploded into the side of my face and spun me around and down like an unstrung puppet. I landed gracelessly a few paces away from where he fell on his side. Fully half of my sword ended up buried in his chest.

He lay still, and for a few seconds I thought I'd actually pulled it off. "Oww," he grumbled. He looked down at the blade. I tried to get to my feet, but he'd seriously messed up my equilibrium, so I sort of just crouched there and waited for the hillside to stop rocking.

"You almost ran me through," he noted. "Good work."

Until he rolled up to a sitting position, I was holding out hope that I'd caused some nerve damage or something, but no. He was almost completely unharmed.

I made it to my feet, still fairly wobbly. "Does that hurt?"

"Oh, yeah," he said matter-of-factly. He reached down and grabbed the sword by the blade and pulled. Slowly, it slid out of him.

At least I'd drawn blood this time.

He climbed to his feet again, my sword and all hope of winning this battle still in his hand. He broke the blade over his knee.

Tossing the pieces aside, he asked, "Any other ideas?"

My vision finally clearing up, I said, "I thought I'd fall back on running." And then I did just that.

I sprinted down toward to the pier. He didn't start after me immediately, not because he was too worn out, but because he was clearly aggravated that I wouldn't just surrender already.

Other than the pier, my only real option was to head up toward Mount Byrsa and maybe just keep on running until I reached a landmark I recognized, like the Nile. I was pretty sure I still had long-distance running skills to my advantage. It'd be like old times, when I'd have to spend six or seven days running after food until the food finally got too tired to run. But that would take too long. Plus, I'd have to return to Carthage eventually—if only to pick up my stuff—and I'd still have a demon problem on my hands. Better to find a place to hide for the night, steal back into the city in the morning, and not leave again until I found out who hired Whomp or until I was sure I'd outlived him. Finding such a hiding place would be the hard part.

Meandering through the small collection of boathouses, I reached the dock, which had only my ship in port at the time. This significantly reduced my options. With two or three boats, I could conceivably hide in the hold of one of them, but hiding in the only boat available was maybe not the best idea ever. And I'd end up cornered.

I could hear him coming. With the houses in the way, he was temporarily obscured from sight, but it sounded like he was heading straight for me. Evidently, demons are good trackers.

Out of choices, I jumped onto my ship and climbed the mainmast.

Whomp reached the dock a few minutes later.

"There you are," he said, looking up.

He stepped aboard the ship, checking out the surroundings to see if I had any other surprises left, like a small army hidden below deck. What I wouldn't have given to have a small army hidden below deck. "You run pretty fast. How old did you say you were?"

"I don't know how old I am. Lost count."

"Yeah?"

"I'm immortal."

I figured it was a good conversation topic, and the more

talking he did, the less killing he did. He looked confused rather than impressed.

"Im-what?"

He was circling under the mast while talking, making me wonder if he was going to attempt to climb it.

"Immortal," I repeated. "I don't get old and die."

"No kidding."

No, definitely not impressed. And it looked like I wasn't going to get a "well, since you lived *that* long" free pass from him.

I was clinging to the very top of the mast.

We didn't have crow's nests in those days. We barely had sails. Just pieces of silk we threw up on the odd chance the wind was going the same way we were. Usually, we rowed. Consequently, if he were patient enough, I'd eventually fall because it's not easy to hold that position. But demons are not known for their patience. Makes them great for storming sieges.

"How's that worked out for you?" he asked, as regards my immortality. It looked as if he'd decided how to approach this problem.

"Not bad so far," I said.

"What happens if you fall from, say, the top of a tall mast onto a hard wooden deck?"

"I don't know. Never tried it. Hey, can I ask you something? Before you kill me?"

"Sure."

"How come there aren't more of you?"

"What, you mean in Carthage?"

"I mean in general. Since you're so hard to kill and all."

"It's a secret," he said, honestly sounding like nobody ever asked him that before, which was possible.

"Yeah, but you're gonna kill me anyway," I pointed out.

"That's right."

He reared back to take a swing at the base of the mast. "You didn't answer my question," I shouted.

"The answer is, I don't know," he said. Then he punched the mast.

The whole thing wobbled mightily, especially at the top. It was all I could do to hang on. I fortunately had plenty of tree-climbing experience to draw from.

"Hmm," he muttered. He stepped back to try again, but before he could, a loud CRACK sounded out from the center of the mast.

He'd hit a weak point in the wood grain. The whole thing was splitting up the middle and coming down like the felled tree it once was.

I swung around to one side and, with my hands gripping the top of the mast and my feet touching just below my hands, tried to offer some guidance to the chosen direction of the mast's descent.

A few seconds later the mast sounded out another loud CRACK and down it went, pretty much falling the way I hoped it would. I landed not on the deck but in the water, a little stunned, but otherwise none the worse.

The top fourth of the mast had snapped off after impacting with the side of the ship. I found it floating beside me in the water.

"You lucky devil," Whomp declared, on verifying my continued good health. I grabbed onto the mast tip.

Something occurred to me. "Hey," I shouted. "Can demons swim?"

"No," he said. "But you can't stay in the water forever."

"I don't have to. I can swim to the city from here."

I used the mast like a kick board just to illustrate my point.

This was not an outcome that pleased Whomp. "I'll destroy your ship and your house, kill all your slaves and everyone else who gets in my way if you don't get out of the water and let me kill you!"

Not the most convincing argument.

"Go ahead," I said. "The boat's already half-destroyed anyway."

He picked up the heavy base of the mast and hurled it into the water. He missed me, but I gave him points for effort.

"You're not nearly as charming when you're not about to kill somebody," I said.

"Get back here!"

"Can't. Gotta go. But it was nice meeting you."

Swimming off, I could hear him tearing apart my vessel piece by piece, his roaring growing more distant with each stroke.

~

It took the rest of the night and part of the next morning to reach the city's inner harbor. By then Whomp had destroyed most of the homes on the pier and killed dozens of people, many of whom didn't even work for me. Midday, around the time I reached my main house in Carthage, the sufets had figured out that something horrible was happening outside the city walls and a garrison of soldiers was sent to deal with the problem. It took a couple of days, and there were a tremendous number of human casualties, but they did eventually take care of Whomp for me.

The subsequent inquiry uncovered the name of the merchant who was foolish enough to hire a demon. Guy had been a guest in my home dozens of times, which explained how he knew so much about my ledgers. He was sentenced to death.

And I got a good discount on two of his ships. So, like any good businessman, I came out ahead in the end.

But I never did learn why there are so few demons in the world.

CHAPTER 13

Got a visit from the man himself today. He wanted to see how I was holding up, or so he said. His real motive might have had something to do with Viktor, who I might just be getting to. Can't have your top scientist asking difficult questions when you're so close to success.

So, he kept going on about how this situation I'm in is "just temporary" and how I should "relax." Because I'm supposed to be naïve enough to think he'll actually let me walk out of here when this is all over. I told him to go to hell. Not the best way to get an extra helping at dinner, but whatever.

~

I looked again at the frozen image of Gary's crushed face. What idiot set a demon on me? It seemed unlikely that a bounty was put on my head at the same time a demon was sent to hunt me down, so the most apparent conclusion was that the demon was another bounty hunter. Or at least he was hired by the same person.

This is as stupid in modern times as it had been in ancient

Carthage. Demons don't do subtle. They may be motivated by money, but they're also motivated by bloodlust, and usually the bloodlust wins. Possibly, the person who was behind all of this knew perfectly well that sending a demon would result in some collateral damage, and possibly he or she considered that acceptable. This did not compel me to surrender.

"Do you have any more?" I asked Tchekhy, waving the empty bottle at him.

He looked up for the first time in two hours. "You need more?"

"I do," I said. "Turns out there's a demon chasing me."

"There is a demon chasing all of us, my friend."

"I mean literally. You find anything?"

"Oh, yes."

"Feel like telling me what?"

He lit another cigarette and paused dramatically. Tchekhy can be very theatrical.

"Come," he said. "I'll show you."

I got up and half-staggered across the room as the vodka said hello to my motor skills. Perhaps another bottle wouldn't be a good idea.

Tchekhy pointed to one of the monitors. "You are familiar with the Internet?"

"Of course I am," I replied indignantly.

I was, in fact, only somewhat familiar with it. Try to look at this from my perspective. I remember getting drunk several of years ago with a guy named Bob who declared that "everything" in the world of computers changes completely "every eighteen months." He went on with "honestly, you blink and you're hopelessly behind."

That describes just about my whole existence. Nod off during the Restoration, next thing you know you're right in the middle of the French Revolution, and you're wondering what the hell happened.

"Good," Tchekhy said. "What you are looking at here is a MUD."

"Okay."

"Multi-User Dimension."

"Okay."

"It is fantasy. Role-playing. You understand?"

"Not even a little bit."

He sighed heavily. "Many different people join a group, all right? It is a group where everyone pretends to be someone else in someplace else at some other time or some other world."

"Why?"

"Why not? It is fun, these games of fantasy. I belong to two myself. I am a merchant in one and a warrior in another."

"And this is fun? Because I've been both and they weren't all that thrilling."

"Very much. You trade, you fight monsters, solve puzzles ... a welcome distraction."

"I'll take your word for it. Why are you showing me one?"

"Because this MUD is not like any I have seen before. It is playing out in the modern world."

"Sounds healthy," I noted, a tad sarcastically.

"Yes, but still with fantasy elements. There are vampires and demons and other magical creatures. And one immortal."

"Pardon?"

"It would appear that one of the central goals of this MUD is to track an immortal man. Just reading along, it seems most of the participants treat this as a work of interactive fiction, but a few are taking it very seriously."

He clicked an entry titled *Recent Pic*. It came with an attachment and in that attachment was a poorly reproduced image —of me.

"Oh crap," I said.

"Oh crap, indeed," agreed Tchekhy. "There is some out-of-character speculation that you are merely the person who is running the MUD, encouraging people to seek you out for some egotistic goal. But the ones who take it seriously accept you as an immortal, and seem to believe in the vampires and fairies as well."

"They're called pixies," I said.

He looked at me carefully. "They are real?"

"Sure."

"And demons?"

I held up the photo of Gary's face. He grimaced. I returned to my computerized picture. "Does that photo include when and where it was taken?"

"It was captured seven months ago in Cleveland."

That explained where the photograph in Stan's kit had come from, as well as the "last known location" identifier.

"So, these ... MUD people are tracking me?"

"That is the idea. Much honor is accorded anybody who captures your image and reports your current location. The rumor that you were in Boston had the Boston members wandering the streets with their digital cameras for several days. Shall I write that you have since left for New York?"

"I wish you wouldn't." I was feeling sick. Might have been the vodka, but I didn't think so. "How long has this been going on?"

"For over a year."

"These people have been following me for a year? Whose idea was this?"

"That, I cannot know for certain. I have identified the screen name of the person running the MUD, but his email is fairly generic." He referred to a second monitor. "Over here I am attempting to track the origin of the email. I sent a request to join this MUD and obtained an automated response. From that, I analyzed the source, a software company in South Dakota called InfoGen."

"And this company is running the MUD."

"No. A person with an email address within this company is running the MUD. And that might not be the case either."

"You lost me again."

"Say you know a computer technician within a certain company, and say that person is in charge of assigning email accounts for that company. Your technician friend could hypothetically establish a perfectly valid email address for you with no one else in the company being the wiser. And you in turn could have your email from that account forwarded to another address. It would effectively be a blind mail drop. Nearly untraceable."

"Only nearly?"

"I am breaking into their system to ascertain the owner of the account. If that leads to another account, I shall be forced to do the same. With some luck, I will eventually get a location and possibly a name."

"And how long will that take?"

"Minutes. Hours. Days. There is no *a priori* answer for that question. But there is another bottle of vodka in the cooler, and you are already familiar with the couch. You are free to stay, if you wish."

~

Tchekhy woke me from a sound, alcohol-induced sleep sometime later. I had no clear idea exactly *how* much later, not with the air conditioner blocking the window.

"Did you find anything?" I muttered, not particularly willing to move.

"A new message on the MUD," he said. "You were spotted at the train station."

"Glorious. What about the email thing?"

"I am still tracing that."

There was clearly something more. He couldn't have woken me up just for that. "And?"

"And there is someone here to see you."

I tried to sit up, but my head wouldn't let me. "She wouldn't be blonde and built like a supermodel, by chance, would she? Because otherwise I'm not moving."

"After a fashion, yes, she is," he said.

I realized how freaked my old friend looked. Then something buzzed past his ear and I understood.

"Hello, Iza," I said. "What are you doing here?"

"H'lo," she chimed.

"Remember what I said about pixies, Tchekhy?" I asked. "Meet Iza."

"We have met," he stammered, clutching a gold cross around his neck.

You'd think a guy who knew an immortal personally would be more difficult to shake up. He was lucky Brenda didn't come.

Iza was darting madly about the room, which I recognized as the pixie version of a nervous twitch indicative of impending bad news like "you're living at the base of an active volcano."

"What's wrong, Iza?" I asked. "And how did you find me?"

"I follow. Early, when you leave girl. Girl asks Iza to follow. Iza follow to train. Iza read and tell girl."

I actually understood that. Possibly because I was drunk. I would have to remember that trick.

Brenda—who I hadn't told where I was going—asked Iza to find out what train I took. Stupid of me not to consider the possibility I would be tailed by a pixie. Except Iza was sort of coerced into helping me in the first place. I wondered what Brenda did to gain her confidence. Perhaps showing her the mushroom trick was a bad idea.

"So, you didn't get on the train with me," I said.

"Nono, I tell girl."

"Then why are you here now?"

"The man," she pouted.

"What man?"

"Big man. Big smelly man. Hurt girl."

I sat up. "Someone hurt Brenda? She's not ..."

"Girl run away. Make me use train."

"It must have been the demon. Are you sure she's okay?"

"She hide," Iza emphasized. That was the best she could do, comfort-wise. Had I known half of the goddamn Internet was following me around, I would have given her more cash and demanded she change addresses immediately.

"Demon?" Tchekhy asked.

"Yes," I said. "And he attacked a friend. He must be one tough bastard to get the best of her."

"A woman against a demon?"

"She's not a woman. Brenda's a vampire."

"Ah. Of course." Tchekhy picked up the bottle of vodka from the cot and promptly downed the remainder. He was probably planning to pick up a few more crosses later at wherever one goes to buy crosses. I'm a bull in the Judeo-Christian worldview china shop.

"Iza, how did you find me here?" I asked, remembering that this was a fairly big city.

"I smell," she said.

Great Zeus, did everything have a better sense of smell than I did?

I thought of Whomp and how quickly he'd followed me to the pier. Could this one track me as easily? Could he track Iza?

"Tchekhy, I need strong coffee and a quick answer on that email question," I said, rubbing my eyes as if that had some sort of magical sobering effect. "It doesn't look like it's going to be safe for me to stay here much longer."

"*Da,*" he answered meekly.

"Also, what the hell time is it?"

~

It was pushing seven in the evening, which I discovered as soon as I remembered I was wearing a watch. It felt like later, but I hadn't gotten much sleep over the past couple of days. All I really wanted was another bottle of Tchekhy's vodka and a good long nap on his couch, but it was thinking like that which got me into this little jam in the first place, so instead I sipped my coffee and tried to clear the woozies as quickly as possible. It was time to start thinking straight before things spun any more out of control. I could figure my way out of this. Or that's what I told myself.

The whole thing shook me up pretty badly when I thought hard enough about it. Between the devoted little Internet cult tracking me, the bounty hunters, the demon, and the letters in the newspaper, I felt more trapped than I had in a long time.

As I said, I've managed to escape long-term imprisonment in my many years, but lack of firsthand experience doesn't dampen my fear of it in the least bit. Throw in the instinctive reaction to being cornered and the times in the past when I've been an actual slave, and it was enough to make an immortal crazy.

My strongest impulse was to get up and just run. Well, run and drink more vodka, but mainly just run. But I was no longer entirely comfortable doing that either. I was running when I left Boston, and it was possible Brenda paid for that decision with her life. If I ran again the next person at risk might be Tchekhy, and I liked his odds against a demon considerably less than Brenda's.

That was the biggest problem—the demon. I could get away from human bounty hunters, and I could live with the people from the MUD snapping my picture because neither had shown any particular talent for tracking me, thus far relying mainly on luck and tip-offs. But the demon might have gotten my scent, and if I wasn't careful he'd leave a trail of bodies in his wake.

I was clearly going to have to figure out a way to kill it. Possibly, modern weaponry could do now what swords and arrows could not.

With the first inkling of a plan tricking through my brain, it occurred to me it might be helpful to know if the demon was in New York yet.

"Iza, are you still here?" It'd been an hour since she arrived with the news, and in that time I mostly sat still and sobered up while Tchekhy continued to violate the law and pretend there wasn't a pixie in the room.

"Uh-huh," I heard her little voice declare. She zipped over from whatever distant corner of the room she'd been camping in.

"Do you remember what the demon smells like?"

"Deeman?"

"The big man who hurt Brenda."

"Uh-huh."

"If I asked you to fly around the city and look for him, could you do that? I can get you some more mushrooms."

"Uh-huh, okay."

"And then tell me when you find him," I added. You have to be very specific with pixies.

"Uh-huh."

She buzzed off.

Once it was clear she was safely out of the room, Tchekhy looked up from his hacking.

"It is not natural," he muttered.

"What, her? She's no less natural than you are," I said.

"I know my Bible, Efgeniy. You should not traffic with such beings."

"I'm a lot older than the Bible, my friend, and I can tell you from experience the world is a good deal stranger and more interesting than anything in that book."

He fell silent and continued to work. That's usually what happens when someone brings up the Bible with me, mainly because I was around for most of it. Let's just say if you're looking for historical accuracy there, you're looking in the wrong place. And the stuff that *is* accurate—or at least fact-based—is horribly skewed. Take Joshua, from battle of Jericho fame. Joshua was a ruthless and violent man who was looking to carve out an empire without any particular concern about how much blood was shed to do it, just like every other megalomaniacal world-conqueror from that time. Having the God of the Old Testament on his side didn't make any kind of difference, nor did it make the blood on Joshua's hands justifiable.

I'm willing to concede that the wisdom contained within the Bible is worth at least a little pondering, but anyone who thinks, for instance, that because pixies aren't featured they are therefore bad in some way needs to re-evaluate.

I returned to the matter at hand.

"So, where are we?"

"I am on my third company," he said. "I was able to trace the first email address to a forwarding address at a tech firm in Colorado, and from there to a savings-and-loan in New Mexico."

"This guy knows a lot of email administrators," I said.

"*Da.* But fortunately, things are going faster now, because ..." He stopped and did a staring-off-into-the-distance thing.

"Because what?" I asked, but it was as if I was no longer in the room. He started typing faster, and then paused. Then he wheeled over to another computer and engaged a search engine.

"There," he said. "I should have figured it out earlier."

"What?"

"All three of the companies have the same security profile. They contracted the same firm to establish their firewalls."

I almost understood that. "Is that unusual?"

"Possibly it is simply a coincidence. Do you believe in coincidences?"

"Not really."

"Nor do I."

I looked at the search engine results. "Securidot," I read.

"They are in Seattle. I believe your mystery pursuer is associated with them. He or she must have established a back door to the security program the company sells and is using it to create the phantom email accounts."

"Can you tell exactly who it is within the company?"

"I doubt they would be foolish enough to allow for that possibility. The very fact that there is a back door access into a supposedly impregnable firewall program puts the entire company in danger. Discovery might even land them in prison."

"Can you keep tracking the emails anyway?" I asked. "And keep a record of all of them. It might come in handy."

"Of course."

I sat at the computer with the Securidot web page displayed and started reading, while Tchekhy returned to his work.

According to their website, Securidot was started in the mid-1990s by Robert Grindel. His story read like the prototypical dot-com success story. Geeky guy comes up with a neat-o idea, lots of companies pay lots of money for the product of his neat-o idea, geeky guy makes a bundle, and buys a professional sports franchise. All except for the sports franchise part.

Aside from this well-burnished history, the site itself wasn't very useful, especially since I wasn't a major corporation looking for a good security program.

"Anything else?" I asked. "This is pretty basic stuff."

"Try Lexis/Nexis," he suggested. "You can look up old newspaper articles there. I have an account."

"A legal account?" I asked.

"Does that matter?"

I followed a bookmark to Tchekhy's illegal Lexis/Nexis account. (Honestly I don't think he pays for anything.) Results there proved more interesting. Securidot had just hit the jackpot on a buyout deal with a company called Secure Systems International doing the buying. I wondered if SSI knew Securidot's program came with a back door.

Information on Grindel himself was a bit more compelling. For starters, the legend on the Securidot website was, as I'd suspected, a very polished version of the truth. He'd actually founded the company with a man named Brian Standish. Brian was the techno-geek and the founder of the technology the company made its millions on. Robert was a different kind of ideas man. He got the backers, founded the company, ran the business, and eventually marginalized Brian entirely.

Brian Standish took a buyout six months before Securidot was sold. Reading between the lines, I got the impression Robert knew he was going to sell out and forced out Brian beforehand.

Which was only sort of interesting. Nothing in the articles I found was a smoking gun. Still, I began to think Robert Grindel was the guy I was looking for. Or rather, the guy who was looking for me. He just seemed like the type. I bounced the idea off Tchekhy.

"It's possible," he said. "But I think you should be looking for someone who is more wealthy. Perhaps even a government."

"Maybe so."

The bounty on my head was roughly one fifth of what Grindel earned from the sale. Tchekhy had a good point.

"You know," Tchekhy said, "there is a very easy way to find out more about who is after you. We could simply call him."

He picked up the phone I'd taken from Stan and tossed it to me.

The phone had been the proverbial 300-pound gorilla in the room for the entire day. We both knew it was the fastest way to get quick information but we also knew that using it could be entirely too dangerous. If the person on the other end of the line recognized that neither of us was Stan they might be able to do something we weren't prepared for. Like activate a tracking device. Or set off an explosive charge in the phone. It sounded paranoid, but at this particular juncture, paranoia was a useful impulse.

Hesitantly, I flipped the phone open. "Oh, hell," I said.

"What?"

I held up the phone so he could read the small display screen. It read: *NYC*.

"Does this mean a demon is about to arrive at my front door, Efgeniy?"

He'd been ignoring the possibility, just as I was avoiding having to admit I'd put him in danger.

"Um, maybe," I said.

He looked rather cross.

"Then you should leave," he suggested. "Contact me later and perhaps I'll have finished this trace."

"Not that easy," I said. "He might still show up here."

"I can care for myself," he argued.

I held up the photos of Gary and Nate. "You haven't dealt with anything like this."

"The Lord will protect me," he declared stubbornly. "I will be fine."

"Yes, well ... just in case He's busy, maybe I should come up with something else."

"Then you had better come up with it quickly."

I'd been working on an idea for the last hour, actually.

"Did you say you could post to this MUD thing?"

"Yes. Why?"

"How far is Central Park from here?"

CHAPTER 14

Viktor just showed me a speculative article he wrote for Discover magazine. It's about me, which is a little scary considering he wrote it five years ago. Well technically speaking it isn't about me. It's about someone like me. A purely theoretical me, if you will.

The gist of it was that a lot of the knowledge he needed to do the research he's now doing was already out there. As he put it, there is a time for every scientific idea and now is the time for this one. This is the latest volley in our argument. I'm still not buying.

Anyway, it went a long way toward explaining how he ended up getting attached to this project.

~

I reached the pond at the southern edge of Central Park at around ten. By then the darkness was nearly complete, and a decent chill had settled over the whole city. There was a waning moon to see by but it was playing chicken with a bank of clouds, so there were times when I had nothing but the street lamps.

I had with me the bag with all my stuff plus the still-unused satellite phone and a heavy red parka on loan from Tchekhy with Stan's gun stuffed in one of the pockets. The red parka stood out, as it was supposed to. An hour earlier a digital photo of me wearing it was uploaded onto the MUD along with the message "taken today just outside of Central Park!" Tchekhy posted it under the name of a regular New York contributor to the site, which made more sense than setting up a new account and immediately posting information on the dodgy immortal, something we both agreed would arouse suspicion as to the provenance of that information. The only one who would be wise to it was the guy whose account we used, and since Tchekhy disabled his account right after posting, it would take days for the truth to come out. I only needed one evening.

Passing by the pond, I headed north. The plan was to parade myself up and down the park. That would still make me a tough find because it's a big place, but I didn't need much, just a couple of MUD groupies to snap some pictures and at least one or two bounty hunters. And no muggers. That'd be good.

At the half hour point, I passed a police officer on horseback. I resisted the urge to ask him how many cops patrolled the park at night because that could be a major problem. Hopefully if there were a lot of them, they weren't very quick responders.

I had a conversation once with the guy who designed the landscape for Central Park. His name was Frederick Olmstead, and by God could he talk. I had the misfortune of sharing a passenger compartment on a train ride from St. Louis to Chicago, and I think I got in maybe three words edgewise. Everything with him was nature, nature, nature, which I guess one could expect from a landscaper, but he really went over the top with all of it. He seemed to think his arrangements let "nature speak for itself" as compared to the gigantic, artificial floral displays of exotic plants that he seemed to show great disdain for. If I'd managed get a word in I would have told him I heard nature speak for itself on a number of occasions, and I suspect he wouldn't like what nature really had to say.

I doubt he would have liked what happened to Central Park in the years since he passed either. Even in the dark I could tell that much of his original vision had been allowed to slip away with time. But everything does, doesn't it?

At one hour from the time I'd first entered the park I reached the northern edge and turned around, choosing a different path. If Tchekhy was wrong about any of this it was going to be a long night.

I found an unoccupied bench and took a seat. It was time to check. I pulled out the satellite phone and flipped it open. The backlit display verified that things were going as planned. It read: *Cntrl Pk-Now.*

~

Another hour later I'd moved to a different bench, this one in the middle of the park and overlooking the lake. I could see the moisture in the clouds that had engulfed the visible sky, and I could see my breath. It was going to snow, unless it got too cold for it. I'd worry that I was going to catch my death in the form of a cold, if I caught colds.

The closest I had come to any interesting activity involved a lengthy conversation with a wino who thought I was his wife, and two separate flashbulb incidents involving unseen cameramen who probably scurried off immediately to post their images of the legendary immortal.

I was tired. I'd ingested nothing substantial beyond pizza, vodka, and coffee, and walking the breadth of Central Park with that as sustenance can be taxing. If nobody showed soon I was going to take a nap.

But then I heard something. It was footfall coming from my left, faint but unmistakable, and definitely not belonging to any horse or demon. It was getting louder. Someone was approaching.

I watched as a young woman came into view. The bench was on a low hill, so while she'd probably been on the path for a while it wasn't until she was about fifty feet away that I could even see her. She was wearing tight-fitting acid-wash jeans, sneakers, and a faded green army jacket that looked surprisingly good on her, given that green army jackets are not generally meant to be flattering. Underneath the coat was a black turtleneck. She had long, dirty blonde hair that obscured part of her face.

I had reason to suspect everyone because Central Park at night—no matter how many cops are around—is not a very safe place to take a nighttime stroll. But it was difficult to see potential danger in this attractive, five-foot-three package heading my way.

Once she got close enough for it to be entirely too obvious that I was staring, I shifted my gaze to the lights reflecting off the surface of the water, relying on the occasional stolen glance and my peripheral vision to track her progress.

I have a failing when it comes to attractive women. I'm a starer. Can't help it. You'd think after a few dozen centuries I'd be able to do something about this, because most women can sense when they're being stared at and some react negatively to it. But while I can look at another man's face and see twenty people I'd known over the centuries who looked exactly like him, every woman looks fairly unique to me. So, when I stare, it's either out of mild wonder or outright awe, depending on how drunk I am.

When she reached the bench, she sat down next to me. I was doing my damnedest to pretend I didn't notice anything, which is stupid, because pretending not to stare is even more obvious than staring. So I turned and gave her the *hey, how ya doin'?* nod that mankind has perfected over centuries of hanging out together in public places. Given neither of us was exactly waiting for a bus, this came off as silly—to me, at least—but I had to acknowledge her somehow.

We sat for another minute, staring at the lake.

"I thought you'd be shorter," she said finally.

I looked at her.

"I'm sorry, what?" Brown eyes. Very nice.

"Living so long and all," she explained. "People were shorter way back when. I figured you'd be shorter."

"Do I know you?"

She brushed the hair back from her face and smiled. She had a fascinating triangular structure to her face, with high cheekbones and a chin that tapered to a point. "Sure. I'm Jonas Milagro."

A man's name, last I checked. But that sort of thing changes so often I no longer assume.

"Should that sound familiar?" I asked. And it sort of did.

"It ought to. A few hours ago somebody using my name posted a photo of you on the Internet."

That's where I'd heard it.

"But, I have two accounts," she said. "I also go by the name of Alan Guff."

That's definitely a guy's name. "You don't look like an Alan."

"Well thank you," she smiled. "I don't think I look like a Jonas either."

"Not really, no."

"It's not unusual. You go on a MUD to pretend to be somebody else, right? So, I switch genders sometimes. Usually it's the other way around. I belong to ten different MUDs, and I think maybe twenty percent of the 'women' on them are actually women."

"So ... you're here because your account was hijacked?" I asked.

"No. But maybe you can introduce me to whoever did that for you sometime. Neat trick. I'm here because I think you're the real thing. And I want to know what made you decide to drag half of

Manhattan into Central Park tonight with your little *come and get me* post."

"Maybe I was just bored."

"Oh? Were you?" She looked me in the eyes. "Just bored? Because it looked a little desperate to me."

"What's your real name?"

"Clara."

"Clara, if I told you that tonight, the most dangerous place in this entire city is next to me on a park bench, would you believe me?"

A strange expression passed over her. It was fear, but not exactly fear. Like the prospect of danger was something erotic. "I might," she said with a grin. "What kind of danger are we talking about?"

"The kind that could be permanent," I said.

"You'll have to do better than that, Mr. Immortal. Girl doesn't take a nighttime stroll in Central Park if she's afraid of a little danger."

I could see that. Clara was starting to remind me of a repressed French duchess I used to spend time with. She liked being spanked with an ivory hairbrush.

"All right," I said. "It's a trap."

She looked a tad skeptical. "For who?" she asked. "You?"

"No, I set the trap. It's for someone else."

"And you're springing this trap alone? Or are there soldiers hidden in the lake or something? Because you don't look like all that much, if you don't mind my saying."

"It's complicated."

"Sure it is." Clara took my hand in hers and gave me a flirty smile, and the possibility dawned on me that I was dealing with a groupie. Go figure. "How about we take off before the bad people come?"

Did she think I went through all this trouble just to pick up a woman?

I heard, to the right of the bench and just off the path, a gun cock.

"Do not move, sir." It was a man's voice with a hint of Mississippi.

I looked at Clara. "Too late," I said. "They're here."

CHAPTER 15

Iza finally found her way. It's difficult to piece together from her syntax, but I think there were exhaust fans that were tough to navigate around. It's a very small, closed system—my cell is technically a stand-alone building— so you'd think it wouldn't have been all that difficult. There are only so many places to try.

So, her basic message was, "tell me what to do."

I've decided that since Clara went through the trouble to smuggle my tamed pixie into the place that I should trust her. (Although knowing about Iza at all means Clara had to have been eavesdropping on me. Two demerits for that.) Besides, I didn't have much to lose. It's not like they can do anything worse to me.

The problem is pixies aren't good with complex instructions. This is going to take a while.

~

The guy with the voice and the gun was still behind me.

"Put your hands on your head," he ordered.

"I can't," I said. "You told me not to move."

I felt the barrel of the gun up against my head. "Funny man," he said.

Maybe not Mississippi. Georgia?

"Go on and do it," he commanded.

I did as I was told while still looking into Clara's eyes. She was looking at the man behind me, and she appeared scared but not out-of-her-mind scared. This I took to mean two things. One, I had a human behind me, and two, maybe she was telling the truth about knowing how to handle herself.

"Miss, you'll want to run off now," the man suggested. "This is not your concern."

"Why don't you run off instead?" she offered. "I found him first."

"Please, ma'am. I am not above killing a woman."

"You would not," she said a tad less defiantly than I think she was aiming for.

"Do not make me prove it to you," he barked.

"Clara, listen to him," I suggested. "He's not kidding." He pressed the barrel deeper into my scalp.

"Quiet," he whispered. "I know about what happened in Boston. Trust me when I tell you I will not make the same mistake. Now be still for a moment, please."

I felt a sharp prick in the back of my right hand.

"Owww!" I exclaimed. "Not again with the damn shot."

"It's required," he said simply. "Now sit tight."

Fifteen seconds later he said, "Good enough. Get to your feet. You too, miss."

"Hang on ... " Clara protested.

"Get. Up."

She got up. So did I, hands still behind my head.

"Turn around," he ordered, to me.

I turned. He was a skinny black man a couple of inches shorter than me. Had a scar running down the right side of his face that made him look a bit more badass, but only just a bit. I figured I could take him if he gave me a chance. Possibly aware of this he stepped back, his gun pointed at my heart. He pulled a pair of plastic handcuffs out of his jacket pocket and tossed them over my shoulder to Clara.

"If you're going to stick around, darling, I may as well put you to work. Handcuff him." He looked at me. "Bring your hands down behind your back, sir. I trust you'll be less lethal once properly trussed."

"It's not me you have to worry about," I said, having taken note of some telltale movement just over my captor's shoulder.

He smiled, looking very relaxed and unconcerned. "As the lady said, do you have an army of soldiers hidden in the lake?"

"No. But I'd check the trees if I were you."

A loud ZIP sound echoed through the night. I watched the bounty hunter's expression change from confidence to the shock that usually transpires when one's heart unexpectedly explodes. He collapsed forward.

"Sniper," I said to him, lowering my hands. "Told you to check the trees."

"Oh, Jesus," Clara exclaimed, now officially in panic mode. "I should ... we have to ..."

I spun around. "Don't move ... !" but she had already turned to run.

Another loud ZIP and the sod at her feet kicked into the air. She cried out in surprise and stumbled backward, landing gracelessly on her very pretty backside.

"That's a marksman up there," I pointed out. "You're in luck. They only miss if they feel like it, so this one must like you."

"Stay where you are!" a man at the opposite end of the clearing demanded. He emerged from a set of trees nowhere near the sniper. He was dressed in black pajamas and carried what looked like an M-4 in his hands, looking very Delta Force.

"Two of you?" I asked.

"Yes, sir," he said fairly amicably, as he marched toward us.

Suddenly everybody wanted to call me sir. "We're here to take you into custody, sir. I trust you'll come quietly."

Climbing to her feet, Clara backed away from him, hands raised, until she was next to me.

"What's going on here?" she muttered.

"Told you this was a bad place to be."

"You weren't just being mysterious?"

"Nope."

"Why are they after you?"

"I don't know," I said. "But your MUD is what helped them track me, which is why I used it. It's not what it seems."

"I thought this was a trap."

"It is, but not for them—for something else. They're here to help me kill it. They just don't know that yet. And you don't want to be here when it arrives."

"Something worse than them?"

"Oh yes."

The soldier marching to the bench looked pretty intent on "taking me in" as he put it, except that he kept swatting around his head, like a mosquito was bothering him. It seemed out of character.

"Ma'am, this is a government matter," he said officiously, drawing up to a stop a few feet from us. Again with the swatting.

"Like hell it is," Clara said.

"I don't want to get rough with you, ma'am."

"Yeah that's what he said." She pointed to the recently deceased man behind us.

Close enough now, I heard the buzzing more clearly.

"Iza," I said loudly. "It's okay, Iza."

He looked puzzled. "Who are you talking to?"

"Nobody," I said cheerily.

He raised his gun. "Is there someone else here?"

"Not yet. But don't worry, he's on his way."

He looked around. "Who?"

"You'll see. Unless you want to take off now. I'd really recommend that, actually."

"Is that a threat?" he half-shouted. He wasn't about to shoot me, but that didn't mean his gung-ho aggressiveness didn't come off as a little disturbing. (Guns and short fuses never go well together.) He also knew there were other people out there looking for me who were willing to do the same thing to him that he and his partner had just done to the first guy, and that was clearly making him edgy.

"It's no threat. It's a warning," I said. "There are other things out here tonight that are worse than you."

"No shit," he scoffed. "That's why I invited my friend to help secure the perimeter."

"Is that what you're calling murder now?" Clara asked.

"No ma'am. I call that business." He pointed his M-4 at her. "You know another one of my favorite terms? Collateral damage. Maybe you want to take the deal that fella on the ground there offered you and start running. This doesn't concern you."

The ZIP of his partner's rifle halted any further negotiation. Clara and I winced instinctively at the sound, but no dirt kicked up and neither of us collapsed suddenly in a heap. It was followed by three more shots. The sniper was shooting at somebody else.

G.I. Joe in front of us put his finger to his ear. "Falcon Two, what's going on?"

How cute. Only two of them and they still came up with team codes.

I took a look at the distant tree I'd spotted Falcon Two in. "What's he say?"

"There's someone moving out there," Falcon One said. (I'm assuming he was Falcon One.)

"I hear it," Clara said, turning to look as well.

I did, too. Something very large was barreling through the Central Park trees.

We heard two more reports from the rifle and then the tree

Falcon Two was in shuddered. This was followed by a loud thump and then a sickening whump and a high-pitched, very brief scream pierced the air.

"Falcon Two!" Falcon One shouted into his ear-mike. "Billy, what happened?"

Silence.

"Billy's dead," I said.

"Like hell," he said, even as he readied his rifle.

"No, he's really dead," I insisted. "That second sound was his chest cavity being forcefully imploded. It's not the sort of thing you mistake for something else."

"Fuck you."

"If you were listening carefully, you probably heard the ribs snap."

Falcon One stepped in front of us and aimed his rifle at the tree area where his friend had just died, not particularly concerned that I could disarm him from that position. It was disturbingly quiet.

"Clara," I whispered. "Human beings don't like killing pretty young women. What's coming doesn't give a damn."

"What is it?" she asked, sounding panicky.

"Just run. Get out of here. I'm not kidding."

"Yeah," she said, backing away. "Yeah, I think you're right." She tugged at my sleeve. "Come with me."

"I can't. It's after me. If they can't deal with it, I'm going to have to."

"How?"

"I don't know yet."

She looked at me, now thoroughly terrified. Clearly this was a good deal more trouble than she had been looking for. She nodded, then turned and ran.

"Maybe you want to tell me what this is?" barked Falcon One over his shoulder.

"Sorry, pal," I said. "I already gave you your warning."

He spun around and pointed the barrel at my chest. "Tell me what it is!" he demanded.

Having his buddy killed kind of shook him up for some reason.

"You wouldn't believe me. But I can give you some advice."

"Go on."

"He's big, he's much faster than he should be, and you should try and aim for his head. I don't know if a chest shot will do much good."

The truth was, I was hoping this guy could take care of my demon problem for me. That was basically the plan: attract a bunch of armed men into a secluded location and then invite the demon to come and play. I was hoping guns had more of an effect than swords, maces, and spears did. Of course, in my mind I pictured a lot more armed men. I also didn't think they'd be so unconcerned about killing one another. Really, they couldn't figure out how to split five million?

We were about twenty yards from the trees where the demon was hidden, so it had a major open space to traverse in order to get within striking range, provided it wasn't armed. I was going with the assumption it wasn't, because guns have triggers and triggers require little, human-sized fingers, and demons don't have human-sized fingers.

The two of us stared at the trees and waited. And waited. "Screw this," he said, finally. "We're going."

Just then a loud roar pierced the air. My gun-toting maniac companion freaked and started firing indiscriminately into the woods, which made a hell of a lot of noise because unlike his partner, he wasn't using a silenced sniper rifle. That would surely send the police our way.

The problem was he wasn't firing anywhere near the demon. It had moved to our right, a fact we both discovered a second too late when it emerged and started charging.

Falcon One showed less than iron fortitude, I have to say. He did turn and fire in basically the correct direction, but in terms of marksmanship most Boy Scouts would have done better. I mean we're talking about a big target moving forward on a direct path. Pitiful. I used to face charging lions in the Serengeti with nothing more than a stone axe and a loincloth. People today disappoint me.

His best chance to score a decent hit—while the demon was closing the gap—fell apart when it threw something that struck the soldier square in the face, knocking him onto his back. It took me a second to realize what the demon had thrown. It was Falcon Two's head. I never saw a lion do that.

I stepped back and waited as the demon neatly dispatched Falcon One in a manner that I don't think you need to have described. I will say that it took a few minutes, because even after the guy was dead the demon needed a little extra time to play with the corpse in what can only be called vivisection by fist. It was not unlike what happened to Gary and Nate.

When he finally calmed down, I asked, "Are you finished?"

"Yeah," he grunted. "Ain't you gonna run?"

"You'll just keep chasing me," I said.

"Yep."

He stood. He was a bit shorter than the ones I remembered, and not quite as stocky. He was also fully clothed, which took a little getting used to. In the poor lighting he actually did look human. I imagined during the day he wore lots of hats, and maybe mittens or something.

"So, we goin' now?" he asked.

"Not just yet," I said.

Okay where were all the bounty hunters now? You'd think at least one would have a bazooka. But no, it was just the demon and me. Perhaps they all realized five million wasn't worth dismemberment. I could have told them that.

"You killed a couple of friends of mine," I commented.

"Did I?" He looked down at the body at his feet.

"Not them. In Boston."

"Oh." He still looked puzzled, like maybe he'd killed a whole bunch of people in Boston and wasn't sure which ones I was talking about.

"College kids. In an apartment. They had a futon in the living room?"

"Ohhh, yeah. Okay. Futon. Yeah."

"Okay? What, no remorse?"

"What do you care? You're supposed to be real old, right? You've seen lotsa people die."

Demon logic.

"Yes, but these were friends of mine, as I said."

"And how 'bout that girl, huh? What a handful."

"Brenda?" I asked, taken aback. "Did you ..."

"I'll go back for her later. I owe her. I was looking, but then I got tipped you was here. Strong. What the hell is she?"

"A vampire," I said.

He laughed. Never heard a demon laugh and I don't want to ever again. "C'mon," he said. "There's no such thing as vampires."

The irony was totally lost on him.

He asked again, "So, are we going now?"

"Almost," I said. I was stalling. I'd even take a patrolman on horseback at this point. "Let me ask you the same thing I asked the last demon I came across."

"What's that?"

"How come there are so few of you? Your kind are so hard to kill, I don't know why you haven't overrun the planet by now."

"It's a secret." Same damn thing the last one said. They hadn't gotten any cleverer with time. "Now enough. Let's go. Move."

"Okay," I said. Quickly—and expertly, if you don't mind my bragging— I drew Stan's gun from my pocket and fired directly at the spot between the demon's eyes.

His head rocked and he fell over backward, landing with a

sick squish onto the remnants of Falcon One. And for a second there I was ready to join the Smith & Wesson fan club.

"Fuck!" he shouted. "That fucking hurt!"

Uh-oh.

He leapt to his feet. I made an effort to flee but that effort only took me about three paces before he had his hand on my collar. He spun me around and shook the bag and the gun from my hands and with one powerful mitt lifted me up by my own neck.

"I gotta bring you in *alive*, but he didn't say anything about *one piece*, pal! See you try some shit like that with two broken arms, huh?"

Cop? Bounty hunter? Anyone? Clara?

I was in some major trouble. I thought for sure a gunshot at close range would do the trick. Instead, I'd just pissed off a very strong creature with serious anger-management issues.

"Then, I'll do the legs!" he shouted, his eyes positively aglow with the possibilities. "Yeah, and maybe the spine!"

I would have offered a clever retort or even an apology, but I couldn't actually breathe. My mind was racing through the possibilities again, drifting back to the old question. Why *weren't* there more demons? What was their weakness?

It's been said that in times of extreme stress the mind goes in unusual directions. Mine drifted, for reasons I'll never know, to *War of the Worlds*. (Not the movie. The book. And not because I read it but because I remembered chatting with H.G. Wells about it. He stole the ending from me. Honest.)

The demon pulled me close until we were nose-to-nose, and I got to find out what a genuine treat demon breath is. "How's a wheelchair for eternity sound to you?"

It was worth a try. I sneezed right into his face.

The demon's reaction was immediate and surprising. He dropped me and staggered backward, rubbing at his face and eyes like he'd been scalded with acid.

Fighting for breath, I climbed to my feet at around the same time he ceased his personal ministrations.

"Hey!" he said. "You can't get sick. I read that!"

"True," I said. "But you can, can't you?"

"I'm gonna rip your whole arm off for that," he said.

Having precious little time to act, I bit into my right wrist. Blood seeped into my mouth, helped along by the same puncture wounds Brenda made a few days earlier. I sucked hard until my mouth was half full.

The demon picked me up by the neck again. He was done talking. Glee spread across his face as he pondered the options regarding non-lethal tortures available to him. He was so excited he was panting.

I spit into his mouth.

"Aww, what the ..." he spat my blood back out and was about to offer a new debilitating injury for me when his eyes widened. He dropped me again.

"Shitty immune system, huh?" I said. "That's a shame."

I'm kind of disappointed that it took me so long to figure out a demon's weakness. In my defense, the germ theory of disease wasn't well known in Carthage.

He staggered backward as the toxin in my blood attacked him from the inside. It had been diluted by having been in my system for the last few minutes and probably wouldn't have been lethal to a human in that state, but apparently all it took to kill the demon was a few particles of the stuff.

He clutched his throat, barely capable of breath. I could see his tongue swelling and hanging out like a sick dog's. He collapsed onto his back, digging at his own throat, drawing blood.

I kneeled down to look him in the panicked eyes. "It's why there are so few of you, isn't it? I bet most of you die before puberty."

His breathing had stopped completely, but he wasn't quite dead yet.

"Just so we're clear, this is what happens when you kill friends of mine," I added.

He might have grunted some kind of response, but it was difficult to tell with him unable to breathe and all. I hovered over him long enough to watch his pupils stop moving. Long enough to be absolutely sure he was dead. It was oddly satisfying. I mean, I've killed a lot of things in my lifetime, but this was my first demon.

"Oh, clever," said a man with an accent I figured for Southern England. He was behind me, and I pretty much assumed he had a gun pointed at my back. Sure, *now* another bounty hunter shows up.

"You think so?" I stood, but didn't bother to turn.

"Very much so," he said. "I'm rather impressed."

"Impressed enough to let me go?"

"No. Not that impressed. So sorry."

There was a loud bonk and the sound of someone falling over. I turned around.

The Englishman was lying on his side, no longer conscious and no longer holding his gun. Standing over him was Clara. She was holding a large piece of driftwood and looking jumpy.

"Did I kill him?" she asked, hopping from foot-to-foot the way one might if one desperately needed to pee. I leaned over him and checked. He was still breathing, but there was a nasty wound at the base of his skull. The way his hand was twitching, there might have been some nerve damage.

"No," I said, "but he may have trouble walking for a while."

"Okay." She dropped the driftwood. "Okay. Okay, let's—"

"How far away is home for you?" I asked.

"Not far."

"If we try and run there, can you keep up?"

"I ... um ..."

"Focus, Clara. I need first aid for my wrist, and I need to get out of the park as soon as possible, and the only friendly place I know of is too far. There are more bounty hunters out tonight, and they're probably all headed here. Not to mention the police, who are probably interested in the gunshots. Can you help me?"

She snapped out of the stunned reverie she'd been caught up in. "Yes. And ... and I jog. I'll be all right."

"Good," I said, shedding the red parka and picking up my bag. "Lead on."

CHAPTER 16

We went through the science again this morning. Viktor wants me to understand how it works—how I work—for some reason. I keep explaining to him that if he wants to really get me to understand medicine, he's going to have to start with leeches and work up from there. I exaggerate, but only slightly. I mean, I understand what disease is and what causes it, and I have a vague comprehension of how the human body fights disease, but his tedious lectures approach a complexity I just don't care to absorb. Although he did have a few interesting thoughts on my metabolism and why it seems like I can't get any fatter or stronger. But I'm never going to get the thing about telomeres. He should just stop trying.

~

For our mad dash through the northern portion of Central Park, we stayed away from well-lit paths as much as possible and basically waded through every bush, shrub, and bramble we could. It wasn't just a matter of evading whatever remaining bounty hunter types who might surface: New

York's Finest had finally gotten their act together. Seems the sound of automatic gunfire in the middle of Central Park causes them to mobilize in large numbers.

The street surrounding the north entrance to the park was, perhaps not surprisingly, lined with cop cars, fire trucks, and ambulances. And bystanders, fortunately for us. We were able to merge effectively with the steadily increasing mass of onlookers, and once we'd pushed through them, we were basically home free.

We walked the remaining three blocks to Clara's apartment.

She lived in a nondescript building on a street full of nondescript buildings. I honestly didn't know how she told them apart.

"It's on the top floor," she said, as we climbed into an elevator that didn't look like it was up for a trip all the way to the top. "It's not much, but I have roof access, which is cool."

Not much turned out to be only a little bit bigger than Brenda's hole in Chinatown. The kitchen, living room, and bedroom were basically all the same room. And Clara's bachelor-like tendencies made it seem even smaller than it was. To wit, there was a stack of pizza boxes in the corner, and that was the only spot on the floor not covered in unwashed clothing. At least she had her own bathroom, small though it was. (Sink, toilet, shower, but no tub. Again, only a small step up from Brenda's, but a step nonetheless. Plus, this bathroom was clean.)

I helped myself to the bathroom sink, rinsing my wrist carefully. I'd taken a good bite out of myself, but it looked like it was already starting to heal.

"I don't have any bandages," Clara called from the kitchen area.

"How about some ice and a hand towel?"

"That I have."

She appeared momentarily with ice bundled in a towel, offered with a slightly trembling hand. I'd have worried that the towel wasn't clean, but infection is another one of those things that I don't have to be concerned with.

"Let me see," she said, pointing at my wrist. I held it up.

"Ugh. Didn't that hurt?"

"Not as much as getting peeled by a demon would have."

She reached out to touch it.

"Don't."

She jumped back.

"My blood might still be toxic," I said.

I pressed the ice up against the wound and stepped past her and out of the bathroom.

"Are you okay?" I asked, stopping beside her as she used the doorjamb to support herself. Her cheeks were flushed with blood and her hands were still shaking.

"Yeah, I ... just ..."

"Take some deep breaths," I said. "You look ready to faint."

"It's the adrenaline," she said. "I'm still a little buzzed."

"Near-death experiences will do that. Even to me."

She nodded. "Was that thing ... that was a demon?"

"Yeah. Aren't they fun?"

"I didn't think ... I mean, we talk about them on the MUD, but I never ..."

"I know. It's like discovering Santa's real, isn't it?"

I was looking for a place to sit. My options were the bed or an uncomfortable-looking bar stool in front of the kitchen counter.

"Yeah," she smiled, relieved to have it put into context. "Um, but Santa isn't real, right?"

"Not so far as I know." That's actually a complicated question. Long story.

"Oh, good. Because I've been sorta naughty. Here." She swept a pile of clothes off the bed. "It's laundry day."

I wanted to say it looked like laundry day had passed her by a month ago, but I was a guest. Instead, I sat, which felt uncommonly good. I was fighting a little dizziness myself.

We went through an awkward silence, with her back by the bathroom door and me trying to hold onto my equilibrium.

"Oh, hey," she said, breaking the moment. She fell to her knees, put one hand on my thigh, and reached between my legs and under the bed. She emerged with a laptop. "We should check the MUD."

She sat down beside me. It was not the firmest mattress ever built so we ended up sagging together until our thighs and shoulders touched. At around that moment a certain part of my anatomy reminded me that she was an exceptionally attractive young woman.

She flipped open the laptop and started typing away.

"I don't know a lot about computers," I said, "but shouldn't that be hooked up to something?"

"It's WiFi," she explained.

"Okay." No clue.

"Wireless," she elaborated. "Pirated, actually. The guy two floors down has wireless network access. I'm kinda stealing it."

I was reminded of a conversation I had with a guy once who couldn't stop talking about this new thing where you could send your voice through the air and have it heard on the other side of town. I thought he was certifiable. Twenty years later everyone had a radio. So I knew better than to say "oh, c'mon, how does it really work?" even though the concept of stealing Internet access out of midair sounded preposterous.

The familiar MUD frame popped up on her screen. She scanned the messages carefully. "Looks like nobody has posted much of anything yet. Should I say something?"

"No," I said. "That would be incredibly dangerous."

"They'd never believe me."

"Who?"

"My friends. If I told them I had the immortal in my room, sitting on my bed ... !"

"You can't," I said seriously. "It would put both of us at risk."

She checked my face to see how not kidding I was. I tried to look grave, as opposed to tired, hungry, and mildly hung over. Evidently I passed, as she closed the laptop and slipped it back under the bed. "Yeah," she said, sounding disappointed. "I guess."

She pushed away from me until she was sitting at the head of the bed, where she sulked for exactly two seconds before returning to the main theme, which was, "Oh my God, I can't believe you're here!"

"Is it really that exciting?" Her adrenaline had returned in force, while mine was nowhere to be seen. Ah, youth.

"Yes!" she declared. "Oh, I have *so* many questions! Like, what do I call you? Do you have a name?"

"I have a lot of them," I said dully. "I've been going by Adam lately."

"Hah! Like Adam and Eve?"

That hadn't actually occurred to me. "Sure." I was fading badly. It had been a very long day.

Clara kept on talking. She had a lot of questions, and they came one after the other in rapid succession with no real pause in between for a proper response, which was okay by me because at some point I leaned backward onto the bed. I don't know exactly when I fell asleep.

~

I woke up to sunlight streaming into the room through the un-curtained windows. I was under the blankets and evidently no longer fully clothed. Underwear, yes. Pants, no. Shirt, no. I had no memory of arriving in that state on my own. I looked around and spied my pants and shirt neatly folded atop my bag in the corner where there had been a stack of pizza boxes the night before. And not only the boxes were missing; the whole room had been picked up, revealing a previously obscured hardwood floor.

I could see Clara over the half wall in the half kitchen, whisking something in a bowl. She had her hair pulled back in a ponytail—which complemented her high cheekbones nicely—and was wearing a sleeveless half shirt with no evidence of a bra. This complemented her nicely, too.

"Hey," I said.

She looked up and smiled. "Hey! You eat eggs? Scrambled okay?"

"Sure."

"Great, that's the only kind of egg I can make." After fiddling for a second, she got a frying pan heated and the eggs into the pan and then stepped around the half wall, at which point I discovered she was practically naked, wearing only a pair of pink bikini briefs. The rest was long tan legs and a lovely midriff. My goodness.

About the tan. I've never been able to understand this. Some women just have tans somehow. And this has always been true, well before tanning salons and whatnot, even at times when tan skin wasn't the slightest bit in vogue. (For a time, pale skin was the It Look. It meant the woman in question was wealthy enough to never have to go outside without something covering her, like a parasol. It also meant they were generally unathletic, near-starved, and possibly suffering from consumption. Yes, people found that attractive.) My point is Clara lived in New York City, which is not exactly a beach town. And it was early December. So where in the hell did the tan come from? Not that I was complaining in the slightest bit. I was always the guy snapping up the hot-blooded, deeply tanned servant girl in the cupboard while the lady of the house complained of vapors and slept all day.

Clara announced, "It'll be done in a minute," acting totally ignorant of her own near-nakedness. "You slept well?"

"Yeah. Sorry about that. It's been a long couple of days."

"Don't worry about it," she chimed.

I sat up. "Um ... we didn't ..."

"No, silly." She returned to the stove. "I mean I could have taken advantage of you, I guess. You were out cold. I did take some pictures for my web site. Hope that was okay."

"You what?"

"Kidding. But I picked up."

"I noticed," I said. "I was wondering where you hid all the clothes."

"Stacked in the closet," she said, pointing to the small closet near the front door. "I wouldn't recommend opening it. Could be very dangerous."

She emerged from the kitchen with a plate full of eggs and handed it over. I went at them eagerly, as I was apparently rather hungry. She sat down on the bed and watched me eat.

"What time is it?" I asked, mouth full of eggs. All sorts of dining proprieties go out the window when you and your host are both almost naked.

"Around two," she said.

"Guess I was pretty tired."

"Yeah ... I've been up for hours. I'm not real big on sleep."

I would have told her to expect that to change in another seven or eight years, but I was too busy stuffing my face. Can't imagine that was a pretty sight, but she didn't seem to mind all that much.

It took me all of thirty seconds to finish off the eggs. She swept the plate off to the kitchen.

"So what do you do?" I asked, because that seemed like a good question, better than *why are you walking around in your underwear like that?*

"Grad student. NYU," she clarified, dumping the plate unceremoniously into the sink and returning to the bed. "Economics."

"That's interesting."

"No, it's not."

"Okay, no it's not."

She smiled. I smiled back. Long smiling pause. "That was pretty amazing, last night," she said.

"Which part?"

"All of it. The demon thing and all." The early morning encounter we shared still had her blood pumping. "Was that the first time you ever ..."

"What, killed one? Or met one?"

"I dunno. Either," she said, her hands fiddling with the sheet. Nervous tic. I made her nervous? "I gotta admit the whole 'immortal' thing is kinda hard to get my mind around. It's like I have to use a whole different vocabulary to get it right. I mean, is there *anything* you haven't done before?"

"Well, seen demons before. Mostly from a distance, which is usually the best way to meet one. It's the first time I ever killed one, or even figured out exactly how. I expected one of those helpful, heavily armed fellows to do it for me."

"Yeah, who were they? You said something about a bounty."

"Someone put a price on my head recently. They were there to collect."

Her expression clouded with something that looked like concern. "And the MUD ... you said that has something to do with all of this?"

"It does. I think whoever set it up, did so to keep track of me. To make me easier to find for the people he hired."

"God ... I feel terrible."

"Don't. It's not your fault."

Although I admit, complex Internet role-playing games don't sound too healthy to me. Must be a generational thing.

"I guess ... I mean, most of them? Most of them think it's just a joke, or ... another make-believe world and all. There are a few of us who had our suspicions. You know, that maybe it wasn't so pretend, that maybe there was such a thing as an actual immortal man. Especially when that photo turned up."

"You mean one of those digital images?"

"No, not those. Someone found an old photograph in a book from 1892 and scanned it. Pretty much everyone figured it was a fake, because, you know, you can do a lot with photos nowadays. But I know the girl who posted it, and she swore it was legit."

I thought about it. "That was ... oh, the Chicago World's Fair."

"Yeah, exactly!"

It was the first time I'd seen a portable camera, and I didn't quite believe someone could capture an image with it. Foolishly —and after having had quite a bit to drink at the German pavilion—I dared the photographer to prove it to me. Interesting how a mistake over a hundred years ago could come back to haunt me like that. I've since been very careful to avoid cameras. (In hindsight, I should have avoided beer, too.) Or, careful up until I became a wanted man and MUD geeks started hunting me with digital cameras. But short of walking around with a veil on, that was pretty much unavoidable.

"So there are a few of you who took the whole thing seriously."

"Sort of seriously. I mean, we never thought we were putting you in any danger or anything. It was all just for fun. We even started up a little mini- group within the MUD."

"Really."

She blushed slightly. "We call it the Cult of the Immortal."

I grinned.

"You're kidding."

"No, but it was just for fun! None of us ever expected to actually meet you one day."

"And what did the Cult of the Immortal do?"

"Oh, God, I cannot believe I'm even telling you this," she said.

"You brought it up."

She mock-sighed. I couldn't help but think she'd intentionally manipulated the conversation in this direction. She said, "It's mostly stuff about what it must be like to be you. All the things you must know, what you must have seen ... how you kiss ..."

"Excuse me?"

"Yeah! You're an experienced older man with the body of a thirty-year-old. How cool is that?"

I never thought of it that way, in no small part because I'd never been with a woman who went into the transaction knowing in advance that I was immortal. If I ever told—and I rarely did—it was after the fact.

"Are you telling me I'm some kind of sex symbol?" I asked.

"I wouldn't put it that way."

"How would you put it?"

She thought about it. "Okay, I guess that's about right."

"Is this cult all women?"

"I think it might be. There's no way to be sure."

I didn't know whether to be fascinated, aroused, or concerned. "Maybe I should be glad you're the one who found me."

Clara smiled. Mischief danced in her eyes. "How glad?"

Before I could think of an appropriately pithy reply, she leaned forward and kissed me. Not a peck, but a man-the-guns-and-take-no-prisoners kiss. The kind that comes off as aggressive and soft at the same time, leaving you to wonder how that's even possible. It was a very good kiss, in other words. I held up my end of the exchange pretty well once my mind registered what was happening and got all the blood flowing in all the right places.

After a good twenty seconds, we separated. Mainly for air. "Oh my," I said.

"Yeah," she agreed. Color had rushed to her face and her nipples were erect and, well, so was I.

"It's been a while," I admitted.

"I'm sure you remember how."

She pulled off the shirt that had only barely covered her in the first place. "I think I can figure it out," I agreed.

She leaned in for a gentler, less manic kiss, while my hands found their way to her naked breasts.

A word about breasts. I have gazed at, held, touched, squeezed, tugged on, licked, or otherwise fondled a lot of them in my lifetime, and I am no closer now to understanding their appeal than I ever was. One might think I'd have grown tired of them after all that time, but these elegant curves still hold more fascination for me than the entire Alexandrian Library ever did.

Clara's breasts were firm and fantastic. She pushed herself forward, rubbing up against my bare chest, which is another exciting sensation I can't seem to get enough of.

I leaned back on the bed and pulled her on top of me, kicking the blankets away as expertly as I could, considering my hands were still occupied. Then we took turns removing each other's underwear and I thanked God for twenty-first century clothing. Until you've attempted to undress a Victorian era noblewoman, you can't possibly understand how wonderful a simple pair of cotton briefs is.

As I found my way into her, we worked up to a complementary rhythm, with her doing most of the work while I held onto various body parts, eyes open, appreciating the way the rivulets of sweat on her body glistened in the sunlight.

She was right about me. I do know a lot about a lot of things, and sex is one of those things. It's difficult to have lived this long and not gotten good at something you enjoy doing as much as I enjoy sex. Given a decent supply of fresh water, I could probably prolong the act for a couple of days. Not that I'm bragging, just pointing out that while it had indeed been nearly thirty years since my last sexual encounter, I was fully capable of pausing to admire things like sweat glistening in the sun, or the jiggle of a pair of well-formed breasts as the toned muscles beneath them flex with increasing ferocity. Or the mixed expression of pleasure and pain on a woman's face as she reaches her first climax.

I have probably not always been a great lover. I think a

turning point for me was the discovery that women can find sex enjoyable, too, if one does one's job properly. I know that sounds terribly naïve, but you have to appreciate where I'm coming from. In terms of pleasuring equally, I was at least a millennium ahead of the curve.

Once she reached her first orgasm, I dutifully took my turn on top, and then we tried out a few inventive positions that it definitely helps to be in shape for. More than an hour passed—as measured by the sun's movement—before I gave in to my own climax. I could have continued for a good deal longer but I didn't think she could. Again, not bragging. Just being honest here.

Moderately exhausted, we lay still on the bed for another ten minutes before Clara spoke up again.

"Goodness," she whispered.

"I guess the Cult of the Immortal had a few things right," I said.

Now I was bragging.

"I'll say," she agreed, which was good to hear. "This will certainly help recruitment. Nice to see infertility hasn't hurt your drive any."

"Nope."

"Hey, maybe I can loan you out to other cult members."

"The female ones? I'm game."

She punched me lightly on the shoulder. "Hey! I'm keeping you to myself, buddy."

"Your customs are so strange to me," I joked.

"Cut it out." She rolled out of bed and walked to the kitchen, returning with two bottles of water. She tossed me one of them, and I drank eagerly while she polished off the other bottle.

"God," she said. "I'm wiped."

Curling up beside me, she nuzzled her head under my arm and dozed off with a pretty little contented smile on her face. I watched her.

I tried to imagine what might be going on inside that lovely head of hers. Like how much she really knew about me and where that information had come from. I wondered how much of what she'd told me about the MUD was even true. Because a great body and an afternoon of marathon sex might drive me to distraction, but not enough to recall that I'd never told her I was sterile.

CHAPTER 17

I wish I could say I'm naturally more trusting of women with whom I happen to be sleeping, but invariably I find just the opposite to be the case. It's not that I think anyone who would willingly engage in intercourse with me is therefore untrustworthy—although the idea has merit—it's just that I've been burned before. And betrayal at the hands of someone I'm intimate with ends up being more memorable for some reason. One might even call it "intimacy issues," if one were so inclined.

I think I developed this problem after I was forced to leave ancient Egypt. This was around the time of what's now called the fourth dynasty, under the rule of King Khufu. (We didn't call them Pharaohs back then. Nor did we call it Egypt. It was Kemet.) I had been living in and around the Nile Delta for quite a long time by then, because for many centuries there was simply no better place to be.

I started out there on the losing side of a local conflict during the first expansion of the Kemet Empire and ended up introduced to the Nile region as a slave, the property of a landowner named Hefuz. Hefuz was a brutal, unpleasant man who treated women and slaves more or less the same and who sired more than two dozen legitimate and illegitimate children in his time on Earth before passing things on to his eldest son, Hefiz.

The son was only slightly less brutal toward women and considerably nicer to the help—especially the male ones, as Hefiz clearly swung in that direction. In the latter years of his life, Hefiz was kind enough to grant me a small plot of land and my freedom, Kemet being one of the few places where a slave could work his way out of bondage given time and a kind owner. Patience, decent farming, irrigation skills and a little crafty maneuvering, and a century later I owned most of the land old Hefuz once did. It's one of those small ironies I get to appreciate from time to time.

Living a public life as a landowner in Kemet, as an immortal, was slightly trickier than it would be later in Carthage, and for a couple of reasons. First, Kemet had the most advanced culture I had ever seen up to that point in time, and I had to learn how to master it. One might think more culture means more people and more people means more ways to disguise oneself, and to an extent that's true. But it also means more laws, more outside concerns over one's identity and place in the world, more politics, more people in places of power to view you as a threat, or worse. Look at what I have to do today to avoid official notice and you'll understand that increased population size doesn't necessarily translate into decreased danger.

Second, Kemet's system of government was much more religiously oriented than Carthage would ever be. The more religious the population, the more dangerous a high-profile life is for someone like me.

After living for three generations on Hefuz's land, I started over again from scratch. I handed my slaves their own parcels of land and took off with the modern equivalent of a handful of cash: two ducks, an ox, and two bushels of barley. I soon found work as an apprentice to a pottery maker, and when that grew tiresome, I moved on to jewelry, then textiles, then basket-weaving, and so on. Over the subsequent three centuries, I learned how to do every handcraft you can name, and I also discovered how good beer can be when it's made properly.

I eventually tried my hand in politics. Through a series of maneuvers that would be incredibly boring to list, I worked my way into the court of King Khufu, initially as an astronomer, later as vizier. In that position I had less trouble with the whole immortality thing. Surrounded by people who already believed the king was a living god, it wasn't difficult to convince them I'd simply managed, through wisdom and a superior knowledge of the ways of the world, to figure out how to cheat aging and death. I even had fun with it, telling those who asked that one of the secrets was swallowing a live scarab each evening before I went to bed. I think a few might have actually tried this.

If you go by Hollywood, the position of vizier translates into "grand wizard" of some kind, but this is pretty much a load of crap. (I watched *The Mummy* in a movie theater and laughed out loud for the entire film. This did not endear me to anybody else in attendance.) I was a political figure, less there to administer advice than to run things while Khufu was busy with his various wives. The modern analogue would be prime minister.

And I had a lot to do, because Khufu was always busy. Being raised with the understanding that one is a god can do wonders for one's perspective of oneself, especially *vis-à-vis* all matters sexual. He—and all kings before and after him—was permitted as many wives as he wanted provided he had a Wife Number One to bear him a formal offspring, said offspring being the official heir to the throne. Wife Number One was, per requisite, a blood member of the royal family. In Khufu's case she was his half-sister. This is not quite as icky as it sounds, given the number of wives and attendant offspring each of the kings had.

I got quite a bit of tail myself, if you don't mind my being slightly crude about it. As vizier, I was at the top of the, well, the top of the pyramid, second only to those with royal blood. That kind of power is one heck of an aphrodisiac.

There was one woman in particular I was very fond of. Her name was Nampheta, a fifteen-year-old wonder of a girl. (Do not, please, get hung up on her age. Judging the past by the present understanding of sexual adulthood is unfair and it doesn't take into account the fact that people didn't always live as long then as they do now. For contrast, consider Khufu took his first wife when he was eleven. Even were I not immortal, my grand old age of thirty-something would have identified me as an elder.) Nampheta had dark eyes, straight black hair down to her navel, skin the color of coffee, and a manner that mimicked the royal upbringing she had never had.

She was a slave. Her position was that of attendant to Khufu's third wife, Heptamre. Consequently, few paid her much heed, as one learns to ignore slaves. My personal downfall came in assuming that because of her status, she was without power.

For at least a little while, I was in love with Nampheta. She would come to my chambers as often as was possible, stealing away two and three times a week, or as often as Heptamre's schedule—Heptamre was a harpy, by the way—would permit. And I had a private room that ensured us complete privacy for all manner of intimacies, sexual and otherwise.

I do believe Nampheta was the most creative lover I ever had. She was like a walking Kama Sutra, but without the annoying religious undertones. And more flexible than you could imagine. We spent many an evening developing exotic new uses for whatever prop might be on hand, such that I could never look at a spear, a clay urn, or a cat quite the same way again. And when we were too exhausted to move, we talked. It was a decent little arrangement.

Until one evening, when everything went awry. It was after a particularly exhausting effort, which included what may have been the first historical example of a trapeze, that Nampheta asked the question.

"Lord Vizier, will you soon take a wife?"

My bachelorhood had approached something legendary within the palace of Khufu. As most of the residents knew, I was far older than any man they'd ever met, so rumors combining the two facts freely circulated. My favorite, and the one most commonly repeated, had me being castrated by the god Re himself in exchange for eternal life. Nampheta—and maybe four or five other women in the palace—knew from personal experience that this was untrue, but I didn't go through much trouble debunking it.

Anyway, I had no intention of taking a wife and starting a family. The family part was entirely out of the question, not to mention physically impossible. Emotionally, I wasn't up for it either.

Okay, so maybe my intimacy issues predated Nampheta.

"I had no plans to," I said.

Nampheta sat up on the stone floor, still quite naked, her sweaty body half-visible and glistening in the shafts of moonlight from the window. I couldn't see her face, as I'd lit no brazier for our evening's calisthenics. Maybe if I had, I'd have been able to glean from her expression how much more serious this conversation was to her than it was to me.

"Never?" she asked quietly.

"What would I do with a wife?" I was busy trying to fill a basin with water. Other than jumping in the river, linen cloths and fresh water was the closest thing to a bath one got in Kemet. Just one step up from licking oneself clean.

"I see," she said quietly. She rose and began assembling her clothing without another word.

Sensing that something was amiss—and yes, you did have to hit me over the head with it in those days—I stopped what I was doing and went to her.

"You wish for something more?" I asked, trying to reach for her elbow and getting shoved off.

"Of course I do," she said. "Would you not, were our roles reversed? I am a slave."

And I was one also once, I wanted to say. But that didn't go well with the all-wise vizier-guy role, so I kept it to myself. "Perhaps I could help you in some other way," I offered. "I could buy ..."

"I don't want you to buy me. I want you to marry me!"

"Nampheta ... I do love you, you know that."

"Do you? Then make me your wife."

"I can't," I said. "It's not that simple. You're a ... a common slave."

"Common, am I?" she snapped icily.

"A bad choice of words." I was never great at talking to women, by the way. "What I mean is, politically, it would be a sign of weakness. It would ..."

"You are the grand vizier, second only to the king, looked on by most as a god. None would dare question you."

And what happens when you get old and I don't? I didn't say. What I did say was, "It's far more complicated than that."

She fastened the belt around the waist of her linen dress, and then dried her eyes with a swipe. "Well then, this common slave must go now to see to her queen. I would not want to become a complication."

And without another word she marched out through the unguarded servant's exit, never to return to my bedchamber.

It was weeks before I discovered how badly I'd screwed up.

~

I was collecting taxes when I received word that King Khufu wished to speak to me.

Tax collecting did not involve my going out and knocking on doors or any such thing. I mainly stood at the steps of the temple and counted duties from various parts of Kemet as they were brought in. We didn't employ a true currency system of any sort, so this mainly entailed the receipt of various goods. Foods, mostly, but also finished crafts and precious metals. One of my responsibilities was value assessment—whether, say, two geese equaled a bushel of wheat—and this was a real strength for a man who was familiar with nearly every manual skill known at that time.

Taxes were high that year and food was much more precious than other goods because we were building up a supply. The plan was to use the stored food to feed the farm laborers who were soon to be idle thanks to the floodwaters of the Nile. This was no welfare plan, because then the farmers would be put to a different sort of work altogether—building Khufu's pyramid. (It was the world's first public works program, after a fashion.) A lot of labor was needed because Khufu's pyramid was designed—by him and his priest—to be the biggest thing anybody had ever seen. It had to be to fit that ego of his.

Knowing full well how unusual it was to get called back to the palace—and the message was delivered by two of his guards rather than a runner, which didn't make me feel much better—I left the temple immediately. (And with no assistants to fall back on, a lot of people were going to be waiting an awfully long time for me to return. This happened on occasion, and I never heard one complaint about it. People didn't mind lines all that much back then. Bet the motor vehicles registry would appreciate this kind of respect.)

I went on foot, which didn't take long as the temple was right next to the palace, but which invariably got the royals all chatty about the impropriety of it all. Nobody, and I mean nobody, went around on foot if they could afford not to. We all had these chairs to get carried around in. I hated them. I was always expecting somebody in front to trip and send me flying into an ox or something.

I reached Khufu's antechamber fairly quickly and found him alone but for one solitary slave—Nampheta.

She knelt beside his throne, leaning forward and with her face down in a position of maximum supplication. Khufu, who had been pacing, stood before his small dais and watched me as I entered.

"Lord Vizier," he greeted.

"My king," I replied, bowing deeply. I noticed the guards who had escorted me shut the doors behind them on their way out of the royal chamber. Nothing about this looked even a little bit good.

"You have something to tell me, I think," Khufu said. It wasn't a question.

I should mention that like many persons of royal blood I have met in my life, underneath it all King Khufu was moderately insecure. I think it's because so many of them spend their lives trying to aspire to the greatness that is frankly assumed because of their family background, the problem being that blood alone doesn't guarantee greatness in a man. Deep down inside, most of them realize this. Some overcompensate. Khufu was like that.

He had a lot to compensate for. He was a little man, not terribly bright, and not the slightest bit clever. I often had to go out of my way not to appear too smart so as to avoid his wrath. This was not always so easy.

In this case, I had no idea what he was talking about.

"I don't believe so," I said.

"No?"

He glared at me, but soon decided this wasn't terribly threatening given I was a head taller, so he retreated to his raised throne and sat. I waited for more details.

"You have been plotting against me," he stated, as though it were a fact. It was complete nonsense. My sense of political intrigue didn't extend beyond making sure my ass remained securely covered.

"I've been doing nothing of the sort."

My eyes strayed to Nampheta on the floor. She wouldn't look up to me, or move much beyond breathing. What had she been telling him?

"Liar!" he shouted. Sweet Re—the man was angry. "I know about the meetings you have been having with my snake of a half brother! Behind my back! Did you think I would not learn of this treachery?"

"With Khalfu?"

Khalfu was the eldest son of Khufu's father's second wife. (One needed a chart to keep track, especially since none of them were very creative in the name department.)

"Yes, why don't you tell me what you were plotting, Lord Vizier?" He had taken my positive identification of his half brother to be a confession of some sort. Again, not the brightest guy in Kemet.

"The last I spoke with Khalfu was last week," I said. "He requested information on the crop blight in the south. Two provinces had been lax in their duties."

"Again you lie! Why would Khalfu concern himself with such matters!"

"Because you asked him to look into it, my king."

He paused in mid-bluster as soon as he realized that yes, he had done exactly that, while I stifled the urge to giggle. He recovered quickly.

"There were other meetings," he insisted. "Private meetings."

"When might these have occurred?"

"Suffice it to say I know they did. Unfortunate for you both that I have a witness whose loyalty is far greater than yours."

Which brought us back to the supine figure by the throne. Nampheta had still not moved a muscle, but she was certainly listening.

"Do you mean the slave on the floor, my king?" I asked mildly.

"She overheard your treachery, Lord Vizier."

"Did she?" I asked. "Tell me, when did the great Khufu decide that the word of a palace slave was greater than his vizier? Greater than even his own brother's?"

"My brother is a dog!" he shouted. "And you, vizier, no one *knows* what you are!"

This was very bad, and it was going to get worse very soon if I didn't figure out a way to calm him down. Unfortunately, I was getting pissed off myself, although not so much at him. How could Nampheta do this?

"Khufu, she is a slave! What is the matter with you?"

"I have long expected this from you," he spat.

"Then you are foolish and paranoid, and listening to lies!"

Oops. Never call a king paranoid. Even when they are.

He leapt to his feet. "Guards!"

The two Cro-Magnons from outside the room came running in, spears at the ready.

"Hold this traitor!" Khufu demanded, pointing at me.

Well, I couldn't have that. I mean it was already obvious I was in major trouble, but while I didn't see any ready solution, I could be pretty positive the options would go from few to none as soon as I let Khufu's palace guards chain me up. Fortunately, he employed only humans. Two of them I could handle.

When the first guard reached me, I grabbed his spear, yanked it over his head and kneed him in the groin. He let go of the spear in time for me to swing it around like a baseball bat and swat down the second guard with a blow to the side of the head, shattering the wood haft and knocking him out. With a quick spinning kick, I broke the nose of the first guard before he had an opportunity to do much more than grab his privates and whimper. He was unconscious by the time he hit the floor.

Khufu was too stunned by my actions to find his voice, which afforded me the time to pick up the half of the broken spear that had a point on the end of it. A quick jump up to the throne and I had the tip pressed up against the front of his throat.

"Sit down, Khufu," I ordered. He did as I requested, which had to be the first time since he was a whelp that he took orders from anybody.

"Nampheta," I barked, "get to your feet."

She rose slowly. Tears were streaming down her face and she looked more terrified than I had ever seen her, which was appropriate. The foolish thing had put both our lives in danger.

"Look at me."

Her eyes found their way from her feet up to my face. Frightened indeed. Of me.

This would have been, incidentally, the very best time for Khufu to grab the spear, as I wasn't paying him much attention. He didn't budge. Can't say I was surprised.

"Why?" I asked her.

She trembled mightily, but couldn't put to words what had to be a complex stew of emotions. It didn't matter. I could guess most of it. After leaving me she must have found her way into Khufu's bed. It was the only way a slave could have gotten his ear, and it was the only way she could have found out his deepest fear: that the people he trusted were plotting against him. I refused to believe she really wanted me dead—doubted, in fact, that she even thought through any of this to the proper conclusion. She just wanted to hurt me, and perhaps, also show that she had more power than I'd given her credit for. But then I had more power than she'd given me credit for as well.

I decided that was absolutely the only thing I had going for me. Nobody knew what I really was. Khufu had said so himself.

"Vizier," Khufu began.

"Shut up," I said.

"You dare speak to me like that?" he asked, his voice rising to its former heights.

"I'll speak to you however I wish," I replied. I pressed the point a tiny bit further into his throat to emphasize my resolve.

"I am about to offer you a deal, Khufu," I said. "I recommend you take it."

"A deal?" he repeated, shocked.

"Spare her life and I will spare yours."

He scoffed at the notion. "In a moment this room will be full of guards, and you will be dead. You are in no position to bargain."

I pressed the tip of the spear forward a bit more, opening a pinhole in his throat. "Your guards cannot kill me," I said. "Now make the deal."

"All right," he whispered.

I looked at Nampheta. "Go," I said to her. "The king's word is his bond, now run. Leave this place and never return."

Hesitating only momentarily, she fled the chamber. If I was very, very lucky she wouldn't alert the guards for at least a few more minutes.

"I would not have had her killed," he insisted. "She's done nothing wrong."

"We disagree," I said. "And after you let me go, you will need someone on whom to target your wrath."

"After I let you go? Lord Vizier, you have truly gone mad."

"My real name is Seth," I said, trying hard to sound as sinister as I could. "Why don't you try calling me that instead?"

He laughed, but only for long enough to decide I wasn't joking.

~

It's hard to overemphasize the hold the old myths had over the people of Kemet. Try to imagine a society of fundamentalist Christians and then imagine that the Bible included a thorough plan for a system of government and you'd be close. In order for the king to hold onto his power, the old stories had to be essentially factual; otherwise, the whole king equals god thing would have to be untrue as well. And if it were possible for the king to be the living incarnation of Horus or Osiris or Re, then it was also possible for the living incarnation of Seth to walk the Earth.

As the legend had it, Seth—god of the desert, god of violence, basically god of everything unpleasant—betrayed and then slew Osiris and chopped his body up in a million pieces, scattering the remains all over Kemet. Osiris's wife—Isis—eventually found all the pieces (except, interestingly, his penis, for reasons I'm unclear on) and restored her husband.

Kings associate themselves with one god or another. Sometimes Re, but generally Osiris or his father Horus. It's not unlike popes picking the names of earlier pontiffs with whom they feel a kinship. Khufu—and this was good news for me—believed himself to be the living incarnation of Osiris.

So you can imagine how he felt being told that the man holding a pointy thing to his neck was the god Seth himself.

~

"I don't believe you," he said defiantly. His tone said he wasn't so sure.

"Believe what you see, Khufu. You see what I did to your guards. You see that I have not aged a day since we first met."

I pulled myself up to his ear and pressed the blade a bit harder into his throat, because it seemed like a good and sinister thing to do.

"Believe that all you will do by striking me down today is anger me," I whispered, laying it on as thick as I thought I could. "And if you do, when I return I will not be interested in honoring the deal we made today."

"Deal?" he whined.

"Your life for hers," I repeated. "You remember?"

"Oh ... yes."

I could hear footsteps from outside the chamber. We were cutting this close.

"Consider yourself lucky, Khufu," I said, trying to pick up the pace without being too obvious about it. "I keep my word. Escape my wrath on this day—let me leave freely—and you shall live a long life."

"Halt!" shouted about a dozen guards, more or less simultaneously, from behind me.

I released Khufu, stepped off the stage, and tossed down the spear half. A trickle of blood escaped the small wound I'd put in his throat. Immediately I was grabbed by three guards, my arms pinned. I watched Khufu.

Reflexively, he reached down and touched his throat, discovering the blood. I hoped the little twerp wasn't the type to faint at the sight of it.

Two more guards joined in to wrestle me to the ground and there was a good possibility I had only a few seconds left to live.

"Khufu!" I barked. He was testing the royal blood's texture, looking rather out of sorts. "Remember what I said!"

A particularly large palace guard stepped in front of me with a sword, looking prepared to remove my head on the spot. Drawing the king's blood was customarily an immediate death sentence, so that was probably precisely what he had in mind. I'd hoped that brazenly wounding Khufu would lend credence to my claim of godhood, the big drawback being the instant execution thing.

"Stop," Khufu said a bit too quietly. "I said STOP!"

Everybody froze.

"Release him."

They did just that, immediately. Nobody had a word to say, either. That's another thing presumed divinity will buy you.

Khufu stood. There was a matter of saving face that still needed taking care of. "I have decided to let this man live," he said grandly. "He is to be exiled immediately. Unharmed. Is that clear?"

The lead guard bowed his head, meaning he understood. No guard dared speak directly.

"I thank you," I said, bowing myself. "My king."

Not willing to push my luck any further, I walked as calmly as possible from his throne room and headed directly for the nearest exit, escorted by the entire palace guard.

I didn't stop until I reached the coast.

~

It would be several centuries before I returned to Egypt, long after Khufu and his entire bloodline had died out, and long after Nampheta passed on. I never learned what happened to her, but I hoped she took my advice and fled to someplace safe.

I noted, with some amusement, that Khufu managed to get his pyramid built, although I understand it took him twenty years—about ten years longer than expected. (Again blazing the trail for modern public works programs.) The damn thing is huge and still standing. It's the big one at Giza. It's been completely looted, of course, which is what happens when you announce to the world precisely where you and all your worldly possessions have been buried. I believe I even told Khufu this would happen. That's what he gets for not listening to me.

CHAPTER 18

I guess one of the reasons they keep bringing me into the lab and trying out new tests—and I swear, these lab guys are more creative than Torquemada when it comes to designing things to do to the human body—is because of cancer. Seems their issue is I haven't ever had it, and this is some kind of problem. I never gave it much thought before, but I'm not a scientist, am I?

The problem is that cancer isn't something the immune system can fight. This was news to me, and please don't ask me why or how this is the case, but apparently it is. I'm taking their word for it.

Viktor was abuzz this morning because someone named "Warren" had had a brainstorm the night before. (I don't know which one Warren is. I can barely tell them apart outside of Viktor.) The solution is amazingly simple. If they'd asked me the right way, I probably could have figured it out for them: I'm older than cancer.

That's only half of the answer, because it only explains genetically acquired cancer. Cancer via exposure to a carcinogen is a different problem. Still, pretty funny, no? After all those tests?

The view from the rooftop of Clara's building was impressive, and even more so when she pulled a telescope out of that magical closet (her dirty clothes were still stacked in there) and carried it up. I initially planned to use it to see firsthand how the investigation into the *massacre by the lake*—as the papers were calling it—was going, but unfortunately the row of buildings across the street blocked most of Central Park. So instead I used it to focus on things at random and to kill time.

It had been three days since I'd fled from the park to Clara's apartment, and except for the roof, I hadn't gone anywhere. She was good enough to run out and pick up things for me—extra clothes, some food, everything but liquor. Apparently, at some point, I made an irrational statement about quitting for a while, and she had far more resolve about it than I did. She compensated with ridiculous amounts of sex. It was a fair exchange, and probably healthier, too.

"What are you looking for?" Clara asked. She was shivering behind me, in the open door.

It was a particularly cold day. The threatening snow I'd seen from the Central Park bench manifested the following morning—which I had to think made the murder investigation all that more hellish—and the thermometer hadn't risen enough since to make a dent in the accumulation total. But it made the top of the city look nicer, which never hurt.

I'm always amused by the way people today react to snow. Six inches? Gimme a break. You want to talk snow? I lived through half an ice age, for Baal's sake. Two feet on a good day. And I'm talking about in Northern Africa. Imagine what Europe was like.

"I'm just looking."

I was cold, too, but it was something I could tolerate.

"This city is a marvel," I lied.

"It was a marvel yesterday," she complained.

I looked up from the eyepiece.

"I won't be long. Go on down if you like. Make some coffee." It was the third time I'd offered a variation of this statement. Once more and she'd think I was hiding something.

Clara looked hesitant. "Yeah?"

"You worried I'm going to jump?"

"No ... it's just odd. Standing up here in the cold and eating raw mushrooms."

"You want to try one?" I asked.

"God, no. Maybe fried."

"They're good like this."

Actually, they're dreadful. Never liked mushrooms, even when I was foraging for a living. (Truffles I'm fond of, but you don't much find those anymore.) I popped one into my mouth and made a happy face.

"I'll take your word for it," she said. "Okay, I give up. I'm going in. Don't be long."

"Only until sunset," I said.

She backed in through the door and pulled it shut.

It was about time. I counted to ten and then walked to the edge of the roof.

"Iza?" I said in a normal voice. One might think it impossible, given their incredibly small ears, but pixies have good hearing. I put the bag of mushrooms down on the roof and waited. A moment later she alit beside the bag.

"There you are," I said.

"Lady gone?" Iza asked. It had taken me fifteen minutes yesterday to explain to her that she couldn't appear when Clara was around. Not that I didn't trust Clara. Well, okay, yes, that was exactly why. I've never been able to get Nampheta's betrayal entirely out of my head, so the first sign of dissembling and I turn into Secret Agent Man—even now, four thousand years later.

"She's gone inside," I said. "Is that for me?" Iza was carrying a small metal device.

"Uh-huh."

I took it from her and flipped it around in my hand. It took a couple of minutes to figure out that I was looking at a digital recorder. My, but we'd come a long way since papyrus.

"How's it work?" I might as well have asked the mushrooms.

"Don't know," she managed to say, her tiny mouth being full. There is a certain inexplicable fascination inherent in watching a pixie devour an entire bag of mushrooms. Like the ant carrying several times his body weight, pixies can consume astounding quantities of fresh vegetables. I suppose they burn it all off immediately. I've never seen a fat pixie.

After fiddling with the seemingly button-free recorder, I realized the entire front portion was hinged, and so I squeezed it and heard a little click, and then Tchekhy's voice. I held it up to my ear.

He jumped right in. "Provided the information you have provided me with is accurate, the girl you met is indeed Clarabelle Wassermann. She was truthful as well regarding her status as a registered student at New York University, but according to her running transcript, she has not attended classes for two semesters. She is the fourth child of a very wealthy family from Connecticut, which pays for the credit card she uses exclusively."

I didn't even want to know how many laws he broke to find all that out.

"I cannot definitively ascertain whether she is the individual behind the MUD character we borrowed, but that account is still disabled, and I have seen no recorded attempts by the owner to access or reactivate the account. This would appear to parallel your request that she not contribute.

"As to your question regarding this Cult of the Immortal she spoke of, I found a private chat room log bearing such a title within the MUD. The discussions there appear innocent, if not a bit banal. Based on certain anatomical speculations, it is apparent these persons have not met you."

Nice.

"Another detail which might bear some interest. I found a monthly fee on her credit card for an organization called All-Mother. Based on their web site, it is some form of proto-feminist group. I did not probe too deeply as it appears they have a very persistent firewall, but I can if you wish. Beware militant feminists, my old friend."

I found it hard to believe there was any firewall Tchekhy couldn't get past with a little work. Could be he didn't try hard enough. Or he thought it was a dead end. He was probably right.

"As to the other matter, I tracked the ownership of the MUD as far as I could. I am afraid I could not put a name with the email, but I can tell you the trail does end at Securidot to someone within that company with access to the email administrative files. And, as I am sure you are curious, other than the MUD I could not find anything connecting Ms. Wassermann to Securidot.

"If you need any additional information you may send this device back with your ... pixie. Click thrice rapidly to record, once to stop. I hope this finds you well."

So Clara checked out, Securidot was probably a dead end, and I should beware militant feminists. Not the kind of information I was hoping for but it would have to do, unless I felt like spending a week passing the tape recorder back and forth. I wasn't going to risk visiting Tchekhy directly, not after almost leading a demon straight to him. At least I was reasonably sure nobody could find me at Clara's. If they could, they already would have.

I needed to find out more about Robert Grindel. Tchekhy wasn't convinced that Grindel was the man behind the curtain, but Tchekhy is an old cold warrior at heart and thus would always be inclined toward blaming a government apparatus whenever possible. (And he did have some historical precedent to fall back on.) I was less conspiracy-minded, preferring to put my stock in the proverbial wild-eyed madman. Grindel seemed like the type.

The question was how to research without leaving the apartment. I would need Clara's laptop. And possibly Clara. I just had to convince myself I could trust her.

Iza had finished off the mushrooms and was buzzing around with renewed fervor.

"Shouldn't you wait a half hour before you do that?" I asked.

"Huh?"

"Nothing."

"I go back?" she asked.

"Not now," I said, pocketing the recorder. "Thank you, Iza."

"All done?"

"If I need you, I'll leave some mushrooms up here. Okay?" Because you never know when a pixie will come in handy, especially a tame one.

"Okay." Without so much as a fare-thee-well, she buzzed off. Whoever said ignorance is bliss had been talking to a pixie.

~

"You freeze anything off?" Clara asked as I re-entered the apartment with the telescope in tow. She was sitting at the kitchen counter eating a slice of cold pizza and reading the laptop screen. Stark naked.

You can draw your own conclusions regarding a woman who prefers to walk about her curtain-free apartment without a stitch on. My thoughts drifted between wondering what deep-rooted factors from her past led to such exhibitionistic behavior and quietly applauding my good fortune. I could only imagine what the people in the building across the street thought.

"No frostbite that I'm aware of," I said as casually as one can when speaking to a naked woman. "What'cha doing?"

"Reading my mail," she said. "Got about a hundred inquiries about you from the MUD folks. And the boards have gone nuts over the Central Park massacre. Since everybody knew you were there, the consensus seems to be that you're dead, and that's led to a massive freak-out regarding the philosophical consequences of a dead immortal. It's pretty interesting. You sure I can't respond?"

"Please don't," I said, unbuttoning my shirt. She pushed away the laptop.

"Again, why?"

"I told you. Somebody is after me and I don't know who."

"You know that sounds kinda paranoid, right?"

"You were there," I said. "How many more armed men do you think would have shown up if we stuck around? Aside from the police?"

"I know that, but it's not like my web access can be traced."

"They'll find the building," I said. "That's close enough."

She sighed theatrically, in a manner reminiscent of Marie Antoinette. (I've found while women's faces tend to be fairly unique, their expressions of exasperation are often not.) With youth comes restlessness. In the last forty-eight hours we'd had six versions of this conversation. I was putting up with it because I sort of liked her a lot. Same as with Marie.

"Hanging with an immortal not as exciting as you thought?"

"No, Adam, it's not that. I don't understand why you're just ... waiting. If somebody is after you, do something about it."

Having attained total personal nakedness myself, I walked past her to the refrigerator for some water and a decent pregnant pause while I tried to find an analogy that fit the current century and got me out of the conversation at the same time.

"I saw a cat pin a mouse behind a radiator once," I said, having chosen the first clunky analogy I could think of. "The cat couldn't reach the mouse and the mouse had no place to go except out from behind the radiator. *Détente*."

"Okay."

"So the cat just sat there and waited for the mouse to panic and make a break for it. For hours."

She closed her laptop and fixed me with an arch look. "And you're the mouse."

"And the best thing to do is not panic. Plus, I can wait for a very, very long time."

"You just made that story up."

I smiled. "How could you tell?"

"You would have saved the mouse," she declared confidently.

"You know me that well, do you?"

"I do." She got off the chair and walked around the kitchen bar and up to me until our bodies were just touching. It might have been mildly exciting with clothing. It was considerably more so without. "You would have rescued the mouse because that's what you do. You're the hero."

"Not *a* hero?" I asked. "*The* hero?"

"That's right." She took the water bottle from my hand and put it down on the counter. "You're the one who comes to the rescue. The knight in shining armor."

"I was never a knight."

She lifted her leg and wrapped it around my hip, pulling herself onto me. "Liar," she whispered.

~

Much later, after a lengthy and elaborate workout that involved every flat surface in the apartment and about half of the vertical ones, we lay together on the bed and enjoyed a little post-coital peace.

"What was your first name?" Clara asked from her position under my arm. Her breathing had been so regular I thought she was asleep.

"When?"

"In the beginning."

"I didn't really have one."

"Everyone has a name. You didn't grow up in a preverbal society."

I sat up and looked down at her. "How do you know?"

"Because," she said, rolling onto her back. "You have the capacity for language. Did you know that if you don't introduce language to a person by the age of twelve, they never develop it?"

"Now who's making things up?"

"I did not make that up. I'll show you the study."

"Well, then they just made it up," I insisted.

I have a real love/hate relationship with science. On the one hand, I can speak from personal experience that scientific and technological advances have made life a whole hell of a lot easier in just about every way imaginable. (Just two words illustrate that point amply—indoor plumbing.) But I also remember when science meant bleeding people to get the sickness out of them, boring holes in heads to free the evil spirits, and serving powdered human remains to cure gout. If there's one thing I've been thankful for in my many years, it's that I never had to experience the hundreds of dubious medical solutions offered for the supposed benefit of mankind.

I realized she was still waiting for an answer, so I gave her one. "I don't know if I'd call it language," I said. "We were barely even self-aware. I can remember some specific events, but not very much, and only if I work at it. But I did have a name, sort of. More of a sound than anything. It sounded like 'urrr'."

"Ur."

"No, with a longer *R*. Urrr. Ur was a Sumerian city-state."

"Maybe they named it after you."

"Hope not. The Sumerians were pretty obnoxious."

She seemed satisfied, and lay still for a while. Again, I thought she was asleep until she started speaking.

"So why are you hiding?" she asked. "Really, this time."

I sighed, although I didn't mean to. "I thought we went through this."

She propped herself up on her elbow. "It doesn't seem like you."

"You've known me for three days."

"Know what I think? I think that whole mouse story was your way of telling me to shut up about it."

"It worked."

"Only because I was horny. I think you already know the name of the guy that's after you. You just haven't decided what to do about it."

"That's not true," I lied. "And who said it was a guy? Could be a woman. Or a whole government."

"Then why aren't you doing something? Let me help you find out who it is. Then you can ... I don't know, exact vengeance, or whatever it is you plan to do to them."

"I don't plan to do anything to them," I said. "I'm going to find a spot on the farthest end of the planet *from* them, and live there for long enough to know that everybody involved is dead."

This was basically true. The reason I wanted to find out more about Robert Grindel was to determine exactly how far his reach extended. And maybe suss out his vulnerabilities.

"No, you aren't," she said as regards my plan, such that it was.

"Why not? It's worked before."

She sat up. "Look, that demon was about the scariest thing I've ever seen, and you faced him down when you could have just run away and waited it out. Whoever hired the demon is just as bad, so you can't expect me to believe you're going to hop a plane to Borneo as soon as you get his name."

"The demon was different," I said. "He would have been relentless. I had to face him eventually."

"No, you didn't. Demons don't live forever."

"He killed some friends," I said, after a pause. "That's why I did what I did. He proved that as long as he was looking for me, everyone I met was in danger."

"Ah-hah!" she exclaimed.

"What?"

"I told you. You're the hero. If all you cared about was self-preservation ..."

"Then I would have run. I get your point. It's wrong, but I get your point."

"Why am I wrong?"

"I'm just ... I'm not a hero."

I'm really not. I've done enough terrible things in my life to take myself out of the hero sweepstakes for an eternity. But Clara was a romantic.

"You put your life at risk for others," she said stubbornly. "How is that not heroic?"

"I thought my way out of a situation and that's all."

"A situation you would never have been in if you weren't interested in righting a wrong," she declared.

I sighed again. We could go back and forth with this all night. "If it makes you feel better to think of me as a hero, okay. But exacting vengeance, as you put it, would be unnecessarily dangerous."

She fell back on the bed, and after a while said, "But you're curious."

"About what?"

"About whoever set this up," she said. "Five million dollars? For you? You gotta wonder why, right?"

"Not really."

"Liar."

"Okay, not curious enough," I said. "Curiosity killed the cat."

"I thought you were the mouse behind the radiator."

"Now I'm the cat."

"Okay," she said. "You're the cat who already knows the name of the dog, then."

"There's a dog now?"

She glared at me. "You know his name, Adam," she insisted.

I sagged back into the bed and let her question hang in the air for a few seconds.

"All right," I said. "Answer me this. How did you know about my infertility?"

"Your what?"

"You mentioned it, the first day I was here. I never told you about it. How did you know?"

"Is that ... ?" She fell back against the pillow. "From the MUD, Adam! Jesus, you're paranoid."

"I prefer to think of it as extra careful," I argued weakly.

"You've been nailing me for three days and ... God, I can't even *speak* to you right now." She turned away from me on the bed and sulked. I think women are born knowing how to sulk expertly.

We lay there quietly for a few minutes. I made a mental note. Next time I accused a lover of deception, I was going to have to pick a better time. Like when we were both wearing clothes. And possibly in a public place. You'd think I would have learned this by now.

"So I have some trust issues," I said after a time.

"No kidding," she agreed.

"That's on the MUD? Because that's not the kind of information I share with anybody."

She turned back. "Look, Adam. You're going to have to trust somebody eventually. Obviously whoever is after you knows a whole lot more about you than you realize, and that makes them dangerous. So if I can help you find them, *let* me."

I nodded, because she was right. There was no other way. I crossed my fingers and hoped this time it was the right decision.

"Have you ever heard of a company called Securidot?"

CHAPTER 19

Clara hadn't heard of Securidot, but she was a veritable wizard with her little laptop, so it wasn't long before we both knew a whole lot more about the company.

"This buyout you read about before is big news," Clara said. It was well into the night by then, and she was all business with her computer up on the kitchen counter, with her hair pulled up, her hand working a pen on a pad of paper, and her body still entirely naked. I was more tastefully dressed in a pair of pants.

She continued, "Both Securidot and Secure Systems International were hit pretty hard by the recession."

"Are we in a recession?"

"We were. Plus, there was the dot-com implosion a few years back. That didn't help."

I only recently learned the word "dot-com" but had no idea there'd been an "implosion." I would have asked for clarification but it didn't seem worth my time.

She continued. "They're competing companies with competing products, but with different market shares. SSI is mostly consumer stuff—small firms and what have you. Securidot has a few smaller customers, but mostly lives off large corporations and government contracts. The buyout of Securidot ended up saving both companies. And it looks like it made a bundle of coin for someone named Robert Grindel. I guess he was the CEO of Securidot until recently. He got a decent buyout."

She looked up from her computer. "That's him, isn't it?"

"I don't know," I said. "It had been impressed upon me that Grindel doesn't have enough money to pull off something like this."

"No," she agreed. "Not if all he's got is what came out of this deal. Hang on."

More typing. I sipped from my water and waited patiently. Having someone else do the searching was probably a good thing. When the Internet was first explained to me, it was a half an hour before I got anywhere close to grasping the concept. I kept getting it confused with the old party phone lines that used to be common before everyone got their own telephones.

"All right," she began, after another lengthy bout of researching, "This guy isn't just a dot-commer. He's got a wide range of interests. I Googled him and it looks like ..."

"I'm sorry," I interrupted. "You what to him?"

"Googled. I put his name into a search engine."

"Never mind, go on."

"Okay. I see his name popping up all over the place associated with five or six different proposals and investment vehicles. So that means he has more money than what he made on the Securidot sale."

"Enough money?"

"There's really no way to tell. This is mostly back-channel stuff. Think of him as a facilitator. Someone comes to him with an idea—or he goes out and finds a workable idea himself—and he puts together investors for it. If he's successful, he gets a cut or a percentage and moves on. Doesn't even matter if the proposal turns into something successful. He gets paid either way."

"Nice gig," I said.

"Yeah. I bet his rolodex is worth millions all by itself. Probably built up his contact list through his association with Securidot."

"So by catching me, he could be closing out another deal. And it doesn't even have to be his idea."

"It's probably not. But he would already need to know you exist. No telling whether it was him or someone else that brought that knowledge to the table." She looked up at me. "You look convinced."

"I pretty much am. Can we figure out what he's working on right now?"

"Not with public access resources like this, no," she said. "What you need is somebody with enough money to be considered a viable investor. A venture capitalist."

I was unfamiliar with the term, and said so. She explained, "VCs look for places to put their money, basically. All they really care about is if an idea can turn into something they can make money off of. Although there's something to be said for an idea that *sounds* good but doesn't work out, because tax write-offs are sometimes just as valuable. I did a term paper on this stuff if you want to read it."

"Another time," I said. "So they're like patricians?"

"Kind of. Except a patrician might support an artist for the sake of art. These guys are definitely in it for the money."

"Can anybody be a venture capitalist?"

"Anybody with gobs of hard money, sure. Do you know of anyone?"

"Yeah. Can I use your phone?"

~

An hour later, I had a new best friend in a Swiss banker named Heintz, and a workable plan. Heintz would be spending the next day or two trying to find out what Grindel's latest investment vehicle was—preferably without spending any of my money first. While Heintz was doing this, I planned to be on a fast plane heading straight out of this hemisphere. The last part didn't sit well with Clara.

"Look," I said, "You said yourself he doesn't have the money for this bounty on his own. That's his weakness. If he can't get me, he can't maintain the bounty, because the investors will pull out."

"It's a stupid idea," she insisted. "You don't even know for sure if he's who you think he is. Or where he is."

"Yeah, but I just need to know where his money is. And who else could it be? We know it's someone connected with Securi-dot. You think a low-level programmer has the money to do this when the CEO doesn't?"

"I don't know, maybe," she said. "I think the only way to be sure is to find him. We can do it together."

"Oh, for Baal's sake, we cannot. And for five million he doesn't want to just have a chat."

"What if he doesn't even have it?" she asked. "What if the money is a bluff?"

I shook my head. "You don't hire these kinds of people with bluff money. Not if you want to live through the experience."

Clara pouted. My death-proof, long-term but capture-free plan wasn't flying with her. I couldn't imagine why. My keeping out of his clutches should—if I was reading this situation correctly—bankrupt him fairly quickly. And if I had to I could invest directly myself and take him apart from the inside. It was a good plan.

"Which part of this don't you like?" I asked. "The bloodless part or the part where I run off?"

"It just seems cowardly," she said after a time.

"Oh, please," I said. "A word like *coward* doesn't mean anything to me. Neither does *brave* or *valorous.* They're what you use to describe a dead person. 'Oh, so-and-so acted bravely when he charged that crowd of Huns armed with only a half-sword and a pair of sandals. Sure he's dead now, but what valor!' Well, maybe the dead guy charging the Huns did it to inspire the men he fought with, or maybe he just realized he was already dead and decided to take out as many of his enemies as he could first. And maybe the coward who ran away warned the people behind him that the Huns were coming, and at the end of the day saved more lives for it. Call it cowardice all you want, but I'll still be breathing when it's done, and that's my favorite kind of plan."

"He'll keep chasing you," she said quietly. I'd raised my voice a bit, which I think scared her. The word *coward* annoys me for some reason. Not that she could have known that.

"Let him," I said. "I'll outlive him."

She looked defeated.

"I didn't think ... when I offered to help, I didn't think it would be helping you to get away from me. I'm not ready to say good-bye to you yet, Adam."

And there it was, the root of our argument. I had been hanging out, enjoying some good sex, trying to decide when would be the best time to disappear for a century or two. She had apparently been working from a different agenda.

Not to say that women fall in love with me routinely or even that I'm particularly easy to fall in love with, but this has happened before. Even arguing that only one out of ten women with whom I've been intimate also fell in love with me at some point, you'd still be looking at decent numbers. The only way to prevent it was to swear off female companionship altogether. I just can't do that.

"I'm sorry you feel that way, but I wasn't planning to stay for much longer anyway." True, now that I had a strategy to work with, it was time to go. I had been holding out for good-bye sex, but it didn't sound like that was going to happen once I was finished breaking her heart.

Ah well.

She wasn't buying. "You expect me to believe I don't mean anything to you?"

"You can believe what you want," I said.

"I don't."

"I'm sorry, but ... I just needed a place to stay."

I tried to sound convincing and, well, it was half true in that even if I hadn't been sleeping with the host, I still would have stayed. But I did have feelings for her.

Was love one of those feelings? Hard to say. It was possible I simply no longer remembered what love felt like. What I did remember was what losing someone I loved felt like, and that memory was strong enough to get me heading for the door whenever I found myself in this situation. Like I said—intimacy issues.

"You still can't trust me, can you?" she asked.

"No, I trust you." Also true.

We suffered through a lengthy silence.

"Look," I said finally, "I have to get going."

I couldn't even look at her when I said this.

"Now?"

"I think it has to be now, don't you?"

She looked down and wiped a tear. I'm not entirely heartless. This was killing me.

"I guess you do," she said quietly. She reopened her laptop. "Where do you want to go?"

CHAPTER 20

Here's what I don't get. I've been listening to these guys talk and talk about how my body works, but whenever I bring up the next step they get all vague with me, using phrases like "transformational genetic event," which doesn't sound like anything with which I'm familiar. I do know that whatever this "event" is, it has something to do with a virus. Beyond that? No idea. But I'm wondering if it has to do with what's in the reinforced building next to mine.

I need to think about it some more. I've got time. I can figure this out.

~

After much thought, we decided I should take a flight from JFK to Heathrow and pick my destination from there. Clara wanted to know where I was going to ultimately end up, but she also didn't. Something about lots of beer and daddy's credit card and having a weak moment. I tried to sympathize without sounding like I wanted her to come with me. (I did sort of want her to come with me.) And I didn't actually know where I was going to go once I reached London, although it crossed my mind to visit my money in Switzerland. Or to return to Amsterdam. Have I mentioned how much I love Amsterdam?

I actually thought it would be a miracle if I made it onto the plane, but I didn't tell her that. With the demon out of the way, all I had to worry about was ingenuity on the part of my human pursuers, or simply luck smiling on the wrong person at the wrong moment, and that seemed like pretty good odds when I thought about it in the abstract. But now that I was actually going out into the world, in a more-or-less mad dash for the border, I was beginning to have my doubts. And since I'd already done a fabulous job of burning my bridge with Clara, I couldn't stay any longer either.

Clara reserved a ticket for me under one of the passports I hadn't used lately, meaning I had to brush up on my Spanish as I was going to have to be Gaspar Esperanzo for a little while. This is not as easy as it sounds, not when you're fluent in almost every European dialect there ever was. I had to look up some Spanish-language web sites to get my head in the right century. I also had to give Clara some cash since it was the aforementioned daddy's credit card that bought my ticket. (It's surprisingly difficult to buy a ticket online with cash.)

Three in the morning, with large portions of the city sleeping, it was time to say good-bye. Significantly, she'd managed to put on some clothes for the occasion.

"Will you let me know you're okay?" she asked.

"Do you want me to?"

"Of course."

"Then I will," I said, although I probably wouldn't. It was unspoken, but while making the formal arrangements for my departure, a sense of resignation imposed itself on the proceedings. She'd stopped arguing, and I had stopped forcing myself to be so callous. "I think it would be best if you tried to get on with your life," I added helpfully. "And maybe I'll catch up with you someday. When you're married and insanely happy."

She hugged me, and I hugged her back. "I don't think that will ever happen," she said.

"It always does." I kissed her on the forehead. A paternal gesture. Appropriate, given our age difference.

She kissed her finger and touched my cheek with it. "I've about figured out this immortality thing," she said with a smile that managed to look sad. "All I have to do is stop getting older."

"That's all there is to it."

"When I get that down, I'll look you up."

I smiled. "It's not as fun as it sounds."

"Nothing ever is."

We hugged tighter, and then I left.

~

The flight wasn't until ten in the morning, but I didn't want anybody to see me leaving Clara's apartment during the day, so to throw off the scent I snuck out during the night and descended into the pit of hell itself. The subway.

Like just about everything else conjured up in the past century, the underground subway system of the modern city is an unfathomable engineering miracle covered in several inches of filth, urine, and spray paint. Despite being a certified member of the human race, I'll never fully understand why miracles of this magnitude are treated so casually.

For the first couple of hours on the train, I expounded at length on that point with a drunk named Lester, who heartily agreed with me. Lester also let me in on important secrets about what the government is putting in the drinking water and how all communists are homosexuals and vice versa. Lester was a sharp guy, in a "wow, you're nuts" sort of way. It was like speaking to outtakes from *Dr. Strangelove*.

Lester also had a bottle, which he offered kindly to share. I declined, for an odd reason—I didn't want to disappoint Clara. I reminded myself I never planned to see her again, but it didn't help.

Sometime in the third hour, Lester suddenly decided we were at "his stop"—although we'd been by it four times—and wandered off. I think he sobered up enough to wonder if maybe I was a homosexual communist government operative checking up on him. Could have been the tape recorder I suddenly pulled out of my pocket that gave him that impression. Yeah, it was sort of cruel, but he was starting to bore me.

Alone again, I got my hands on an abandoned early edition of the Times, and out of curiosity flipped through the pages to see if there were any new messages in Latin waiting for me. I found it on page seventeen. It was another full pager—must have cost a fortune—and it said pretty much exactly the same thing.

For the Eternal Man

You have nothing to fear from us. We will not hurt you. Your health is the most important thing. If you stop running, you will realize we have much to discuss. Wait where you are.

I had to think that somewhere in New York was a very confused Latin professor with a Times subscription.

I stayed underground for all of rush hour, which was a startling contrast to me and Lester alone in a car. Calling them sardines in business suits would be a bit cliché and besides which, inaccurate. More like a perpetual feeding frenzy. Or the way we used to bring down big game back in the day—everyone charge.

I shifted with the business-clad tide for a while, hopping off at stops here and there and basically making life miserable for anybody who might be following me. Then, with two hours to go before my flight, I popped back up to the surface and hailed a cab for JFK. Thus ended the easiest part of my day.

~

In the cab my thoughts drifted somewhat predictably back to Clara and how much I was expecting to miss her.

It would be easier if I didn't care about anybody. I've met men like that, and none of them had immortality going for them. Me, I've got a ready-made excuse to be a serial dater. Yet, every time I leave someone behind, I feel pangs of regret followed by years of "hey, that looks sort of like ..." sightings, until I either convince myself to go back and find the girl I abandoned or until I do the math and figure out she's been dead for a while. Which is always a profoundly depressing revelation.

I wish I could say I'd never met anyone like her—meaning Clara the person, not Clara the uniquely attractive woman—but the tragedy of memory precludes such considerations. Yes, she reminded me of other women, women I slept with and women I simply knew fairly well. One might think that takes the wonder out of romance. In a way it does, but in its place is the cozy familiarity of seeing someone again after a long time apart. It's thoughts like these that make me wonder if there is such a thing as reincarnation.

Anyway, I'd miss her, just like I miss all of them.

My cab driver was a lunatic named Mohammed who seemed to show equal amounts of disdain for all the other cars on the road and for all the traffic laws. If I didn't know better, I'd think he was trying to kill me. But he wasn't. He liked me. I always get along well with cab drivers because I always speak their language, whatever language that might be. Mohammed's was Arabic. I entertained the prospect of telling him I met the original Mohammed, but I was pretty sure he wouldn't believe me. (Nice guy, old Mohammed was. A tad zealous and more than a bit touched in the head, but otherwise all right. He and Lester the subway drunk would have gotten along well.)

We arrived at the curb with a little over an hour to spare before my flight. It looked like my luck had held. All I had to do was make it to the gate and I was home free. I figured the best anyone could do once I was inside was try and talk me into going with them, seeing as how they'd never get a gun past the metal detectors. And if the woman I was sleeping with couldn't convince me to go to Grindel, what chance did anyone else have?

After tipping Mohammed, I stepped past a man pushing a baby stroller and nearly made it through the sliding doors leading inside when I heard a familiar voice.

"That's him."

I should have run straight for the gate. Instead, I turned around and found myself staring at the barrel of a gun. It was wrapped up in a receiving blanket, so I was the only one who could see it.

The man with the stroller smiled. "Don't move," he said.

"Why not?" I asked. "You going to shoot me here, in front of the skycaps? You think I'm stupid?"

The happy faux father was still smiling. He was dressed in generic upper-middle class, looked to be about six feet tall and decently muscular, in a daily jogging yuppie kind of way. Probably knew something about hand-to-hand combat. I could take him.

"No," he answered. "I know you are not stupid." Trace of a German accent.

He held up his other hand, the hand that had been holding the baby stroller. In it was an eight-by-ten black-and-white photograph of Clara. Clara tied up and gagged with electrical tape.

"Hah! Shit, Adam, you should see your face!"

It wasn't the man with the gun who said that. It was the familiar voice that had caused me to turn around in the first place. It was the baby. I looked down.

"Hello, Jerry," I said. "You make one ugly newborn, you know that?"

CHAPTER 21

Clara finally managed to get a map through to me. I'm guessing since she was able to draw it, she also has a good deal more freedom than anything I'm working with. I'm wondering again if maybe she's not even a prisoner at all. That would be a nettlesome complication. Especially if she tells anyone about my escape plan, which has plenty of holes in it already and certainly won't need her help to go horribly wrong.

And even if it goes exactly the way it's supposed to, I don't expect I'll be surviving it. The best I can reasonably hope for is to take out as many people when I go as I can.

~

An hour later I was in the backseat of a minivan and taking in the less scenic portions of northern New Jersey. (The snow covering helped, from a beautification standpoint, but only marginally.) Beside me, in a baby's car seat, was Jerry. I can't even begin to tell you how funny this looked. My captor—who introduced himself as John—was handling the driving. He was doing the limit with a fresh-faced all-American smile on his face. Joe Anybody on a Sunday afternoon jaunt. Which made me the brother-in-law, just in from the airport. Or the other half of a gay couple, depending on who asked.

My bag was at my feet. John hadn't bothered to search it, which was just as well. I didn't have anything I could use in there. I'd left the gun in the park, and it would take hours to kill John with Tchekhy's tape recorder. The only thing I'd rather they didn't know I had was the satellite phone. Of course, they had one of their own.

It had been assumed from the outset that I would be going quietly.

Seemed like a reasonable assumption, as they had my girlfriend hostage and I was supposedly the chivalrous sort and all. And really, you had to give them credit for thinking of getting a hostage since we all know I'm not an easy guy to forcibly transport. They were pretty close to being right about the chivalry part, but that was about it. I certainly wasn't going peacefully.

"So where are we headed?" I asked John No-Last-Name.

"To see my employer," he said with a smile one reserves for friendly chats about the weather.

"That's self-evident," I said. "I was looking for something more specific. Like what region of the country, or even what country in general. I just want to know how to dress for the occasion."

"You needn't worry," he said. "We've made all the arrangements."

"Uh-huh. Hope you have a lot of cash."

"I'm sorry?"

"A lot of cash," I said. "This thing gets what? Twelve miles to the gallon? For a cross-country drive, it's just not very practical." John recognized a clumsy fishing expedition for what it was and didn't answer. So I continued. "Not to mention dangerous for the environment. You know, I've been reading up on these—"

"Hey, Adam," Jerry interjected, "was she good or what?"

He was examining the photograph of Clara and doing things to himself that I'm willing to bet the designers of the baby seat never envisioned.

"You like that, do you?" I was decidedly unhappy with my erstwhile friend. "You like to have them tied up like that?"

"I'm more of a handcuff guy myself," he admitted. "Crashed a women's prison once? Un-fucking-believable. You know what I mean?"

I took the photo from him.

I guess you're probably wondering how I ever ended up trusting something as unpleasant as Jerry in the first place. You may have also noticed that while I have some fascinating tales about various other uncommon beings—vampires, pixies, demons—I haven't told you any about iffrits. This is because there are no interesting stories. Iffrits are completely and utterly useless. They have never, to my knowledge, done anything particularly brave or particularly evil. Or anything at all. No iffrit has made an impact that I know of on history in any way whatsoever. Evolutionarily speaking, I believe their specific niche in the world is to serve as excellent drinking partners, which is exactly how I've always treated them. I trusted Jerry in that capacity and never anticipated betrayal from him because betrayal would just be too much work for an iffrit.

"So how'd this play out, Jerry?"

"How'd what play out?"

"How did you get involved with all of this?"

"Yer pissed, ain't-cha?"

"However could you tell?"

He popped the harness loose and scampered out of the seat. Another thing the designers probably hadn't counted on. "Awww, don't be that way, Adam," he said, leaning across my knee to try to look me in the eye. "It's just money, is all."

"Just money," I repeated. I really wanted to strangle the little prick. "When did iffrits ever care about money? You don't even have any pockets to put it in."

"I'm getting entrepreneurial."

"I'd be amazed if you even knew what that word meant."

"I figure with enough cash I can maybe buy my own beer truck or something. Or a bar."

Now that sounded more like an iffrit. "You'd sell me out for a beer truck?"

"So it's not the best thing I ever done. Look, somebody who knows somebody tipped me off that you were worth some money, okay? That's all."

"Who?"

"You don't know the guy. Turned up in Sully's one night asking about you. I told him to fuck off, course, but then I got to thinking about it and decided it might be worth looking into. So I followed him and stole his little phone thingie. And the guy on the other end told me what was what, gave me his private number, and here I am. Guess he figured since I knew you I'd be good to keep in touch with."

"Uh-huh. And when was this?"

"Couple of months ago."

"A couple of ..." *Sonofabitch.*

I couldn't help it. I grabbed him by the neck and held him up. This caught the attention of my cheery driver.

"Please don't do that," he said. "I'd rather you weren't spotted throttling our baby." Not *don't kill my partner*, just *don't blow my cover*. I wondered if Jerry was even aware how expendable he'd made himself. Probably not.

I picked my bag up off the floor and tossed it on the seat beside me, shoved Jerry down where the bag had been, and put my foot on his throat.

"Is this better?" I asked John.

"Much better, thank you."

"Hey!" Jerry complained.

"Shut up," I said. "Two months ago, Jerry? You led these people to me in Boston, didn't you?"

"Yeah," he choked.

"And to the apartment. You called him from Gary and Nate's apartment and do you know what happened then? Rather than contact one of his bounty hunters, he sent a demon. A demon, Jerry."

He was starting to get my point. "Hey, now c'mon, those guys were dicks!"

I stepped harder. He made a gagging noise and then something that may have been a hairball spat out of his mouth and narrowly missed my pant leg.

"They're dead now, you little asshole."

He tried speaking but found it too difficult until I eased up. "You were supposed to *be* there!" he said. "How was I supposed to know you was gonna leave?"

Had I crushed his windpipe at that moment, I doubt it would have elicited much more than a thank-you from the driver for doing his job for him. But I had more questions saved up, so I released Jerry. He sat up, coughing and hacking and surely disappointed to have lost his erection, while I returned to the view outside the window and entertained happy thoughts about iffrit dismemberment.

Based on the road signs, it appeared we were still heading south. I don't know a lot about state highways, but I do know driving to Seattle—which was where Robert Grindel last resided—would involve heading west. So maybe we weren't driving there.

"Is she safe?" I asked the driver, of Clara.

"Of course," he said. "We're not cruel people. Just insistent."

"You guys must have finally figured out you need to work together, huh?"

"I don't understand your meaning, friend," he said cheerily, as if we really were friends. Did he think being personable would keep him alive longer?

"Somebody had to get Clara to wherever it is we're going. I left her less than ten hours ago. So unless she's in the trunk, you have some help. Other than the iffrit, I mean."

He didn't feel like talking any more. I tried a different question. "When will I see her?"

He sighed heavily. "After you have been delivered," he said. "All right?"

Now, if you're paying attention, that was a mistake. Up until then I wasn't sure Clara was being brought to the same location as I was. John figured there was no reason not to tell me that because I couldn't possibly know where we were going or how to find out. He was wrong on both counts, and had he bothered to search my bag, he would have known that.

"How will I know you'll release her?" I was just killing time now.

"As I said, we are not cruel people. She's an instrument to facilitate your delivery."

"Can't you use *hostage* and *blackmail* like everybody else?"

He smiled. I could tell because the sides of his face twitched upward.

Jerry, in the meantime, crawled off the floor and sulked his way back to the baby seat. He seemed to be under the impression that I was mad at him. Either that or he was pissed I'd taken away the photo of Clara.

Up ahead I saw a small plane descending, to the left of the highway. We were near an airfield. So that was how he was taking me west. A private plane.

That wouldn't do.

I lifted my bag from the seat and made like I was slipping the photograph of Clara into it. I was, but more importantly, I was removing the arm strap. (It was the kind that clipped on, the kind airports always make you remove beforehand.) Since Jerry was sulking and John was watching the road and making the proper turnoff toward the airfield, nobody noticed.

The off-ramp led to an overpass, which fed a two-lane road that ran perpendicular to the highway. Then we hung an unexpected left onto a private road that barely qualified as one lane and quickly devolved from marginally paved to mostly dirt covered with a crust of snow. With the poor traction, John slowed to fifteen. Honestly, he was making this much too easy.

Conveniently isolated from potential witnesses, I waited until a decent pothole and then leapt forward. Being a very conscientious motor vehicle operator, John was focused entirely on maintaining control of the car when we hit the pothole, so he couldn't do much other than take note of the fact that when he settled back down in his seat he had the strap from my bag wrapped around his neck. I yanked back hard.

"Better ease off the gas there, John," I suggested.

"You idiot," he muttered, managing to keep the car on the road despite the imminent threat to his life. In fact, he picked up speed. Impressive. I yanked tighter.

Jerry, not real quick on the uptake, finally noticed his ride was about to get a lot bumpier. He went into attack mode—such as it was—and launched himself at my face, but I warded him off with my free hand. He clung on and sank his teeth into my forearm.

"Ow!" I exclaimed. You would, too. I took my eyes off the driver just long enough to swing Jerry against the side of the baby seat, stunning him into letting go.

The distraction Jerry provided was sufficient for the driver to get his hands on his gun and raise it over his shoulder. I saw it just in time to duck.

He fired. The bullet put a good hole in the roof but fortunately not in me. Unwilling to see if he could improve upon his aim, I gripped the strap with both hands and tugged sharply back and to the right until I heard John's neck snap.

We were up to twenty miles an hour. Spotting a turn ahead

that we were definitely not going to make, I threw myself on the floor and curled up in a fetal position.

Impact with a decent-sized tree came shortly thereafter.

I didn't hear the car hit the tree, the airbags deploy, or Jerry's scream as he was thrown forward. The gunshot had temporarily deafened me. But once things were settled I could see that I was okay, the driver was still dead, and Jerry was decidedly unhappy. He was lying on the back seat— he'd bounced off the back of the passenger seat—looking dazed and resting awkwardly on his arm, which appeared broken. I left him where he was, pulled myself up, and let myself out.

The minivan had a tree-shaped dent in the front. It wasn't totaled, but it also was no longer a viable transportation option in the immediate future. I had hoped to avoid that, but walking away intact was still a pretty good result, all things considered.

Opening the driver's side door, I pushed over my friendly ex-captor and searched him, finding a wad of cash, a spare clip for the gun, a regular cell phone, and his satellite phone. I took each item, plus the gun itself from the floor of the minivan, then reattached my extremely useful bag strap. I would have to send a thank you note to the manufacturer. (*This strap is very sturdy and makes for an excellent murder weapon ...*)

My hearing returning, I focused attention to the injured iffrit in the back seat.

"Adam, man, you fucked up ..." he whined, prone on the seat and looking up at me.

I pulled him out of the car and dropped him unceremoniously onto the smoking hood. He yelped in pain.

"Did I?" I asked. "Tell me how."

Wincing from the broken arm I had dropped him on, he said, "Whatta ya gonna do now? You don't even know where to go!"

"Let me worry about that. Did you really see her?" I asked.

"Who?"

"The red-haired woman. You said in Boston that you'd seen her."

"Oh her ... of course I did ..."

He was lying. I held the gun to his head to emphasize my feelings regarding his veracity.

"Okay, okay!" he cried. "I needed an excuse to be there, all right? Plus, you get even more shit-faced than usual every time you think about her, and I figured that'd make you stay put until they came to take you away. But I tried to warn you!"

"Warn me? When?"

"I told you to stay away from her."

"That's not a warning."

"Best I could come up with and still get paid."

Iffrit logic.

"You described her eyes to me," I said. "How did you know what color her eyes were?"

"What?" he laughed. "You told me that yourself, you stupid prick. Jesus, do you have any idea how much you talk about yourself when you're drunk? You act like this whole immortality gig is one big fucking secret, and then you go tell anybody who'll buy you a bottle. Half the fucking western world knows your deal by now. Are you really surprised at all this shit?"

I almost pulled the trigger, mainly out of spite. He was right though. I hadn't been careful for a very long time. It used to be it wasn't a big deal to spout off in a tavern somewhere, because odds were, nobody of consequence would be within earshot. But it also used to be true that a boat trip across the Mediterranean would be an effective way to disappear, and that it was possible to change your name just by deciding to call yourself something different. The world had changed, and I'd lost track again. Eventually something like this was bound to happen.

"Okay." I slipped the gun into my bag. "You can live."

"Geez, thanks," he muttered. I started to walk away, toward the air field.

"Hey, Adam," Jerry called out after me.

"What?"

"Why're you doing this?"

"Doing what?"

"The girl. You were already done with her. Why do you even care?"

I smiled. "Because I'm the hero."

CHAPTER 22

I'm a little worried. I deliberately led Ringo closer to the second cell this morning. The last two times we did this, the creature in that cell hit the door hard. Since Ringo hates it when that happens, I can only do this once in a while because otherwise he'll figure out it's intentional. Anyhow, it's just about the only way to make sure it's still alive in there. And today, nothing. The door didn't rock at all. And the late night booming noises stopped some time ago. Hope it's not dead. That would mean it's not what I thought it was, which would screw up everything.

~

I followed the snow-covered dirt path the rest of the way to the airfield. It wasn't much of a walk. Had I waited another thirty seconds to pounce upon my driver, it might have been too late. One does not want to get into a life-or-death struggle in a careening minivan on a landing strip with multiple witnesses and multiple gas-filled and grounded airplanes for targets. This much I have learned.

Actually, the multiple witness part was something I just made up. It turned out this was a very small airfield, clearly privately owned, with a total of three airplanes standing in front of a hangar that looked barely large enough to accommodate two, and a single plowed runway. (I would love to tell you what kind of planes they were, but I'm only just past the "man was not meant to fly, Mr. Wright" phase.) So rather than there being a gaggle of potential witnesses, there was exactly one.

Sitting in a Jeep next to the building was what I at first took to be a smallish man with short hair in a bulky flight jacket, but who, on closer inspection, turned out to be a normal-sized woman. She had flight jockey-type mirrored sunglasses on. As she was facing me, I could only assume she was also watching while I made my way close enough to hold a decent conversation.

"Hello," I said.

"Good morning," she answered, unmoving.

The hangar behind her was attached to a small, windowed office. I could see a radio inside and gathered that if one wanted to take off from this airfield, one must first radio in one's intentions using this. (I learned this by watching movies, so who knows if it was true. Sounded good though.) The door was padlocked and on the door was written the legend "Patti's Chartered Flights." I made an inferential leap.

"You must be Patti," I said.

She nodded. "You must be my twelve-fifteen."

"I must be."

"Except," she went on, "You can't possibly be my twelve-fifteen."

"Oh? Why not?"

"Because I was contracted to take two men."

"The other guy couldn't make it."

"Uh-huh." She looked over my shoulder at the road I'd just emerged from. "Must have been a long walk from the highway."

"I like walking. Very healthy."

"It's thirty degrees out, there's snow on the ground, and you have no coat."

"Well, sure," I agreed, "it's a little chilly."

Patti repositioned herself uneasily in the Jeep. I wasn't winning her over with my world-class charm. "Sounded like there was some kind of accident up the road there," she said. "Should I call an ambulance? Or just skip on ahead and phone the police?"

"That depends," I said. "What's your position on guns?"

"Pardon me?"

"Let's say I have a handgun in my bag here. Would you take my word for it, or do I have to pull it out and show it to you?"

She thought about it. "Honestly, I think you'd have to show it to me."

"All right." I produced the gun from the bag. "Do you need for me to point it at you, too, or shall we just proceed to the next step?"

She stared at the gun for a few seconds. "No, that's fine. What can I do for you?"

"You were chartered to take two men?"

"Yeah."

"By whom?" I asked.

"Guy named John Filcher. Blond, moderately handsome, forgettable personality."

"Sounds like the right guy. Where were we going?"

"He said he'd file a flight plan before takeoff. I usually don't do business like that, but his money was good and there was a lot of it." She seemed remarkably unconcerned about the gun, all things considered.

I looked at one of the planes. "What's the range on these?"

"Full tank, I could take you as far as the Keys."

"Florida?"

"Yes, those Keys."

"How about Seattle?"

"Maybe halfway with a tailwind."

So, provided Grindel was my man—and he was still in the Seattle area— John had planned a multi-leg trip. He'd probably lined up two or three private flights through other charter companies so no one pilot would know he'd begun the day in Jersey. That's what I would do.

"Did he pay in advance?"

"Sure did."

"How bright of you," I said.

"I like to think so."

I slipped the gun back into the bag. "As it turns out, I may just need an airplane."

Patti looked at me skeptically. "Drugs?"

"What?" Was she offering me some?

"Is this about drugs?"

"Ah. No."

"Are we doing something illegal, illicit, or otherwise immoral?"

"No, no, and I don't think so."

"Yet, if I drove a few hundred yards that way I would find what? A dead guy in a wrecked car?"

"You just might, yes."

"Care to explain that?"

"I'd love to," I said, "but I honestly think I don't have the time right now."

She stared at me for several seconds, until it felt like she was the one with the gun. Finally, she said, "Okay, so where are we going?"

"I'm not sure yet. I could use about an hour. I have my own phone."

~

Safely tucked in the corner of Patti's office—away from the window and in front of the space heater—I reached into my bag and pulled out the one-button mystery phone.

The display on it read "EN RTE."

It occurred to me that Robert Grindel—or whoever would be on the other end of the phone when I used it—had done something extremely foolish. He'd taken the simple task of picking me up and having me delivered, and turned it into a contest. All the soldiers-of-fortune that had come after me had been working independent of one another and, more to the point, against one another. It was like a Bruce Lee movie, where everyone attacked two or three at a time instead of just bum rushing the guy. And Bruce always came out on top. (When I watch his movies, I wonder what Bruce would have done if he'd faced a Mongol horde. Those guys knew how to use overwhelming force.)

I checked outside the window. Patti was busy prepping the airplane and had not yet done something unpleasant like contacting the police, so far as I could tell. I could have made her stay in the office where I could keep an eye on her, but something made me think she was trustworthy. Don't know what, but then I never do. She just didn't seem like the type. Also, given the circumstances, it must have made more sense to her to be able to claim she was in the air when the man on her private road turned up with a broken neck.

Enough stalling. I flipped open the phone and hit the button.

The phone didn't ring. Instead I was treated to about ten seconds of white noise, followed by a recording of a woman's voice telling me to "please stand by" followed by another ten seconds of white noise. I remembered how impressed Tchekhy was when he looked at the device and how I'd been told it was a satellite phone, and that it was probably an encrypted one. I had to remember to send it to Tchekhy when I was done so he could check out the insides. He'd probably accept that as full payment for services rendered.

Finally a man answered.

"Hello, Adam," he said. "Or is that not what you're calling yourself now?"

"That'll do," I said. I shouldn't have been surprised he knew who was on the other end of the line, but I was. "And you must be Robert Grindel."

There was a slight delay on his end of the call.

"Touché," he said. "How is the man I assigned to bring you here?"

"Dead. Sorry about that."

"Well," he said. "One in Boston, four in Central Park—plus the one you crippled—and now this. You're leaving quite a trail of bodies behind you, Adam."

You ever talk to someone and think, his voice just isn't that deep? That was the impression Robert Grindel was giving me.

"Whose fault is that?" I asked.

"Mine, I suppose. Can't guarantee law enforcement will see it that way. Should I call them? Tell them who they should be looking for?"

"You wouldn't do that, Robert."

"No. I guess I wouldn't. Killing the demon was particularly impressive. He's been quite a mystery for the local coroner."

"Has he?"

"Oh, yes. I've been reading their files. Nobody protects anything properly any more, you know. The lack of security is really amazing. They say half his body had disintegrated before it even reached their office, and the entire thing dissolved completely overnight. I don't know about you, but I find that fascinating."

Actually, it was sort of fascinating. The idea that demons had a self-destruct mechanism would explain how a creature that large could go virtually unnoticed by the modern scientific community.

"What do you want, Robert?" I asked, getting back to the point. "Why have you been doing this?"

He laughed, temporarily straying into a more natural higher octave. "I want you to come visit me."

"And this is how you go about asking?"

"I couldn't have you saying no," he said.

"I might not have."

"Your instinct is to run, Adam. I think that's been firmly established. Look at what you did to my man in Boston before you even understood what was happening."

"I suppose you read that report, too?"

"I did. And I understand. I really do. Underneath that veneer of modern sophistication, you are still the feral ape man lashing out instinctively when cornered."

"Gosh, you make it sound so romantic."

"It is," he said, sounding genuinely impressed. "Your brutality is a marvel. It's one of the things I admire about you."

Zeus, was he going to ask me out on a date, or what? "Look, Robert, let's skip ahead. Is the girl with you?"

"Not yet, but I expect her here very soon. I look forward to meeting her."

"Great," I said. "Listen, I probably don't need to tell you this, but if you hurt her you're going to get an up-close look at that brutality thing you find so marvelous."

"Of course. But I highly recommend haste on your part. I can't guarantee her safety forever."

"Two days," I said. "And you'd better call off your hunters. I'm coming in on my own."

"I'm glad. Once you're here I'm sure you'll appreciate what I'm trying to accomplish."

I didn't think so. I was planning on going in, getting the girl, and leaving. "What might that be?"

"Something historic. But I can't go into details now. You understand. Now, let me give you the coordinates."

He dictated a series of numbers to me, which I dutifully wrote down despite not having a clear idea what they meant. He assured me anyone with a basic understanding of navigation could figure them out, but was kind enough to give me a hint. It was somewhere in Arizona. Guess he'd left Seattle.

"Don't be late," he recommended before hanging up. "I don't want to hurt her, but... you understand my position."

I hung up by pressing the button a second time. As soon as the call was disconnected the digital display blinked out. The phone was a one-use-only device, as I'd thought. Which was okay, because I really didn't relish another conversation with Mr. Grindel. But I had two days to worry about that.

Tossing the device back into my bag, I retrieved the cell phone I'd taken from John in the minivan. I checked my watch. It was six in the evening in Zurich. They'd take my call anyway. Money buys lots of things.

CHAPTER 23

The first thing Patti did, when I handed her the coordinates, was check her map and confirm.

"There's no airfield at that location."

"It's in Arizona somewhere," I offered helpfully.

"I know it's in Arizona. It's probably a dried lake bed or something. Not my point."

She sat down and made a few calculations and then a few phone calls, and in another twenty minutes, she had the itinerary planned out. Patti seemed very competent, which was good. I always look for competence in someone who's going to be flying me somewhere. I'm still pretty sure man was not meant to fly, so the confidence that the person doing that flying is not also a raving nut job helps me cope. I knew more than a couple of self-professed geniuses in my day who managed to turn glue and some bird feathers into inadvertent suicide.

The problem with the lack of an airport, as Patti explained shortly after takeoff, was refueling. If she wasn't landing on an airstrip she needed to get to the coordinates with enough fuel to cover a trip to the nearest one. "It changes the dynamics of the flight plan a bit."

It turns out it doesn't take all that long to make it across the United States. This is one of those things I still can't quite get used to. For most of my life, distances were calculated by how long it took to walk from one place to the next. Then it was how long a good horse could take you in a day. Now it's motorized vehicles and planes, and I've only had a century to adjust. Flying in general doesn't bother me so much—as long as I don't think about it all too long—because it's conceptually so far removed from any other experience that I have nothing to compare it to. It's the efficiency that messes me up.

As Patti pointed out when handing me the itinerary, she could have drawn up a plan to get us there in under a day if I wanted. I didn't, mainly because as expected, the cell phone I was using couldn't pick up a signal at thirty-thousand feet. And I had a follow-up phone call or two to place.

~

We made small talk for most of the flight. Patti was decidedly professional about the whole thing, not once bringing up the gun in my bag or her suspicion that whatever I was involved in, it was in all likelihood illegal.

Instead, we talked about Patti and her sordid love life. The bulk of her tale lasted about three hours and took us through two states. Which was plenty of time to learn more than anybody who isn't a priest or a lover should have any right to know about another person. The good news was I hardly had to talk at all. Sure, I could have volunteered something to the conversation—I have learned enough to know that when a woman talks, one should at least nod and grunt appreciatively from time to time—but once she got into a rhythm there was no stopping her.

"Oh, listen to me!" she said finally, shortly after the amusing tale of Dan, the garbage man who liked to dress in a tutu at night.

"I've been doing all the talking. Sorry, it's a nervous thing. I talk a lot when I'm nervous."

"I make you nervous?"

"Not you exactly, no," she said, without elaboration. She meant the gun. "So what's your story?"

"You don't really want to know, do you?"

She glanced over at me.

"Kinda," she said. "You just don't seem the type."

"The type for what?"

"To be involved in ... whatever. Crime, I guess. There's a big black cloud of trouble around your head."

"You reading my aura now?"

She smiled. "Pilots know clouds."

I laughed. "How does a person who is, as you say, involved in crime, act ordinarily?"

"There's two types—nervous or way too calm. The nervous ones spend the whole time bouncing up and down and staring at shit on the dashboard and asking stupid questions. I hate that. But the calm ones are worse. They just sit there and don't move, or talk, or anything. The whole flight is one uncomfortable pause. I hate that more."

"Okay. Which category do I fit in?"

She stared at me for a five count, the way someone might if they were attempting to count your eyelashes. "Maybe neither. Except for the cloud, I'd put you somewhere between tourist and businessman," she concluded.

"Maybe that's all I am," I offered. "A businessman on vacation."

"Right," she said sarcastically.

She quieted down for a while, checking random dials or whatever one is supposed to check when one flies an airplane. She hadn't touched the stick in over an hour, which made me wonder how much pilots actually have to do to fly planes. Not like she had to swerve to avoid things. Seemed pretty easy to me.

"How old are you?" Patti asked, finally.

"Isn't that an impolite question?"

"There are no impolite questions at this altitude."

"Okay. How old do I look?"

She frowned. "You have a habit of answering questions with questions, you know that? Maybe thirty-five."

"Okay. Thirty-five, then."

"Except you don't act thirty-five, so that can't be right."

"How should I act?" I was trying not to be too forthcoming, because I'd only recently learned exactly how much trouble it caused when I was. It helped that I was currently sober, and thus less likely to run off at the mouth. Plus, this was sort of interesting.

"Oh, I know what it is!" she exclaimed. "You're a vet."

"A pet doctor?"

"Don't play dumb. What was it? Iraq?"

That was a tricky one to answer. If I said yes, we might have gotten bogged down in questions about divisions and units, and I didn't know enough about regular army to lie convincingly. And once you start talking about this stuff, you quickly find the person you're speaking to knows someone who knows someone you might have served with. But I couldn't very well tell her that the last time I fought in something that was big enough to come with a name was during the Peloponnesian War.

"What about me cries out veteran, exactly?"

"Dunno. But I know a few. There was this World War vet I used to know. He didn't give a damn about much of anything. Or maybe it was just that he knew nothing that came next would ever be quite so bad. It was a confidence thing. That's it, that's the vibe I'm getting."

I decided it was time to cut off the conversation entirely. Either that or start talking about the Greeks.

"You're wrong," I said curtly. "I never fought in a war."

"Oh," she said. "Okay."

And then we settled into one of those uncomfortable silences she had been talking about earlier.

~

Patti set us up at a hotel near the airfield after the first leg of the trip. Separate rooms, of course. As soon as I was alone, I arranged a call to Switzerland.

As you may have already guessed, I'm sort of terrible about money. I can never really keep decent track of what is, and isn't, a lot of it, which is just not my fault. Seriously, I remember when I could buy a horse with what a loaf of bread costs now. So when I first called the Swiss bank from Clara's apartment and gave them the necessary account information, I learned two things. The first was I now had my own private banker, Heintz, whose only job was to kiss up to me. This was because of the second thing: the exact balance in my account. Heintz had to read it to me five times because I'd never heard a number that large before, and I frankly didn't know what to make of it. "That's a lot, isn't it?" was about all I could say.

So the money was nice, but far more important was what that money got me, i.e., a Swiss banker who wanted to keep me happy at all times. Which was why I felt comfortable having him look into Robert Grindel's finances.

What I learned on my follow-up call from the hotel room was that Clara and I had been correct about at least one thing. Grindel was indeed swimming in venture capital money.

The question was, what was Grindel offering his current investors? Heintz's best guess put the project somewhere in the field of medicine, based mainly on the types of projects these investors had previously shown interest in.

"For us to learn more, we must first show an active interest in investing," he said. "Would you like for me to make the necessary arrangements?"

If I were at that moment sitting on a beach in Fiji, I'd have said yes. But as I was about to get the answers I needed on my own, it seemed superfluous. Plus, this was in all likelihood the last chance I would have to speak to Heintz for some time.

"Put out some feelers," I said. "Mostly I'm interested in how one gets this sort of money from these sorts of people. How fluid is the situation?"

"I am not sure I understand."

"I assume one has to provide the investors with solid evidence that one's project is worth investing into. How much proof? And what would constitute a breach of contract? What would make the investors decide to ask for their money back?"

"Ah," he said. "That varies wildly from circumstance to circumstance. Mostly, it is up to each venture capitalist as regards their personal comfort level in the arena of standards of proof. A person who has shown past success in a particular avenue, and who has a new idea that merely looks good on paper, can do quite well. For others, a prototype, or an experiment proving the viability of a theory. It depends on the hypothetical product. And again, on how stringent the investor's vetting procedures are."

"And breach of contract?"

"That would take quite a lot. One would need to prove not only did the concept that initially warranted the investment fail to bear fruit, but the party which proposed it was consciously aware the product would not succeed. This is exceedingly difficult to prove. Investors are notoriously skittish for just this reason. Most arrangements involve a gradual influx of funding contingent upon pre-established goals being met along the way. Using this Mr. Grindel as an example, he could have his funding cut quite suddenly from one or all of the investors if at one point he failed to deliver an aspect of the project as promised."

"All right," I said. "I think I understand. Now let me ask you something, Heintz, understanding first that this is an entirely hypothetical question."

"Of course."

"Let's just say I wanted to destroy Robert Grindel, immediately. Can this be done?"

"Do you intend 'destroy' to mean financially or some other way?" His tone didn't change in the slightest, even when discussing what had to be an allusion to murder. I so very liked this whole personal Swiss banker thing. I made a mental note to pay more attention to my money in the future.

"I mean financially," I said. "Is he vulnerable?"

"Most assuredly. Any time the bulk of one's finances comes from a source outside of one's own fortune, one is vulnerable. Immediacy is another matter."

"I was afraid you were going to say that."

"Things do not happen quickly in high finance," he said. Heintz had very rapidly come to grips with my naïveté. Actually, given that according to my account I was roughly a hundred-and-forty-seven years old, he'd come to grips with a large number of seemingly impossible things already, so my lack of financial acumen was probably comparatively minor. He continued, "Even were I to devise a way to cut off all of his funding today, in all likelihood he would have access to several months of advanced funds. And it would take years for the investors to successfully reclaim their initial investments, if at all."

"Even in a case of fraud?"

"At this level, that word is effectively meaningless. And realistically, the worst I could do was inspire his investors to apply a more hands-on approach to his project. Enforce timetables, that sort of thing. It would be a nuisance, but that's all it would be, provided he has a viable product."

"And we can't find out what that product is," I reiterated.

"Not without some time."

I would have told him I just wanted some idea of what I was walking into, but that might have welcomed more questions than I needed to answer. Instead, I left him to make his inquiries. If I survived the experience, it might be worth understanding the finances behind this whole mess.

~

The second leg of our journey was much shorter, and took us to within fifty miles of the designated landing site. It was there that Patti topped off her gas tank for what would be a very quick round trip into the veritable middle of nowhere.

"Here," I said, as she climbed back into the pilot's seat and started up the engine. I was handing her a wad of cash.

"What's that, a tip?" she said. "I've already been paid."

"It's a little extra. For your discretion."

She shrugged it off. "Give it to me when we get there."

"Take it now," I urged. "When we land, I want you to slow down enough to let me off and then get out of there."

"Seriously?"

"I'm very serious. I don't want them to see you. If it's at all possible, I want you to pick a landing point at least a quarter mile off target. I'll walk the rest of the way."

"Why is this, again?"

"If someone sees the tail numbers on your plane they can trace it back to you, right?"

"Yeah, of course."

"Well, let's make sure nobody can do that, shall we?"

She fixed me with a quizzical look but didn't pursue the point any further. And maybe I was being unduly paranoid but, as I've said, sometimes paranoia is worth the trouble. It got me through most of the fifteenth century.

We covered the last leg in under an hour. As requested, she put us down a good distance from the meeting point.

"Here we are," she said, as we rolled to a stop.

"You do fine work," I said, unbuckling myself.

"I know. Hey, tell me something, before you go."

"If I can."

"How much trouble are you in?"

I smiled. "I don't really know yet."

"Whatever this is about, I hope it goes well for you."

We shook hands.

"Believe it or not," I said, "it's about a girl."

"That figures," she rolled her eyes. "Be careful."

I slammed the door to the plane and watched until she successfully reached altitude. Then I pointed myself in the right direction and started walking.

CHAPTER 24

It was a shock to go from a snowy day in the middle of New Jersey, to a hot salt flat in the heart of Arizona, in just under two days. And I was wearing equal-opportunity clothing, in the sense that it wasn't appropriate for either climate. Especially my shoes, which might have made sense in a mall or an office building. A desert? Not so much.

But I didn't have far to go. There was some risk I'd start walking in the wrong direction—a fairly common occurrence in deserts, if memory served—but I was aided greatly by the occasional reflection I saw on the horizon. Somebody out there was watching me through a pair of binoculars. I headed toward them.

I'm not a huge fan of deserts. They're hell for my memory, for one thing, because I'm just old enough to remember when a couple of the smaller ones were bodies of water. And there's nothing more upsetting than to think you're about to come up on a nice cool lake, only to discover that the beach has taken over the place. Historically, I tended to stick to the more fertile regions—coastlines and the like—with Egypt being a notable exception. There are lots of ways to end up dead while living near the sea, but at least then it takes an exceptional event (volcanoes, floods, severe storms) to do it. In a desert, surviving the day is the exceptional event.

The ground was reasonably hard—good for walking—but entirely flat, so it never felt like I was making any progress at all, right up until I was close enough to see who was waiting for me. Two men standing next to a Humvee. At first, I thought the clothes they wore were army-issue gear, which introduced a whole slew of problems. I knew Grindel had private financial backers, but if one of those backers was the United States Government, I was in serious trouble. Because no matter how powerful a person or company in the private sector might be, they're still limited—theoretically—by laws. Governments don't have that kind of problem.

But, they weren't army-issue at all, as I realized when I got closer. No insignias of any kind. It was more like hunting gear, or an outfit you'd find for sale in the back of *Soldier of Fortune*.

Both were armed and made no effort to disguise this. The guns weren't army-issue either.

"Hello, boys," I said, once in earshot. The first one—a squat, deeply tanned man with an entire can of chewing tobacco in his cheek and a set of binoculars around his neck—had the business end of what looked to be a fully automatic Uzi pointed at my chest. I added, "I know I don't really keep up with all the gun laws, but aren't those things illegal?"

The other guy was a tall, rail-thin black man who appeared much more relaxed in demeanor than his counterpart. I got the idea that he was in charge. He was holding a handgun at rest at his side. In his other hand he had a radio.

"State your name," the tall one barked.

"Adam," I said. "Mr. Grindel is expecting me."

He nodded. "Delivery confirmed," he said into the radio.

"Why'd you walk?" the short one asked.

"Seemed like a nice day for one," I said. "Got any water?"

He glanced at the guy with the radio—definitely confirming

for me who was in charge—and, gaining assent, pulled a bottle of Poland Springs from his back pocket. He tossed it to me.

I drank the whole thing in a few seconds. Never ever take clean water for granted. Just trust me on this.

I tossed the empty back to him, which he swatted away. Litterer.

"Please tell me that thing behind you has air conditioning."

He spat some black spittle on the ground and stepped aside, pulling open the back door. "Get in," he said, a trail of spit still on his lip, which was moderately disgusting.

The tall one hooked the radio to his belt. "Come on, we're on a schedule."

I stepped to the open door and prepared to climb in.

"Bag," the one with the Uzi and the spittle said.

"What?"

"Hand over the bag."

I did. He tossed it over his shoulder to the second man, who zipped it open.

"Wow," he said. "You got a lot of cash in here, pal."

"I'm not big on credit."

Tall black guy fished the gun from the bag. He fixed me with an arch look and then tossed the gun as far away from the Humvee as he could. He did the same with the tape recorder and the cell phone—I had mailed Grindel's no-longer-utile phone, along with dead John's unused one, to Tchekhy from the motel the night before—and then shoved the bag into the front seat through the open window.

"You won't need the money where you're going," he said, "so we'll be hanging onto it for you."

"Can I get a receipt?"

Shorty shoved the barrel of his gun into my ribs. "Shut up and get in."

I was going to do just that, largely because I wanted to get out of the sun.

But then another option occurred to me.

"Hey," I said, "you know what I just realized?" I slammed the door. "You guys can't shoot me."

With my right hand I pushed the barrel of the Uzi into the side of the Humvee, spun around and swung my left elbow into tobacco boy's ear. He got two impacts for one when the other side of his head hit the roof of the truck. He sagged to the ground. His partner, rather than fire on me, did just about what I was expecting him to do: he tried to club me with the gun. If he was smart about it, he would have tried to wound me with a shot to the leg or something, but no doubt his orders specifically forbade such an act. I ducked his swing, and he hit the car instead. So far the Humvee was getting the worst end of this deal.

I jabbed my fingers into his solar plexus, which effectively reduced the amount of oxygen he had to work with to zero. Then it was just a matter of pinching the right spot on his wrist to get him to release the handgun. I spun him around, wrapped my arm around his neck, and shoved the barrel of the gun into his ear.

"The radio," I said. "Toss it to the ground."

Still gasping unpleasantly for air to the extent he was having trouble standing up straight, he fumbled about until the radio was freed. It landed a few feet from the front tire. I fired a bullet into it. He flinched just a bit with the report, as he should have.

"Does he have one?" I asked, meaning the unconscious guy at his feet.

He nodded.

"Get it."

I released him so he could pat down his partner and unearth the second radio. He held it up.

"Put it on the ground and stomp on it," I said

"They're expecting us to radio in on the way."

"No, they aren't. You already told them you were en route, and we can't be that far. Now destroy it. I don't want your buddy to wake up and tip off anybody."

He complied, reluctantly.

"Now what?" he asked. "You gonna drive there yourself?"

"No," I said. "You're driving. But first, why don't you bend down and get that Uzi for me?"

~

The Humvee was indeed air conditioned, which was a truly marvelous thing. Would that someone had invented it earlier. Khufu would have never left the palace if it had central air, probably. I certainly wouldn't have.

I sat in the back and kept the Uzi pointed at the driver's seat while my tall friend drove us to wherever the hell it was we were going.

"I don't see the point in this," he said calmly as he steered. He had decided I wasn't planning to shoot him, which was approximately true for the moment. "You're going to end up in the same place either way."

"True, but I always like to be the one holding the gun. I'm quirky like that. So what are you, a merc?"

"Private security detail," he said. "We guard the whole compound."

"You don't strike me as a security guard."

"It's a pretty high-end company," he said. "We do a lot of overseas work. Middle East, mainly."

"Hence the hardware."

"Yeah. First job I've been on where everybody spoke English."

"Tell me about the compound."

He smiled and rubbed the back of his neck. The gesture said, *oops, did I say compound?* "It's an old army base."

"Uh-huh. And what goes on there?"

"I dunno."

"Excuse me?"

I poked his lower back through the seat. This did almost no

good at all, as it appeared the back of his chair had some metal in it. I would have to remember that in the event I needed to actually shoot him.

"Seriously," he said. "I'm pretty new to this assignment."

"All right, what do you *think* is going on there?"

He hesitated briefly, working out whether there was any point in being unhelpful. "I think it's a laboratory. But everyone involved is very Manhattan Project about it. I honestly couldn't tell you what they're working on."

He shot a look back at me. "Do you know?"

I wondered if this was what all the security team members did with their free time—sit around and guess what they were guarding.

"Would I be asking if I did?"

"I figured ... I don't know what your deal is with all of this, man. All we were told was to pick up a hostile. But I didn't see anybody holding a gun to you when you walked up."

"Do I seem hostile now?"

"Hey, I guess you have your reasons."

We'd been driving along the salt flats for a good twenty minutes. Up ahead I could see the beginnings of an actual hill.

"Seen anybody else lately?" I asked. "New people brought into the place in the past day or two?"

"Yeah. Early this morning. They brought in some woman by helicopter."

"Cute?"

"Didn't see her myself. Guy who told me about it seemed to think so, but you spend enough time out here and that could mean anything. Male-female ratio's about forty to one. Couple a cooks, that's it. And they're old."

We drove around the hill. Up ahead, surrounded by a tall fence, was our destination.

Considering the whole place was in the middle of a mess of nothing, the fence seemed superfluous, unless it was designed more to keep people in, than keep people out. To that extent, it did have a sort of prison-like feel to it. I could only see a couple of buildings past the entrance and a small guard booth at the gate. The buildings looked like old Quonset huts that had arrived straight from a black-and-white war movie.

"Just how old is this base?" I asked.

"Real old."

"And you all stay here 24-7?"

"There's a barracks building up and to the right. It sleeps a lot more than what we have, but that's where we've been staying. The mess is there, too."

"What about the other buildings?"

"On the perimeter, not much else is in use. And we mostly stick to the perimeter."

"There's no security in the middle?"

"I didn't say that. We just don't cover that territory."

The guard at the gate opened the tollbooth arm and waved us through. We were most definitely expected. He didn't seem to notice we were short a passenger.

From the gate, the driver took a left on a well-defined road that skirted along the outside of the compound. To our right it was nothing but one drab, one-story gray building after another. This was clearly a place designed by someone from the Army Corps of Engineers.

"So, these are what, more barracks?"

"Some. We just passed the officers' club. Not in use."

"And you've been here how long?"

"Personally? Only four months. Guess the contract is older."

"How old?"

"Three years or so."

That was curious. The way I had it figured, Grindel had only been actively looking for me for about six months. Whatever this project was, he didn't need me for the first thirty months of it.

The driver slowed and took a right, and then we were negotiating our way between two of the similar huts. Ahead, a lone individual was standing there, waiting for us. He was wearing a three-piece suit and sunglasses and did not strike me as all that physically imposing in general. But he did look like he was born to wear the suit. It had to be Robert Grindel.

"Here we are," the man behind the wheel announced, coming to a stop a few feet from Grindel and turning off the engine. "Now what?"

"Now I pick up the lady you described and get the hell out of here," I said, adding, "you've been very forthcoming. I appreciate that."

"No problem. It's not the first time I've been in a hostage situation. I find it's best to just answer the questions."

"Good advice. Now I'd like to get out of this car without having to shoot you, seeing as you've been so nice about everything so far. We're going to get out of our respective doors on the count of three, and if you do anything stupid I'm going to cut you in half. Got that?"

He nodded.

"Leave the keys in the ignition. We go on three."

I counted to three and the two of us slid smoothly out of the Humvee with nary a bump. He really *had* done this before.

I shut my door and pressed the Uzi into his side.

"Adam!" the man in the suit said. "Glad you could make it. I'm Robert Grindel."

"I gathered." After three steps toward him, I pushed the driver to the ground and drew the handgun from where it was stuffed in my belt. I pointed it at Grindel. The Uzi I kept trained on the driver, who wisely stayed down on his knees.

Grindel's expression clouded, but he stood his ground.

"There's no need for that," he said, in a tsk-tsk sort of voice one reserves for children.

"Sure there is," I said. "What did you think, we'd have a nice chat? I'm here for the girl and then I'm leaving."

"Oh, I don't think so," he said, smiling. There was something particular about him that bothered me, and it was around then that I realized exactly what it was.

"We've met before," I said.

"Very good," he said. "I looked more classically nerdish back then. And you were a drunk who spent the evening talking about immortality. I didn't take you seriously, not until much later when I discovered such a thing as yourself was theoretically possible. And here we are."

Inwardly I was kicking myself. All this time wondering who told this guy about me and all I had to do was look in the mirror.

"Have you read any of the speculative work of Doctor Viktor Kopalev?" Grindel asked. "It's very enlightening."

"I'm not much for scientific papers,."

"Ah. Well, you'll meet him soon enough. He'll tell you all about it. *Fascinating* stuff."

"Where's Clara?" I asked by way of changing the subject.

"Safe."

I stepped closer. He still didn't appear particularly concerned.

"Get her," I demanded.

"Adam, look around you. Did you think I didn't know you were capable of overpowering a two-man security detail?"

I chanced a few sidelong glances and realized that, yes, I'd misjudged the situation rather seriously. What had been a big empty clearing a minute earlier was now a perimeter of armed men. They must have been in the buildings when we drove up.

"They can't stop me from killing you," I insisted. "And I'm pretty sure they're not going to kill me."

"Why not?"

"The bounty hunters were told to take me alive, and so were the men you sent for me just now. Whatever you need me to do, I'm of no use dead."

"That's true. But if I'm dead… that's a different situation, isn't it?" He smiled. "You can't kill me without killing yourself. I'd call this a stalemate."

"You'd make a decent hostage," I said. "Now once again. Where is Clara?"

He sighed heavily. "You seem to be under a certain misapprehension. Ms. Wassermann isn't here as a prisoner. She's a volunteer."

I blinked about six times. When you're holding two guns and watching a closing circle of armed men in your peripheral vision, this is about the only way to record surprise. "You're lying."

"I'm not. She contacted me shortly after you left. I guess the reward money was too much to pass up. She's a few buildings behind me, having a nice meal and probably contemplating how to best spend it. She's even asked if she can stay on. This is an exciting project, you see. Once I explained it to her, she was quite interested."

"I don't believe you," I said, even though I sort of did.

"Why not?" he asked. "If she's the only reason you came here in the first place, why would I tell you such a thing, if it wasn't true?"

He had a point. "All right. Then you and *I* are leaving. Right now."

"Adam," he said patiently, as if I'd disappointed him terribly. "We have her here."

"Who?" I asked. "Clara? You just told me—"

"Not Clara. Can I show you something?"

"Maybe later," I said. "I'm a little pressed for time right now."

The perimeter had closed to about fifteen feet, which was really more of an intimidation thing than anything else, because if they all started firing, they'd probably shoot each other. They hadn't cut off my access to the car yet, though.

Grindel said, "I'm going to reach into my jacket pocket for a small device. Looks like a miniature television set."

"Slowly," I said.

"Of course." He slipped his left hand into his pocket and emerged with what looked to be a PDA. He held it out. "Take a look."

I dropped the Uzi to free up my hand—I only needed one hostage at this point—took the device, and looked at the image captured on the screen.

"That's a live local video feed," he said. "I know it doesn't seem like a video image, but that's only because she rarely moves."

It was the red-haired woman.

She was sitting cross-legged on the floor of a white room next to a cot, looking directly at the camera. There was no way it could have been anybody else.

Grindel said, "We have a few tests we need to run on you. That's all. And when we're done, I'll let you meet her. I know that's something you've been waiting a long time to do."

"She's here," I said dully. "She's *alive*."

I couldn't take my eyes off the screen.

"Yes, on both counts, although I'm not about to tell you precisely where. I'm sure you understand why."

I wavered. "Bring her here," I muttered. "I'll ..."

"I'm not going to do that, Adam. I was never going to give you Clara, and I'm not going to let you have your red-haired friend either. Not until after we're done." He leaned in closer, which he could do as I'd apparently lowered my gun. "A minute ago you were willing to die before surrendering. Do you still think it's worth it?"

I dropped the gun. "You win."

~

And that was my final mistake. Bob isn't going to let me walk out of here when we're done, and I don't think he's going to grant me my audience with the red-haired woman either. It's just not in his nature.

I remember reading an article about how the big drug companies don't tend to pursue experiments on herbal remedies because it's impossible to patent a substance that can be found in nature. Well, I can't be patented either. But there's only one of me, and I can be destroyed.

It's the only way he can possibly protect his investment.

PART III

FREEDOM'S JUST ANOTHER WORD

CHAPTER 25

I've been staring at a keyhole for two hours. Or maybe it only feels like two hours. I can't tell for sure, because the passage of time is one of those things I need the sun or the moon for, and I can't see either of them from where I'm sitting. A watch would do the trick but they took mine away a long time ago, which I'm convinced they did just because they knew it would annoy me. My own fault for becoming attached to the concept of time. Back in the African bush I didn't care what day it was, and the concept of seasons was fairly dim in a region where the seasonal change was minimal.

Right about now, with every day beginning and ending more or less the same way, I'm finding myself envious of that particular mindset.

Anyway, my point—two hours is probably a generous estimate. Let's just say it's been a while and move on.

The keyhole is attached to the only door to my padded cell. There is nothing extraordinary whatsoever about the room aside from the padding, the lack of a window, and the fact that I have been stuck inside of it for a long time. I've certainly checked. The most interesting thing about the room is that on the other side of the padding is a layer of concrete, which came as a surprise when I first discovered it because from the outside the standalone building looks like a basic Quonset hut with old wood plank walls and a couple of windows that didn't used to be fake. If there was only the padding and the wood planks in my way, I would have been out of here a long time ago. Clearly, Bob had the interior redone in anticipation of my arrival.

Bob's a good details man. A quick look at the outside of the second hut, which is about five feet away from mine, illustrates that point well. Unlike all the others—there are four prison huts altogether, in a row, near the center of the compound—the second hut is reinforced on the inside with steel rather than cement. Whatever's inside of it is considerably stronger than I am and would probably look longingly at a cement wall the same way I look at wood planking. It's also a whole lot stronger than Ringo, my demon guard, based on the damage it's caused from the inside. The door and all of the walls have been pounded on mercilessly, to the point where metal can be seen bursting through the wood planks, like a balloon popping out of a papier-mâché shell.

Things have been quiet in cell number two for a long time now. It's either dead or it's hoping somebody with a key comes to that conclusion and opens the door.

I'm pretty sure the red-haired woman is in hut number four, because I heard some very unladylike moaning coming from the third cell a couple of weeks ago. I never heard the red-haired woman speak, but I'm pretty positive she wouldn't sound like that if enticed to moan. She seems more of the mezzo-soprano type and this was something of an alto. An alto being castrated, maybe. God only knows what actually made that noise.

I am trying to get used to calling her Eve. That's what Viktor and the lab techs call her. It's a bit hokey, and probably only given to her because I'm going by the name of Adam—I think if I'd been using Othello they'd be calling her Desdemona—but as I'd never seen fit to assign any name to her after ten millennia, it's about time I started trying one out. Repeatedly referring to her as "the red-haired woman," after all, is a little unwieldy, and makes me sound a bit like a *Peanuts* character. (I didn't know Charles Schulz, but I like to think sometimes that Charlie Brown's obsession with the red-haired little girl was the universe's homage to me personally.)

These are the things I think about when I have nothing else to do outside of staring at keyholes. And I've had nothing else to do for some time now. Aside from the daily trips to the lab. Those barely count.

~

Underneath me, between the cot mattress and the springs, is a folded up sheet of onion paper, and on the sheet of onion paper, drawn in black magic marker, is a scale map of the entire compound. I could stare at the map instead of the keyhole, except that the map is the closest thing I've had to reading material this whole time. I have thus committed it to memory several times over and am prepared to argue that the keyhole is more interesting.

I have by now translated the contents of the map into a mental three-dimensional construct that I think is accurate enough to bet my life on, which is exactly what I'll be doing, provided something exciting happens involving the keyhole somewhat soon.

Just by counting paces, I could navigate the whole compound with my eyes closed. It's exactly ninety-seven paces from the door of my cell to the door of the lab. I verify that every day. (It's also either sixty-three or sixty-five demon paces, depending on Ringo's mood. Not relevant, but collecting useless data is a good way to pass the time, so there you go.) Knowing the paces between two points on the map, I was able to extrapolate distances to other buildings fairly easily, even though I've never been to any of them.

The administrative building, for example. Never been there. Hope to soon. It's across the way from the laboratory and it's where Bob Grindel works. He's got an office right above the central awning that covers the front door. Nice big picture window and everything. I look up every day and stare at that window, and even though nine times out of ten the sunrise makes it impossible to look through the glass—the admin building faces east and we're in Arizona, which has so much sun I'm starting to miss New England—I've been able to get a couple of glimpses of him looking down at me. Even flipped him the finger once. Didn't change my situation at all, except that it made me feel better.

I haven't had many chances to talk to Bob. He stopped by a couple of times to talk about how he's going to be setting me free just as soon as Viktor is done in the lab. On neither occasion did I have an opportunity to do much more than sneer and try out a few old insults in some dead languages. This is mainly because Bob tends to travel around with Brutus, the other demon of the inner compound. Brutus and Ringo constitute the only security in the inner circle of buildings, which is pretty much exactly how my security force hostage described it when I first arrived. The human security—there are about twenty-five of them, if Clara's count is accurate—cover the perimeter, the demons roam the center, and ne'er the twain shall meet. That may be because Bob doesn't want any of the guards to see a demon, and to thus declare loudly, "sweet Jesus, what is that thing?" as this can be awkward. More likely, Bob doesn't want any humans to notice he's keeping prisoners, as this is generally considered illegal if one is not an actual government. And sometimes not even then.

Speaking of Clara, I'm still not sure what to do about her. She did smuggle Iza into the place, for which I'm enormously grateful. That she even knew Iza existed meant she eavesdropped on me while I was on the roof of her building, but that's a minor indiscretion, all things considered. Far more serious is the fact that I probably wouldn't be sitting in this cell staring at a keyhole if Clara hadn't tricked me into rescuing her in the first place. So I don't know why she sent me Iza, or drew the map (which Iza carried in, hence the onion sheet) or gave me all the information about the size of the security force. I don't like trusting someone only because I have nobody else around to trust.

It is only with great trepidation that I've been slipping back out to Clara a few of the details of my escape plan. I need her to help secure transportation and a few other things, because while Iza can find me a Humvee, she can't drive one. Once I'm out, speed will be an issue, as the less time I spend out in the open, the better my chances are. Not that my chances are at all good either way.

The plan, incidentally, is incredibly stupid, and it's very probably going to end up getting me killed. But it's the best one I can come up with. And when I'm not kicking myself for being unable to think up a better one, I'm blaming Viktor for not listening to me.

~

Doctor Viktor Kopalev is hypothetically just as responsible for my situation as Bob Grindel, because the original idea was Viktor's. All Bob knows is computers and money, and is apparently nearly as clueless as I am when it comes to biology. But he knows a good idea when he sees it.

I guess a few years back he caught a whiff of some of the work Viktor had been doing in immune system research and the seemingly unrelated field of human aging. At the time, that work was ninety percent speculative, because Viktor didn't know I existed. That, and a killer business plan, is what Bob brought to the table. So while Bob secured investors—and test subjects— Viktor put together the team and supervised the building of the laboratory. All the science, basically. And he didn't once stop to wonder whether he should.

And then they nabbed Eve. I never asked—none of the lab boys have been willing to talk about Eve, other than to comment that she hardly speaks—but I'm guessing they were looking for both of us from the outset and found her first. I don't know how they did that. But I stopped looking after becoming erroneously convinced she was dead. Maybe it wasn't that hard. A good deal more difficult, I'm sure, was catching the thing in cell number two. Difficult to know when—or how—they did that.

At some point Viktor and his team realized they needed more than just Eve to complete the project. As they're on something of a timetable, Bob redoubled his efforts to catch me. Ergo, bounty hunters and demons and hostages and so on.

As to the project itself, based on the amount of research that would have had to continue well after the death of Viktor Kopalev—had Eve and I never existed—I'd say it's about a hundred years before its time. Sometimes that's a good thing. This isn't one of those times.

I've seen lots of big ideas come and go. As a rule, they tend to arrive at, or just before, the world is ready for them. Take something really simple, like the wheel. The first version of the wheel I ever saw was a part of a child's wooden toy, and I didn't see another one for about fifty years when somebody got the splendid idea to put a couple of them under a wood platform and have an ox pull it. We could have probably come up with the wheel hundreds of years before then but we didn't need to, because we had no domesticated animals, and as foragers, we didn't have any need to transport things from place to place. We just ate whatever we could find, wherever we could find it, just as soon as it was found. Much like fast food. So it wasn't that mankind was too stupid to come up with a concept as significant as the wheel before a certain time. We invented it when there was a practical need for it.

In this case, the wheel is my immune system, which is where the whole analogy sort of breaks down, making me think I should have come up with a better one. Anyway, Viktor and his team have figured out how to give my immune reaction to other people. As he described it, it was just a matter of turning on the right gene sequence in a normal human's body. Finding the gene was the easy part, because they have two living samples to work from. Much harder was figuring out how to get it turned on throughout the whole body. They haven't said so, but I think that's what the monster in the second cell is for.

Harder still was determining how to grant immortality. That's where those damned telomeres Viktor keeps talking about come in. I've absolutely no idea what the science behind this part is because I zoned out whenever he tried to explain. Suffice to say it's complicated, and it involves several courses of treatment and something called "gene therapy." It's much more difficult to accomplish than the immunity treatment, which I'm told can be distributed in the same manner as your standard vaccine.

So to return to the wheel comparison, say the child's toy version of the wheel had the power to destroy the world as we know it. Now you see what I mean about a bad analogy.

Try instead to imagine what it would be like if you could go back in time and give the entire Confederate Army a supply of fully automatic machine guns and all the ammo they would ever need. That's a bit closer to what I'm talking about. Basically, there is a time for everything, and now is not the right time for what Viktor and his team have concocted.

I've told Viktor this more times and in more ways than you can possibly imagine, with no luck whatsoever. He's been focusing on the whole "nobody ever gets sick any more, ever" aspect, which I admit sounds pretty good, up until half the population starves.

That's assuming everybody gets a dose, which isn't how it's going to happen. Bob is a capitalist, not a humanitarian. He won't be giving this away. He'll find the highest bidder, sell out and move on, just like with every other business deal he's ever cut. Then comes the unappetizing prospect of an immunized population coming up against a non-immunized population, and now you're looking in the dictionary for a word that means "something worse than genocide."

Throw into that the unfortunate possibility that the very richest among us—the ones who can afford the special gene therapy treatment—also never happen to die. As I've said before, death is just about the only constant in my immortal life, and while I might complain about it from time to time, I think that happens to be a pretty good arrangement. Because whether you're a Hitler or an Alexander, eventually the universe will do away with you just as it did for Jesus and Gandhi. Death is the great leveler.

Maybe I'm being selfish about my own personal immortality. Maybe I just don't want to share it. But I also haven't abused it—much—and I certainly haven't done any world conquering and mass slaughtering. I frankly don't think enough of my fellow man to believe others, when handed the same gifts, will act as wisely.

So, where Viktor—who is the worst kind of idealist—sees a future with less pain and suffering, I see only chaos and class warfare and murder and war. He calls me a pessimist and maybe he's right. But assuming the worst of people has gotten me pretty far.

Since I've failed to convince him that he's managed to create the worst kind of weapon, I'm going to have to deal with the problem directly. Provided I ever get out of my cell.

~

Which brings me back to the keyhole. It's not your everyday keyhole, unless you happen to live every day in the nineteenth century. All the doors in the inner compound have outsized keyholes to fit the outsized keys that are currently on a large ring attached to Ringo's belt. They had to be big because demons are not known for their fine motor coordination.

This is why they typically break down doors to get through them. It's not necessarily belligerence—although one must never discount belligerence in a demon as a motivating factor—so much as that most keys are simply too small for their fingers to manipulate. I've been told some of them can't even work doorknobs.

Though unusually large, the keyholes are still entirely too small for a human to jam his finger into. (I've tried and have two formerly sprained pinky fingers to show for it.) But they're plenty big enough to accommodate a pixie's arm.

Just so you know—in case you ever want to try—it's a hell of a thing to teach a pixie how to pick a lock. It's not so much that they don't understand how locks work; it's that they don't know what locks are. They don't even have clothing, for Baal's sake. So just explaining the basic principles took a week. And without a lock for Iza to practice on—other than the one for my cell door, which I don't want her opening prematurely—I had to enlist Clara's help. Which is another thing I've relied on my Judas to do for me. No, I'm not comfortable about this at all.

I'm staring at the keyhole because any minute now Iza is going to be unlocking the door. I hope. I gave her the word that tonight is the night about two hours ago, (or however long I've been staring) and she flitted off to inform Clara that she needs to ready herself.

I did this because this afternoon on my last trip to the lab, Viktor was kind enough to inform me that the tests are over. He now has everything he needs from me and Eve to finish his work. Which means sometime in the next couple of days, Robert Grindel will be arriving to, as he once put it, "discuss compensation" for my time. I fully expect this compensation to prominently feature a bullet in the back of the head.

You may be wondering why I waited this long. If you had an escape plan that was as likely to get you killed as mine, you'd wait, too. What I've been waiting for is anybody's guess. A miracle, I suppose.

The way the plan works, Iza is supposed to wait until Ringo checks out. I had her observe the actions outside my cell for about a week and report her findings, which is how I learned I'm not being guarded a full twenty-four hours a day. Ringo goes to bed (I assume demons sleep) right around the same time the team from the lab exits for the evening, which is generally sometime after sunset.

After getting me out, Iza will open Eve's cell and then the lab, where the two of us will hide out—possibly having a decent conversation in a place where Eve can't disappear on me—while Iza completes phase two, which is the part of the plan where lots of people die. Everything after that is kind of dicey.

But first comes getting my door open. I'm beginning to worry that this isn't going to be happening.

Scratch that.

I hear a click. The lock is being manipulated. I jump to my feet and am about to cross the distance and pull open the door—Iza isn't strong enough to actually do it herself—when the door swings open on its own.

"Hello, Adam," says the figure in the door.

She steps into the light and I wonder for a second whether Iza simply misunderstood the plan. Otherwise, how could Eve be standing in front of me?

CHAPTER 26

About three seconds pass before I figure out what's actually happening. All it takes is for Bob to step out from behind Eve, revealing the handgun he's got pointed at the back of her head.

"Glad to see you're still awake," he says. "It's time we settled that matter of compensation."

Now I'm thinking I did put off the escape plan a tad too long.

~

With Bob Grindel, and his handgun, standing behind us next to the ever-present Brutus, Eve and I are marched through the compound in a direction that indicates we're heading for the outer perimeter fence.

"I did promise you'd have an opportunity to meet, Adam," Bob says, coming off as unspeakably smug. He reminds me a bit of Caligula. Not the movie, the guy. "You can't say I've been dishonest."

"No, Bob, I guess I can't."

Definitely out of the inner compound. We've already passed

two inner circle buildings that had previously only existed in the map in my head. If I have it figured right, in another fifty paces we'd be passing through the outer ring.

Just looking around, I can tell why it is Bob decided to do this tonight. It's the last night of a new moon. Visibility stinks, especially since most of the lights in the place are extremely localized, concerned primarily with keeping front stoops lit. The two exceptions are the center of the compound (the midway point between the administrative building and the lab) which is perpetually lit by spotlights atop a centrally located light stand, and the perimeter fence, which has a light stanchion every twenty yards. All provided Clara's map is accurate.

I keep glancing at Eve to my right. She's dressed in the same sort of generic white cottons I'd been handed the day I first checked in, but somehow she manages to look simply amazing in it, carrying herself with a certain grace that makes me wonder if her feet are actually touching the ground. I fall in love again five or six times.

Unfortunately, since her initial greeting, she hasn't said a word. This is not the kind of conversation I had in mind.

"She doesn't talk much," Bob says, noting my interest. "I should have mentioned that earlier."

"Maybe she just isn't interested in talking to you," I say.

Still a good distance from the fence, I manage to pick up the telltale buzzing of an adult pixie in flight. If asked to describe the noise, I'd say it falls somewhere between the sound of the wind through a pine tree and the low rasp of corduroy pant legs rubbing together. It's the sort of thing you have to know you're hearing in order to catch it, and I'm fairly confident Bob and Brutus don't. Eve does. She shoots a sidelong glance at me and I can swear I see the barest traces of a grin.

"So tell me, Bob," I say, a bit louder. "Now that you've gotten the first phase of this little project out of the way, when do you go to phase two?"

I sincerely hope Iza hears the last part of my sentence and puts it into the proper context. As pixies are not known for being able to follow conversational threads very closely, it's a good hope.

"Phase one, as you put it, isn't completed yet," Bob says. "First I have to eliminate the remaining liabilities." That means us, presumably. "This technology is very much desired by a number of multinational consortiums. I expect to do rather well for myself."

"Of course you do," I say. "And the rest of the world be damned, right?"

I can no longer hear Iza. Either she's lost interest and is now flying back to Clara, or she caught my request. I would find out soon.

"It's true that there may be some unexpected political consequences," Bob agrees. "But that's inevitable in the face of progress. Might as well do the best I can financially."

"Sure," I say. "And when one of your interested parties decides to unleash a biological weapon, you're going to say what? 'Oh well'?"

"Yes," he agrees. "That's exactly right. Now stop. This is close enough."

We had walked south, through the unused end of the camp. Human security is supposed to patrol this section, but I haven't seen anybody, so I'm guessing Grindel told them to stay away for a few hours.

He'd stopped us facing the perimeter fence, just beyond two vacant huts. At the foot of the fence a very deep hole has been dug in the sand, which must have been a challenge to accomplish given the concrete quality of the ground. Probably took Brutus all afternoon.

It's a new first for me. I've never stared into my own grave before.

"You have two minutes, Adam," Bob says.

"Excuse me?" I ask, turning.

"I'm giving you the face time you've been waiting for."

"Seriously?"

"Yes. Now quit stalling before I change my mind."

Bob takes two gracious steps backward in the interest of giving us some privacy. I'd have preferred he take forty or fifty steps, but whatever.

I look Eve in the eye, and she looks back. Which is the closest thing to a meaningful conversation we've ever had. As always, her expression reveals nothing.

"I thought you were dead," I say, after deciding she isn't going to be speaking without a prompt.

She smiles. Apparently nobody told her we're on a clock here.

"Do you have anything to say?" I ask.

She looks at me quizzically, the pale white of her skin contrasting remarkably with her red hair in the half-light.

"Why are you here?" she asks finally.

She has a musical cadence to her speech that would give a linguist fits. I recognize it as the rhythm of a language that died before the written word. I just can't quite figure out which one.

In answering, I could have explained that I'd come to save a woman I thought was in serious danger, but who turned out to have deliberately tricked me into following her—and who might even have tipped off Bob that I was planning on making a break tonight, thus putting the two of us in this position—when I should have followed my instinct and bolted, remembering that I'm *not* the hero, that the hero eventually ends up dead, and the person who put that notion in my head in the first place is the selfsame traitorous woman.

But that would take too long. Instead I say, "I'm here to rescue you."

"I see," she says. "How ironic."

"What do you mean?"

"I knew you would turn up in this place. Even against your own better judgment. It's why I chose to stay."

An alarm from the center of the camp startles us both, and more importantly, prevents me from asking just what in the hell she means. Implicit in being a prisoner is that one doesn't simply decide to stay. Unless there's a get-out-of-jail pass nobody told me about.

The alarm catches the attention of Grindel and his large demon bodyguard. Brutus looks especially tense, which isn't something you see all that often in his species.

"It's for the cage," Brutus says.

"The cage? Who could have opened that?" Grindel asks.

"I did," I say, even though nobody's talking to me.

"Really? How did you ... Never mind." He brings his handgun to bear. "Sorry, Adam. The two of you have run out of time."

Pointing his gun at my head causes the ground at his feet to erupt. It takes a second to register, but evidently somebody's shooting at him. He jumps backward, and fortunately, doesn't pull the trigger himself.

"Let her go!" someone shouts.

Clara?

Bob looks around, trying to pinpoint the source of the voice. It came from the corner window of the hut to Bob's right, but he can't seem to figure this out.

"Miss Wassermann," he shouts, turning in a slow circle, arms raised. It's an invitation to take another shot. "You shouldn't involve yourself in something you don't understand."

There's a moment when he leaves himself exposed, but Brutus steps between us before I can do anything, so I just stand still and hope Clara knows what the hell she's doing. Because when this is over I'm going to have to ask her why she's more interested in saving Eve than in saving me, and that will be a lot easier to ask if both of us are still alive.

"I understand plenty, Bob," Clara shouts back. "Now walk away."

Bob spins around and shoots three times in the direction of the voice. He had been baiting her into talking some more, which should have been obvious.

We're all treated to a lengthy silence, and for a second I worry he's gotten lucky.

"Nice try," Clara says finally. "The fuck, you think I'm stupid?"

"What are you waiting for?" I shout. "Shoot him!"

Bob stares at the side of the building he's just riddled, then declares, "She can't. She's bluffing."

He points the gun at me again, and now I'm wondering if there's any place convenient to jump. Just before he fires, say. People in the movies can dodge bullets, so why not me? I don't get a chance to ascertain the feasibility of this plan, which is good as I really don't think it'll work. A shot rings out, but again it isn't Bob shooting. And this time Clara hasn't aimed at his feet.

The bullet glances off the side of his shoulder, and the impact causes him to drop the handgun. I dive for it, snatch it up and scramble to my feet, but of the two of us, Brutus is a good deal quicker. He picks up his wounded boss, pulls him into a hug, and starts running back toward the center of the compound. I don't even get a shot off.

But Clara does. Quite a few shots. Bullets are flying all over the place and at first I'm thinking she's just shooting indiscriminately, but no. She's hitting her target. The lead is just bouncing off Brutus's tough hide.

With friendly fire all around us, I dive at Eve—who hasn't moved during any of this—and carry her into our erstwhile grave until the shooting stops.

Long silence. Except for the siren, which is still wailing away in the distance.

"Are you wounded?" I ask Eve once I'm finally certain Clara's finished.

"No," she says, adding, "please get off of me."

I pull myself out of the hole, then reach down and give her a hand out. She looks a touch perturbed by the whole thing, which just annoys me. I wasn't coming on to her. I was trying to save her life.

The alarm has been joined by the far-off reports of automatic gunfire and the occasional piercing scream. It's begun. And I'm about as far from the lab as I can be while still inside the fence. Not good.

"Okay, what the hell is going on?" Clara asks, lowering herself to the ground from the roof of the hut with what looks to be an M-16 on her back.

"Rampant chaos," I say. "And if we're lucky, it's going to get worse pretty fast. When did you learn how to throw your voice?"

She lands clumsily, then pulls herself to her feet and ambles over. I notice she's wearing the same kind of uniform the security team wore the last time I saw one of them. Not sure what's stranger, seeing her in a uniform or seeing her in any clothes at all.

"When did I what?" she asks. "Oh." She holds up a radio. "I set it to an unused frequency and put another one in the window."

"Smart girl," I admit. But Clara isn't paying attention to me any longer. She's too busy staring at Eve.

"All-mother," she says reverently.

Tchekhy's warning about militant feminists springs rather suddenly to mind. That, coupled with the realization that I'd have saved myself a bunch of trouble if I'd asked him to hack into the All-Mother website, is enough to make me nauseous.

"Child," Eve says. "Tell me you didn't come all this way ..."

"Of course. I'm here to save you."

"Uh, hello?" I interrupt. There would be time for this later. "Ladies, we're a bit exposed out here."

Clara, still entirely ignoring me, genuflects at Eve's feet. What the hell, I ask myself, is going on here?

"Oh, my dear. Get up, please," Eve says. "I didn't mean for this to happen. I was never in any real danger."

We are saved further elaboration on the matter of Eve's apparent inability to comprehend a life-threatening situation by a scream from the center of camp. A terribly loud, achingly horrible scream that one cannot help but to turn toward. Which I do.

"What was that?" Clara asks quietly, getting to her feet and looking in roughly the same direction. I think she's finally getting it through her head that we're in a spot of trouble. Plus, she's acknowledging my existence again, which is nice.

"Something I haven't heard in a very long time," I say, which is true. Not something I'm bound to forget, either. "We have to hurry. Eve, if you ..."

I trail off, as it appears Eve is no longer standing right next to me. And, when one finds out one is talking to an empty space rather than a person, one is disinclined to finish one's sentence.

"Where'd she go?" Clara asks, turning.

We're standing in an open area fifty feet from any building and with a clear view of the lit perimeter road a hundred feet in either direction. Straight ahead, the other side of the chain link fence offers a view of the desert that extends nearly that far before fading into darkness. (The fence is entirely too tall to scale anyway, and topped with barbed wire that actively discourages any bold attempts to do so.) Eve is nowhere.

I peek over the edge of the grave, but she's not in there either. And there's no way she's fast enough to have escaped from view in three seconds. Not if, as Viktor reassured me a couple of times, she and I are the same sort of being.

"Where did she go!" Clara shouts, repeating herself.

"She's just ... gone," I say, as nothing more clever is coming to mind. I find myself staring at the ground where she'd been standing a moment earlier. The imprints of her shoes are still there. It's just that Eve has ceased to occupy them.

"How?" Clara asks. She's getting a tad hysterical.

"If I knew how she did that, I'd do it myself."

"But—"

A second alarm sounds, up near the front entrance of the camp. This snaps me back into the situation like a slap across the face. There will be time later to ponder the implications of what we just witnessed, but to get to that point I'm going to have to figure out a way to survive the next few hours.

Clara's not quite there yet. "It's impossible!" she insists.

"Oh, absolutely. But we can talk about it later. Like, not when we're about to get killed. We have to get out of here. Now."

"She—"

"Clara. Now."

~

Running from building to building, we use the cover each structure provides us as well as we can. And each step that takes us closer to the center, also brings us closer to the sounds of utter mayhem. Alarms are sounding, guns are firing, people are screaming. It seems like it's happening all around us.

"Are we under attack?" Clara asks as we run.

"You could say that."

"By what?"

We reach the corner of one of the larger inner buildings. An unused physics lab. I peer around the corner to see if the center compound is occupied. It doesn't appear to be.

"What made that noise?" Clara continues. "The screaming you said you'd heard before. What was that?"

"That was the sound of a demon being eviscerated."

"Jesus."

More gunfire, to our right and pretty close. We hear a man scream before abruptly losing his voice and—based on the somewhat sickening noise that follows—his life. It's nice to imagine I'm hearing Bob Grindel being killed, but more likely it's a security team member. They're probably all over the place by now, as one's patrol assignment tends to go out the window when one is fleeing for one's life. It's another variable to consider.

"It's eating," I say, noting the sucking sounds. "Let's move. Quickly."

Taking Clara by the hand, I lead us in a sprint over the remaining distance to the center. Clara pulls free and stops when she sees the four huts.

"You had Iza open all the doors," she notes. "I didn't know you were going to do that."

"She didn't need to tell you."

"You didn't trust me?"

"Of course I didn't. Would you?"

She thinks about it. "Maybe not."

A noise, that might be described as howling on multiple frequencies, cuts through the air. It's from behind us, roughly where we heard the death of a man a minute earlier.

"It's coming," I say. And the lab's too far to reach.

I push Clara into the nearest doorway—for cell number three —and follow her in, closing the door behind us. And then we hold our breath for a thirty count.

"It's gone," Clara whispers.

"Maybe."

"So what is it?"

"It's a vampire," I say. "A very, very hungry vampire. They were keeping it in the second cell."

"There's such a thing as vampires?"

"Sure."

It takes her a couple of seconds to readjust her world view and then, "Why the hell are we headed into the middle of the compound?"

"We can't climb that fence," I say. "And even if we tried, is that where you want to be when the vampire comes by? Better to find a place to hide until it's all over."

"So ... wait. What is this room for?"

She'd taken her eyes off the door for long enough to have a look around.

I follow her gaze.

The inside of the third cell looks like the interior of an intensive care ward. (Or rather, what they look like on TV. I've never been in one.) The room is full of tubes and wires and machines for registering vital statistics. A large bed takes up the center of the room. The bed's empty.

"You've never been in here?" Clara asks.

"Nope. You?"

"No. I wonder who it was for?"

"I heard moaning coming from this cell. Maybe there was another experiment going on. One I didn't know about."

"But on who?" she reiterates.

"Dunno. They're not here now. And we both know Bob likes to destroy things when he's done with them, so ..."

We hear some more gunfire. I'm beginning to think everyone on the base is armed with an automatic weapon except for me.

"Sounds like that's a good ways off," I say. "We should try and chance it now."

"Chance what?" she asked. "We're safe here, aren't we?"

"I'd feel safer in the lab," I say. Which is sort of true, as the lab is built of sterner stuff and has a big metal door and all that. But I have another reason for wanting to get in there.

I crack open the door and do not end up savagely killed, so I try opening it wider. Still no sudden death. We step out. More screaming from somewhere to our left, and definitely not close.

"There are like forty or fifty people here," Clara notes. "Is it me, or does it sound like they're being killed one-by-one?"

"It's not just you."

I turn the corner past the row of huts and nearly trip over

what's left of Ringo. Clara nearly does the same, and then in seeing what she had avoided immediately starts screaming. I clap my hand over her mouth as quickly as I can.

"Quiet down," I whisper, "Or you'll bring it right to us."

I get a nod of understanding from her, so I pull back my hand and kneel down to examine the remains.

He came to final rest on his side, or at least the largest portion of what's left of him did. One of his arms has been torn completely off, both his legs are broken and lying at strange angles, and it appears as if several internal organs have been removed with a blunt instrument. It looks like he died in horrible pain, and for a second, I actually feel sympathetic.

I roll the torso. This causes more of the viscera to roll out onto the ground, and I hear Clara actively attempting to control her gag reflex. I also learn the answer to my own personal age-old question: demons do have hearts. I see Ringo's with my own eyes. But that's less important than what else I find—the key ring, still attached to his belt. I pick up the ring.

"Adam?" Clara says, her voice freaking out all over the place. "How ... are vampires that strong? I mean ..."

"They get stronger and faster as they get older," I say. "This one must be pretty old. Now keep your gun ready. We just need to make it to the lab."

CHAPTER 27

At a full sprint, it takes us only about thirty seconds to cross the gap to the door of the laboratory. Feels like a whole lot longer. Unsurprisingly, it's locked.

"C'mon, open it," Clara says nervously. I'm holding the key ring up in the light to see if there are any markings to help identify the correct key, but if there is an indicator, I can't see it. So I just start trying out keys. There are roughly twenty to choose from.

If things had gone according to plan, Iza would have opened the door—for me and Eve rather than me and Clara—before freeing the hungry vampire that's probably seconds away from eating us both. Iza's nowhere to be found, but at least I have the key ring. It almost balances out.

"Just shoot it open," Clara says.

"It's a steel door," I point out. "That'll waste bullets, make too much noise, and the ricochet will probably hit one of us."

"Shh! Listen." More automatic gunfire could be heard to our left. Two, maybe three different shooters.

"It's not anywhere near us," I say.

"How do you know?"

"What do you think they're shooting at?"

All the damn keys look identical. I can't even imagine how something as big and stupid as Ringo could be expected to tell them apart.

"So what's with the uniform?" I ask, as much to keep her from panicking as out of actual curiosity. Or maybe I'm trying to keep myself from panicking.

"I got it from the laundry," she says distractedly.

"How'd you pull that off?"

"Easy. I've had free run of this place since I got here."

"Yeah?" Five keys and no luck. It's going to end up being the twentieth one I try.

Clara says, "Bob was trying to get into my pants. Guess he figured that'd be easier if I didn't think of him as a complete son of a bitch. So he took pains to not treat me like a captive."

"He told me you were here because you wanted to be."

"Yeah, he told himself that, too."

"How about the gun?" I ask. "Or did you find that in the laundry also?"

"It's a loaner," she says.

"Somebody loaned you an automatic rifle?"

"You'd be surprised what a cute girl like me can get away with in a camp full of men," she says with a smile, sounding a bit more like the Clara I remember from New York.

"I knew Helen of Troy, so no, I'm not all that surprised."

Eleven. If Ringo doesn't have the key to the lab on this ring, I'm not sure what my next step is going to be. As it is, we're frighteningly exposed under the lab's door stoop light.

"They teach you to fire it, too?" I ask, regarding Clara's gun.

"I had a few lessons. Target practice out in the desert."

"They seem to have taught you well."

"Not really. I meant to kill Bob, not just wound him. Are you almost done?"

"It *has* to be one of these," I insist, more for my own benefit.

She stiffens up. "Someone's coming!" she whispers. I'm on my fifteenth key.

"Hang on ..."

She raises her gun. Out of the corner of my eye I can see the barrel shaking all over the place. We're cutting this close.

And then the lock clicks and the door opens. Seventeen turns out to be the lucky number. I grab her and pull the two of us into the antechamber.

"It's running for us!" she shouts.

We throw our combined weight on the door and spin the lock. After a good long pause in which nothing happens other than the two of us not breathing, we relax.

"You saw it?" I ask.

"I don't know," she says. "Maybe. Somebody's out there, that I'm sure of."

"This door should keep it out, until it runs out of easier victims."

"This was your plan? How were you going to keep it from killing you?"

"It's not the best plan in the world. Come on."

I lead her through the next door.

In order to get into the lab proper, one has to go through three sets of double doors. The first set is the one we just locked. The second set of doors is glass, and they separate the antechamber from an area called a walkthrough. The purpose of the walkthrough is to keep airborne contamination down to a minimum. After the doors leading into it, there's a second set of doors leading out of it, and at no time can both sets of doors be open.

The rest of the lab, then, is what's referred to in the parlance as a clean room. This I find comical, because I've always likened science to its predecessor—alchemy. I knew a lot of alchemists, and not one of them ever worried about cross-contamination. If anything, one tended to need a bath *after* spending time in an alchemist's lab.

Once in the walkthrough I peer into the lab, which is pretty easy to do, as every wall is glass at this point. The laboratory is lit dimly by a moderate selection of fluorescent lights and table lamps. And it looks like a few experiments are still running, based on the various indicator lights on the equipment. But, as I'd hoped, it's deserted.

When Grindel first bought this place out, he had the interior tailored to Viktor's specifications. The second floor was removed—Viktor said the ceiling was a mess of loose particulate matter, which I remembered because I don't know what particulate matter is—and replaced with a new drop ceiling. All the walls for separate rooms were also removed, making it one giant space. Areas are now defined by counters and equipment. And one curtain, off in the right corner of the lab, hiding an examination table. I spent a good deal of time on that table being poked and prodded. To that end, the curtain is for privacy. There are a couple of female lab techs, but even if it were an all-male staff, it would still be no fun being the only naked guy in the place.

"What are we doing here?" Clara asks. "Other than hiding from the vampire."

"I'm reclaiming some private property," I say. I open the inner door of the walkthrough. "Do me a favor. Stand here and hold this door open."

"Okay."

"And loan me that gun."

She hands over the M-16. I take it and use the butt of the gun to shatter the glass in the outer door. Then I go to work on the lock.

"What the hell are you doing?" she asks.

"Making sure we're not interrupted."

It takes a couple of minutes to adequately destroy the locking mechanism on the door. That accomplished, I enter the lab. Clara lets the door close. I hear the lock engage.

"All right," I say. "Let's get to work."

~

I learned an awful lot about cell biology and genetics during my month of daily visits to the lab. About eighty percent of it went completely over my head—especially the theoretical aspects—but I paid attention and asked enough questions to make it seem as if my curiosity was very general, instead of highly specific. It helps that scientists apparently love to talk about what they do. (Alchemists were the same way.) I imagine this comes from not having many people to talk to—outside of other scientists—who would actually look interested in the minutia.

Among the things I learned was where all the samples of my body's cells are being kept and what I would have to do if I wanted to destroy them.

Having Clara with me, rather than Eve, is actually a huge bonus. Of course, according to the original plan, Clara is supposed to be securing transportation right about now. But you take what you get.

"You've been here before, right?" I ask her.

"Couple times."

"Did you see their computers?"

"Yeah. Pretty standard."

"While I'm busy, do you want to see if you can find all of the data they've been accumulating over the past month?"

"I just have to turn it on," she says.

"Yeah, but my point is, I probably wouldn't know how to do that."

"Right. Okay. What are you going to be doing?"

"Just hurry."

Ten minutes later I'd collected all the samples I could find—both my blood and Eve's—and deposited them into a convenient and very large biohazard waste bucket.

"So. All-mother?" I ask, while searching the cabinets for a nice big jug of bleach.

Clara's still typing away at the computer. "It's what we call her," she says simply.

"Cute name. Aside from the disturbing religious undertones, I almost like it better than Eve." I open a refrigerator, because I can't remember if one is supposed to keep bleach cold or not. The answer appears to be no, but I do find a useful collection of diseases.

Viktor and his team inflicted every virus and bacteria on me that they could get their hands on, and when they were done, they tried inventing new ones to see what effect they would have. None of them did a thing regardless of the concentration. I found this mostly annoying, but it was also sort of cool. Having some very smart guys actively trying to infect me with something, and failing, is a pretty big ego boost.

I pocket a vial of chicken pox and move on.

"So, do you want to explain what happened earlier?" I ask Clara.

"Not so sure you want to know."

"Sure I do."

"It's kind of complicated."

"You mean you'd rather not upset me while I'm packing a gun."

"Mine's bigger than yours," she says. "But no, I just meant that while committing industrial espionage and running for our lives from a homicidal vampire, I might not have the time to be able to explain it with the proper degree of nuance."

"*Here* it is," I say. In one of the cabinets holding an array of more benign liquid compounds, I discover two big jugs of bleach. I pull them both out and carry them to the waste bin.

"I've got all the files," she says. "What do you want to do with them?"

"Can you delete them?" I ask.

"I'll try."

I start dumping the bleach over all the stuff in the bin. As I understand it, this is the only way to totally destroy the cells, right down to the DNA. I discovered this by asking one of the scientists how they went about ensuring there was no contamination on reused slides.

"So what you mean is," I begin, picking up the earlier subject, "you think it might be bad, at this juncture, to admit your whole goal from the time we met, was finding and rescuing Eve, even to the point of putting my life in jeopardy. Is that right?"

"Like I said, it's more complicated than that."

"How much more?"

I toss aside the first jug—now empty—and crack open the second.

"Okay," she says, turning away from the computer, "here's how it was. She disappeared. Nobody knew what happened to her and nobody had any sure leads. Then a few of us stumbled upon the MUD. We already knew a lot about you based on what she'd told us, and when we saw that somebody was trying to use Internet users to track your movements, we figured out that whoever wanted you, probably also had her. The idea was that one of us would touch base with you before you were taken, learn what you knew, and use that information to find her."

"There, that wasn't so bad," I say. "Was sleeping with me step three of the plan or step four?"

"See? That's what I'm talking about! You're not going to understand, so forget it."

"I'm sorry," I say, while polishing off the second jug. "Please continue. But can you type at the same time? We're on the clock here."

"You brought it up," she says, returning to the computer.

"That I did."

Looking around, I realize I've forgotten all about the stuff in the liquid nitrogen. I move to rectify that situation.

"Sleeping with you was never part of any plan," Clara says. "I did that because I wanted to. You needed a place to hole up and I needed to get information, and everything else that happened in my apartment was just for fun."

"Ah," I say, pulling on the gigantic oven mitts I'd seen Viktor use a number of times. "But that was a problem, wasn't it? I didn't know much more than you did."

"You knew a bit more. I don't know who got you Grindel's name, but whoever it was, he did a better job than any of us."

"You probably weren't breaking enough laws."

"But I still needed to know where he was keeping her. And it was obvious convincing you to go after him wasn't going to work. That's when I hit on the idea of making myself a hostage."

"Tricking me into trying to rescue you. Nice plan."

"If I could have figured out a way to get taken in without involving you, I would have," she claims. "Problem."

"What?" I ask, elbow-deep in the thick run-off from the nitrogen.

"This terminal is part of a network," she says. "And the servers aren't in this building."

"Where are they?" I'm not altogether certain what a server is, but wondering where it's kept seems like a good question.

"Don't know. Probably across the way."

"In the admin building."

"Yeah. Looks like there are four terminals with open access to this system. Three of them are in this room. The fourth is probably the computer in Bob's office."

I lift the test tubes out of the nitrogen like I'd seen Viktor do and walk them over to the bleach tub. Inside the tubes are synthetic versions of what's in mine and Eve's blood mixed with whatever they took from the vampire. They're the only vials of Viktor's final product currently in existence.

"Probably?"

"It's a good guess. He's got a computer over there. That I know. But it's set up beyond the firewall."

"You can tell that from here?"

"No, but I've tried and I can't reach the Internet from here. Bob can. I've seen him use his computer to get stock info. Since he probably set this up, I'm sure he knows the passwords needed to get into this network from there."

I dump the first batch of test tubes into the bleach and go back for more.

"Is there any way to know if he's transmitted the data anywhere? I need to know if it exists outside of this compound."

"No, but I doubt it. He'd be risking a lot if he put any of this out there."

"Okay." Back in the nitrogen again. It's hard to see through the gas, but it looks as if I'm almost finished. "So can you still delete it?"

"Not completely. I took care of what was here, but the data could still be reconstructed. I'd need to access the server tower. And I have no way of knowing if a copy of it exists anywhere else. Bob also has a zip drive on his desk."

"You seem to know an awful lot about Bob's desk."

"I've been kicking around for a month," she says. "And, like I told you, he's spent most of that time trying to get into my pants. I paid attention."

"When did you find out what was going to happen tonight?"

"About an hour before you did. Bob actually came right out and told me. I think he wanted me to be impressed that he was the kind of man who could execute somebody. I couldn't find Iza in time to warn you."

I'm done with the nitrogen. Provided my scientist friend was telling the truth about the deleterious effects of bleach on human cells, there is now no direct sample of my blood in the compound other than what's in my own body.

"What's that?" Clara asks. She's facing the door, specifically because of the sound of somebody working the lock.

"Get your gun ready," I suggest, discarding the mitts and raising my own gun.

We both take an involuntarily deep breath and wait. Presumably the vampire isn't going to use a key to get in, but there are other things on the base to worry about.

And then the door swings open and Viktor walks in.

He won't make it past the inner airlock doors, so I'm sort of happy to see him.

"My God, Adam!" he exclaims, stepping through the broken glass that used to look like a door.

"How's it going outside, Doc?" I ask, sliding the gun back into my waist string.

"It's madness! What has happened?"

"Hostile takeover," I say. "Clara, you want to help me out here?"

"I saw you entering the lab ..." Viktor begins.

"Oh, was that you? Clara saw you coming. Thought you were someone else."

"I ... yes, I went back for the key."

"What do we do about him?" Clara asks, her gun still raised.

"He can't get in. Don't worry about it."

"Bob and his demon are still out there somewhere. What if he went and found them?"

"Good point." I step up to the glass wall. "Viktor, you know that creature you boys have been keeping locked up in the second cell? It's running loose right now. That's what all those screams you've been hearing are about. So I guess if you want to run off to Bob, you're welcome to do so. But I'm willing to bet you won't make it."

"You ... you released the vampire?"

"Sure did. And it sounds like it's awfully hungry."

Viktor crosses himself compulsively, which I find faintly amusing, as he never struck me as a particularly religious man.

Despite the name, Viktor was actually raised in eastern Pennsylvania by a couple of highly practical parents who nearly put themselves into the poor house paying for his education. In a lot of ways he still feels the weight of that debt, which I think is one of the subtle psychological factors in his life's work. The need to make a permanent mark on the world to justify their sacrifice and all that. It's touching, really. If I didn't think his life's work would also bring about the indirect deaths of millions of people, I'd be rooting for him.

"Clara, I don't think he's going anywhere," I say. Poor Viktor looks completely paralyzed.

"Good enough for me," she says, putting her gun down. "What are we doing next?"

"Come help me."

I lead her to the flammables cabinet. It contains exactly what something with that name should contain.

"Adam," Viktor half-shouts, which he needs to do to be heard through the glass. "What has been going on in there?"

"Just cleaning up," I say, pulling out a jug of methanol and handing it to Clara.

"Start at the far end," I tell her, "And cover everything."

"Got it."

"No!" Viktor shouts. He reaches for the door and tries to get in, but of course, it's not going to budge. The security system of the walkthrough thinks the outer door—with its busted lock—is still open.

"Sorry, Viktor," I say. "You know how I feel about all of this."

"You're insane!"

"Not this century," I say. Stepping past the flammables, I check out the oxygen tanks. The lab has two very large tanks of pure oxygen, which I was told was used for experiments under the hood. (The "hood" is a small chamber that looks like a delicatessen hot plate area.) "By the way, Doc, how old is that vampire?"

Viktor's too busy staring at the waste bin and the empty bleach cans with a widening look of horror to respond.

"Viktor?"

"I don't know ..." he says absently. "It was ... we needed the oldest vampire we could find. For the purest ... the purest sample of the virus."

Using the butt of the handgun I whack the screw valve off the first tank.

It starts whistling as the oxygen is released into the air.

On the other side of the room, spreading methanol all over about one quarter of the lab, Clara says, "I don't get it. Why did you need a vampire?"

I whack the other tank open.

"That was the missing piece, wasn't it Viktor?" I say. "You knew what gene to turn on, but you didn't have a way to transform all the cells in the body. Am I right?"

"Adam, please, whatever you're about to do, don't do it." Viktor is a portly, frail octogenarian who usually carries himself with something akin to dignity. That dignity has completely deserted him, and he's on the verge of blubbering. I ignore him as well as I can.

I continue, mostly for Clara's benefit. "But then somebody had a great idea. What if you took a blood-borne virus and used it to do the job for you? Whose idea was that, Viktor? Was that yours?"

"Please," he repeats. Seeing the culmination of his life's work being destroyed before his eyes has to be kind of tough.

"Okay, I get it now," Clara says. She's returned to the cabinet and helped herself to another bottle, while I'm busy spreading ethanol all over the near side of the room. She adds, "Someone gets infected by a vampire, it affects their whole body."

"And it's permanent," I add. "The virus is almost perfect already, except it also makes the body especially sensitive to solar radiation."

"Hey," Clara says, "look what I found." She'd opened up a drawer at one of the desks and is now holding up a bottle of whiskey. "Should I add it to the floor?"

"God, no," I say. "I'll take that."

She tosses me the bottle, adding, "She always said alcohol was a weakness for you."

"Eve? I guess she would know."

I take a good long drink. My goodness but I needed that.

"She's been shadowing me for an eternity. And if we get out of this alive, you and I are going to have a very long talk about her."

"Can't wait," she says. "Are we about done?"

I look around. The oxygen content in the room has gone up markedly, and just about every surface has been covered with some form of flammable liquid. The fumes are making my eyes tear up, which is a pretty good sign that we're done.

"Adam," Viktor pleads, "what you are doing ... you've no right. This can help so many people."

"What do you mean I have no right? You had your turn to play God. Now it's mine. Besides, I've already doused the cells in bleach. This part is just to make sure nobody picks up the pieces later."

Clara, blissfully unconcerned with the philosophical consequences of our actions asks, "So how do we get out?"

"The emergency exit."

The lab has two, one in each corner. One day I leaned on one of the door's bars to make sure they actually opened. They do, and they're also hooked up to an alarm. You can't imagine what kind of trouble that caused.

I say, "Viktor, in a few minutes, it's going to be more dangerous in here than outside. I trust you know how to let yourself out."

Viktor lets out a little whimper. I guess that means he heard me.

I meet Clara at the exit and trade guns with her.

"Get ready to hit that door," I say. Then I switch her gun to fully automatic and start firing indiscriminately into the room.

Creating a spark isn't nearly as easy as it looks in the movies, where every bullet that hits something flares brightly as if the world were made of flint. That not being the case here, I just go to town on the whole room and hope something somewhere flares up.

I had less trouble creating fire in the Stone Age. But after several seconds—and following possibly permanent hearing loss —I manage to hit a piece of electronic equipment that sparks long enough to create the desired effect.

"Okay, go," I say. Clara pushes the fire door open, alarms sound off, and out she goes.

I take one last look at Viktor. It seems like he's going to stay and watch the place melt away. There's no point in warning him again to get out. So instead, I screw open the whiskey, take another deep drag, and toss the bottle into the middle of the room. My last glimpse of the lab is of flames rolling across the floor like someone had spilled a big jar of pure fire.

I step out, shut the door behind me, and lean up against the side of the building next to Clara. I'm about to discuss the next step when she grabs my arm and squeezes hard.

"Don't move," she whispers urgently. "It's here."

CHAPTER 28

I remember a long conversation I once had with a vampire named Bordick, sometime in the late seventeenth century. He was one of the oldest I'd ever met, meaning we had a good deal in common with one another, because how often does one get to compare two-hundred-year-old war stories with someone else?

We got onto the subject of the somewhat unfair public perception of vampires—a perception that was actually worse in the seventeenth century than it is now. It was Bordick's theory that people, in overreacting to vampires, tend to create their own monsters. He meant this rather literally.

As he told it, sometime around his first century, the villagers of a small Latvian hamlet figured out what he was and decided to do something about it. So one afternoon they sealed up the crypt where he was spending his daylight hours. Without elaborating on why they did this—he wasn't bothering anybody and had restricted his nightly drinking mainly to livestock—he pointed out that this is just about the stupidest thing you can possibly do to a vampire, because they don't starve to death like people. They just get hungrier.

Hang out with a vampire who drinks a small allotment of blood two or three times a week and you'll swear there's hardly any difference between him and your average human. But one who hasn't drunk in two or three weeks isn't the best company around. The hungry ones tend to fixate on your neck a lot, which can be very uncomfortable, and it becomes obvious somewhat quickly that they aren't listening to what you're saying because they're too preoccupied listening to your heart pumping. It's like trying to converse with somebody who's tuned into music on headphones, only much more disturbing.

According to Bordick, anything longer than thirty days is utter agony. Two months and this constant pain spawns dementia. Longer than that and you've got a vampire who is, mentally, entirely too far gone to listen to any sort of reason whatsoever.

So after a full calendar year sealed up in that crypt, Bordick was utterly out of his mind.

He couldn't tell me how the crypt was reopened because he has no memory of it. His brain had stopped processing cogent thoughts. And his mind didn't return to him until he woke up two nights later in a pile of bodies. Bordick had slaughtered the entire town. Over five hundred men, women and children, he claimed. It may have been an exaggeration, but the number of people wasn't the point.

The point was, never try to kill a vampire by cutting off its food supply, unless your goal is to create an indiscriminate, nearly unstoppable killing machine.

~

Standing motionless against the side of the laboratory building and staring at the creature huddled in the darkness fifty feet away, Bordick's story is the first thing that springs to mind. I can hear small explosions as the empty plastic methanol and ethanol jugs detonate from the heat inside the lab.

With the oxygen feeding the inferno, standing this close is going to ultimately prove to be a bad idea. But moving anywhere else doesn't seem like such a hot prospect either.

"Should we shoot it?" Clara whispers.

"That didn't seem to make a difference with the security guards."

"Then what do you suggest?"

"I'm fresh out of life-sparing ideas at the moment. You?"

The vampire is difficult to make out. Pale skin, definitely. And it looks to be female. A thick mane of hair covers most of its face and part of what seems to be a naked body. The only sounds it makes—it doesn't breathe—is a sort of puckering, slurpy noise.

I wonder how many lives the vampire has claimed in the past hour. I also wonder why it's still here. Surely it could have gotten past the fences if it wanted to. Perhaps, despite being almost entirely out of its mind, vengeance is still a primary motivational factor.

Well, and feeding. There aren't any people outside of the fence to feed upon.

All this is fairly moot speculation, as I'm surely about to have my throat ripped out by it.

"Maybe it doesn't see us," Clara says.

"It sees us. I think the problem is we haven't attacked or tried to run away. We've confused it."

"Well, we're gonna have to move soon. Those oxygen tanks'll be exploding any minute now, and I don't want to be too close to the building when that happens."

"Neither do I."

We both hear the front door to the lab slam shut.

Viktor.

The vampire hears him, too.

"Viktor!" I shout. "Don't move!"

Either he doesn't hear me or he doesn't care to listen. I spot him about halfway to the administrative building running as fast as an eighty year old geneticist can run. Meaning, not so fast. And not even close to how fast the vampire can go.

I've never seen any creature move so quickly. The vampire catches up with Viktor in about three seconds from what has to be at least thirty yards away. For my part, I raise my gun to shoot at it, but don't have enough time or enough of a target to make it worth the effort to try. Then there's the matter of whether or not a bullet would do any good. Vampires have thinner hides than demons, but I'm pretty sure I've never encountered one this old. Seeing it move I'm wondering if it might actually be older than three centuries.

Catching him from behind, the vampire breaks Viktor's neck with one swift jerk and buries its face into the side of his neck. It is a magnificent and terrible thing to behold. It's also a golden opportunity to run to the nearest building and get some cover before it can come after us, but I'm so dumbfounded by the sheer violence of it all that I can't seem to move.

Clara's not so transfixed. "Come on!" she says, jerking at my sleeve.

With her in the lead, we sprint to the door of the nearest building—an inner perimeter barracks house that is not, to the best of my knowledge, in use. Clara tries the door and finds it to be locked. I pull her around the side of the building and out of the light.

"We make for the admin building," I say.

"Past the vampire?"

"Look at it," I say, thumbing around the corner of the building. "The door's unlocked."

Thanks to the light directly over the front of the door to the administrative building, one can clearly see the door has been left slightly ajar. Clara peeks around the corner and confirms this.

"So? She'll still catch us before we ever get there."

A decent point. Especially since the space between us and that door is probably the best-lit area in the entire base and the vampire is right in the middle of it. The direct route would take us right past her.

"We can cut around. Avoid the compound."

"Worth a try, I guess."

Right then, the tanks in the lab go up. The detonation is not quite tremendous enough to blow open any of the walls—it's one of the few made of bricks, as apparently, when the army built it they took the story of the three little pigs to heart—but it does make the ground shake dramatically enough to knock both of us over.

I get back to my feet and help Clara up.

"This seems like a good time to run," I say.

After rounding the first corner of the barracks building we take off in a dead sprint for the edge of the second barracks—the building where the scientists sleep—with me leading, but Clara in position to pass. Impending death makes one run faster. I think that's probably why they fire a gun before track meets.

I turn the next corner, which puts us on a beeline for the front door of the administrative building.

Or it would have, had I not tripped. I look back to see what I'd caught my leg on. Face down, in pajamas and looking extremely deceased, is one of Viktor's teammates.

"He must have come out the window," Clara says. Indeed, the window to the barracks has been broken out. I peer inside.

I can't say I ever got a chance to really know all of the scientists who were a part of Viktor's group during my stay. But they were always polite and generally decent, and I imagine if this were a different world and all of us ended up walking away, and I ran into one of them sometime later in a bar or something, I would not have a problem sharing a drink with them. So I feel sort of sad, looking in through the shattered window and seeing the carnage inside. I don't think any of them deserved to be murdered. Certainly most of them didn't.

"It went inside after them," Clara whispers.

"No time to worry about that now. We have to get out of the open."

"Why? It doesn't look like buildings pose much of a—"

She stops, staring over my shoulder. I turn around.

The vampire is between us and the open door of the admin building. I didn't think she could suck Viktor dry that quickly.

I position myself in front of Clara, and extend my arms, a little mini-cordon that won't stop the vampire any more than it would stop a flame thrower. But it looks gallant, and I figure I may as well go out acting gallantly. Behind me, Clara's muttering the Lord's Prayer.

"We don't want to hurt you," I say.

The vampire stands from her crouch and takes two hesitant steps toward us.

"Get out of the way and I'll shoot it," Clara mutters.

"No," I say. "Look."

"Look at what?"

"She's not attacking."

Indeed, the vampire has stopped moving and is tilting her head and looking at us with a curiosity that seems absent any real malevolence. We're being studied.

"Are you doing this?" Clara asks.

"I'm not doing anything. She just doesn't want to kill us."

"Why not?"

"Try not to sound offended."

A noise in another part of the base somewhere, well beyond my range of hearing, but clearly not beyond the vampire's, takes her attention away from us. Then she leaps twenty feet nearly straight up and lands on the roof of the barracks. In another second she's out of sight.

"I think I peed my pants," Clara says. "Why'd she do that?"

"I wish I knew. But I'm not about to complain."

"Let's get one of the cars and get out of here before she changes her mind."

"Not yet," I say. "We still have to destroy the data on the server."

~

The front door to the administrative building is covered by a large wood awning with a rounded top, which distinguishes it from every other building in the place insofar as whoever designed it gave a damn about basic aesthetics.

I'm guessing, based on the distribution of the windows and the apparent usage of several of the rooms, that unlike the lab, the inside was left more or less intact after it was purchased by Bob Grindel's group. As I said, Bob tended to enjoy watching me from his picture window above that awning when I was taken to the lab in the morning. He always had this pose—feet apart, hands on hips—that gave off a certain *I am the king of all I survey* attitude that made me want to kill him. I never quite got over that.

So it was with mixed pleasure that I learned from Clara that not only is the main computer storage in the admin building, there's a possibility Bob has made a copy of it in his office. Trying to destroy the computers, and retrieve the disks from Bob, vastly increases the likelihood that I will not survive the evening, but on the bright side, it provides me with an excellent opportunity to kill him. Provided the vampire hasn't caught up to him yet.

"Do you know where the computer-whatever is?" I ask Clara as soon as we're inside.

"The tower? I think so. There's a locked room down the hall. I've never been in it, but I felt the door once, and it was cool."

"In a slang sense?" I ask, confused.

"Air conditioning."

"Um, okay. Can you get into the room on your own?"

"With the key. Where are you going?"

"Upstairs. To check for copies."

She looks at me archly. "You don't even know what a zip disk looks like."

"I'll figure it out."

She holds out her hand and I give up the key ring.

"He's already left the base," she says. "You know that, right? He probably went straight for his helicopter as soon as I wounded him."

"Probably. Can't hurt to check."

I get a frown from her. "Back at the apartment, when I was trying to convince you to come here, it was just so I could follow. You don't actually have to exact revenge, or whatever it is you think you're doing here."

"Do you think I'm doing this to impress you?"

"I'm just sorry I called you cowardly is all."

"Clara, if he's upstairs and I skipped out without even trying to go after him, I'll be kicking myself for the next three centuries."

"Fine," she shrugs. "I'll meet you back here in a few. Then maybe we can get the hell off this base already."

She runs off down the hall while I head up the center staircase that's directly in front of me.

Clara's right. As long as the vampire isn't interested in eating either of us, there's no good reason not to grab the nearest vehicle and escape while we still can. Which means I'm doing exactly what I told her in New York I wasn't going to do—acting out solely in the name of vengeance. And, as I've said before, that's nearly always a mistake. But I'd *really* like to kill Bob, and I'm not looking to be reasonable about it at this point.

I reach the second floor landing, check the gun—still a half-clip left— and slip the vial of chicken pox I took from the lab into my hand. The gun is for Bob, who I'm thinking is no less bullet-proof now than he was an hour ago when Clara winged him. The vial is for Brutus.

The center office is only a few paces from the landing. I sneak up to it and, finding the door ajar, I kick it completely open and spin into the room firing. I reasoned, perhaps stupidly, that if Bob was anywhere he'd be at his desk and that his desk just had to be near the picture window. Completely wrong, naturally. The only thing the bullets hit is the window, which manages to crack spectacularly in several places.

A heavy hand comes down from the right of the doorway and knocks the gun from my grasp. Before I have much of a chance to register this, I'm shoved to the floor myself, albeit several feet away from the gun. Brutus is on top of me a second later, one mitt wrapped around my neck.

"Not yet," says Bob. The lights are out in the room, so the best I can figure is that he's somewhere to the right of the half-shattered window. Behind the desk. If I were even a bit smart, I would have asked Clara how the office was set up before going and assuming things.

"Pick him up."

Brutus complies by lifting me mostly by the neck—not real comfortable, that— and pressing me up against the wall.

My eyes adjust and there's Bob with a very large suitcase open atop the desk. He has a white bandage on his shoulder, which he's bled through.

"It looks like you've been busy," he notes. He points out the window. The fire in the lab flickers obediently, currently in the process of devouring the wood roof.

"Just ... destroying the evidence," I say. Talking is a real challenge.

"Yes, well ... sorry to tell you this, but you've failed. I have all the copies of the research I need right here. At worst, you've scored only a minor setback."

"You still need the blood of an immortal to make it work," I say. "Eve's gone. And you can't have mine."

Bob laughs. A disappointing reaction. "Think, Adam. How do you suppose we proved the treatment worked?"

Uh-oh.

"Yes! Human testing. And who better than me to try it out on?" He picks up the suitcase. "I've got just about all the immortal blood I'm ever going to need. So, as I think I said earlier, you're officially expendable."

He gets face-to-face with me. If I thought I could produce spit at this moment, I would. Bob says, "That was well-played, by the way. The bit about the vampire, I mean. I didn't see that coming. Mind telling me how you freed it?"

"Magic."

He smiles. "I don't need to know that badly. I trust Ms. Wassermann is downstairs right now?"

"She's dead," I whisper.

"You're a bad liar. I saw you come in together. No matter. I'll pick her up on my way out. Good-bye." To Brutus, he says, "Meet me downstairs when you're done with him."

Bob steps out the door and shuts it behind him. Brutus smiles at me, and starts to squeeze.

"Wait," I say, holding up my left hand. The vial is still palmed there.

"What?"

Killing me would take about as long for him as it would for me to crush a centipede. He has time.

"You ever read H. G. Wells?"

"Who?" he asks, and when his mouth opens to form the 'o' sound, I shove the vial into it.

He lets go of me. When I land, I take a few seconds to enjoy breathing and then get to my feet, snatch the gun from the floor, and await the inevitable.

Brutus staggers backward up against the closed door and grabs at his throat. I'm about to say something pithy—the situation calls for it—but then I hear him crunching down on the glass and swishing the contents around in his mouth like he's at a wine-tasting. Then he stands up straight, shoots me a smile, and spits the cork onto the carpet.

"A little bitter," he says, "but not bad. Could've used some pepper."

"Oh shit," I say, succinctly.

"Sorry. You want me to jump around, maybe scratch my throat, wave my arms or something?"

A couple more pieces fit into place. "It was you," I say. "In the third room."

"Yeah. Well, me and Ringo. Doc fixed us up so we don't get sick no more. And that's just the start. Mr. Grindel's gonna take care of all of our friends, too. Time our kind came out of hiding."

"How could he have been so stupid?" I ask. Because it's one thing to try and help people who get sick. It's another to fix the immune system of an otherwise invulnerable race of sociopaths. Bob and Viktor both must have been out of their minds to even consider it.

"Mr. Grindel seems to think there's only a few of us around," he explains. "He's in for a surprise. Too bad this came too late for Jimmy."

"Jimmy?"

"The one you killed in New York. I'm gonna have to hurt you for that, cuz he took that job after I recommended him to Mr. Grindel, so I'm feeling guilty now, and I hate feeling guilty."

With one arm he lifts the desk and throws it up against the wall. Which is bad, as I was in the process of putting the desk between us at the time, and there's nothing else that's big and heavy to hide behind, other than Brutus. "You're gonna have to pay for Ringo, too," he says. "He was a straight-up guy."

"I didn't kill Ringo."

"May as well have."

He takes a step toward me. I raise the gun, but just for show, as it would be a huge waste of bullets unless I managed to hit an eye. (Demon eyes are small and deep-set, as if they evolved in anticipation of just such a moment.)

Brutus is still standing between me and the door, and the office isn't particularly large, so I don't have a lot in the way of maneuverability to work with. Seeing no other option, I take the only exit that's available, the window.

I spin around and run straight at it, hitting the glass as hard as I can with my shoulder. It gives, but not quite as efficiently as I thought it would. This would be my first time through plate glass, and I stupidly assumed it would be as easy as it looks in the movies.

So I end up a bit stunned by the impact. And falling fifteen feet is not a good time to be stunned, just in general. My trajectory takes me to the edge of the awning. I bounce off it—the good news being it slows my descent, the bad being that it feels like I've dislocated my shoulder—and then fall the remaining distance.

I nearly get my feet under me before impact, but not quite. One leg is all I can muster. Something goes pop in my knee and then I'm down in a heap. It's a non-dead heap, and for that I can only be grateful. I just wish every part of my body didn't hurt quite so much.

The gun lands a few feet away. It takes all the energy I have left to reach it. And just as I do I feel the ground tremble.

"That was pretty good," Brutus says.

I look around, which is a treat because I'm on a piece of broken glass, and whenever I shift it digs a bit deeper into my ribcage. Brutus jumped out of the shattered window, and is now standing a few feet away, looking perfectly sound. I am about to die.

"I didn't quite stick the landing," I admit.

"No, but points for trying. Pretty ballsy."

I'm trying to come up with an adequate prayer for this moment, but one doesn't come to mind. Too many faiths to choose from. Too many gods. Don't think any of them are listening.

And then a blur from the corner of my eye becomes a whoosh of air and a loud, violent impact in the center of Brutus's chest. My first thought is that someone has fired a rocket from somewhere.

The demon doesn't move, although in hindsight he probably wishes he had. By not giving in to the impact, he just makes it easier for the vampire to drive her arm straight through him.

They stand still like that for a few seconds. She is rooting around inside of his chest, which is just about exactly as disgusting as it sounds.

Then she jerks her arm out again and takes a tangle of internal organs with her, and punches him flush in the face, causing his pug nose to actually cave in. Brutus gives a little whimper, falls to his knees, and then sags onto his side.

She remains standing over him holding what looks to be his heart, waiting to make sure he can't go on without one. When it's clear he cannot, she tosses the heart aside.

I'm wondering if she still doesn't feel like killing me. And then she speaks.

"Lord Venice ... What is this place?"

My jaw drops.

"Eloise?"

She turns and brushes the hair from her face. It's her all right, as beautiful as ever, but in sore need of a bath to wash away the dried blood.

"I knew your smell, but it did not seem possible. I thought you dead."

"And I you," I respond. By my calculations she's at least two and a half centuries past her expiration date. *"How have you lasted so long?"*

"I was well-schooled in the art of immortality," she quips. A blood tear streaks down her face.

Poor thing. She looks so confused.

"Tell me, my lord, have I gone mad?"

"Don't move, either of you!"

I tilt my head—the best I can do for the moment—to check the source of the voice. Bob has emerged from the building. In front of him, holding the briefcase, is Clara. He has a gun pointed at her head.

"Bob!" I greet. "Where've you been?" I try standing up, but discover two things. First, my knee is not at all happy with me, and second, I'd apparently hit my head on impact, as the world goes all spinny when I try to move too quickly.

"I've got all I need," Bob says. He's edging his way past us, heading—I assume—for the helicopter pad. "So don't screw with me and I won't shoot you or your girlfriend."

"I know this man," Eloise says.

"He is the one who brought you here."

"Tell that thing to back the hell off!" Bob shouts, meaning Eloise. I keep my gaze focused on him and fight the urge to black out, which seems like an inviting option right now. My ears are already ringing, and I imagine in a second or two my vision will start to go. Which is a bad time to try shooting a gun.

"I would like to kill him," Eloise says calmly.

"What did it say?" Bob asks.

"She said she wants to kill you." I'm noticing my lips feel fatter than they should.

"She better not try!" Bob says, pressing the barrel harder against Clara's temple.

"Oww!" Clara says.

The ringing is starting to really annoy me. I figured it was just another symptom of a concussion but now I'm wondering if it's an external sound.

Can anybody else hear it?

"Calm down," I say to Bob. "I'll talk to her."

I switch to French. *"Eloise, are you fast enough to rip out his throat before he damages the girl?"*

"I do not think so."

"Pity. I will have to shoot this fool myself."

Clara giggles. Apparently, she speaks French.

"What did it say?" Bob asks.

"Her name is Eloise, Bob. Be respectful. She may be the oldest vampire you'll ever meet."

"Go to hell. What did it say?"

"She said she'll leave you alone. Okay?"

"Is that the truth?"

"Of course. But, you know, I can't speak for Iza."

It isn't ringing. It's buzzing.

"Iza?" Bob repeats. "Who the hell is Iza?"

"Just a friend. She's been hanging around."

"Sure. Whatever," Bob says. "You're all insane."

He starts backpedaling toward the copter pad in double-time, jerking Clara along and trying to keep us in front.

"Iza," I call out, "the eyes please."

Things happen very quickly after that.

Hearing the low hum of a pixie in flight, Clara suddenly drops to her knees at more or less the same time Iza impacts Bob's left eye. As you can imagine, Bob finds this incredibly painful.

"Aaaaagh!" he declares meaningfully.

He fires his gun. I don't think blowing Clara's head off is actually his intention. It's more like a reflex. And fortunately Clara's head is no longer in line with the barrel when the gun goes off. Singes her hair a bit, but that's all.

While he's clapping his hand over the wounded eye, Clara makes it completely to the ground and out of my way, which is very good thinking on her part.

I raise my gun, take a shot, and miss entirely. In my defense, I would like to point out that I'm firing with the wrong hand, while lying on my side on a piece of glass, and with a dislocated shoulder, trying to hit a guy that is backlit by a small inferno that also happens to be my doing.

Bob, one eye and all, realizes I'm shooting at him and raises his own gun, so I fire again. This time I hit him in the left shoulder. He rocks sideways with the impact, and now he's staring down at the bullet wound, which I don't think is fatal.

But he looks too shocked to take advantage of my poor aim. He says, "But, I'm ..."

"Immortal?" I ask. My words sound all mushy. "But not invincible."

I take careful aim this time, which is easy enough to do, as Bob's just standing there with a stupid look on his face. My vision's getting fuzzy. Feels a little like being drunk. But I can shoot okay when I'm drunk.

I manage to put one between his eyes. This does nothing to alter his expression, but it does seem to have a remarkable effect on the rest of his body. He collapses.

That finished, I drop my own gun and sag back onto my dislocated shoulder, which just about kicks me over my pain threshold. I'm thinking death right about now wouldn't be so bad. It'd certainly hurt less. And then I black out.

~

When I wake up again, I'm alone in the back of one of the Humvees, my legs extended along the back seat and my head cushioned by a rolled-up shirt. Checking the rest of me, I find my arm to be in a sling and my side bandaged. I wonder how long I've been out.

"Adam," a voice says.

This is the sound that woke me up. I heard somebody calling my name.

I look around. "Clara?"

"No, not Clara."

It's Eve. She's standing just outside the truck. The top is down, making her easy enough to spot. I don't know how I missed seeing her immediately. Just to be sure, I blink a bunch of times. Still there.

"Oh," I say. "H'lo."

I'm fairly groggy and there is a decent chance I'm speaking to a hallucination. I go with it anyway. Sometimes hallucinations have interesting things to say.

"I handled this badly," Eve admits. "I forget sometimes how dangerous the world is for ... for other people. For you."

"You're not like me, are you?" I say. "I always thought you were, but you're something else."

"I am older. That's all."

"So, that whole vanishing thing you did earlier ... you're saying I'm going to figure that out eventually?"

Eve smiles. "You will perhaps need to survive a third again as long first. But, yes." She glances over her shoulder. *Is someone coming?*

"You and I, we are owed a long conversation," she says.

"I'm not going anywhere." Especially true if nobody shows up to get behind the wheel of the Humvee.

"No. But now is not that time."

"You're the most annoying hallucination I've ever had, you know that?" She grins. "Why is now not the time?"

"Because I'm not certain I am ready to forgive you yet, Urrr."

What?

"I don't ... I have no idea what you're talking about."

"I know that. One day you will remember. And then you can find me, and we will talk."

"Something I did to you?"

Eve smiles again. She has a fantastic smile. "When you remember, then you will understand."

She turns to go.

"Wait!" I say.

She hesitates.

"Okay, say I figure out what the hell you're talking about. This is the first time I've spoken to you after ten millennia of trying. I don't think I can wait that long again."

She stares at me gravely. "This world we share is getting much too small. If you want to find me again, it will not be that difficult. Provided I want you to. And you are wrong. This isn't the first time we've spoken."

I hear the sound of footsteps in sand, up near the head of the car.

"Be well," Eve says. Then she turns and walks out of view.

"Wait!" I call out uselessly.

"What is it, Adam?" It's Clara talking, from the driver's side door. "Is something wrong?"

"Eve. Stop her."

"What?" She looks around. "There isn't anybody else here."

"You don't ... no, no of course there isn't."

"Must have been a nasty hit you took to the head," she says.

"Yeah," I agree. "That must be it."

EPILOGUE

With a full tank of gas, a map, compass, and a bag of mushrooms for Iza, we drive out of the compound. Our destination is the nearest town, which according to the map, is a good three hours away.

We remain largely silent for the first hour of the trip, all except for Iza, who's a louder eater than you might expect.

It turns out the reason Iza had been absent for most of the night's proceedings, was that I had not been quite as clear in my instructions as I'd thought. What I had told her to do after unlocking the doors was to fly off and locate the nearest idle car, then find Clara and bring her to it, and finally to find me and Eve and lead us to Clara. Thus, as soon as I was done I'd head in the proper direction, rather than stumble about a very large area with a killer vampire and possibly a very angry armed security force to worry about.

The problem was that Iza didn't know what a car was, or where to locate one.

You'd think a pixie who lived in Boston at one time would be fully aware of the concept of an automobile. But, after a few days of patient explanation, it became clear that she thought of cars as simply another type of animal, meaning there was a pretty good chance that when the time came she would end up leading me directly to a stray dog instead. I had to provide her with an extremely detailed description. So detailed, she bypassed a number of perfectly viable vehicular options because a few of the particulars were a little bit off.

But when she finally did spot what she was sent to find, she raced back and arrived just about the same time I tried to fly from a second story window. She explained that she would have told me right then about the car she'd found, but it looked like I was busy.

As to what happened after I passed out, Clara filled in much of the details.

When Bob Grindel fired his gun right next to Clara's temple, she lost her hearing for a good minute or two, and thus remained on the ground covering her head and hoping things were turning out okay. When she finally peeked out she saw me unconscious on the ground with Eloise kneeling over me. Given what she knew about Eloise, she assumed the worst. But when Eloise said, *"He has fainted,"* Clara understood well enough to not panic completely.

A somewhat awkward conversation followed, during which Clara managed to convey the need to get me to the vehicle Iza had come to tell us about. This must have been a treat to listen to. Clara with her rudimentary boarding school French, translating directions from a pixie who is barely fluent in English, to Eloise and her fourteenth century peasant version of the French language. I wish I'd been awake for it.

But Clara got the point across all right. And, once I was in the car, she went to the infirmary to get what she needed for my wounds, patching me up as well as she knew how.

I spoke with Eloise before we left, giving her a quick review of what country she was in and why she was here. I also asked if she remembered what she'd done after Iza had opened the door for her. Much like my old friend Bordick, she had only vague memories of what transpired, but she did recall having an active interest in killing more or less anything she could hear breathing. She was moderately certain she'd succeeded. So, the good news was, we probably weren't going to run into anybody on our way out. Bad news? As Clara said, there were at least fifty people in the camp at the beginning of the night. I only felt bad about this once I saw the carnage myself on our way out of camp. It looked like Gettysburg, only with a more thorough appreciation of the art of dismemberment.

Eloise ultimately decided it might be fun to explore America rather than tag along with us, and I was in no position to stop her. Clara looked relieved. Can't say I blame her.

I did ask how Eloise was going to avoid the sun while in the middle of a desert.

"I will just dig before sunrise."

I'd never thought of that, proving again that I would make one terrible vampire. I told her to look me up once she got settled—and washed all the blood off and found some clothes and all of that. She said she would.

~

Almost two hours into the trip, and my knee is swelling up horribly. I have the pant leg rolled up so I can study it in all its black-and-blue glory. It's unpleasant, bordering on nauseating. And every bump in the road is a special treat, let me tell you.

I've had injuries of this sort before, and usually they heal given enough time, so I'm not too worried. And my shoulder has calmed down a bit. We had to pop it back into place before leaving, which was decidedly unpleasant. But, by comparison, I'm pretty lucky. Not as lucky as Clara, who doesn't have a scratch, but lucky.

With the sky turning brighter from the impending sunrise, Clara finally breaks the silence.

"She doesn't hate you, you know."

I frown. "Eve."

"Yeah. Her description of you, from the website? It's actually quite nice. You know, considering."

"You're going to have to show me that site when we get the chance," I say.

"I will."

I shift in my seat to try to get a little blood flowing, and also so I can look at Clara's eyes in the rearview mirror.

"Seems I did something to her once," I say. "Any idea what?"

"No," she says, her eyes flicking up at the mirror to catch mine. "She won't talk about it. I'm guessing it was something pretty bad."

"You think? She's been nursing a grudge that's older than written history. It's probably something more serious than me pissing in her rose garden."

"But you don't know what," she says flatly. I'm not so sure she believes me.

"Honestly, I don't. I wish I did."

The sunrise starts to brighten up the sky to our left. It's still nice and cool out, but in another hour or two we'll have the windows up (we raised the top before we started driving) and the air conditioner blasting away. Soon after that, hopefully, we'll reach something approximating civilization— and a hospital—provided we're driving in the correct direction.

"You know," I say, "I've been thinking."

"About?"

"Something Bob said that's been bothering me. Maybe it's just the concussion talking but ..." I trail off. I'm not so sure I want to bring this up right now.

"Go on," she prompts.

"He said he needed to test his formula on a human subject."

"Yeah ..."

"And he implied that he was that subject."

Clara says, "He was. Told me so himself. If you were him, wouldn't you want to be the first in line?"

"True, but work through this with me. He nabbed Eve months ago, right? And she's just as immortal as I am. And really, other than her being able to disappear into thin air, there's only one difference between her and me."

"Boy-girl," she offers.

"Exactly. So, fine, they have her, but there's something wrong. They can't get whatever extract or clone sample, or whatever, to work on everybody. So they have to go out and find another immortal, which is when Bob kick-started his search for me. Do you follow?"

"So far."

"I'm thinking I was critical because Eve's sample only worked on other women. Bob needed me—specifically me—so he could become immortal."

"Are you saying that, or asking that?"

"I'm guessing."

"Not a bad guess."

"I didn't think it was." I lean forward some more. "Clara, when Bob was trying to escape in the end there, he had you and he had his suitcase, and he said he had everything he needed. But what he needed was an immortal man AND an immortal woman—plus one vampire—to deliver the product to his investors. He can pick up a new vampire more or less anywhere, if he knows where to look. But he only had an immortal man."

"You're getting to a question in here, right?"

"Yeah, if Bob was the first one in line, who was the second?"

Clara looks up at me in the mirror and gives a sly smile.

"Told you I'd figure out this immortality thing eventually," she says.

BONUS STORY: ON GODS AND MONSTERS

"Tell me about the gods," she purred.

She was curled up next to me, wrapped loosely in a cotton sheet with a pillow under the crook of her arm. The light breeze from my open bay window threatened to lift the sheet off her, because nature abhors a covered succubus.

Her name was Rowena, and I'm not calling her names; she actually was a succubus.

I slid out of the bed and padded over to the pitcher of water on a nearby table. After my third or fourth encounter with Rowena, I learned that keeping drinking water available was a good idea. I had tried wine first. That didn't work out so well.

"Do you want some water?" I asked.

"No. I want you to come back to bed."

I smiled, and drank. We were in a private country house in Northern England that I happened to own, in the middle of the day and the middle of the week. I had nowhere to go and nobody to see, and I expected those facts to remain unchanged for quite a long time. So there was no hurry. Despite this, my heart skipped and I fought the urge to race back to the bed, because she asked for me.

This is how things work with succubi.

The whole business about them being demons is a bit of nonsense, but it contains a grain of truth. A succubus will enjoy sex a lot—nearly as much as whomever they happen to be with—but what she really appreciates is the obsession.

Thus, men (and women, more often than you'd think) might find themselves doing things that turn out to be a touch self-destructive in hindsight. It's not exactly the same as enslaving a man and sucking his soul out of him and causing premature aging and whatever else people are saying nowadays about her species. But when a man throws away his family, career and inheritance just to spend all the uninterrupted time he can with one, it's nearly the same thing.

Not that it always ends up that way. I personally love finding a willing and able succubus whenever I can, because aside from their obviously wonderful physical attributes, the average succubus looks roughly twenty-two human years old for approximately fifty actual years, and that is a fantastic thing for a guy who's been alive as long as I have. Despite that, even if I completely lost control with one, unlike an ordinary human, I could outlive her.

That's my solution. I don't know how mortals do it, though.

Rowena was not a long-term companion for me in that sense. She spent most of her time enthralling high-ranking members of the Anglican Church, including at least one Bishop I knew of. That was no less scandalous then—this was 1862—than it is now.

I was her vacation.

"Why do you want to know about the gods?" I asked, returning to the bed. She sat up and let the sheet fall away, revealing a deeply tanned body and two perfect, pert breasts, and for a moment I forgot what we were talking about. I slipped under the sheet beside her. "And which gods do you mean?"

"I'm curious," she said, curling under my arm. Her hand slid down my chest and to my crotch. "And we have a few minutes, it seems."

I brushed the red hair from her eyes and lifted her chin so I could see her properly.

"This isn't a casual bedside inquiry, Rowena. Why don't you ask what you want to ask instead of hoping I stumble upon it?"

She grinned and I fell in love, for just a half second.

"Plato," she said.

"Plato?"

"You've read him?"

"I knew him."

She pushed away and tucked her knees in until she was sitting up and opposite me and my heart broke, for just a half second. Although she was still entirely naked, and fully apparent as such, and that eased the pain.

"Did he believe in the gods of the Greeks?" she asked. The switch from coy flirtation to intellectual curiosity was mildly jarring, but I didn't mind all that much. The truth was, there were few beings on Earth with greater native intelligence, on average, than succubi. It was the sort of thing one was better off knowing in advance.

"He didn't," I said, "but many still did in his day, as did most of their ancestors."

"And Aristotle? Or Socrates? Or, I don't know, Parmenides, Eratosthenes, Pythagoras, Heraclitus ..."

"You've been bedding a scholar, haven't you?"

It had been a very long time since anyone had rattled off such a long list of Greeks to me.

"I've been reading," she said a touch sternly. She slipped off her knees and lay back on the blankets, looking up at the ceiling.

"I can tell. No, most of the great thinkers did not believe in the old gods. They preferred to set up their own private cults instead, since the body politic at large did still believe.

Pythagoras's cult was particularly notorious, but he was also a lunatic."

"I thought he was interesting," she said. She reached over her head with one arm and found my leg, which she rubbed gently the way one might tickle a pet. It was as if she was daring me to form complete sentences.

"Interesting yes, sane no," I said. "The Pythagoreans worshipped numbers instead of gods."

"That doesn't sound so crazy to me. Not in comparison."

"Except they had a tendency to draw their swords on non-initiates. They were particularly protective of the dodecahedron."

Rowena laughed. She had a rich, velvety laugh that caused men to run toward the sound, even if they couldn't walk unaided prior to hearing it.

"All right," she said, "I accept your opinion on Pythagoras. But ... what I don't understand is how anyone could in seriousness think the Pantheon was a reasonable thing."

Her other hand had managed to discover her cleavage, her fingers teasing along the breastbone, the thumb tracing the outside of her left breast. It was possible she wasn't even aware she was doing it, but it was all I was aware of. Consequently, my response was nothing more than, "The Pantheon." Because when you cannot think of what to say, repeating back what you had just heard was nearly always a safe option.

"Zeus," she offered. "Hermes, Poseidon, Hera, Athena ..."

"Yes, I know who you mean, I just don't know *what* you mean."

"Oh, goodness. Petulant, irrational, cruel beings living on top of a mountain lusting after mortals and giving them silly quests or hurling thunderbolts at them or turning them into pigs or cows or trees. It's the sort of thing you tell a child you want to frighten into obedience."

I leaned forward until I was next to her, looking down at her lovely body.

"Maybe that's how they saw the world," I said. My right hand, on its own initiative, traced its way along her flat stomach and to her hipbone as my lips contemplated giving some serious attention to her nipples. Her skin felt like satin and smelled like cinnamon.

She lifted my hand up to her face. Smiling, she pulled a finger into her mouth and sucked on it for a moment, and then pulled it out and kissed the palm. "You were there," she said. "Don't tell me maybe."

Rolling out from below me, she reached the end of the bed and got to her feet. My heart broke again, along with a few other organs.

I sighed grandly as I watched her walk away. She stopped at the pitcher and slowly poured herself the glass of water she'd turned down so recently.

"All right," I said. "The behavior of the gods was mankind's way of explaining the apparent random cruelty of day-to-day life. Will that do?"

"No." She leaned back against the wall, sipping from her glass, smiling. I sat up and swung my feet around, meaning to walk to her. "And you have to stay on the bed," she added.

"Why is that?"

"Because you're not taking my questions seriously, so you will stay there until I'm satisfied."

"It seems to me you've been fairly well satisfied so far," I suggested.

"Oh, indeed, milord. But in that regard I can also satisfy myself right here, without additional assistance."

To punctuate this point, she dipped two fingers into the water and began drawing a line down her belly, stopping just shy of very interesting. I think I may have moaned audibly.

"Ask me again," I said.

"I want you to explain to me how a civilization that gave birth to the greatest thinkers in history, could possibly subscribe to such a juvenile religious faith."

"That will take a while," I confessed, without exaggeration.

"I have nowhere to be."

Nor did I, but this was not how I expected to be spending all the free time I had set aside. "All right. But this will come at a price."

"Whatever you feel is appropriate," she said with a satisfying grin. I decided on an approach.

"The short explanation," I began, "is that they believed in the gods because the Greeks had met their gods."

She looked disappointed.

"Now you're just patronizing me," she said.

"I'm not."

"Zeus, Athena and all of that? We are talking about the same gods?"

"Yes."

"I think I would prefer the longer explanation."

"All right, another approach: how do you think the gods were created?"

She laughed. "I imagine some overly creative little boy dreamed them up."

"It's a serious question, Rowena. How do you create a god?"

She pondered this, while tasting her water by dipping a finger in the glass and then sucking on it. I've never seen anyone enjoy fresh water as much as her.

"I guess I don't know," she admitted. "The stories of the gods were told for a long time, weren't they? There wasn't a ... a bible of any kind."

"No, there wasn't. The myths were passed on orally. But how did they start?"

She glided away from the wall and settled in the bench in front of the bay window. With legs crossed—said legs being of the long, muscular sort generally seen on dancers, the kind that made men drop whatever they were carrying when she walked by—she leaned back and looked out the window for some time, while sunlight tricked across her naked body with great eagerness. If I had the time, I would have commissioned a painter.

"I know mankind to be notorious when it comes to properly interpreting the natural world," she said. "Am I a demon?"

"You are definitely not," I answered. "Although I'm less certain regarding incubi."

She smiled. Insulting an incubus when talking to a succubus is always a good way to get ahead, because while they are of the same species, they don't get along in any real sense.

I don't like them either; most I've met have turned out to be dim, charmless rakes. But I understand them.

Essentially the responsibility of carrying on the species falls on the incubi, because succubi can't become pregnant. Thus, the average incubus spends all of his time charming and bedding women in order to impregnate them, and roughly one out of ten offspring ends up being a succubus or an incubus. They tend to prefer married women whose husbands are men of means so that their children will have a decent upbringing, given the incubus isn't going to be helping raise anybody. I frankly don't see why any woman would be interested in one, but I am not a woman.

"So," she continued, "I could easily imagine these gods began as misapprehended stories that developed into something supernatural in the retelling."

"That's a large part of it," I agreed. "But what did the stories begin as?"

"Ah! As men!"

"Exactly. The deeds of great men and women, passed down through history."

"Great women?"

"History has had many matriarchies, and quite a few women have actively participated in warrior cultures. It wasn't always as it is now."

She stood and walked over to the bed, stopping just shy of arm's reach. I was uncovered and so it was fairly clear I was ready for her to return.

"This answer nearly pleases me," she said.

"Nearly?"

I could have reached out and grabbed her by the arm and pulled her into the bed. And she would have relented, and even acted as if that was what she had wanted all along. But it would have been the last time we were together.

Instead of acceding to the bed, she sat down on her knees beside it, in a position of supplication I found entirely irresistible.

"You mean to say that all of the gods of the Pantheon were true persons of Greek history," she said.

"No," I countered. "True persons of history, but not all of Greek history. The Greeks were conquerors before written history, and their gods came from many different traditions. It would be impossible to tease out all of the stories after the fact."

"Impossible for you?" she asked. "You were there."

"I was, but no. Even if I cared to remember, there are too many threads." She looked disappointed.

"That's a shame." She sighed grandly, adding, "And I reject your premise."

"What?"

"Which is unfortunate; I was looking forward to rejoining you." She spread her thighs just slightly, and her hand felt its way down. I strongly considered leaving the conversation at that and simply watching her.

"Where do you disagree?" I asked.

"You told me the Greeks had met their gods in person ..." she hesitated to tickle herself, which we both enjoyed. And then her hand slid back up to her belly. "But you've also said the gods came from traditions older than the Greeks themselves. Are you suggesting these gods are all immortals? Because you have told me often there is no one like you and I believe you."

"All of that is true," I agreed—although it wasn't. "You can continue doing that if you wish."

"I do," she said. "But I'd like you to administer to the contradiction before I administer myself."

I've talked philosophy with a lot of people, and while it was often a frustrating undertaking, I couldn't recall any of those conversations being quite this maddening, for reasons having little to do with the subject itself.

"This Bishop you've made friends with," I said.

"Yes? Would you like to see what I do for him? I'm already on my knees."

I ignored the offer, as painful as that was. "Does he talk to you about Jesus?"

"Sometimes. But only in passing. He doesn't believe I have a soul. I think that makes it easier for him."

I asked, "Has he ever met Jesus?"

This question had a significant effect on her mood, which came as a surprise as it didn't occur to me, prior to asking, that a succubus could also be an adherent of the Christian faith. Her hands, just moments ago finding interesting places on her body to rub and massage, fell to her sides.

"That is not the same thing," she said.

I felt the urge to backtrack, but it was too late.

"Nor is it all that different," I said. "It's been nearly two millennia since Jesus of Nazareth walked the Earth, but finding someone today who would declare he never truly existed, and that he wasn't a god, would be difficult."

"*The* God. He also never lived atop a great big mountain and hurled lightning at people," she said, hopping to her feet and walking over to the water pitcher again. Her carriage had changed from enticing and graceful to simple and efficient, and I realized for the first time just how much of what a succubus is and does is a performance. However, she was still naked; the situation could be salvaged.

"You're missing my larger point, Rowena," I said. "The Greeks may not have met their gods face-to-face, but their ancestors did, in the same way the ancestors of your Cardinal met Jesus."

"I understand your point," she said without turning.

Something in her tone of voice recommended I keep quiet for a while, and so I did. Presently, she turned again and leaned back up against the wall, stretched dramatically—it was reminiscent of a cat somehow—and looked at me. A grin crept back onto her face.

"I am beginning to question the wisdom of debating gods with an immortal man," she said.

"Do you accept my premise?" I asked.

"I do, conditionally."

"Conditionally."

She walked slowly across the room, hips swinging slightly. Despite the lack of clothing, she carried herself with the allure of a well-dressed courtesan on a Parisian ballroom floor. I gathered from this that she had decided she was no longer cross with me. Committing one knee to the bed, she leaned forward, breasts dangling nearly within reach.

"My fear is that should I compare the philosophical underpinnings of Christianity to the warrior gods of legend, you will find a way to prove them equal in merit, and I don't think I'd like to hear any of that."

She leaned in and kissed me deeply. I reached around and grabbed her perfect little behind and pulled her onto the bed properly. Her legs separated and her knees slid in beside my hips.

"So let's save any more ... probing ... on the matter for another time, milord."

With a free hand she pulled away the sheet that separated us and settled on top of me. A little moan of satisfaction escaped her lips—a portion of the performance or not, I no longer cared—and then she was tilting her head back and panting and I was lifting myself up to meet her downward thrusts. And my last cogent thought, before I gave in to what would be a largely mindless afternoon of carnality, was that I was very glad Rowena found my explanation satisfactory.

Because the last thing I wanted was to have to tell her the truth: some gods were more real than others.

ABOUT THE AUTHOR

Gene Doucette is a hybrid author, albeit in a somewhat roundabout way. From 2010 through 2014, Gene published four full-length novels (*Immortal, Hellenic Immortal, Fixer,* and *Immortal at the Edge of the World*) with a small indie publisher. Then, in 2014, Gene started self-publishing novellas that were set in the same universe as the *Immortal* series, at which point he was a hybrid.

When the novellas proved more lucrative than the novels, Gene tried self-publishing a full novel, *The Spaceship Next Door,* in 2015. This went well. So well, that in 2016, Gene reacquired the rights to the earlier four novels from the publisher, and re-released them, at which point he wasn't a hybrid any longer.

Additional self-published novels followed: *Immortal and the Island of Impossible Things* (2016); *Unfiction* (2017); and *The Frequency of Aliens* (2017).

In 2018, John Joseph Adams Books (an imprint of Houghton Mifflin Harcourt) acquired the rights to *The Spaceship Next Door.* The reprint was published in September of that year, at which point Gene was once again a hybrid author.

Since then, a number of things have happened. Gene published three more novels—*Immortal From Hell* (2018), *Fixer Redux* (2019), and *Immortal: Last Call* (2020)—and wrote a new novel called *The Apocalypse Seven* that he did not self-publish; it was acquired by JJA/HMH in September of 2019. Publication date is May 25, 2021.

Gene lives in Cambridge, MA.

For the latest on Gene Doucette, follow him online

genedoucette.me
genedoucette@me.com

ALSO BY GENE DOUCETTE

SCI-FI

The Spaceship Next Door

The world changed on a Tuesday.

When a spaceship landed in an open field in the quiet mill town of Sorrow Falls, Massachusetts, everyone realized humankind was not alone in the universe. With that realization, everyone freaked out for a little while.

Or, almost everyone. The residents of Sorrow Falls took the news pretty well. This could have been due to a certain local quality of unflappability, or it could have been that in three years, the ship did exactly nothing other than sit quietly in that field, and nobody understood the full extent of this nothing the ship was doing better than the people who lived right next door.

Sixteen-year old Annie Collins is one of the ship's closest neighbors. Once upon a time she took every last theory about the ship seriously, whether it was advanced by an adult ,or by a peer. Surely one of the theories would be proven true eventually—if not several of them—the very minute the ship decided to do something. Annie is starting to think this will never happen.

One late August morning, a little over three years since the ship landed, Edgar Somerville arrived in town. Ed's a government operative posing as a journalist, which is obvious to Annie—and pretty much everyone else he meets—almost immediately. He has a lot of questions that need answers, because he thinks everyone is wrong: the ship is doing something, and he needs Annie's help to figure out what that is.

Annie is a good choice for tour guide. She already knows everyone in town and when Ed's theory is proven correct—something is apocalyptically wrong in Sorrow Falls—she's a pretty good person to have around.

As a matter of fact, Annie Collins might be the most important person on the planet. She just doesn't know it.

~

The Frequency of Aliens

Annie Collins is back!

Becoming an overnight celebrity at age sixteen should have been a lot more fun. Yes, there were times when it was extremely cool, but when the newness of it all wore off, Annie Collins was left with a permanent security detail and the kind of constant scrutiny that makes the college experience especially awkward.

Not helping matters: she's the only kid in school with her own pet spaceship.

She would love it if things found some kind of normal, but as long as she has control of the most lethal—and only—interstellar vehicle in existence, that isn't going to happen. Worse, things appear to be going in the other direction. Instead of everyone getting used to the idea of the ship, the complaints are getting louder. Public opinion is turning, and the demands that Annie turn over the ship are becoming more frequent. It doesn't help that everyone seems to think Annie is giving them nightmares.

Nightmares aren't the only weird things going on lately. A government telescope in California has been abandoned, and nobody seems to know why.

The man called on to investigate—Edgar Somerville—has become the go-to guy whenever there's something odd going on, which has been pretty common lately. So far, nothing has panned out: no aliens or zombies or anything else that might be deemed legitimately peculiar… but now may be different, and not just because Ed can't find an easy explanation. This isn't the only telescope where people have gone missing, and the clues left behind lead back to Annie.

It all adds up to a new threat that the world may just need saving from, requiring the help of all the Sorrow Falls survivors. The question is: are they saving the world with Annie Collins, or are they saving it from her?

The Frequency of Aliens is the exciting sequel to *The Spaceship Next Door.*

Unfiction

When Oliver Naughton joins the Tenth Avenue Writers Underground, headed by literary wunderkind Wilson Knight, Oliver figures he'll finally get some of the wild imaginings out of his head and onto paper.

But when Wilson takes an intense interest in Oliver's writing and his genre stories of dragons, aliens, and spies, things get weird. Oliver's stories don't just need to be finished: they insist on it.

With the help of Minerva, Wilson's girlfriend, Oliver has to find the connection between reality, fiction, the mythical Cydonian Kingdom, and the non-mythical nightclub called M Pallas. That is, if he can survive the alien invasion, the ghosts, and the fact that he thinks he might be in love with Minerva.

Unfiction is a wild ride through the collision of science fiction, fantasy, thriller, horror and romance. It's what happens when one writer's fiction interferes with everyone's reality.

Fixer

What would you do if you could see into the future?

As a child, he dreamed of being a superhero. Most people never get to realize their childhood dreams, but Corrigan Bain has come close. He is a fixer. His job is to prevent accidents—to see the future and "fix" things before people get hurt. But the ability to see into the future, however limited, isn't always so simple. Sometimes not everyone can be saved.

"Don't let them know you can see them."

Graduate students from a local university are dying, and former lover and FBI agent Maggie Trent is the only person who believes their deaths aren't as accidental as they appear. But the truth can only be found in something from Corrigan Bain's past, and he's not interested in sharing that past, not even with Maggie.

To stop the deaths, Corrigan will have to face up to some old horrors, confront the possibility that he may be going mad, and find a way to stop a killer no one can see.

Corrigan Bain is going insane ... or is he?

Because there's something in the future that doesn't want to be seen. It isn't human. It's got a taste for mayhem. And it is very, very angry.

Fixer Redux

Someone's altering the future, and it isn't Corrigan Bain

Corrigan Bain was retired.

It wasn't something he ever thought he'd be able to do. The problem was that the *job* he wanted to retire from wasn't actually a job at all: nobody paid him to do it, and nobody else did it. With very few exceptions, nobody even knew he was doing it.

Corrigan called himself a fixer, because he fixed accidents that were about to happen. It was complicated and unrewarding, and even though doing it right meant saving someone, he didn't enjoy it. He couldn't stop —he thought—because there would always be accidents, and he would never find someone to take over as fixer. Anyone trying would have to be capable of seeing the future, like he did, and that kind of person was hard to find.

Still, he did it. He's never been happier.

His girlfriend, Maggie Trent of the FBI, has not retired. Her task force just shut down the most dangerous domestic terrorist cell in the country, and she's up for an award, and a big promotion.

Everything's going their way now, and the future looks even brighter.

Unfortunately, that future is about to blow up in their faces…literally. And somehow, Corrigan Bain, fixer, the man who can see the future, is taken completely by surprise.

Fixer Redux is the long-awaited sequel to ***Fixer***. Catch up with Corrigan, as he tries to understand a future that no longer makes sense.

~

FANTASY

The Immortal Novel Series

~

Immortal

"I don't know how old I am. My earliest memory is something along the lines of fire good, ice bad, so I think I predate written history, but I don't know by how much. I like to brag that I've been there from the beginning, and while this may very well be true, I generally just say it to pick up girls."

Surviving sixty thousand years takes cunning and more than a little luck. But in the twenty-first century, Adam confronts new dangers—someone has found out what he is, a demon is after him, and he has run out of places to hide. Worst of all, he has had entirely too much to drink.

Immortal is a first person confessional penned by a man who is immortal, but not invincible. In an artful blending of sci-fi, adventure, fantasy, and humor, IMMORTAL introduces us to a world with vampires, demons and other "magical" creatures, yet a world without actual magic.

At the center of the book is Adam.

Adam is a sixty thousand year old man. (Approximately.) He doesn't age or get sick, but is otherwise entirely capable of being killed. His survival has hinged on an innate ability to adapt, his wits, and a fairly large dollop of luck. He makes for an excellent guide through history ... when he's sober.

Immortal is a contemporary fantasy for non-fantasy readers and fantasy enthusiasts alike.

~

Hellenic Immortal

"Very occasionally, I will pop up in the historical record. Most of the time I'm not at all easy to spot, because most of the time I'm just a guy who does a thing and then disappears again into the background behind someone-or-other who's busy doing something much more important. But there are a couple of rare occasions when I get a starring role."

An oracle has predicted the sojourner's end, which is a problem for Adam insofar as he has never encountered an oracular prediction that didn't come true ... and he is the sojourner. To survive, he's going to have to figure out what a beautiful ex-government analyst, an eco-terrorist, a rogue FBI agent, and the world's oldest religious cult all want with him, and fast.

And all he wanted when he came to Vegas was to forget about a girl. And maybe have a drink or two.

The second book in the Immortal series, Hellenic Immortal follows the continuing adventures of Adam, a sixty-thousand-year-old man with a wry sense of humor, a flair for storytelling, and a knack for staying alive. Hellenic Immortal is a clever blend of history, mythology, sci-fi, fantasy, adventure, mystery and romance. A little something, in other words, for every reader.

~

Immortal at the Edge of the World

"What I was currently doing with my time and money ... didn't really deserve anyone else's attention. If I was feeling romantic about it, I'd call it a quest, but all I was really doing was trying to answer a question I'd been ignoring for a thousand years."

In his very long life, Adam had encountered only one person who appeared to share his longevity: the mysterious red-haired woman. She appeared throughout history, usually from a distance, nearly always vanishing before he could speak to her.

In his last encounter, she actually did vanish—into thin air, right in front of him. The question was how did she do it? To answer, Adam will have to complete a quest he gave up on a thousand years earlier, for an object that may no longer exist.

If he can find it, he might be able to do what the red-haired woman did, and if he can do that, maybe he can find her again and ask her who she is ... and why she seems to hate him.

But Adam isn't the only one who wants the red-haired woman. There are other forces at work, and after a warning from one of the few men he trusts, Adam realizes how much danger everyone is in. To save his friends and finish his quest he may be forced to bankrupt himself, call in every favor he can, and ultimately trade the one thing he'd never been able to give up before: his life.

~

Immortal and the island of Impossible Things

"I thought I'd miss the world."

Adam is on vacation in an island paradise, with nothing to do and plenty of time to do nothing.

It's exactly what he needed: beautiful weather, beautiful girlfriend, plenty of books to read, and alcohol to drink. Most importantly, either nobody on the island knows who he is, or, nobody cares.

"This probably sounds boring, and maybe it is. It's possible I have no compass to help determine boring, or maybe I have a different threshold than most people. From my perspective, though, the vast majority of human history has been boring, by which I mean nothing happened, and sure, that can be dull. On the other hand, nothing happening includes nobody trying to kill anybody, and specifically, nobody trying to kill me. That's the kind of boring a guy can get behind."

Nothing last forever, though, and that includes the opportunity to *do* nothing. One day, unwelcome visitors arrive in secret, with impossible knowledge of impossible events, and then the impossible things arrive: a new species.

It's *all* impossible, especially to the immortal man who thought he'd seen all there was to see in the world. Now, Adam is going to have to figure out what's happening and make things right before he and everyone he loves ends up dead in the hot sun of this island paradise.

~

Immortal From Hell

Not all of Adam's stories have happy endings

"Paris is romantic and quests are cool. But the threat of a global pandemic kind of sours the whole thing. The good news was, if all life on Earth were felled by a plague, it looked like this one could take me out too. It'd be pretty lonely otherwise."

--Adam the immortal

When Adam decides to leave the safety of the island, it's for a good reason: Eve, the only other immortal on the planet, appears to be dying, and nobody seems to understand why. But when Adam—with his extremely capable girlfriend Mirella—tries to retrace Eve's steps, he discovers a world that's a whole lot deadlier than he remembered.

Adam is supposed to be dead. He went through a lot of trouble to fake that death, but now that he's back it's clear someone remains unconvinced. That wouldn't be so terrible, except that whoever it is, they have a great deal of influence, and an abiding interest in ensuring that his death sticks this time around.

Adam and Mirella will have to figure out how to travel halfway across the world in secret, with almost no resources or friends. The good news is, Adam solved the travel problem a thousand years earlier. The bad news is, one of his oldest assumptions will turn out to be untrue.

Immortal From Hell is the darkest entry in the Immortal series.

~

Immortal: Last Call

"I'm something like sixty-thousand years old, and I've probably thought more

about my own death than any living being has thought about any subject, ever. I used to be unduly preoccupied with what might constitute a "good death", although interestingly, this has always been an after-the-fact analysis. What I mean is, following a near-death experience, I'll generally perform a quiet review of the circumstances and judge whether that death would have been objectively good, by whatever metric one uses for that kind of thing. I'm not nearly that self-reflective while in the midst of said near-death experience. Facing death, the predominant thought is always not like this."

A disease threatening the lives of everyone—human and non-human—has been loosed upon the world, by an arch-enemy Adam didn't even know he had.

That's just the first of his problems. Adam's also in jail, facing multiple counts of murder, at least a few of which are accurate. He may never see the inside of a courtroom, because there remains a bounty on his head—put there by the aforementioned arch-enemy—that someone is bound to try to collect while he's stuck behind bars.

Meanwhile, Adam's sitting on some tantalizing evidence that there might be a cure, but to find it, he's going to have to get out of jail, get out of the country, and track down the man responsible. He can't do any of that alone, but he also can't rely on any of his non-human friends for help, not when they're all getting sick.

What he needs is a particularly gifted human, who can do things no other human is capable of. He knows one such person. He calls himself a fixer, and he's Adam's—and possibly the world's—last hope. That's provided he believes any of it.

Immortal: Last Call is the sixth book in the *Immortal Novel Series*, and also the end of a long journey for one immortal man.

~

Immortal Stories

~

Eve

"...if your next question is, what could that possibly make me, if I'm not an angel or a god? The answer is the same as what I said before: many have considered me a god, and probably a few have thought of me as an angel. I'm neither, if those positions are defined by any kind of supernormal magical power. True magic of that kind doesn't exist, but I can do things that may appear magic to someone slightly more tethered to their mortality. I'm a woman, and that's all. What may make me different from the next woman is that it's possible I'm the very first one..."

For most of humankind, the woman calling herself Eve has been nothing more than a shock of red hair glimpsed out of the corner of the eye, in a crowd, or from a great distance. She's been worshipped, feared, and hunted, but perhaps never understood. Now, she's trying to reconnect with the world, and finding that more challenging than anticipated.

Can the oldest human on Earth rediscover her own humanity? Or will she decide the world isn't worth it?

~

The Immortal Chronicles

~

Immortal at Sea (volume 1)

Adam's adventures on the high seas have taken him from the Mediterranean to the Barbary Coast, and if there's one thing he learned, it's that maybe the sea is trying to tell him to stay on dry land.

~

Hard-Boiled Immortal (volume 2)

The year was 1942, there was a war on, and Adam was having a lot of trouble avoiding the attention of some important people. The kind of people with guns, and ways to make a fella disappear. He was caught somewhere between the mob and the government, and the only way out involved a red-haired dame he was pretty sure he couldn't trust.

~

Immortal and the Madman (volume 3)

On a nice quiet trip to the English countryside to cope with the likelihood that he has gone a little insane, Adam meets a man who definitely has. The madman's name is John Corrigan, and he is convinced he's going to die soon.

He could be right. Because there's trouble coming, and unless Adam can get his own head together in time, they may die together.

~

Yuletide Immortal (volume 4)

When he's in a funk, Adam the immortal man mostly just wants a place to drink and the occasional drinking buddy. When that buddy turns out to be Santa Claus, Adam is forced to face one of the biggest challenges of extremely long life: Christmas cheer. Will Santa break him out of his bad mood? Or will he be responsible for depressing the most positive man on the planet?

~

Regency Immortal (volume 5)

Adam has accidentally stumbled upon an important period in history: Vienna in 1814. Mostly, he'd just like to continue to enjoy the local pubs, but that becomes impossible when he meets Anna, an intriguing woman with an unreasonable number of secrets and sharp objects.

Anna is hunting down a man who isn't exactly a man, and if Adam doesn't help her, all of Europe will suffer. If Adam *does* help, the cost may be his own life. It's not a fantastic set of options. Also, he's probably fallen in love with her, which just complicates everything.